THE KINGDOM OF LIGHT

Giulio Leoni is a professor of Italian literature and
history. He lives in Rome with his family.

Shaun Whiteside's most recent translations from
Italian include *Venice is a Fish* by Tiziano Scarpa and
The Solitude of Prime Numbers by Paolo Giordano.

ALSO BY GIULIO LEONI

The Third Heaven Conspiracy

GIULIO LEONI

The Kingdom
of Light

TRANSLATED FROM THE ITALIAN BY
Shaun Whiteside

VINTAGE BOOKS
London

Published by Vintage 2010

2 4 6 8 10 9 7 5 3

First published in Italy as *I Delitti Della Luce* in 2005 by Arnoldo
Mondadori Editore S.p.A, Milano. This edition published by
arrangement with Piergiorgio Nicolazzini Literary Agency

First published in Great Britain in 2009 by
Harvill Secker

Vintage
Random House, 20 Vauxhall Bridge Road,
London SW1V 2SA

www.vintage-books.co.uk

Addresses for companies within The Random House Group Limited
can be found at: www.randomhouse.co.uk/offices.htm

The Random House Group Limited Reg. No. 954009

A CIP catalogue record for this book
is available from the British Library

ISBN 9780099516460

The Random House Group Limited supports The Forest
Stewardship Council (FSC), the leading international forest
certification organisation. All our titles that are printed on
Greenpeace approved FSC certified paper carry the FSC logo.
Our paper procurement policy can be found at:
www.rbooks.co.uk/environment

Mixed Sources
Product group from well-managed
forests and other controlled sources
www.fsc.org   Cert no. TT-COC-2139
© 1996 Forest Stewardship Council
FSC

Printed and bound in Great Britain by
CPI Bookmarque, Croydon, CR0 4TD

For Riccarda

Si probitas, sensus, virtutum gratia, census,
nobilitas orti possint resistere morti,
non foret extinctus Federicus, qui iacet intus.

If probity, reason, abundance of virtue, nobility of birth,
could prevent death, Frederick, who lies here,
would not have died.

Inscription on Frederick's tomb.

CAST OF CHARACTERS

DANTE ALIGHIERI (c.1265–1321) – prior of Florence, poet and author of *The Divine Comedy*, often referred to in the book as Messer Durante, because his full name was Durante degli Alighieri

Some real persons are described in greater detail in the Glossary at the back of the book (see page 315).

CARDINAL D'ACQUASPARTA – the Pope's representative in the city of Florence

MAESTRO ALBERTO – a Lombard *mechanicus* who keeps an inn at Santa Maria

ARRIGO DA JESI – formerly held the chair of natural philosophy at the Faculty of Arts and Theology in Paris, where he taught Dante; known in the novel as 'the philosopher'

THE BARGELLO – chief of the guards for the Commune

BONIFACE VIII – Pope of the Roman Catholic Church from 1294 until 1303; sometimes referred to in the novel as Caetani, because he was born Benedetto Caetani

BRANDANO – a monk and preacher of miracles; the leader of a group of pilgrims seeking to free the Holy Land from the pagans

CECCHERINO – the owner of a disreputable tavern
CECCO ANGIOLIERI – a poet and acquaintance of Dante
NOFFO DEI – the head of the inquisitors in Florence
MESSER DUCCIO – town clerk and secretary of the
   Council
FREDERICK II – Holy Roman Emperor 1220–50 and
   monarch of Italy from 1215
HAMID – a young Saracen slave captured off the coast
   of Egypt and now working for Maestro Alberto
MONNA LAGIA – a local brothel-keeper
PIETRA – one of Monna Lagia's whores and Dante's
   lover

AT THE ANGEL INN

BRUNETTO DA PALERMO – a painter
FRANCESCHINO COLONNA – a student from Rome
FABIO DAL POZZO – a cloth merchant from the North
MANETTO DEL MOLINO – keeper of the Angel Inn, on
   behalf of the Cavalcanti
MESSER MARCELLO – a scholar and doctor from the
   North; known in the novel as 'the doctor'
JACQUES MONERRE – a scholar and astronomer from
   Toulouse
RIGO DI COLA – a wool merchant
BERNARDO RINUCCIO – a writer and scholar; known in
   the novel as 'the historian'

Palermo, summer 1240

*T*HE GLARE *of sunset pierced the foliage, inflaming the gilded surface of the fruits on the lemon tree.*

In the garden, closed off by a marble colonnade, an intense scent of flowers floated through the air, carried on the sea breeze.

Reclining on purple cushions, the Emperor was distractedly tracing geometrical drawings on the ground. He stretched his hand towards a citrus fruit lying on the ground and showed it to the younger man who stood beside him.

'So what shape is the earth?' he asked after a moment's reflection.

'A solid sphere, curved at every point,' confirmed Guido Bonatti, the court astrologer.

Frederick meditated upon these words. Then he suddenly opened his fingers, dropping the fruit. 'So what holds it up, then?' he went on, turning towards his other companion in thought, who sat slightly apart from the others. A pale man, freckled face and red hair.

'The hand of God,' replied the foremost scientist of Christendom, the pride of his court. Michael Scotus. Slender as one of the reeds that held up the pergola of the vines.

'And how high are the skies where God dwells? Can you tell me that, Guido?'

'As far as their light reaches, Majesty,' replied the astrologer, picking up the fruit with his left hand. 'Which is the light of God.'

'And what lies beyond that light?'

'Beyond it lies only darkness. As the Scriptures tell us, what remained after light was called into being,' replied Michael Scotus, pointing a finger up into the air.

An enigmatic smile lit up Frederick's face. A little way off, a man dressed in the rough habit of the Minorites had witnessed the scene in silence.

The Emperor turned towards him. 'Tell me your measurement, Brother Elias. The measurement of the height of God.'

I

Morning of 5th August, 1300, in the marshes west of Florence

THEY HAD turned away from the houses beside a cottage on the road to Pisa, when the sun was already high in the sky. From there they had headed towards the river, which flowed a few leagues away, invisible among the cane thickets and the patches of marshy vegetation.

For over two hours the little column trudged across the waterlogged terrain, weighed down by their heavy armour, seeking a path among the swamps. At their head Dante Alighieri, wearing the banner of the priory, stayed about twenty yards ahead of the group.

'Prior, please wait, slow down. Why such a hurry?' wheezed the Bargello, a squat man covered with armour that made him even clumsier than he would otherwise have been. The Bargello, chief of the guards, slipped as he attempted to catch up with the prior.

A little waterway blocked their path. Dante turned round, wiping the sweat from his brow with his sleeve.

THE KINGDOM OF LIGHT

Then with a resolute gesture he pulled the hem of his robe up above his knees and waded through the stream, followed by the others. Further ahead the horizon was hidden by a scrubby hillock.

'That's the tower of Santa Croce . . . we should be there by now,' panted the chief of the guards, pointing at a far-off building.

The prior had stopped a little further off, halfway up the slope, and was pulling his shoes out of the mud and water.

With a grimace of disgust he pulled a leech from his calf and threw it far away. At the point where the sucker had bitten his flesh, a thin stream of blood stained his skin. He washed the wound with a little water, then stared impatiently at the awkward movements of the Bargello, who was breathlessly trying to catch up with him.

'So where is it?'

In front of them, in an opening among the reed-thickets, the bank of the Arno could be seen, folding into a loop hidden by a bump in the ground.

'It should be here . . . behind this clump.'

Dante looked in the direction indicated. The muddy dune seemed to be trying to drag them down. For the last few steps he had to use his hands, clutching the spiny tufts that covered its summit; then finally he was able to take a look from the other side.

About three hundred yards away a dark outline lay beached on the pebbly shore, partly hidden by the vegetation.

'So it was true . . . there it is,' stammered the Bargello.

Dante was also having difficulty believing his own eyes. Leaning slightly to one side, a war galley lay against the river bank, its whole array of oars outstretched as though about to take to the open sea.

'The devil must have brought it here,' the Bargello murmured with a shudder. Dante couldn't suppress a smile. He knew the legends that were told about this place. But if the devil really did exist, at least he would catch a glimpse of him.

'I can't see anyone on board. It looks abandoned,' remarked one of the guards.

'Yes, not a trace of life,' the poet confirmed, studying the deserted fo'c'sle. On the narrow central corridor not a soul could be seen, and there was no one at the helm. The nave looked in perfect condition, as if the ship had only recently docked, its big triangular sail neatly furled on the boom. Dante felt a shiver running down his spine. Such large vessels couldn't possibly sail on the Arno. Its presence here was . . . yes, it was *impossible*. He sought a sign that might reveal where the ship had come from, but there was nothing but a black flag dangling slackly from the yard.

'Let's go over. I have to see . . . and I have to know,' he said, and slipped quickly down on his back, plunging into the canal, followed reluctantly by the others.

He had grabbed a sword from one of the men, and

opened up a path for himself by impetuously scything the plants, wading through water up to his knees. Streams of sweat trickled down his body, but the excitement of the discovery seemed to have swept all exhaustion away.

He couldn't see where he was going. Then he dealt one final blow and stopped with a jerk, as the horrified cries of the *bargellini* rose up behind him.

A bearded giant had appeared in front of him, more than six ells in height. On the creature's monstrous, crowned head two hideous faces looking in opposite directions took in the whole of the horizon with their twofold malevolent gaze. The giant sat on a massive carved tree-trunk that ended in a bronze tip half-hidden in the mud of the river bank.

An insistent hum echoed in the air. The insects that had been tormenting the men all the way along their march now seemed even more numerous and aggressive. They clustered around the figurehead in a repellent throng.

'Beelzebub, the lord of the flies,' said Dante, disgustedly waving away a cloud of them. A gust of wind pierced the air, bringing with it a terrible stench of decomposition. 'We've got to get on board,' said the prior, after a moment's hesitation.

A rope ladder hung from the anchor mouth at the prow. Dante wrapped his mouth and nose with the veil of his biretta, then hoisted himself up on the remains of the truncated ram and from there began struggling up the ship's rail. Halfway up he turned round, urging on the Bargello, who was still staring dazedly at the figurehead. Dante waited for the other man to begin climbing, and with one last effort hoisted himself on to the fo'c'sle.

The chief of the guards had also reached the deck, puffing. He came and stood next to him so that he could see too, then brought his hand to his mouth with a sob. 'But they're . . .'

'They're dead. As your men said they were.'

Dozens of oarsmen, lined up on their benches, seemed intently engaged in some kind of macabre parody, bent over their oars as if in the convulsive effort of rowing. Other figures lay supine towards the stern and around the helm. The corpses were swollen and covered with an oily liquid, as if they had been exposed to the boiling sun for many days.

Disoriented, Dante looked around. A breath of hot wind swept the deck, raising a foul breath of putrefaction. 'There's plague on board!' whispered the Bargello, putting his hand over his face in an attempt to stem the stench that rose up from below.

Dante shook his head. The ship must have been manoeuvred with extreme skill to rise all the way up the river. How could it have done that if the crew was ill? No, there must be some other cause for this massacre. Death must have come on board like a silent guest, gliding its limbs along for a while before finally striking. He looked up, drawn by the rattle of the flag against the yard. Before the banner sank down again he just had time to see the image of a skull, above two bones in the shape of a cross.

Halfway along the deck there was a hatch leading to the hold. Perhaps the cargo of the ship would reveal its mystery? Picking up a wooden peg, he quickly wrapped it in a strip of tarred cloth that lay on the ground. With a few blows of his flint he lit the makeshift torch, then leaned into the cavity and cast a light inside.

He saw no tools, yardarms or spare sails, or any kind of foodstuffs, or stores of water or wine. No kind of lodging for the crew, no galley or weapons. Even the ballast stones had been removed, turning the ship into a big, empty husk.

It seemed as if its commander's sole concern had been to reduce the load as far as possible so as to come upriver. He turned to look towards the wardroom, below the quarterdeck. The door to the captain's quarters swung slightly, as if someone inside were beckoning him in.

The cabin was plunged in shadow. In the middle of the wardroom, beneath a torch-holder that hung above their heads, three men sat motionless around a small table, slumped on their carved benches, as if they had just interrupted a conversation over beakers of wine, when sleep had suddenly come upon them. At their feet a mass lay in the middle of a pool of light.

Curious, Dante leaned over and brought the torch close

to it. It was a kind of crude device of levers and toothed wheels, whose surfaces of gleaming wood and brass flickered in the flame in a thousand reflections. The thing was two feet high, perhaps as wide and deep, but it was hard to get a clear idea of its original shape, because someone seemed to have attacked it with considerable force, smashing it to pieces. The axe that had inflicted the damage still lay on the ground.

Dante picked up one of the gear-wheels, testing the bite of the thin teeth on his fingers. On the edge there were tiny letters that he couldn't decipher.

At that moment the galley swayed with a groan, as if the river had begun to eddy.

The Bargello had approached, and now looked around in puzzlement. 'But . . . they're Saracens! All dead,' he exclaimed, ignoring the shattered machine.

Dante looked up at the corpses. Two of them wore the insignia of marine officers: they must have been the commander and his second-in-command. The third was dressed in sumptuous clothes that seemed to float around him like outspread wings. Clothes of an unfamiliar shape, like the big turban wrapped around his head. His face bore the marks of advanced old age.

'All . . . all dead,' the Bargello said, stunned.

'Shh,' hissed Dante irritably. 'Let me listen.'

'What to?'

'To what the dead are saying. This man wasn't part of

the crew. He certainly wasn't a sailor. Have you seen his hands? And his clothes? He was a passenger. And they were all dead by the time the ship was beached. With one exception.' He pointed to an empty chair and one of the cups on the table, still full. 'There were four of them. But one of them didn't drink. And look over there,' he added, pointing towards the far side of the cabin. 'There are four hammocks, all slept in. The man who didn't drink is still alive.'

Dante turned the old man's head towards the light and loosened the tightened jaws. Through the half-open mouth he glimpsed a cloister of irregular teeth, coated with a reddish foam. There were deep cuts on the purple lips, as if the unfortunate man had bitten them to the quick during the last moments of his life. Then he sniffed the remains of the liquid in the cup.

'How did they die?'

The poet indicated the corpse to the Bargello, bringing the torch close to his face. 'You see the swollen lips and tongue? As if he had drowned in coagulated air,' he explained, moving the flame away from the face of the dead man, whose beard had begun to curl in the heat of the flame. 'Poison. Not an insult to the innards; a substance that extinguished the force of the breath.'

As he let the dead man's head fall back, something slipped from the corpse's neck, twisting like a snake. It looked like a gilded medallion, covered with tiny signs and Arabic characters, held by a leather lace.

An astrolabe, he noted, and one of very refined manufacture. The alidade, the moving pointer, had been damaged by a blow that had bent one of its two fins. But the rete, a filigree bundle precisely cut like a precious jewel, was intact, with its incredible profusion of spines and flames to mark the fixed stars. Making a rapid calculation, Dante worked out that there were at least a hundred of them. He had never seen an astrolabe with more than thirty. If an angel had needed to determine the route between the stars, he could have found nothing better.

An angel . . . or a demon.

Dante quickly examined the other two corpses. On those, too, death had left the same cruel mark.

'The fourth man killed his companions by poisoning the wine supply. It's customary for drink to be distributed to the men when they have reached their destination. So the crew followed them into the same abyss,' murmured Dante. 'Let's try and find out something about the ship.'

He looked around. At the end of the cabin, fixed to the wall, there was a cabinet reinforced with strips of iron. Forcing in the tip of his dagger, he pulled out the hinges of the door. Inside there was a leather-bound book. It must have been the ship's log. After taking a quick look, he put that in his bag as well.

The stench of decomposition had become unbearable. Dante was seized with a violent attack of retching, as the feeling of nausea become more intense. He managed only to ascertain that their clothes contained no other objects worthy of interest, before he was forced to leave the cabin.

As soon as he was outside he stopped for a moment to catch his breath. His mind ran to the terrible deaths of the oarsmen. Now he understood the awful contraction of their limbs. Anyone who had escaped the poison was left in chains to die of thirst beneath the roasting sun, and the murderer hadn't bothered to unlock their fetters. They had tried to free themselves until the very last, and their desperate cries must have filled the swamp for days. But their incomprehensible language, rather than bringing anyone running over, would have frightened the few inhabitants, terrified as they were by a fear of ghosts.

Dante thought he could still hear the cries rising up from the benches. He turned to the Bargello: 'Order your men to bring back very carefully every fragment of the machine in the wardroom, and have it brought to Florence with the utmost care. Strip off one of the sails and turn it into a bag.'

'And . . . these people?'

The poet looked hesitantly around. He could do nothing more for those wretches. But he wouldn't leave them there to rot among their chains. 'Set fire to the ship. Let it turn into a funeral pyre, and let their God receive them along with their souls,' he commanded. 'And let people know as little as possible about this story for the time being.'

'But the galley was empty. No precious cargo, nothing but rubbish. Why such secrecy?' the chief of the guards objected suspiciously. 'Apart from those corpses.'

'Yes. Apart from those corpses,' the prior interrupted, starting to climb down.

The men hurried to accomplish their task, impatient to get away from that accursed place.

'Let's get back to our horses,' Dante said when he saw the flames beginning to attack the ship. As they moved away, he darted one final glance at the top of the dune. Red tongues rose higher and higher as the fire took hold of the carcase. They looked like fingers rising from the funeral pyre in a plea for justice.

Or revenge.

THEY REACHED Florence early the following day, after a forced night-march that had exhausted both men and horses, while the constellations of the Zodiac waned above their heads. The tops of the walls gleamed in the rays of the early-morning sun, as if they were made of copper rather than brick and stone.

During the night a sandy rain had fallen, with intervals of clarity. While the starry vault had been visible, Dante had looked up to work out how much time had passed. At that moment Gemini, his birth-constellation, was shining in the sky. The twofold splendour of Castor and Pollux seemed to guide him, giving him the strength to conquer the unease that had lately taken hold of him. Several times the Bargello had suggested a rest, encouraged by the protests of his men. But each time Dante had rejected the idea, determined as he was to keep going.

The pyre of the ship had erased the visible traces of the slaughter, but not the right of those souls to be avenged. He had to find the man responsible, the man who had fled after committing that savage crime.

In front of him swayed the bag containing the fragments of the mechanism. The horse swerved nervously each time its cargo groaned with its metallic voice, as if sensing that it was carrying shards of hell.

'Open the door in the name of the city of Florence!' Dante called with the last of his strength at the sentinel on the tower, who peered down, poking his torch through a gap in the crenellations. In the semi-darkness the line of exhausted men and horses was a muddled collection of dark silhouettes. 'And jump to it when I give you an order,' the poet shouted.

'Bugger off!' shouted the man high above them, cupping his hands around his mouth, the better to be heard. 'It isn't market day today, and you can't get in before the third hour. You and your rabble go and camp far from the walls, or I'll come out with the guard and stroke your bones.'

'You whore-son!' yelled Dante, bouncing furiously up

and down on his saddle. The unexpected noise and movement terrified his mount, which shifted sideways and made
his foot slip from his stirrup. He landed heavily, sending
up splashes of mud, only just managing to stay on his
feet. Behind him the malevolent laughter of the *bargellini*
exploded in sympathy with their fellow-guard. Even the
Bargello had been unable to suppress a barely stifled
chuckle.

Meanwhile, drawn by the hubbub, the other soldiers of
the guard corps were crowding round, amidst sounds
of yawning and the rattle of armour. Purple faces, still filled
with sleep, appeared between the merlons, hurling down
insults and making obscene gestures at the people below.

'Open this door, you rogues!' the Bargello finally decided
to shout, letting them know who he was. From above, the
yelling suddenly stopped, replaced a few moments later
by the sound of the chain being removed. Dante, drawing
his horse by the bridle, moved slowly beneath the low
arch. He tried to look in the guards' faces to memorise
each one of them, cursing them under his breath.

At that very moment, a distant chant rose up behind
him, a kind of psalmody of indistinguishable words. For
a moment he thought he was hallucinating and turned
round. Beyond the bend in the road he saw a curious line
of people slowly approaching. It was from them that the
chant was coming.

The group seemed to be made up of the survivors of a

shipwreck. At their head came a tall man, wearing a rough, dark habit, his bearded face half-concealed by its hood. He came forward leaning on a long stick topped with a cross placed in a circle. Behind him a little crowd of men and women were dressed as if their guide had assembled them while they were still going about their daily business. Peasants and merchants, nobles and fishermen, warriors and prostitutes, doctors and usurers, a kind of confused and sorrowful representation of humanity.

In the middle of the crowd of dusty wayfarers were a number of mules loaded up improbably with luggage and parcels. One in particular was constantly shifting sideways, under the weight of a big chest, in spite of the firm hand of the military-looking man who was leading it by the reins. Its load was covered by a white linen sheet emblazoned with a red cross.

After a brief interruption the psalmody had resumed, led by the monk at the head. The procession moved slowly beneath the gate unimpeded by any of the guards.

'Who are they?' asked the poet.

'Pilgrims on their way back from Rome, I should imagine,' replied the Bargello.

'All in search of salvation at the court of Boniface?'

'They travel in groups, hoping in that way to get through the mountain passes without being robbed. Whatever those beggars have worth stealing,' replied the head of the guards, glancing with contempt at the rabble that had passed through the gate. 'And if they escape the brigands, our innkeepers will soon finish the job!' he added with a snigger.

Dante went on watching after the group, then remounted his horse.

'Where do we unload all our stuff?' asked the Bargello after they had walked a hundred yards or so into the city, as if he couldn't wait to rid himself of that cargo of scrap metal.

'Escort me as far as the priors' palace, at San Piero. Deliver the bag to Maestro Alberto, the Lombard who keeps an inn in Santa Croce. Ensure that he looks after it with the greatest care. I will call in to see him tomorrow.'

THE MONASTERY of San Piero was lit on one side by the sun, which now stood above the roof of the building. The poet stepped into the area that still lay in shade, and walked to the stairs leading up to the cells. He had only just begun to climb them when his way was blocked by someone coming down in a hurry. It was a girl, wearing nothing but a few rags. The prior opened his eyes wide in surprise, as he recognised the skinny features of the girl's face, her green eyes bright with lust.

'Pietra . . .' he barely managed to murmur in a cracked voice. The girl laughed stupidly in his face, before resuming her dash towards the exit. A whiff of winy breath wounded his nostrils. For a moment he was tempted to follow her, but was held back by a heavy sound of footsteps. At the top of the stairs a breathless man had appeared, he too half-naked, and seeing the prior he suddenly stopped. He gave Dante a complicit little smile when the poet walked on, without thinking him worthy of a look, straight to his own cell. 'Oh, Messer Alighieri, you have no need to be so grand, when we have to stay shut away here for two months – we're not like the villains locked up in the Stinche prison!' the man called after him. 'It looks as if you've found a way of getting out at least, at night . . .'

Dante swung round and took a few steps towards the man. The blood had started pulsing in his temples with the roar of a waterfall. His eyes too were dimmed with exhaustion and unease. His strength was leaving him, he realised with the detachment of an outside observer, as he stretched his hands out towards the other man, who quickly turned to go down the stairs, towards the guards.

'You won't be jealous of your whore, will you? You can find her whenever you like, in Paradise!' yelled the man, still keeping a prudent distance away. 'Where I found her!'

Dante clenched his fists and resumed his walk towards his destination. 'Lapo, only the irony of fate has decreed that we should find ourselves part of the same authority. Which I try to honour with merit and intelligence, while you offend it with pettiness and vice. But anyway, in church with the saints and in the inn with the gluttons.'

He had articulated the words coldly, in a loud voice. No door opened as he passed, but he hoped that the others were already awake, and that they had heard. He threw open his door, glancing anxiously around the interior of his little cell. Nothing seemed to be missing. He checked his papers, stacked up on his desk beside the loophole, and his precious manuscript of the *Aeneid*. He brushed his finger over the parchment, worn away by countless consultations. They were all there, yes, but not in the order in which he remembered leaving them. During his absence someone must have ransacked his cell in search of his secrets, with a view to using them against him.

A mocking smile rippled across his soft lips. Blind and ignorant. His secrets were written in the book of his memory, protected from everyone.

The message was also still in its place, hidden among the lines of the sixth canto. His unease grew as he felt his strength deserting him. He buried the text in his cabinet and threw himself exhausted on the bed, finally slipping into sleep.

2

7th August, late morning

H<small>E WAS</small> woken by a piercing blade of light that stung his eyes. The sun was already high in the sky, but not even the third-hour bell had managed to conquer the weariness that he felt. He had spent the whole of the previous day in the grip of a dream-filled fever. He got up and sat on the bed. The room spun around him, rolling like the ship that had obsessively passed through his visions. A black hull, heavy with ghosts, emerging with its cargo of ruined faces each time his consciousness faded into a dull torpor.

He waited for things to stop moving, his eyelids tightly shut. Then he tottered to the cabinet and took out his manuscript of the *Aeneid*. Between the pages he had concealed a sheet of paper upon his return from the ship.

It had been found by one of the customs guards in an anonymous-looking bale of silk. He read it for the umpteenth time:

Entrust yourselves to our work, O Fedeli d'Amore, and welcome from the four points of the horizon anyone who comes to accomplish the plan. First the new Temple will be built, then its magnificent gates. Last of all will come the nave, and the incredible dimensions will have been achieved. There lies the key to the treasure of Frederick, which opens the portal to the Kingdom of Light.

A sealed parchment, with no recipient identified. A sign that he knew it was on its way, and was waiting for it in the warehouse, had a casual inspection not got to it before he did.

He reached his hand towards the bag that he had thrown on to the big chest at the end of the bed, and took out the notebook that he had found on the galley. He began delicately opening the pages, which were stuck together by the dampness of the sea. It must have been the logbook, judging by the navigational notes that were repeated with monotonous regularity. Here and there the ink had been diluted, making the writing illegible. He deciphered a few Mediterranean place-names and an inventory of goods. One of the last notes listed some names, perhaps the members of the crew, followed by a short record of repairs carried out in Malta.

A Christian ship. With an unusual crew, however, if those names were really what they seemed to be. A lot of

Frenchmen from the Languedoc. And then the passengers, indicated as 'people from beyond the sea'.

But why would a Christian ship have been carrying pagans, and not as galley-slaves, but staying in the captain's cabin? And under that macabre banner, too. The imperial treasure had been entrusted to them. And what was the Kingdom of Light?

And yet there was something comprehensible in that text. That name, the Fedeli d'Amore. The sect of which he too had been a member in his youth, the secret group struggling against the despotism of the popes. Frenetic thoughts, passions of love. He had known nothing more about them since leaving to devote himself to the political struggle in his city. And now they were coming back, in the company of death.

Death. For some time it had been his travelling companion. He heard its silent footstep as he crossed the sun-drenched streets of Florence, he noticed its breath when his hair stood on end for no reason, like a dog's pelt.

It lived in every line of his next work. The big poem about heaven and earth. A pilgrim's dialogue with the great souls of antiquity, in which he would reveal all the secrets of the beyond.

His eye slipped over the pile of sheets on the desk, papers and parchments collected from everywhere possible, carefully scraped so that they could be used again. He ran a few pages through his fingers.

On one of the first he had traced a picture of the earth, perfectly divided into land and water. And in its belly the vast cave in which the damned would be placed, arranged in circles in a vast amphitheatre, around the dreadful well where Lucifer groans for all eternity. And then the huge cliff rising from the waters, in which sins are purged by climbing. And then . . . and then nothing. His imagination seemed blind, unable to find anything that might with the same precision convey the state of beatitude and the visible form of the heavens.

Evil was so much simpler.

FOR SOME time Dante had heard the unusual sound of people moving, apparently heading towards the Ponte Vecchio. As if a crowd was coming back up from the Oltrarno, heading for the northern districts. First of all, immersed in the rereading of his own writings, he had paid no attention to the sounds and voices. But now the hubbub had grown intense. Instinctively he glanced at the door. Perhaps there was a riot going on, or worse, an uprising by the wool-carders, who were always on the brink of revolt. He ran outside, to find himself in the middle of an excited crowd running down the narrow street like a river in flood.

Amongst the throng of people, most of them dressed in the modest clothing of workers, every now and again one could see the more refined outfits of some members of the upper classes, and the uniform of the district guards. Among them he recognised a face.

'Messer Duccio, what are you doing here? What's everyone doing?'

The secretary of the Council, a middle-aged man, completely bald, had almost fallen on top of him, pushed by the crowd.

'They're all going to Santa Maddalena, Prior!' the man panted at him. 'The reliquary of the East has arrived!'

Dante slipped to the side, dodging the crowd that was moving like a tidal wave along the street.

'Hunting for relics? This gang?' the poet muttered in disbelief.

The secretary braced his shoulders, as he shoved a peasant out of their way. The man didn't even seem to notice, so anxious was he to run ahead with the others.

'The monk Brandano, the preacher of miracles, has arrived from the lands of France!'

'Nothing good has ever come from the lands of France, only the corruption of our honest customs and the worst kind of pestilence. And less than ever since the treacherous Philip has reigned there. They all seem to have gone mad.'

'You're right, they all seem to have gone mad. But when you've seen it for yourself . . .'

'What am I supposed to see?'

'The miraculous Virgin. Come on!'

Dante stared at him, startled. But the other man had already slipped ahead, driven forward by the crowd, and was gesturing to him to follow.

'Come on, you come too!' he heard the secretary calling again as he was sucked in by the crowd.

THE ABBEY of Santa Maddalena rose up behind the old Forum, just beyond Santa Maria in Campidoglio. A massive construction, built on the foundations of an ancient Roman *insula*, whose rectangular perimeter it repeated. In front of it loomed the abbey church with its simple baked-tile façade, followed by a second construction beyond the apse, which had once housed a small community of Benedictine monks. A tall, blind wall on the left closed from sight the cloister, caught between the church and the adjacent buildings.

'Tell me, Messer Duccio,' Dante called to his companion, as he pushed his way through the crowd that thronged before the portal, trying to enter. 'I thought the abbey was abandoned.'

'It is. The community that lived there has almost disappeared. The last abbot died about ten years ago, in the days of Giano della Bella.'

'So who owns it now?'

The town clerk shrugged. 'Hard to say. It was supposed

to return to the ownership of San Pietro. But in practice, adjoining the houses of the Cavalcanti, it was annexed to their possessions in the two adjoining streets.'

Dante looked up towards the neighbouring buildings. He knew those walls very well. The two-hundred-foot truncated tower and the other houses crowding round it, connected by buttresses and walkways. By walling up the outward openings and fortifying the doors, the family dwellings had been transformed into a fortress in the heart of the old city.

'Perhaps Messer Cavalcanti felt the desire to own a family chapel before dying. But it was abandoned, now that his son Guido, the ruffian, has been exiled for factionalism,' Messer Duccio went on.

Dante merely nodded. He himself had signed the banning order. And his heart was still trapped in a vice of suffering.

INSIDE THE church a crowd of men and women thronged into the nave, crushed against the pillars and the unadorned stone walls by the pressure of the people still pouring in. Between the two last pillars an iron chain had been hung, which cut the space, preventing anyone from passing beyond it to the altar. Behind the plain marble table a little wall closed off the space of the choir, obstructing the view from the apse like the wings of a theatre.

Beyond the chain, beside the altar, a wooden chest had been placed, almost as tall as a man, covered by a white linen sheet embroidered with a large scarlet cross. Dante had the sense of having seen that strange object before. He was trying to remember where when he was pushed towards the barrier by a shove from behind. Next to him, a young man wearing student clothes had forced his way to the front, and came and stood next to Dante with a swift word of apology.

Dante turned back in search of Messer Duccio, but the man had disappeared behind the sea of heads. He heard a hum of voices starting up among the crowd.

Another figure had appeared from behind the altar, dressed from head to toe in the coarse cloth tunic of the Holy Land pilgrims, tied around his waist by a hempen rope that held a big wooden cross. All that was could be seen of the man was the part of his face left uncovered by his hood, with a flowing, jet-black beard that reached halfway down his chest. His hands were hidden by the wide sleeves.

He was the monk seen at the head of the unusual crowd of pilgrims, at the city gate. Dante was sure of it. And the chest was the same one he had seen at the Porta al Prato. But now, standing before the altar, the monk's face had nothing of the gaunt obsessiveness that had appeared before Dante in the uncertain light of dawn.

With a dramatic gesture the man threw back his hood,

uncovering a completely bald skull and a majestic brow. It looked as if the marble statue of an ancient Roman had emerged from the earth to walk again among men. There was nothing humble about him, Dante thought, observing him carefully. He represented the perfect icon of the warrior monk, with his big wrestler's shoulders, his imposing stature and, above all, the erect position of someone who comes more to challenge than to ask.

Without a word the man approached the chest and pulled away the cloth, revealing a richly decorated aedicule, like those little portable chapels that Dante had seen being used by itinerant preachers. Then he opened its doors.

Inside, on a table with a central pediment, lay a bronze reliquary almost three feet high. The image, finely chiselled and decorated with a large number of multicoloured stones, reproduced the bust of a woman. The poet had seen something similar before, works of art born to preserve the remains of saints. Coverings for legs, hands, sometimes heads. But this one was big enough to hold an entire human bust.

The strangeness of the face that was represented disconcerted him. The artist had bestowed upon it lineaments of the most unbridled lust and perfidy. Along with an intense pain, in the twisted mouth from which mother-of-pearl teeth gleamed. The hand that carved this must have been extraordinarily skilful, to have evoked so perfectly in metal a goddess from hell. Dante looked round, studying the reaction of the crowd, but it seemed that no one around him was shocked by this indecent object in a holy place.

After waiting for the crowd to absorb the emotion of the moment, the monk approached the reliquary, touching it with his hands as if to warm the cold bronze. First he appeared to undo a buckle that must have secured the base to the bust. Then, manipulating invisible fastenings, he opened an orifice in the head, making part of the sculpted head vibrate. Inside the cavity something white gleamed. The skull of some saint or martyr, Dante thought, irritably. He had never appreciated that custom of breaking bodies apart, rather than leaving them to wait in their entirety for the trump of the Day of Judgement. But perhaps it was only an ivory statue, like those of ancient gods.

Meanwhile the monk had stretched out his arms, to ask the crowd for silence. Then he brought his hand to the reliquary, activating a kind of little handle that protruded from the bust. He drew it to himself, opening it up and putting its contents in full view.

It looked like the torso of a young adolescent girl, cut at waist-height. The beautiful, impassive face seemed covered by a thin layer of translucent material, paler than ivory, which sealed the girl's eyes in tranquil sleep. The head was enclosed in an embroidered bonnet of pearls and gold threads that revealed barely a strip of the gently rounded forehead. The hands, crossed on the chest in the same position reproduced on the reliquary, closed to conceal the sweetness of the little bosom. A statue in wax, to judge by the pallid colour of the complexion and the fixity of the expression.

'Look, the relic!' he heard several voices exclaiming around him.

'The prophet!' cried others.

Dante began to observe the naked bust more closely, this time with a sense of annoyance. Like this, it wasn't a statue, but a bit of mummified body, he thought with disgust. And the stretched skin of the face, the fullness of the cheeks and the eyeballs that he imagined under the closed lids gave it a living appearance quite at odds with the chiselled horrors that were displayed more and more often in churches.

A passage opened up in the mass of people, leading to the chain. A few feet away from him the prophet, as the crowd had called him, had spread his arms, face raised to the sky.

'Behold the Virgin of Antioch crying vengeance for the unhappy Holy Land!' he exclaimed in an inspired tone. He had a deep voice, run through with notes of roughness that revealed his southern origins. 'She is here, a warning to your consciences!'

A pause for effect followed, as if the man wanted to collect all his forces.

'When the pagans, having broken down our defences,

burst into our streets and houses, the horrendous slaughter began. And the terrible wrongs. This young saint had hidden in her house, but when the pagans invaded it, it was her father himself who rescued her from the torments that the demons would have inflicted upon her. With a blow of his sword he divided her virgin body in two. And then the miracle occurred, blinding her assailants. Witness the power of God!'

All of a sudden the preacher lowered his arms, pointing the right one towards the statue. After a moment Dante clearly saw the Virgin's eyelids open, their irises illuminated by a glaring light.

A startled silence had frozen the hundreds of people crowding into the nave. Then a rumble overwhelmed everything, joining all the voices in a single exclamation of wonder.

Even the poet had murmured something, surprised, fascinated by the relic, which continued to move. After opening its eyes completely and looking around, it relaxed the grip of its hands with a fluid motion, raising its right hand in the act of blessing those present. The delicate chest, the breasts barely prominent, seemed to be moving rhythmically.

'It breathes . . . it's alive!' he heard someone shouting beside him, among the thousand other exclamations exploding all around. The relic had begun to turn its head, studying with its motionless eyes the space in front of it, as if in search of someone. It really was alive, however incredible that might have seemed.

The first rows had fallen to their feet, overwhelmed by the crowd of people pushing violently forward, stretching their necks to get a better view.

'The blade cut through her body at the level of her loins. And yet she went on living, through God's will! She uttered terrible words against the pagans, shattering their blind arrogance, confusing them in their terror. And as they groped their way through the darkness, the few who had escaped were able to reach safety, carrying her with them to lands lit by the grace of God!'

The Virgin continued to scan the crowd with her icy gaze. The blue of her irises was so pale as to appear almost white. When her eyes met Dante's, for a moment the poet had a sense that they were looking for him, out of everyone.

'She will lead us to recapture the lost East. We will go back there to free the Sepulchre and make ours once more all the wealth that the pagans stole from our brothers. Listen to her words, when they are announced to you! And meanwhile help her cause with the contributions that each one of you can give,' Brandano went on, pointing at a low, squat figure covered down to his feet by a habit similar to his own, which hid him completely from view.

For some moments the newcomer had begun to move around the crowd, waving a bag in which he was collecting the money that so many hurried to give him. Dante noticed that the figure was keeping his distance from him, head plunged deep in its hood, as if afraid to meet his eye. Perhaps because one could clearly read on his face all the perplexity that stirred within him, Dante thought.

Meanwhile the ritual of the exhibition of the Virgin seemed to be reaching an end. The relic slowly closed its eyes, and once more pressed its hands against its chest. It seemed to have returned to its endless sleep, lost once more in its dreams of Gloria and justice. After closing the doors and securing the belts that held together the various bits of battered marble, the monk Brandano turned to face the still-agitated crowd, pulling behind him the door that closed the aedicule, and covered the miraculous chest once more with the embroidered cloth.

Dante was disconcerted. But he did not share the stupid astonishment of the ecstatic crowd around him. At fairgrounds he had seen maimed and deformed creatures so many times before, apparent insults to life itself. There must be some explanation that reason could – and had to – find.

And yet the Virgin really did seem to be a triumph of the impossible. How could a body survive without half its vital organs, its most intimate fibres slashed to pieces? And breathe without contorting in the most dreadful pain? How could that creature feed itself, unless the hand of

God really did intervene at every moment of its deformed life?

The ancients too had confronted wonders, and even Aristotle had admitted that, in the face of the supernatural, reasons for believing and reasons for denying were equivalent to one another.

But why would a superior power choose that mode in which to manifest itself? His mind refused to accept it. Could God's majesty really reveal itself in those convulsive ways, in the horrendous mutilation of the flesh? In the form of an acrobatic spectacle? All to rouse the rabble to an enterprise that should instead have prompted ardour and virtue? Did God really need this, to free the birthplace of the Son from his enemies? 'It brings misfortune . . . it's cursed,' someone murmured behind him.

Dante turned round in search of the source of the voice. Those words gave form to the sense of unease to which he had fallen prey since seeing the relic. It was an old man, bent double with his years, dressed in modest but not plebeian clothes. 'The Virgin? Why is she cursed?' he enquired.

The old man was staring at the passage along which the two men had vanished with the reliquary. 'Not the Virgin of Antioch . . . whoever she might be, but the obscene wrapping in which she is kept. I have seen that form before, in the days of my youth. I know the hand that carved that face. I saw it more than half a century ago, at the workshop of Maestro Andrea the bell-maker, where we learned the art of casting metal, he and I.'

'Who was he?'

'Guido Bigarelli. *Magister summus. Magister figurae mortis.*'

'Guido Bigarelli? Architect to Frederick the Second? The great Bigarelli?'

'Oh, great, certainly . . . at designing evil. That reliquary – I know how he made it . . .'

The old man shook his head from side to side. Dante was perplexed: perhaps the man's mind had reached its twilight, or already descended into darkness. But that name, Guido Bigarelli, echoed like distant bells.

The Emperor's architect, Frederick's right-hand man in all his most perverse dreams. Bigarelli was said to have decorated his secret chapel in Palermo, after the Swabian had returned from across the sea. Dante had known him too, when for a brief period the sculptor had worked for the friars of Santa Croce. In those days the poet was barely a boy, first getting to grips with the verbal arts. But he clearly remembered the broken nose and unruly beard that gave the man the air of a satyr, his eyes lost in troubled images.

'Master of the face of death . . . why?' Dante asked again. He no longer heard anything of the hubbub around them, gripped solely by that single question.

'I know how he did it,' the old man repeated. 'He cast

it from the body of his dead lover. Lost flesh rather than wax . . . I saw it.'

AT THAT moment some people moved between them, pushed by others who were pressing forward, shouting behind them. The prior noticed the young student who had bumped into him before. He was staring at them as if he had been listening carefully to the speech of the old man, who was now disappearing into the crowd. There were other things Dante would have liked to ask him, but he refrained from following the old man when he heard his own name called out.

He turned round, trying to look beyond the throng, and gave a start. The man who had called him, and who was staring at him with his dark eyes, stood out a good six inches above the heads of the crowd. Dante moved in his direction until he finally reached him.

'Messer Alighieri, you too at the court of miracles?' the man asked with a smile, as they both went and stood in the shelter of a pillar.

Dante had half-closed his mouth in surprise. 'Yes . . . like you, incidentally,' he murmured, unable to think of anything better.

The other man went on smiling, shaking from his face the mass of still-black hair that was beginning to be veined with whitish stripes, in curious contrast to his beard, which was as white as snow. He moved towards Dante, dragging his right leg, which was slightly shorter than its fellow. 'Curiosity is the first foundation of all science. You should know that: you too have tried to penetrate the secrets of nature, when we knew one another in Paris.'

Images of that brief period at the Faculty of Arts quickly passed through the poet's mind. And amongst those the face of this man, Arrigo da Jesi, who had in those days held the chair of natural philosophy.

'How long ago did you leave Paris?' asked the poet.

'Times have changed in the lands of France. After the attacks by the Pope's followers, it became impossible to teach in peace. So I crossed the Alps and stayed for some time in various cities in the North. Most recently I taught in Toulouse.'

Dante's initial surprise was melting away as the man's paternal image required consistency in his memory. Arrigo had been the teacher who had struck him the most, in those days, by the lucidity with which he expounded the theses of the great ancient philosophers.

'Why did you not look for me, Maestro?' the poet affectionately rebuked him. 'I would have welcomed you with the respect that you deserve, allowing for my modest means.'

Arrigo smiled again and cordially slapped his shoulder. 'Thank you, but you mustn't see me as an unhappy exile. I have sufficient resources to live, and from time to time I still give lectures. In fact I hoped to meet you at one of them, and thus renew our acquaintance in the space of words, the only space worthy of the wise man. His only kingdom,' he concluded after a brief pause, looking at the chaos around them.

'Public service has kept me from that kingdom. But I certainly haven't forgotten the lesson you taught me. As I see that you haven't forgotten my name.'

'Could I have forgotten my most brilliant pupil?'

'It seems that your attention does not turn solely to the mysteries of nature and of God,' Dante went on, nodding at the spectacle behind them.

'Knowledge is the wise man's mission. And knowing everything is his most noble ambition,' the philosopher replied after a moment.

'Knowing everything is another name for omniscience. And omniscience is the attribute of God alone, as Thomas Aquinas and Saint Bonaventura teach, amongst many others,' the poet replied. Without noticing, he had begun to cross minds with his former teacher, returning to an interrupted challenge.

'There are also other teachers to lighten our darkness. Others have sought and continue to seek the light, besides the great men to whom you have just alluded. We spoke of some of them, back then. But others it was not wise to mention, not even in the lands of France.'

'And here in Florence?'

'Perhaps.'

Dante felt that he had stepped on to a slippery slope. 'So what do you think about what we just saw?' he asked, changing the subject.

'What we saw . . . Are you sure we both saw the same thing?'

'Certainly our eyes are different, as are our hands and our noses. But essentially the image that our minds draw, from what our senses convey to them, must be the same: because our mind is the mirror of God's, which is one.'

'And what if there were no God?' replied Arrigo, calmly.

'You blaspheme, Arrigo!' Dante raised a threatening finger, and there was a chuckle in his voice. He didn't believe that a man with a chair in the Faculty of Theology could really nurture such a doubt. But the other man didn't share his hilarity. 'I mean, if there were not a single God. If, as with light and shade, the divine principle were also divided into a realm of goodness and its opposite? If that were the case, which of the two dominions would what we have just witnessed belong to?'

Arrigo shrugged. 'Forgive me, Messer Alighieri. It is the continuous use of doubt that may easily become a habit of mind in anyone who, like me, uses it for the investigation of nature. But let us return to the monstrous spectacle that has been presented to us. It seems that God has suspended his laws. Never in my study of the phenomena of nature have I encountered a creature that could survive without half of its organs.'

'Are you, as I am, thinking in terms of a doll, with some sort of mechanism to bring it to life?' asked Dante.

'Maybe. Or maybe not. In France I have seen several of those animated puppets that decorate clock towers. But never one as apparently natural as that. You might almost believe . . .'.

Still immersed in their conversation they tried to reach the exit. But outside the crowd seemed to have come to a standstill, and excited voices rose as if an altercation were in progress. Dante stood on tiptoe, trying to discover the source of the noise, and recognised the Bargello shoving his way through the crowd, flanked by a little group of soldiers and darting his eyes all around.

'Messer Durante!' he cried when he spotted Dante. 'They told me I would find you here!'

'Why so keen to see me?' replied the prior, instinctively becoming defensive.

'We need you at the Angel Inn. There's been a death.'

Dante lowered his head, clenching his fists and his eyelids to conquer the dizziness that had taken control of him. His heart had started thumping like crazy, as a mute rage filled his soul. Again! He struggled to breathe deeply.

As if the streets of Florence were those of Hades. The warm air entering his lungs seemed to have become impossible to breathe. He sought a different image in his memory. Pietra's face, her scornful smile. 'You deal with it – I'm tired.

There will be someone among the priors who can take care of it. Ask one of them.'

'No . . .' The Bargello had already broken off after his monosyllable, as if he couldn't find the words to continue. He cast a suspicious eye at Arrigo, who had stepped discreetly backwards. 'The dead man is someone . . . who shouldn't be there. He's very old. He's wearing Turkish clothes,' he added, emphasising the last two words.

Dante half-closed his eyes. The fourth man. So the reaper's scythe had interrupted his escape? He felt a sudden energy filling his limbs, sparked by that unexpected turn of events. His unease seemed to have waned.

'The Angel Inn, you said . . . Then let's go there. We might be in time to resume our conversation about that ship.'

'But I told you the man is dead!'

'And I want to talk to him. We can always listen to his mute witness, if we are capable of hearing him.'

Meanwhile he had turned towards the portal of the church, taking advantage of a narrow passage through the crowd held open by the *bargellini*, but not before nodding goodbye to the philosopher. The chief of the guards moved behind him, shaking his head.

THE ANGEL Inn opened on to a little street of beaten earth, in the shelter of the ancient Roman walls, next to the street leading to Santa Maria Novella. It must originally have been one of the perimeter watchtowers, whose top had collapsed in the distant past. Now it jutted from the remains of the walls like the last sentinel of a vanished army, submerged by more recent constructions that had gone beyond it towards the countryside. At ground level a big hall had been built around the circular structure with solid wooden planks; this was where the kitchen was, and where the poorer wayfarers were put up on rough beds wide enough to hold as many as three people.

On the other side the lane ran into a low dry-stone wall that ran along a vineyard. Clouds of flies buzzed around the dung that passing horses had deposited on the mud before being tethered to the gate-post.

'Who does this land belong to?' asked the poet, pointing straight ahead.

'The Cavalcantis . . . I think,' replied the Bargello after a moment's reflection. 'The inn must have belonged to the family, some time ago. It was one of their mills, and the tower was a storehouse before being turned into a staging post for pilgrims.'

The Cavalcantis again. And again the same sense of sin and treachery. The prior shook his shoulders to rid himself of it, and began concentrating on the inn once more. The sign showed an angel with its wings spread. An unknown hand had painted over an inscription next to the word 'angel'. But time and weathering had washed it away so that the word was legible once more beneath the blur. The Fallen Angel – that was the inn's original name. A thin smile rose to the poet's lips: he was sure that it was Guido Bigarelli who had insisted on the name – that would be typical of him.

'Where's the body?' he asked, shaking himself abruptly from his thoughts.

'Come with me. There are some cells upstairs in the tower. The innkeeper hires them out to rich travellers who want to sleep alone. It's in one of those, on the top floor.'

Dante hesitated for a moment longer: he wanted an image of the whole to form in his mind before it was overwhelmed by a plethora of sensory impressions. Then, without waiting for the other man to move, he crossed the threshold of the little door and walked alone up the flight of oak stairs that spiralled along the massive wall.

He suddenly became aware of a strange atmosphere, but one that he couldn't quite pinpoint.

He had climbed the stairs very quickly, but halfway up he struggled to breathe in the dense and torrid air. Two small doors opened up on each of the first three floors. The fourth floor had only one door: the whole top floor of the tower consisted of a single room, closed at its apex by imposing chestnut beams. The stagnant air stank, stirred faintly by a feeble draught that came from two little windows set in the front wall.

'Where . . .' he began as he crossed the threshold, but

even before receiving a reply he stopped, struck by the sight that met his eyes. The space before him repeated the circular shape of the building, with a diameter of perhaps ten ells or slightly more. At the end of it there was a little wooden bed, barely big enough for a man of medium height. Nearby, a clothes-chest illuminated by a guttering candle.

In the middle of the room stood a high-backed chair, behind a little desk. In it, a man's body sat stiff and motionless. Dead, but not abandoned to the peace of eternal repose, or prone and crying out for vengeance, because none could have uttered that scream. The man's head, almost severed from his torso by a savage blow, lay sideways on his shoulder.

Dante crossed the threshold to approach the body. Copious amounts of blood had gushed from the wound, spraying the clothes and splashing a page upon which the dead man's right hand still lay, precisely at the centre of an octagon drawn in charcoal on the parchment. The fallen head appeared to turn towards the body from which it had begun to separate. The prior had to conquer a sudden feeling of dizziness before his eyes decided which of the two parts of the body to focus upon.

The body was dressed in fine clothes. They were ample and light, draped around the man's nakedness as majestically as a Roman toga; his forehead was partly wrapped in a woven veil. There was something unusual about the garments' shape, which explained the Bargello's idea that the man was dressed in the Turkish style. In fact they were clothes more suited to travelling than to urban living. Perhaps a wealthy pilgrim, as his presence in the aristocratic area of the inn seemed to indicate. The prior delicately moved the head, brushing aside the long strips of white hair that fell on either side of the face, hiding it from view, and then lifted it towards him.

The victim's face was marked by an anguished grimace, the eyes wide open. And yet, the poet was sure, it was not in pain or surprise. No, that man had tried to go on seeing until the very end. To know the experience of death, or rather to try to escape it. In the black of the pupils Dante sought that shadow of the last image seen, which is said to imprint itself upon the eyes of the dying. But all that his investigations found was a dark cavity. The deep folds in the forehead and at the corners of the half-open mouth, revealing an incomplete, yellowish set of teeth, as well as the grain of the skin marked by the wear of time, indicated advanced age. He recalled the face of the oriental man on the galley, also aged.

And yet the body of the man in front of him seemed massive and well formed. Beneath the clothes one could sense a powerful set of muscles.

For a moment Dante suspected that he might be in the presence of the remains of two different corpses, and that the strip of flesh that still held them together was merely an artifice. He lifted the head, and rested it against the severed throat of the corpse. The lacerations matched up perfectly, and the skin connecting the two parts was intact.

As he performed this operation, his eye concentrated on the dead man's face. The features reminded him of something – a vague ghost of voices and faint colours had begun to stir within him. He placed the head against the shoulder once again and continued to stare at it.

Around him, the little room seemed to have been ransacked. The clothes-chest had been opened and turned upside down, and beside it lay a leather bag with the straps cut, perhaps by the same blade that had slashed the man himself.

Dante looked inside, but it was empty. A thin smell of wax struck his nostrils, along with the more distinct one of ink-gall. There had been papers in there, perhaps removed by the murderer. The hypothesis was reinforced by a dark stain in one corner of the bag, next to a fragment of broken pen. The chest had contained a brass ruler and a compass.

'Call the innkeeper,' he told the Bargello.

A few moments later the other returned, along with a quivering little man, who almost slid along the wall, in an attempt to gaze upon the corpse as little as possible.

The poet cast him an enquiring glance. 'Are you Manetto del Molino, who keeps this inn on behalf of the Cavalcanti?'

The innkeeper nodded. The chattering of his teeth was plainly audible in the silence. It was then that Dante understood the reason for the sense of strangeness that had accompanied him since the moment he had stepped into the inn: there were none of the usual sounds normally heard in such places. No shouting, no laughter, no women's voices. Not even the rattle of crockery or the clatter of hoofs on cobbles. Everything seemed as dead as the victim.

'Who was this man?'

'A pilgrim on his way to Rome. He said his name was Brunetto da Palermo, a painter. I thought he was one of the many who were going to see the Pope to work on the Jubilee . . .'

The poet's eye turned to the dead man's hands. Knotty, covered with the dark marks of old age. But still strong. 'Have you taken anything from here?'

'No, heavens above! I wasn't even brave enough to come in when I was told about . . . about . . .'

'Who discovered the crime?'

'One of Monna Lagia's whores. She had gone to see if any of the guests felt like – well, you know how these things are . . .'

Dante nodded distractedly. 'You mentioned guests. Who's staying in the other rooms?'

The innkeeper cleared his throat. 'There are six guests. Apart from . . . from this one,' he said, pointing to the body, still without looking at it.

'Tell me exactly the names of each of them, and where they're staying.'

'I can do better than that, Prior. I can show you in person. They are drinking together in the big room down below. If you'll follow me . . .'

Dante set off behind him, followed in turn by the Bargello. A wide trapdoor opened in the wooden floor of the first storey, perhaps the loading bay of the old barn. The innkeeper lifted it and beckoned the poet over.

Below them a group of men were sitting around an oak table, drinking from earthenware pitchers. They were sunk in quiet conversation, far from the usual effervescence of tavern noises. They seemed to be biding the time as they waited for something.

'Are those your guests?' the poet asked in a low voice.

The other man, after a quick glance, nodded.

Dante cast his eye over the group, settling on each in turn. He pointed to the one sitting at the top of the table, his head sunk between his shoulders, a vexed expression on his kindly features. Dante thought he had seen him somewhere before. He was the youngest, twenty or younger.

'Franceschino Colonna, from Rome,' the innkeeper murmured. 'On his way back from Bologna. He's a student and he's going back home.'

The prior remembered the young man he had noticed in the miracle church.

'And that one's Fabio dal Pozzo,' added the innkeeper,

following his hand, which had turned towards a squat man sitting beside the first, with a goblet of wine in his hand. 'Cloth merchant. He's come from the North to sell Scottish wool.'

Still in silence, Dante nodded towards the other two, who were sitting on the other side of the table, in the corner, intent on a game of dice. One, wearing clothes that stretched tight as a drum-skin over his large belly, slowly shook the cup as though reluctant to tempt fate. The other man, with features as dark as his own outfit, and terrifyingly thin, distractedly observed his companion's movements.

'Rigo di Cola, the fat one,' whispered the innkeeper. 'Another wool merchant. He's heading to Rome for the Jubilee as well. And the other man's called Bernardo Rinuccio. He's travelling with a lot of paper and ink. I think he's writing something. He's always with the friars, at Santa Croce, rummaging in their paperwork,' he added with a grimace.

The man's angular cheekbones seemed about to pierce the skin of his hollow face. A shiver ran down the poet's spine.

The landlord seemed troubled as well. 'He looks as if he's already dead . . . doesn't he?'

Dante nodded. Boniface was buying up works by artists to beautify Rome in time for the *Centesimus*, the grand Jubilee. His friend, the artist Giotto, was about to leave too. 'And that one?' he whispered, pointing his index finger towards a massive man who, in spite of the infernal heat, sat wrapped in a white woollen cape. His face, with a distinctive aquiline nose, was marked by a long scar that ran from one eyebrow to his cheek. A blow that had only failed by a miracle to kill him.

'Jacques Monerre, a Frenchman,' hissed the innkeeper.

'A Frenchman? And what brings him to these parts?'

The innkeeper shrugged. 'From Toulouse, he said. He's come here from Venice. A *literatus*, like the old man at the end.'

'Toulouse . . . but he's come here from Venice,' repeated the poet, pursing his lips. 'And who's the last one?'

He pointed to the one who had first attracted his attention, an old man with long grey hair parted in the centre that flowed down his thin shoulders. The man was tall and dressed in the sober, dark clothes worn by scholars. His face, illuminated by eyes that shone with youthful light, seemed marked by a network of deep wrinkles. It looked as if he was in the grip of intense cold. His hands were also protected by dark leather gloves.

'Messer Marcello,' replied the little man in a mixture of obsequiousness and diffidence. 'A most learned man, apparently. From the North. He's going to Rome to fulfil a vow. Or at least that's what he's told his companions. One of my serving-girls overheard him.'

Dante glanced once again at the group, then withdrew

to avoid being seen. He didn't want them to know they were being watched. 'Close the door and make sure no one tries to get in. And if anyone does try, take note of it and tell me,' he ordered the little man, before leaving the room again. Then he turned once more towards the Bargello. 'Have the body taken away from here, to the hospital of Santa Maria. In secret, in so far as that's possible in this city of gossips. And without giving any explanation of what's happened.'

'Explanation? We could do with some explanations ourselves,' the chief of the guards replied sarcastically.

'That's true. We haven't got a lead, but the wise man's mind is happy to move through the torments of thought, where the mind of the vulgar man becomes lost and discouraged. And my mind . . . but all in good time.'

'Do you want to question these men? Perhaps . . .'

Dante shook his head. 'If the murderer is one of them, he will have had time to erase every trace by now. And questioning him along with the others would only give him certain advantages. He would jumble his words up with everyone else's, like a wolf among a pack. Better to let him think we know more than we really do. That way we'll make him anxious and give him a false sense of security. And between that Scylla and Charybdis I will stretch my net.'

He moved towards the stairs. On the steps he carefully straightened the folds of his habit and adjusted his biretta, carefully arranging the veil over his right shoulder. Then he started down, moving past the seated men, and made for the light beyond the door.

He had to shield his eyes with his hand before he became accustomed to the glare outside.

3

Morning of 8th August, at the priory

'HERE IS the information you requested about the guests at the inn,' said the town clerk, showing Dante a sheet of paper. 'It hasn't been easy: I've asked all the chief guards at the city gates.'

'Do you expect applause, Messer Duccio?' snorted Dante, taking the sheet from his hands. On it there was a list of names, with a few words next to each. 'Your labours don't seem to have yielded much.'

'Florence is a land of freedom. We don't investigate travellers unless there's a reason involving the security of the Commune,' the other man replied, piqued.

The poet shrugged, then immersed himself in reading. The report added little to what the innkeeper had already revealed.

The only new clue was the record of the date when each of the men had entered the city walls. The pilgrims had arrived by different gates, from the four points of the compass. First Brunetto, the victim, on 2nd August. And with him Rigo di Cola, the wool merchant. The next day Bernardo Rinuccio, followed by the young Colonna and the cloth merchant Fabio dal Pozzo. Then the French knight and finally the old doctor, only two days before. As if they had arranged to meet, waiting for one last pilgrim. Instead, the last to arrive had been death, the most undesirable of guests.

Or perhaps death was already waiting for them there, its yellowish skull hidden behind one of their faces. And it was preparing to take control of their lives in that run-down tower, as it had already done on the ship of the dead.

THE SUN was beginning to set, turning the façades of the houses red. Nearing Orsanmichele, Dante thought of taking the route by the Torre della Castagna, close to the houses of the Cerchi. It could be an opportunity for paying a visit to his relatives, who lived in the same street. But then he changed his mind, seeing that the shadow of the sundial fixed to the loggia was now approaching the seventh hour of the day. He had some way to travel if he was to reach Maestro Alberto in his workshop before the end of the working day.

He plunged into the labyrinth of alleyways behind the remains of the ancient amphitheatre, skirted by a wasp's nest of humble stone houses and wooden shacks where many of the craftsmen of Florence lived and had their workshops. Further south, towards the Arno, the road was blocked by the row of weavers and dyers and by the carders' big water-mills anchored to the river bank. For the last stretch he wandered around the open-air benches of the silk-steamers until he reached a point where the narrow street widened slightly, avoiding the remains of a Roman arch. Immediately after it the way was blocked by a big wall built with the remnants of the old building, where a gate led into a little courtyard. Alberto the Lombard's house opened up on to it.

People were gathered in the little square in front of his workshop. Amidst shouts and laughter, men and women were excitedly watching something in front of them. Thinking that an acrobat was performing and making silly jokes, the prior pushed his way through the people, preparing to order him to move on.

But it wasn't what he had expected. A pillory had been erected on the corner of the street, its wooden pincer constricting the hands and neck of a man in peasant garb, who was lamenting in a loud voice. All around, the laughter of the onlookers rose along with his mounting wails, while stones and dung picked up from the ground were hurled at him.

Dante walked over, resolving to pass by. But someone must have recognised him, because an anxious murmur ran through the crowd, followed by a sudden silence. In that void the voice of the convict suddenly rang out, a confused babble stuffed with Latin terms.

Filled with curiosity, Dante stopped near the pillory. 'What are you complaining about, you rogue? What were you convicted of?' he asked, leaning forward to meet the unfortunate man's eye. When the other man went on staring at the ground, the poet gripped him by the few hairs he still had left, forcing him to lift his head.

Screaming with pain, the man turned his neck as far as he could to return Dante's gaze. On his swollen face one livid eye had been closed by a blow, but the other glittered with malice. 'Oh, Messer, by my faith I am exposed to this derision only because of a *quaestio irresoluta*, a difference of interpretation,' he announced quietly.

'It is over a philosophical disputation that the Bargello has bound you to this cross?' the poet replied in astonishment, relaxing his grip.

'Precisely, Messer. I see from your clothing that you must be a man of culture and learning,' said the convict who, defeated by the uncomfortable position in which he found himself, had turned his face towards the ground once more. 'So you will understand my innocence.'

'Both prisons and hell are full of innocent men, it's well known,' Dante said ironically.

'And yet you will agree with me when you know the history of my disgrace. It all originates in my desire to increase my ancestors' little vine by acquiring a farm on its boundary. My neighbour and I agreed to move the boundary by thirty paces, which I asked to measure personally, with my feet.'

'So?'

'So, I counted out precisely thirty paces, but he declared me a cheat – and here I am.'

'Why? It seems to me that you respected the agreement.'

The other man unexpectedly exploded into mocking laughter, as if all his sufferings had disappeared as he remembered what had happened. 'I ran the thirty paces, Messere. But rather than appreciating the joke, that false neighbour of mine immediately reported me.'

Dante had involuntarily joined in with his laughter. 'It's really a matter of mutual understanding, my friend. Certainly, the measurement increases if the measurer is quick,' he agreed.

The other man seemed content with his judgement. 'Will you intercede on my behalf?' he asked anxiously.

'No. But since you're a philosopher, accept your punishment philosophically and wait for vespers. A few strokes of the whip and you'll be free.'

THE *MECHANICUS* was busy fixing pulleys to a support, for one of the cranes working at the building site of the new Duomo. As the poet walked in, he interrupted his work.

'That consignment I sent you . . . where is it?' Dante broke in.

The other man pointed to a corner of the workshop, between a shelf and a little door. The bag lay there, still tied. 'I haven't touched anything, in accordance with the orders of the *bargellini*,' replied Maestro Alberto. 'But whatever's in there, it would be a good idea to take it out as soon as possible. The cloth is drenched with water.'

The poet quickly untied the laces and began to remove the fragments of the device, passing them to the man who arranged them on the workbench.

As part of the machine passed between his fingers, a grimace of surprise grew on the face of the *mechanicus*. Dante carefully studied his reactions. 'So, what do you think it is?' he asked when the bag was empty.

Without replying, Alberto took from a shelf a lamp with a brass disc behind its wick to concentrate the light. He lit it, even though the workshop was still illuminated by the sun, and concentrated his myopic eyes on the bits of machinery lined up in front of him. 'They look like elements of a tower clock – but different from the ones I know. Apart from . . .'

'What?'

'These carvings, on one of the wheels.'

Dante brought his head close to the point that the other man indicated to him. 'Moorish characters,' he said after a brief examination.

The other man nodded. 'This machine was built by the infidel. Where did you find it?'

The prior didn't reply. The image of the galley had floated into his mind for a moment, with its cargo of death. He gestured vaguely, muttering a few words about confidential commercial matters.

But the *mechanicus* seemed to pay him no heed, gripped as he was by what he had in front of him. 'Besides, they have always excelled at this particular art. Even Frederick the Great had to use Arabs for the clock in Palermo,' he remarked.

'Can you understand what they mean?' asked the poet, touching the incisions with his finger.

'I can't, but my servant can. He can read the writing of his ancestors.'

The *mechanicus* left the room for a moment, before returning in the company of a boy of medium height, with olive skin and the sharp features of someone prey to hunger and rancour. 'This is Hamid, captured off the coast of Egypt. I saved him from the oars when I discovered his skill at working metals. But I don't know if he's grateful to me.'

The old man held the gear-wheel out to the slave, showing him the writing. For a moment the boy stared at the spot he was pointing to, then suddenly looked away. His expression, at first impassive, now seemed perturbed.

'So?' Dante asked him, irritated by his hesitation.

The boy still didn't reply, his frown deepening. 'It's blasphemy. It's an insult to Allah, the powerful, the merciful,' he finally murmured. 'Why do you want to repeat this offence by translating it into the language of the infidel?'

Dante gave a start at the pagan's phrase. But he restrained himself: the boy's face showed signs of sincere discomfort. And perhaps an offence against God really was one in any language.

'The insult against your god will be lessened in my tongue. Out with it!'

'Allah is great,' the Saracen finally decided to say, 'but al-Jazari . . . is greater.' He had drawn his head between his shoulders, as though fearing that Allah might be listening.

'Al-Jazari. Who's that?' Dante asked him.

'I know,' the craftsman exclaimed. 'Al-Jazari, of the great Persian family that made automata. The very greatest of them.'

'Automata?'

'Machines for imitating life. Golden peacocks capable of spreading their lapis-lazuli tails. Bronze lions able to roar on the gates of the thrones of the East, and other diabolic things of that nature. It would appear that the Emperor commissioned something from them to increase the value of his court still further,' Alberto went on. 'He had seen some works by this infidel in Jerusalem, when he went there as a crusader. An extraordinary mind.'

Dante had averted his gaze, staring into the void. He

was thinking about the relic in the church, with its simulacrum of life. The idea that it might have been nothing but a statue animated by a hidden mechanism had never left him.

'But also a . . . a perverse one,' Alberto was saying.

'Perverse. Why?' asked Dante, struck by these words.

'There's something indecent about wanting to simulate life, to invert the order of creation and elevate things of wood and metal to the level of live creatures, even threatening the place of the living.'

'Inverting logic and nature?' the prior asked. Those words had suggested an idea to him. The galley that he had explored also seemed like an incredible inversion of the meaning of things. An object born to protect life on the hostile seas, transformed into an infernal ferry-boat. 'But God instructed us to possess the earth, to name its riches, to regulate its mutability. Even your clocks, Maestro Alberto, are regulators. Is your art not blasphemous, too? Shouldn't you be writing something similar on your toothed wheels?'

Alberto shook his head and was about to reply, but Dante interrupted him. 'Meanwhile tell me if you can grasp the purpose of the machine by studying its remains.'

The other man shrugged, with a dubious expression. He went back to staring at the fragments, rearranging their order a number of times and attempting to link them in different ways. His clenched lips and beetled brow revealed his growing dissatisfaction. At last he stopped, after one final attempt. 'Perhaps. But not entirely. Some essential parts are missing. Certainly, it's like a big clock in some respects. You see this toothed pivot and this fragment of chain? It's the heart of the mechanism, I'm sure of it. Fixed around its axis, this strip of steel activates the first wheel, which transmits the movement to the other, smaller wheels, by means of a sequential application of rotational speed at a calculable rate; if I had all the parts . . .'

'And you say it was built by this al-Jazari,' Dante went on after a brief pause in which he had tried to weigh up the other man's explanations.

'Al-Jazari was the greatest machine-maker in the whole of the known world, the very glory of our trade. If only we had access to his constructions . . .' Alberto resumed staring at the metal fragments, his expression full of religious respect. 'If only he hadn't been killed,' he went on.

'Al-Jazari was killed? Why?'

'He was executed by his co-religionists. Apparently he'd gone mad. Or at least that's what was said years later, in Christian lands.'

The prior stroked his chin reflectively. He pulled so hard on it that he seemed to be trying to stretch his lower jaw. Lost in reflection, he brushed a finger along the incised characters, going over their spirals once more. 'Allah is great, but al-Jazari is greater.' Blasphemy. Blind pride. Even the best were his victims this time.

'When did he die?'

'Around the middle of the century. Just before Emperor Frederick.'

Dante went back to observing the mechanism. So, if it really was al-Jazari's work, as everything suggested, this most complex object must have been constructed at least fifty years before. Where had it been kept for so long? And why had it now come in the company of death, in lands so far from its origins? Above all, what was its purpose?

'There was another thing that was said about him.' The *mechanicus* had spoken in a low voice, but it had been enough to interrupt the thread of the poet's thoughts.

'What?'

'That he was driven mad by one of his discoveries.'

'A machine?'

The other man shook his head. 'No, his machines were his pride, his joy. Al-Jazari went mad because he had discovered the limits of God.'

'The limits of God?'

'That's what they say.'

Dante fell silent for a few moments. The faces of the dead were dancing before him. Then he remembered the astrolabe that the Bargello's men had found on the ship. He looked for it in the bag. Now, in the bright light, he noticed that the tiny marks were not a decoration, but regular carvings of degrees and orbits. Along the rim, once again, Arabic characters. An object of extraordinarily refined manufacture.

He turned round, seeking the young Saracen. Hamid had knelt down on a little rug and was praying with his head turned towards the wall.

Dante walked over to him, holding out the instrument. 'And what's written here?'

The slave hesitated, as if he feared being exposed to another blasphemy. Then, after a rapid glance, he seemed to take heart. 'It's a dedication. "To him who measures the stars." A gift from the Sultan to the head of the astrologers of Damascus.'

The poet and the *mechanicus* stared at one another, waiting for the young man to continue. But there was nothing more to say. Thinking about what he had just heard, Dante looked away, his attention drawn by the room around him. As well as the big workbench, some of the shelves were covered with tools and mechanical parts. In one corner of the room he saw a little niche holding a mat and a rolled-up bed-roll. It must have been the place where the slave-boy slept, he thought, spotting the edge of a manuscript peeping out from beneath the cloth.

Curious, he bent over the mat and lifted it up. It was a decorated manuscript in which the arabesques of the characters merged harmoniously with the ornaments in the margins. The boy had followed his movements apprehensively. Dante caught his eye when he looked up to question him.

'It's a precious, pagan book. What is its title?'

'The story of a dream. It's the *Kitab al-Mi'raj.*'

Without being aware of it, the prior had placed his hands on the text, as if he wished to keep it. Years before, his teacher Brunetto had spoken to him of this rare volume, known in Latin as the *Liber scalae Machometi.* Mohammed's journey into the realm of shadows, to the throne of God. He would have liked to know its contents. And now it was in his hands, but written in a language that he was unable to decipher. He held out the manuscript to the Saracen, but still clutched it tightly. 'You will tell me what is written. If you don't want the Commune to drag you out and burn you, for an act of heresy.' The boy lowered his head. 'But not now. I will come back, to learn what I wish to know.'

Near the hospital of Santa Maria Nuova

'Oh, Dante! Always running, as if the Furies were after you!'

The poet froze, recognising the clumsy voice yelling abuse at him. The newcomer stood, legs spread, on the other side of the street, winking at him with a vulpine expression in his keen eyes. Then he raised his hand, gracefully moving his fingers like a flirtatious girl. His broad face was stamped with an ironic little smile.

'Can I greet you, too? Or are only the Beatrices and your other girlfriends allowed to flash their eyes at you? And yet I too could make the air tremble as they do . . . with my farts, perhaps!'

The poet turned towards him, his fists clenched and his face bright red.

The other man shielded himself, with a comical expression of terror. 'For the love of God, Prior, what a terrible face! The same one that I saw on the plain of Campaldino. That's why we won: the Aretines had no one as terrible as you.'

Meanwhile Dante had reached him. He looked the man up and down, taking in his showy outfit. 'Cecco, are you still here?' he hissed. 'You know there's no place in Florence for debauchees and ne'er-do-wells. I thought you were already on your way to Rome: in the Eternal City there will certainly be more room for you and your enterprises, and the air there is more favourable to corruption.'

Cecco Angiolieri sat down on a stone at the corner of the crossroads, after carefully arranging his stockings and lifting his jerkin, the better to display his breeches.

'And you should know that the laws of Florence forbid indecent and lubricious clothing. What in the devil's name are you dressed like?' the poet pressed him.

But the other man didn't seem at all concerned. He gestured with his hands, indicating the people around him. 'My friend, it is true that in the city of Boniface there are more taverns than stoups and more brothels than confessionals. And in fact it is there that my star revolves, regretting what I have done and gaining the indulgence of the *Centesimus*. But a stay in your virtuous city is obligatory for anyone setting off on the path of goodness and contrition. And as for my breeches,' he went on, stretching out his squat legs and darting Dante a smug glance, 'I must say that no one in Florence has complained, if the truth be known.'

Dante burst out laughing. 'If you frequented our temples and lecture halls rather than our taverns, you would be less full of yourself.'

'Ah, Dante, it's the weight of terrible melancholy that is crushing me and dragging me from the good life. And, above all, an irritating lack of money. If my old man doesn't decide to kick the bucket soon, and leave me the little he has left, I will be forced to beg. Unless you know of a decent opening somewhere. It looks as if things are going really well for you accursed Florentines. It could be that there's a scrap of bread for me, too. I'm here to offer my services.'

'To whom, might one know?'

'Oh, there's always someone who needs a sharp tongue or a ready hand. But you, on the other hand . . .' Cecco winked at Dante, nudging him in the ribs. 'Tell me about your work. What is the prince of Tuscan poets about to offer the world? I heard a rumour, among the Fedeli. A journey into the kingdom of the dead.'

'Of the dead and those who will not die.'

'Nothing less . . .' Cecco murmured in an ironic voice. But Dante had plunged back into his reflections. 'Apparently you want to match the French for arrogance,' said the Sienese, pointing to the walls of the new Duomo, which were rising up behind Santa Reparata. 'Vast cathedrals are being erected, with tall pinnacles and huge pointed vaults. It's as if you want to build a stairway to God, rather than calling to him humbly here below, as we do in our churches.'

Dante, at this last remark, suddenly came to. 'Climbing to God . . . Yes, that's the problem . . .'

'What do you mean?'

'The threefold realm of the dead, in darkness and in light. In my mind I have already drawn the first two states, the lost and those who purge their sins in fire. But of the third realm . . .'

'Paradise? How do you imagine it?'

'That door is still locked to me, Cecco. The realm of Good has still not assumed definitive form in my mind. None of what I have thought so far does justice to the power of God's throne. Sometimes the vague image of a lake of light floats into my mind, with the souls of the just warming themselves around it . . .'

'A circle of idiots around a bonfire, like camel-dealers camped out in the desert. And that would be your Paradise? That's our reward for all the gall and shit that we have to swallow in this life?' the other man exploded with a snigger. 'My word, I can understand the faith of the Mohammedans, with their Paradise rich in milk, honey, wine and beautiful women.'

An expression of nausea appeared on Dante's face. He waved with his hand, shaking his head as if to expunge what had just been said.

Meanwhile he went on walking, sidestepping the crowd of men and beasts that sometimes threatened to run him down. Cecco seemed distracted, as if his thoughts had turned to something a long way off.

Reaching the foot of the steps, Dante stopped, gripping his friend by an arm. 'Cecco, I am here to perform a very sad duty. To inspect the corpse of a murdered man.' He moved towards the entrance of the hospital, but after a few steps he stopped, turning towards Cecco. 'Come inside with me, if you like. For once your cunning and cynicism might be of use to me.'

Without replying, Cecco followed him.

THEY WENT down into the cellar where the bodies of the dead were displayed. The air was almost impossible to breathe, poisoned as it was by the smoke from lamps running on stale oil, and the miasmas that rose up from beneath the stained sheets thrown over the corpses. Protecting his face with his veil, Dante approached the last of the plank beds, where the men of the Misericordia had arranged the naked limbs of the dead man. The head had been reconnected to the torso, and only the frayed strip on one side of the neck bore witness to the horror.

A merciful hand had undressed and washed the body. Dante approached to study that face once more, while Cecco had stopped a certain distance away, his face contorted into a grimace. He observed the heavy features, worn by the abuse of time. And the nose, bent to one side as if broken long ago.

Dante was struck once more by the same sensation that he had felt at the inn. He had seen that face before, he thought as he stroked the gaunt cheeks. Conquering his horror, he gripped the head, bringing it close to his own face. 'Who are you?' he murmured.

He felt as if he was walking in a circle around the edge of a dark well. Then, suddenly, like a bubble of air rising to the surface of a muddy pond, a name appeared in his mind.

He had known this man more than twenty years ago, when he had attended the Francescan school at Santa Croce.

Cecco waited behind him in silence, with a look of

nausea on his face. 'What does it mean?' he murmured at last, while Dante remained silent.

By way of reply the poet merely nodded ahead of him, as if indicating something beyond the cellar wall. He moved his finger as if searching in the air for words that his thoughts had left behind. Then his mind returned from the hypothetical landscape that he had been exploring. 'There, in the church. The reliquary of the virgin. This man is Guido Bigarelli, sculptor of the dead.'

Cecco looked at the victim with perplexity, as if the name suggested nothing to him. Dante, on the other hand, seemed increasingly prey to uneasy astonishment. Could Bigarelli have come back to Florence to be killed there, when one of his works was reappearing in such a marvellous way? It couldn't just be a simple coincidence.

Then his mind returned to the place where they were standing. Cecco continued to stare at the body with an indecipherable expression on his face.

'Bigarelli . . . Bigarelli seemed to be waiting for them,' Dante exclaimed all of a sudden, turning towards him. 'All the others.'

Cecco had bent low over the body. 'But how was he killed? It must have taken enormous strength.'

Now that the wound had been washed of blood and the head put back in its natural position, the trace of the blow that had been delivered looked very impressive. The neck vertebrae gleamed white through the strips of lacerated flesh.

With his index finger the poet touched the edges of the severed neck. 'It's strange . . .' he murmured.

'What?'

'There are signs here of two deep blows. The tip of the blade ran through the neck. Then the murderer moved it to the right, ripping through flesh and bone. Twice, in the same way. Two blows, similar, but clearly different, as if . . .' He broke off.

'As if there were two murderers?' asked Cecco.

Dante shook his head. A sudden idea had come to him. He looked again at the naked body lying in front of him, then turned round in search of something. 'Where are his clothes?'

Cecco looked round as well. In a corner of the room, in a wicker basket, blood-stained clothes were heaped in disarray.

Dante quickly walked over and began to examine them. As he was carefully touching the fabric, beneath his hands he noticed something soft in an inside pocket. It was a folded sheet, with a few signs marked on it. He recognised an octagon, rapidly sketched in pen, with little crosses on some of the vertices. And next to it some words: '*Templum lucis, haec arca thesauri Federici.*'

'This is the temple of light, the casket of the treasure of Frederick.' And then a quick phrase in the common tongue: 'Here opens the door to the realm of darkness.' Those words again, the same as in the message he had hidden in the sixth canto. Something flashed through the poet's mind. Again he examined the dead man's clothes, oriental in style. 'People from beyond the sea' were the words in the galley's log. The corpse that lay here before him – could he be the missing fourth man?

Dante turned towards his friend, who had come over to take a closer look, his face blank.

'Cecco, what brought you here to Florence? I mean – your real reason.'

His friend stared him in the eye. 'To renew my acquaintance with love,' he exclaimed, with his usual mocking air.

Dante shrugged impatiently. He knew that phrase very well, the password of the Fedeli d'Amore.

'But a bit of money wouldn't come amiss, either!' the Sienese concluded.

Midday

THE PRIOR took his leave of his friend. He was uncertain what to do, divided between his desire to deepen the investigation and his need to return to San Piero. The sun beat down on the cobblestones, raising spirals of scorching dust. He noticed the sting of the fine powder in his eye, and without thinking he moved towards the middle of the street to reach an area of shade on the other side. A shout behind him made him start, just in time to keep from being run over by a cart that had appeared out of nowhere. He flattened himself against the wall, cursing the driver who went on urging his horses on without so much as a thought for him.

'Out of the way, villain!' he heard the man cry. Dante was about to run after him, but the cart hurtled violently over a stone, coming perilously close to crashing into him.

'Careful, Messere!' someone yelled at him from the other side. A tall old man, dressed in dark clothes.

Dante shielded his face against the glare with his hand, trying to make out his face. It was the man whom the innkeeper had identified, among the guests, as Marcello, the doctor. He suddenly forgot his rage. 'Thanks for the warning,' he replied, moving towards him. He had a sense that in some way the man was waiting for him. 'I think I know you,' he said when he had reached Marcello, greeting him with a slight bow.

'I know you too, Messer Alighieri. By reputation, if not in person,' the old man replied, bowing his head in turn.

'One's reputation sometimes runs faster than one's feet. And what brings your own feet to these parts?'

'If you know of me, then you also know my art. The study of the tribulations of the body, and of the movements of the stars that determine or cure them. I planned to visit the hospital, to see if my art might be of any use to my unfortunate companion, at the inn. But it would appear that there is nothing more that medical science can do for him, other than confirm his departure from the land of the living.'

'Even with the greatest art imaginable, you could have done nothing for him. He must have died immediately. Did you know him? Was he your friend?'

Marcello remained silent for a moment, as if meditating on his reply. 'Do we not in the end all know each other, everyone on earth?' he asked at last. 'Are we not, by virtue of our humanity, all part of a single family? It seemed to me that it was my duty to go with this man as he took his first steps into eternity.'

'But you knew who he was?' Dante insisted.

The old man hesitated, as if he could not find words to express what he had in mind. 'No, I didn't know him. Except for that brief time when we shared lodgings, in the inn. And yet I had the impression that he knew me. That in fact . . .'

'What?' the poet said by way of encouragement.

'That he had gone to that inn deliberately. To wait for me. As if he knew I would be turning up there,' the other man murmured.

'Explain what you mean.'

'It was something in his manner – the confidential tone with which he addressed me from the evening of our arrival. He was constantly asking me questions, as if he expected me to ask questions of him. He did the same with Bernardo.'

'The *literatus*?'

'He knew of Bernardo's research, and talked to him for a long time, about the past.'

'What did he say?'

'He spoke of his passion, the life of Emperor Frederick. They debated whether the Emperor had ever been to Florence. And now this . . . But it's too late for anything now.'

'A man's death closes his accounts with the art of medicine. But not with justice,' Dante replied, staring at Marcello.

The man nodded. 'It's true. In fact, justice is infinitely more powerful than my humble knowledge.'

Meanwhile Dante had drawn level with the old man, until he could touch his right arm. Beneath his clothes he could feel the solid resistance of his muscles, as if his body were younger than it really was.

Marcello had instinctively recoiled, as if to escape the poet's touch. 'Forgive me, Messere,' he said quickly as he caught the prior's startled expression. 'It's an old habit of mine, contracted when I was healing lepers, beyond the sea.'

'Did you plan to return to your lodgings?' Dante asked him.

'Yes . . . but your city has changed a great deal since I was here last, many years ago now,' the old man replied, glancing at the buildings around him. 'Would you mind accompanying me a little way?'

Without speaking, the prior took his arm, walking slowly towards the ruins of the old baths, along the street that led to the inn.

'What set you on the road to Rome?' asked the poet.

The other man stopped and turned to face him. 'As a man grows older, the time comes to settle his accounts with God and pay off his outstanding bills. I am close now to the *redde rationem*, when Saint Peter will weigh out the debits and credits on his scales. And for that day I want my soul to be washed clean. I am going to Rome to fulfil an old vow and beg forgiveness for the sins I have committed on my long journey through this vale of tears.'

'And how heavy is your burden?'

'What man does not bear one so heavy, especially if, like myself, he has reached a great old age? A long life is a life of many sins.'

Afternoon, outside Santa Croce

IF WHAT he had learned at the inn was true, Bernardo Rinuccio must have been spending almost all his time in the library of the Franciscans. Dante waited outside the door of the scriptorium for the monks to come out once their work was over. Finally Bernardo's bloodless, hollow face appeared on the threshold.

Dante saw him coming, carrying a bundle of parchments and his writing case. Bernardo looked ill and tired, and his step was slow and difficult. And yet he did not seem to be suffering from the heat. From time to time he stopped, leaning his foot on a stone, and took his wax tablets from his bag, writing something on them with a piece of pointed metal.

At a public fountain he avidly approached the bronze pipe, and drank in great gulps. He seemed prey to an insatiable thirst. Dante drew up beside him, greeting him politely. Bernardo returned the greeting, wiping the sweat from his brow with his sleeve.

'I have been wanting to speak to you for some time,' the poet said.

'I know your task, Messer Durante. And I know your voice as a poet. I imagine you want to know the facts related to the horrible death of the painter, Brunetto. But I cannot help you. I only met him at the inn and glimpsed him a few times during meals. My research often takes me outside in search for information. Or closed away in my cubicle, setting down on paper what I have learned,' he added, nodding towards the parchments.

Dante, his curiosity aroused, came closer to him. 'What is the nature of your research?'

'I am attempting to finish the third part of a piece of writing, the *Res gestae Svevorum*. The history of those great Swabian emperors. And particularly of the greatest of them, Frederick. The facts of his life and his death.'

'And what have you found that was useful here in Florence? My city never received the Emperor, to my knowledge.'

'It never welcomed him in his lifetime because he was often hostile to the city, in spite of the presence of many loyal Ghibellines within its walls. But also because the Emperor feared the Scot's prophecy: You will die *sub flore*. But perhaps something of him came here after his death.'

'After his death? What do you mean?'

The historian shrugged and clamped his lips tight shut as if he was afraid of having said too much. 'I found something in the pages of Mainardino's *Chronicles*, and it was that that brought me here.'

'Mainardino da Imola? The bishop loyal to the Emperor, who is said to have spent his last years writing a life of Frederick? But his work is lost, as far as anyone knows. Or perhaps it was never written!'

The other man half-closed his eyelids, glancing cryptically at the poet. Then he looked quickly around, as though to check that no one was listening.

Dante instinctively did the same, but saw no one paying them any attention. Meanwhile Bernardo had pulled a long twig from a bush, and was busy tracing signs in the dust in the road.

'So if that text exists,' the poet pressed, 'and you have been able to read it, what have you learned from it that brings you here? And what if the Emperor came here after his death?'

Bernardo did not reply immediately, trying to find the right words. 'Mainardino wrote something about a treasure belonging to the Emperor. This is how my master put it: '*Thesaurus Federici in Florentia ex oblivione resurget,*' 'Frederick's treasure will emerge from oblivion in Florence.'

'And that's what you're looking for?'

Bernardo firmly shook his head. 'It isn't wealth that I desire. On the margins of life, gold is the most useless of materials. However, I would like my humble work to respond to the question to which even my master could not give a reply. But I want to ask Arrigo da Jesi. I learned that he too is from your city.'

'Why the philosopher?' Dante asked, startled.

'It's in Mainardino's papers. Arrigo was a novice with Elias of Cortona, Frederick's Franciscan friend. And he is said to be very rich. Like Elias. Of whom it was said that he had learned the alchemical secret for making gold. Or perhaps he had found the imperial treasure.' Bernardo seemed to be thinking out loud. 'But perhaps everything is lost,' he said then, shaking his head sadly. 'Everything has vanished into dust with the death of Frederick.'

'And the proof is thought to be here in Florence? Along with his treasure?'

'Mainardino was sure of it. I'm trying to check that certainty. Before death takes me and freezes my lips as it has frozen my master's.'

Dante gripped the man by an arm. 'Do you think you're in danger? Tell me who is threatening you, and all my authority will rise up to shield you!'

The other man smiled sadly. 'Not even all the legions of ancient Rome could come to my aid, Messere. For some time now my piss has smelt of honey and a fire within me is devouring my innards. I only pray to God that he will grant me time to bring my work to its end,' he concluded, bending once more to drink from the fountain.

The prior waited until Bernardo had more or less quenched his burning thirst.

Then the man stood up straight, licking his lips as if to drink every last drop. He seemed to feel better. 'I too should have drawn up the Treaty of Jerusalem,' he murmured.

Dante darted him a quizzical glance, and saw a faint smile lighting up his face. 'In Jerusalem, during his crusade, it is said that Frederick concluded a treaty with the infidels, who in return revealed to him the secret of the panacea, the drug that cures all ills and sends death back beyond the borders of the realm of darkness. Because of this legend, it is believed that Frederick never died, and that he is waiting to come back in the turning of fifty suns since his decease. Just think, Messer Durante: the return of the Antichrist in the year of the Jubilee. Wouldn't it be a terrible joke on Boniface?'

'It occurs to me that the Pope declared his *Centesimus* specifically to exorcise that possibility,' Dante murmured.

*

A LITTLE later Bernardo took his leave and walked wearily away.

For a moment the poet thought of following him, then decided to return to Maestro Alberto. Perhaps there had been some news about the mechanism. And then that book, the *Mi'raj*, kept popping up in his thoughts. The tormented faces of the dead alternated in his mind with the confused image of the heavens in his future work. As if the form of Paradise, still not found, and the dark form of the crime were merging into a single blindness.

He was distracted from his thoughts by the sight of a massive silhouette that had emerged from a side-street to pass along the curve of the ancient amphitheatre. 'Greetings, Messer Monerre!' Dante called to him from behind.

The other man jerked round, looking around to see who in the crowd had called his name. He looked worried, but his circumspection dissolved as soon as he recognised the poet.

'You won't mind exchanging a few words along the way, I hope,' said Dante, catching up with him.

'Messer Durante, it's an honour for me to make your acquaintance. Even if I can imagine the origin of your interest in my humble person. Perhaps in other circumstances learned matters would have been our subject, rather than violence and death.' The man had pronounced those words in correct Tuscan, rendered slightly harsh by his French accent.

'I hear that you speak my language well. But to which learned matters do you refer?' the poet replied.

Monerre raised his finger towards the sky. 'The science of Urania, to which I have dedicated my whole life. In Toulouse, where I was born, then in the Languedoc and finally in Venice. There I studied the chart of the skies on the maps of the ancients, particularly Ptolemy. Sometimes amending imperfections which those great men had disregarded. And I tried to spread that knowledge from my university chair, but without success. And the proof of this is that my name is unknown!'

The man had closed his speech with a bitter smile. As he grimaced, his scar appeared more marked.

An astronomer, thought Dante, surprised by the coincidence.

He must have looked puzzled, because the man smiled. 'If you ask what I am doing in your city, it is only a stage along my final journey.'

'Where are you headed?' asked Dante, increasingly curious. 'And why is this journey your last?'

The word resounded in his ears with a macabre echo. Did this man, like Bernardo, feel that he was close to the end?

Monerre had stopped by the remains of the Roman

gate. In the distance one could glimpse the corner of the Stinche prison, with its grim, blind walls. He ran a hand over his forehead, as though to banish a sudden pain. 'My destination lies in Africa, in the hostile lands of the Moors. And then further south, in the realm of the Manticore, beyond the distant equator, beneath the new southern sky, never beheld by Christian eye. There they speak of the splendour of unknown stars and new constellations imprinting on the heavenly vault the marks of unbelievable destinies. This is the great gap in the catalogue of Hipparchus, which I hope to remedy, at least in part.'

While he spoke, the astronomer's face had brightened, as if his mind's eyes had really flashed with those new lights. Dante heard him absently murmur something in French, before returning to Tuscan. 'And they speak of a divine sign, four stars arranged in a perfect cross. Almost as though to signify the origin of the true faith, or to point to its destiny. But I imagine there is something else that you wish to know.' The emotion had faded from his face. He uttered the last words coldly.

'You spoke of a final journey,' said Dante, engrossed. Florence was becoming an obligatory passage on the way to the end, he thought bitterly.

'I have already travelled in the lands of the infidels. But the injury inflicted on me most recently has damaged the visual ability of my right eye. And through that mysterious sympathy that connects the twin organs, the infection of the one is slowly spreading to the other. Soon I will be in darkness, and the only starlight visible to me will be the one in my memory. That is why I must hurry.'

They went on walking in silence for a long time. The poet tried to keep up with his companion, who walked quickly and vigorously in spite of the infernal heat. 'You're marching like a Berber horse, Messere. Was it on your travels that you developed such a gait?' Dante exploded, after being forced several times to run in order to keep up with the Frenchman.

The other man stopped with a smile. 'Indeed, Prior. There are lands that I have visited in which even an hour's delay can make all the difference between life and death. In the desert, between one oasis and the other, and in the regions infested by pagans, where our bases are precisely a day's journey apart, and any deviation from that means being surprised in the open at night, far from all safety. In those places it is customary for two people to mount a single horse, so that the second may rest and be ready for the remaining part of the march.'

'All lands are hostile in their own way,' Dante murmured. 'You will be aware of what happened in your inn, the murder of your companion.'

Monerre nodded. 'Brunetto. A painter, wasn't he? I often saw him busy at his drawings, in the brief time we shared our lodging.'

'He wasn't a painter. And that wasn't his name. The victim is Guido Bigarelli, the greatest sculptor of our time.'

The Frenchman received the revelation impassively.

'Hadn't you ever suspected anything?' the poet pressed him.

'No. But it isn't unusual for travellers to conceal their identity. For the most various motives.'

'What might those be?'

'To escape the local authorities, if they are in opposition to the governing party. Or the keen eyes of criminals, if they are carrying something precious with them.'

Dante thoughtfully pursed his lips. Bigarelli was an inveterate Ghibelline, passing through a Guelph city. That might well have explained it.

'And perhaps . . . perhaps that was true in his case,' the other man went on.

Dante gave a start. 'What was?'

'The evening before his death, as I went upstairs to my room, I bumped into him. He was standing on the stairs with the fat wool merchant, Rigo di Cola. They were engaged in an animated conversation. When they saw me they stopped suddenly, but not before I was able hear their last words.'

Dante moved closer to him. 'What were they talking about?' he asked anxiously.

'Gold, Messer Alighieri. A mountain of gold. And that in order to have it, they needed to close the light in the circle.'

'What does that mean?' asked the poet, perplexed.

Monerre shrugged. 'I don't know. But that's what I heard. I'm an astronomer, you're the intellectual,' he concluded, with a hint of irony in his voice.

Afternoon and evening

DANTE TOOK his leave of the Frenchman with a vague feeling of dissatisfaction. The idea that the crime might have close connections with the men who, apparently for different reasons, had stayed at the Angel Inn was growing ever stronger.

This idea arose from the sense that in some way, which he could not yet explain, there was something that bound them all together. And yet their characters, their clothes, even their physical appearance were as different as it was possible to imagine. Apart from the fact that they were all foreigners, merely passing through Florence.

He was sure that the form of the crime reflected the mind of the perpetrator. The victim always seems to summon his own executioner, selecting him from those most like himself. The violent man finds death in the brutality of a deliberate act, the amorous spirit ebbs away in lasciviousness and incontinence. So who had the sculptor sought to put an end to his days?

Guido Bigarelli, the master of the figures of the dead,

had returned after a long absence, under a false name, as if to meet death itself. He had courted death throughout his life, in his works. He had made a pact with death, he had silently summoned it to dwell in his bronzes, he had stroked its bones beneath the hot flesh of his lovers. And then death had come, demanding its payment. He remembered the crude hypothesis of the Bargello, which he had at first irritably rejected. But now that possibility was making its presence felt in his mind. Was he the fourth man from the galley? Was he the one who had committed the slaughter, to descend to Avernus in the company of a legion of men?

Dante's mind ran to the miracle of the Virgin. Could the appearance of this old work of Bigarelli's be a mere coincidence, as extraordinary as the human-looking thing that it contained? And do coincidences really exist?

THE ROAD narrowed at a spot where carpenters' poles had been set up and a building was under construction. Another manifestation of the arrogance of the newly wealthy classes, Dante thought. He leaned back against the scaffolding to let a cart pass. Someone ran past him, striking him hard in the face with his elbow. The pain of the blow stunned him for a moment.

As he tried to recover, looking around in an attempt to work out what was happening, a large stone fell with a crash on to the plank wall behind him, followed by another, which grazed his shoulder. He instinctively leaped away from the scaffolding, imagining an imminent collapse.

The square in front of him was the stage for a great tumult: benches overturned, baskets of herbs scattered on the ground amidst fragments of earthenware, and streams of oil and wine trampled by a mass of people engaged in fierce combat, in a whirl of wrestling bodies. All around him, a general stampede of men and women trying to escape.

Another stone, thrown by someone in the middle of the throng, skimmed past him, followed by a large number of other projectiles. From the opposite sides of the square some combatants had begun throwing stones at each other, swinging above their heads slingshots improvised from strips of sheet picked up from the ground among the overturned benches. Making levers out of boards and poles found lying around the place, they had first tried to dig up the cobblestones: then, when the ancient Roman paving stones resisted their efforts, they had fallen upon the remnants of the ancient walls of the Campidoglio, pulling out bricks with their fingers amidst yells and insults.

'What's happening?' shouted Dante, who had taken refuge behind a cart, to an old man who sat hunched up, clutching his head in his hands.

The old man looked up at him, encouraged by the sight

of his clothes. 'The Cerchi and the Donati. They met at the market, and the insults immediately went flying. A fist-fight couldn't be far away.'

'Damned brawlers,' the poet muttered between his teeth. He waited for another volley to land all around them, then resolutely rose to his feet and walked towards the middle of the piazza, hoping that his prior's insignia were very visible. 'Stop, in the name of the law of the Commune!' he shouted in a stentorian voice, gripping the shoulders of one of the fighters who had gone crashing into him, and dispatching him with a kick to the backside.

He felt a hand holding him back by the elbow. With a jerk he pulled away, turning round in fury.

The man behind him raised his hands in a gesture of peace, smiling faintly. 'Excuse me, Durante. I was only trying to help you,' he exclaimed, leaning down to pick up the poet's biretta, which had rolled a short distance away.

The poet recognised the smiling face of the philosopher Arrigo da Jesi. He smiled in turn, trying to brush away from his clothes the dust and filth with which they were covered. 'Forgive me my gesture. But in this insane chaos it isn't easy to discern the just man's hand.'

'Perhaps there aren't so many just men in this city,' Arrigo murmured, looking round at the gangs who had assembled on opposite sides of the square, now giving each other surly glances and shouting threats at one another.

'It looks as if everything's falling apart, as if the plan of the city's founding fathers is collapsing in internecine strife.'

'That plan, if there ever was such a thing, was written on leaves, like the answers of the Sybil, which a gust of wind was enough to throw into confusion,' Dante replied with a shake of his head.

The philosopher also looked round sadly. 'So what has reduced your city to this sorry state?'

Dante pointed angrily at the group of ruffians still wrestling with one another. 'This shameful rabble was unleashed like an irresistible flood within our walls. It came from the four corners of Tuscany, drawn by the ease of profit promised by the decadence of our customs, the idleness of our city governors, the simony of our priests, the corruption of our magistrates and the triumphant ignorance of the learned. It spilled into our streets after overflowing from the sewers in which it first sheltered, taking over the land that our fathers spilled their blood to redeem from barbarism. Florence now looks like a maddened horse.'

The prior broke off, still staring grimly at the young thugs. Meanwhile he rubbed his jaw, wiping away with the back of his hand a little stream of blood that flowed from his cut lip.

Arrigo seemed to have followed his words with great attention. 'Other cities in Italy enjoy no better conditions. But a good ruler could return everyone to reason, if only he had the help of all the men of goodwill. People like you, Messer Alighieri.'

'If people like me, whom you are kind enough to praise, were capable of making themselves heard. If you, rather than these ruffians, had the means and the strength presently conferred by ill-gotten gains.'

'Perhaps the time is near when the eagle will return to rule the skies of Italy, and its claws will blind for ever the dogs of night that have invaded our land.'

Dante smiled weakly, still drying his lip with the tip of his tongue. As he spoke, he continued to follow the movements of the battling parties, which had now moved towards the other end of the square, where they swarmed into the side-alleys. 'Cities are big animals, similar in every respect to the smaller animals that inhabit them,' he said bitterly.

'And they fall victim to the same crimes. You can punch a city, just as you would punch a man,' the philosopher insisted.

Dante stared at him. 'That's true. And by the will of fate, that is a crime that I am currently investigating. Death has passed through the Angel Inn.'

'I know. That poor man Brunetto.'

'That wasn't his real name,' Dante replied indifferently, still brushing the hem of his garment with the palm of his hand.

Arrigo had not reacted to his words. He looked calm, waiting for Dante to go on.

'His name was Guido. Guido Bigarelli.'

'Really?' The philosopher had maintained his placid attitude, as if the name were completely unknown to him. 'And are you on the way to finding the guilty man?' he asked, sitting down in the lee of a low wall.

Dante shrugged and did likewise. 'Fragments of a plot, signifying nothing. No precise motive, neither a how nor a why. Just a sense that the crime had been planned not far from the victim, perhaps by someone known to him, certainly by someone close to him. The dead man's travelling companions: that is where I am being taken by my instinct, and by the reason that lies beneath it.'

'Interrogate them, then, with all the power of your perspicacity.'

'What would be the point? I'd end up with a sticky mixture of truth and lies, in which the light of the just would be corrupted by the artifice of the guilty. I don't have the gift of entering their minds.'

'You seem to have lost all hope.'

'No,' replied the poet. 'I don't need their words. There's a logic that governs things, and that logic is supported by necessity. I must discover the necessity that produced the crimes. Then I will have the logic behind them, finally I will have the words I need.'

'So what's stopping you?'

'Something that is making me lose my bearings. The crimes were committed for a motive both contingent and immediate. And yet the reason behind them lies in something remote. That's what disconcerts me: that a single effect should derive from two causes. Aristotle seems to deny this.'

Arrigo shook his head with a smile. 'I admire your trust in the philosopher. But what do you think of the most modern masters from Paris? Bacon, for example. Does he not teach us that it is the order of nature that gives us the norms for our reasoning? And is Nature not the realm of transformation, and becoming, and contradiction? You have spoken to me of "crimes": is it not, then, only Guido Bigarelli who has crossed Hades' threshold before his time?'

'Not he alone. There was a murder some leagues to the west of the city, perhaps to cover up a single crime. The murderer filled an entire ship with corpses.'

Arrigo opened his mouth to ask a new question, but then clamped his lips shut as if he had changed his mind.

'What is the "Kingdom of Light"?' the poet asked him all of a sudden.

Arrigo turned towards him with a stunned expression. 'A place of the triumph of the spirit, I should imagine. Or, metaphorically, what you call Paradise.'

'We?'

'I mean you theologians, who design its appearance, essence and boundaries. Or even you poets, who attempt to clothe them with words. Why do you ask me?'

'It appears that many people are in search of that place.

94

And what if it were in fact a physical location? Or an object with extraordinary properties? The bastards!'

The philosopher gave a start at this unexpected imprecation, as surprised as the other man by a luke-warm flood of golden droplets raining from the sky, along with the tuneless melody of a popular song. Above them, standing on the remains of the crossbeam of the ancient Roman portico, a member of the Donati family had undone his breeches and was urinating down upon his adversaries, making a magnificent triumphal arch with the jet.

Dante jumped away cursing, careless of the stones still falling around him. He threw himself on all fours, frantically searching for something on the ground, then rose to his feet clutching a fragment of brick in his fist. He froze for an instant, making a quick calculation, then hurled the stone at the man who was still singing as he urinated.

Arrigo saw him taking aim at his target, eyes fixed on the projectile as if guiding its trajectory with the force of his thought. He too lowered his head to follow the object, all the way to the crisp smack and the man's yell as it struck him on the forehead. 'Heavens above, Prior!' he yelled in astonishment. 'A throw of biblical dimensions! You Florentines should have David on your coins, rather than the lily. Or at least erect a statue of him to guard your gates!'

The injured man had fallen to the bottom of the wall, with his face reduced to a mask by the blood that flowed copiously from a gash to his eyebrow. For a moment his cries of pain drowned out the noise of battle.

Arrigo went on staring at the poet with a mixture of surprise and concern. Then he smiled. 'Luckily our differences are restricted to the spiritual sphere. Come away, Prior. Let like go with like. Share your time with me a little longer, on the way to my lodging at Santa Maria Novella.'

Dante cast a last grim glance at the square, then turned towards the philosopher, as the wrinkles on his forehead slowly faded away. 'Yes, perhaps it is best to leave this pack of dogs to bite each other as they wish. Let's go,' he replied, setting off at a good pace.

4

Dawn of 9th August, at the priory

DANTE NOTICED a certain amount of agitation in the courtyard. In one corner, a horse, still saddled and drenched in sweat, struck its hoof against the paving stones. A man in armour was deep in excited conversation with the Bargello. Around them, other soldiers were following their words with interest.

His curiosity aroused, the poet approached the group. 'What's happening?' he asked, following from the corner of his eye the courier who had leaped back into the saddle and spurred his horse, before passing through the cloister portal at a gallop.

'News has reached us of a fire on the Pisa road. Something has been burned on the lands of the Cavalcanti.'

'Something? What do you mean?'

'My men couldn't say. Perhaps a barn. Something big, though. All in ashes.'

The inn where the crime had been committed also belonged to the Cavalcanti, the prior remembered. Perhaps it was a simple coincidence. And yet his mind was uneasy. Like a drawing that has been erased, yet begins to reappear on the page. 'How far away is the fire?'

'A few leagues, just beyond the new city walls.'

Dante remained silent for a while, biting his lips. 'Order an escort of *bargellini* to saddle up two horses for us straight away. I want to go and see.'

'But the fire has been extinguished, there is no danger now,' the other man tried to object.

'It isn't fires that worry me,' Dante replied brusquely.

IT WAS almost an hour before the horses were ready. It was some time past midday when Dante and the Bargello, followed by another six armed men, headed eastwards.

Beyond the fields of Santa Maria Novella loomed the reddish mass of bricks of the walls that the Commune was building to contain the mass of new constructions that had recently risen up around the old city. The stretches of wall were interrupted here and there without any apparent logic, as if they had been built by a capricious giant at play. It looked as if the architects had taken it into their heads to emulate the ancient Romans, scattering the countryside with fresh ruins.

Past the future gate, little of which had been built beyond its foundation, they rode a short way along the beaten path before turning northwards along a country lane that continued on between gorges and brushwood, climbing slightly along some low hills. As they emerged from a small oak forest, their goal finally appeared against the backdrop of a little valley: a large area surrounded by burnt vegetation with the carbonised remains of poles and beams sticking out of it. The building was razed to its foundations.

Whatever it had been, it must have been really imposing. All around, the air was still impregnated by a sharp smell of burning, more intense each time a gust of hot wind returned to raise thin coils of smoke. A certain distance away, untouched by the fire, stood some impressive piles of carpenters' planks.

As he came close to the fire, Dante got down from his mount, approaching the burnt area. Behind him, the Bargello had also clumsily dismounted, with a sigh of impatience that was imitated by the soldiers.

'Have you discovered who built this . . . thing?' asked the prior.

'No, not yet. These are the lands of the Cavalcanti, I told you, they have lain fallow for years, no income for the harvest land register, they're not even taxed. There's only one farmhouse around here, but it's more than two leagues away. It was the farmer who alerted the city guards about the fire.'

'And he didn't know anything more than that? Who was working here?'

The Bargello shrugged. 'These people are crude and primitive. Real animals, barely capable of expressing themselves; not like us city-dwellers. All the farmer was able to say was that there were devils here, and that they were working on the construction of "Satan's ring". He must have come over to spy, but something frightened him and from that moment onwards he kept his distance, until the night of the fire.'

Dante was puzzled. Satan's ring . . . He went back over to study the forest of charred poles that rose around him. An infernal forest struck by the wrath of God. 'Scatter yourselves around,' he called to the men, who stood waiting. 'And search.'

'What are we supposed to be searching for?' asked one of them.

'I don't know. Anything. Anything unusual.'

The men cautiously entered the area of the fire, careful not to stand on any still-glowing embers. It was impossible to imagine, by looking around, what the burnt-down building might have been. Judging by the remains of the beams still wedged in the ground, it looked like some kind of pavilion, or a big barn. Or perhaps a stable, but of a very unusual shape. And had the wood that escaped the fire been destined for storage in the building? Or was it supposed to be used for its as-yet-unfinished construction?

Dante went on walking slowly towards the middle of

the hypothetical building. After ten paces or so he noticed how the blackened tips suddenly stopped emerging from the ground, producing a broad, empty space in the middle.

It really did look a ring. Satan's ring. He irritably repressed that fantastical idea. He had to proceed with the comfort of reason and science. 'Have you got any ropes with you?' he asked the Bargello.

'Each man has a few yards, in his saddlebag.'

'Let's try and get a more precise idea of the shape of this thing,' Dante murmured. 'The shape would normally be irrelevant, but in this instance there might be some substance to it,' he added almost to himself. The Bargello had listened to the last words with puzzlement and was about to reply, but the prior had already darted back outside.

He had noticed that there were some spots among the remains where the beams had been both thicker and more numerous, as though they were a kind of buttress, or elements with a particular function.

'Look along the perimeter of the fire for remains similar to this, and stop beside them. Give me one end of your ropes and stretch them out between you,' he ordered the men.

They all started wandering around among the charred remains, pulling the ropes tied between them. One after another they stopped, raising the ropes to make them more visible.

The shape of a perfect octagon had formed before the poet's eyes.

DANTE WENT on looking for a possible meaning in what he was seeing. Around him the comments of the *bargellini* mingled together, as they shouted to each other from the corners of the building. Dante was growing increasingly puzzled. Suddenly he heard one of the *bargellini* calling to him in a loud voice.

'Here, Prior. This might be something!'

He stepped towards the man who had called to him. He seemed intent on looking for something among the blackened wood and was becoming frantically agitated as he went on shouting.

There really was something there. At first it looked like some kind of burnt plant. Five jointed sticks pointing towards the sky. A charred human hand.

The body lay supine, reduced to a carbon statue. The terrible heat that must have been imprisoned in that spot had dried all fluid from the body, turning it into a fragile mummy. But it hadn't altered the general lines of the body. Perhaps its clothing, apparently a leather jerkin, had melted with the body and protected its shape. The head too was intact, still wrapped in what remained of a strip of fabric.

Dante studied that face, which now looked as if it were

made of black glass. Rigo di Cola, one of the two wool merchants staying at the Angel Inn.

In the end the devil really had appeared in his ring, he thought. And something along those lines must have passed through the minds of the men who had been drawn by his cries. He saw more than one of them making the sign of the cross, certainly to invoke protection for himself, and certainly not in honour of the deceased.

Beside the corpse there were fragments of glass, again covered with what looked like a dark shadow. Dante picked up a piece of the substance on the tip of his finger. 'Lamp-oil,' he said to the Bargello, who had joined him.

'Clear as day,' the man exclaimed, sniffing a piece of glass. 'Our friend set light to the oil to start the fire. But he must have miscalculated. Something went wrong and he fell victim to his own plan. The justice of God has many eyes – it comes when we think it furthest off.'

The poet leaned over the body again, staring at the sharp features of the face, which seemed to have preserved a terrible expression of wonder in the dark cavities left empty by the melting of the eyeballs. Then he turned the body over and went on examining it.

'I'm sure it happened as I told you, Prior,' exclaimed the chief of the guards, in a loud voice so that his men could hear.

Dante pointed his index finger against Rigo's back, at a

level with the heart, showing the Bargello something. Two deep parallel cuts in the burnt jerkin. He drew the dagger from the inside pocket of his habit and delicately inserted the blade into one of the two cuts. The steel entered without encountering any resistance in the lacerated tissue.

Still in silence, he tested the other wound as well, with identical results. Then he turned to stare disdainfully at the Bargello. 'So he was caught up in the torment of the flames, and out of remorse for the crime he had committed he stabbed himself in the back?'

The Bargello didn't say a word.

'Or,' Dante continued implacably, 'have you noticed anything else?'

He stretched his arm out towards the dead man, pointing to something close to the body. The remains of some large sheets of parchment, completely consumed by the flames. Whatever had been written on them was lost.

'More writing?' said the Bargello, looking ill. 'A book?'

The prior shook his head. 'Too big. And no trace of binding between them,' he said, picking up one sheet and examining its edge, which crumbled under his fingers. 'More like drawings of some kind,' he continued. His thoughts had returned to the big, empty bag in Bigarelli's room, with its smell of ink.

'The fourth man? The one who murdered the others? In that case, who killed him?' the Bargello muttered suddenly, confused. He seemed to be waiting for Dante to resolve some inexplicable mystery. But the poet merely reflected, holding his chin between his fingers.

His eyes ceaselessly crossed the space around him, sliding from the burnt remains to the corpse. There had to be a logical connection. He felt he was close to the truth, but it kept slipping through his fingers.

The sun was setting. Soon there would be no point in staying there. After ascertaining that the dead man's pockets were empty, he ordered the body to be buried in the shade of a pine, away from the burnt area.

No one said a prayer over that wretched corpse.

THEY WERE halfway back to the city when Dante heard the intense sound of galloping horses. He barely had time to order his men to stop before a group of horsemen in hunting attire, carrying quivers and bows, emerged from a thicket.

At the sight of them the newcomers reined in their mounts and stopped a few yards away. The poet was sure he had never seen any of them, apart from the youngest, who seemed to be the leader of the group.

'Good evening, Messer Alighieri!' cried the student Franceschino Colonna, ostentatiously removing his cap. 'And you, pay tribute to the Prior of Florence!' he called to his companions. The three men bowed their heads slightly in greeting and muttered something inaudible.

'What brings you to these parts, Colonna? Aren't you a long way from the road to Rome?'

'My city has stood solidly on her hills for twenty centuries, and will remain there for many centuries yet to come. There's no hurry to get there, since your lands are so abundant with game,' the young man exclaimed, drawing a blood-covered rabbit from his saddlebag.

'It doesn't look like much booty for four fat men,' the prior observed, nodding to Franceschino's companions, who remained at a distance. 'Your friends?'

'Jolly travelling companions. They too are pilgrims for the Jubilee, I met them on the road from Bologna. As we wait to resume our journey, we're taking occasional rides in the countryside.'

'Do you know where you are?'

'Somewhere north of the new walls, I think. But we've been wandering about without paying any attention to the road. Have we accidentally trespassed?'

Dante shook his head.

'Then have a safe journey, Messer Alighieri, and I will see you again when God wills,' the young man replied, tugging on his bridle and spurring his horse.

Dante watched him take off before disappearing in the direction of the fire. 'I'll see you again when Florence wills,' he murmured.

His instinct told him they were heading straight for the place where Rigo di Cola had been killed. He had heard that murderers often return to the scene of the crime, because of that mysterious attraction that binds conscience and the sin committed. But he had always thought it mere foolishness.

And yet those men weren't there by chance. He had had time to study the prey that Franceschino had shown him. The animal was covered with dried blood, as if it had been dead for many hours. Whatever their intent, those men had not been hunting.

As SOON as they had passed through the city gate, the Bargello came and stood next to him. 'You know, Prior? I've had an idea. I was thinking about that pile of timber that went up in smoke, and the other lot, ready for use. It would take a clever carpenter to put together a piece of work like that. Who knows what a merchant was doing there in the middle of it.'

'Perhaps he wasn't a merchant after all. And someone must have helped him. But I'm sure it was only at the moment of death.'

'Are you thinking of the cloth merchant Fabio dal Pozzo, who's staying at the Angel Inn?' he asked the poet, who nodded. He too had been thinking of the dead man's companion. 'He's an outsider. He's not one of us. And he's already killed someone, someone close to him.'

Dante thought with a shiver of how justice was done

in his city. 'It might be useful to listen to him. I want to question him once we get to Florence. See to it that he doesn't get away.'

At the priory, early afternoon

HE MUST have been dozing for some time, overcome as he was with exhaustion. He got up from the bed with his mind still confused, still prey to the images of his dream. He threw open the door of his cell and emerged on to the portico, taking deep breaths. In the afternoon air a damp night-time smell was slowly becoming noticeable, but it couldn't yet defeat the fierce heat of the sun, still high in the sky. The usual animation of the streets beyond the monastery wall reached his ears, amplified by the echo of the walls.

He saw that the guards had clustered around the open gate, busy studying something outside. Trying to get his thoughts in order, Dante went down to the cloister. Crowds of men and women could be glimpsed through the portal, walking back from the Oltrarno, passing through the Ponte Vecchio and heading for the northern part of the city. 'Where are they going?' he asked one of the soldiers.

But he already knew the answer. 'Towards the Maddalena. There's a rumour that the Virgin is going to be exhibited again today.'

The image of Bigarelli's broken body had never stopped haunting him. Along with his splendid and horrible work, if what he had been told was true. And then the face of that statue and its curious simulacrum of life. His reason drove the prior to seek the guilty man among the guests at the inn, taking refuge from the ambiguous realm of shadows that had been manifested in the abbey. And yet his instinct cried that the miracle was yet another link in the chain of death. 'Tell the other priors they'll have to manage without me at the meeting. There's something that requires my presence,' was all he managed to convey to the guard.

WHEN HE got there, the church was already full to capacity. Once more the poet elbowed his way through the throng, trying to reach his earlier observation point behind the pillar. The canopy designed to receive Bigarelli's reliquary had already been carried in front of the altar, and someone had drawn the curtains to display it to the view of the faithful. But the monk and the prodigious relic had yet to appear.

Dante took advantage of this to study the mass of humanity all around him. Something had changed since last time: the rumour of the miracle must have spread quickly, reaching the furthest points of the city. Now, apart from the vulgar faces and the coarse greyish clothes of the rabble, the nave was animated with patches of colour, the sumptuous clothes of aristocrats and members of the upper classes.

The halt and the lame had managed to grab a place behind the altar. Here and there was the dark clothing of a notary, and in a corner, unsettlingly, the white habits of two Dominicans.

The poet instinctively withdrew behind the pillar: if even the Inquisition had taken the trouble to come, it was a sure sign that news of the miracle had passed beyond the walls of that little monastery.

At that moment the monk Brandano entered through the back door, on slow and majestic footsteps, followed by the two men charged with the duty of carrying the reliquary. The same procedure was repeated, but this time the expectant atmosphere in the auditorium was more palpable, practically frantic. The eagerness of those who had already witnessed the miracle was now joined by the morbid curiosity of those who had heard of its wonders and by the hope of salvation of those who believed that God had really descended to the midst of hell.

Meanwhile the men had uncovered the Virgin's torso, offering to the eyes of the crowd the limpidity of her waxen skin. After a moment, as if responding to a nod from the monk, the Virgin's eyelids slowly lifted, revealing first the white of the corneas and then the blue flash of the irises. Dante admiringly observed the perfection of the mechanism that was surely concealed within the head, which could perform such a gentle motion, so similar to the human gesture. If it really had been al-Jazari who had made this marvel, his fame was truly deserved, as indeed was his condemnation for blasphemy.

But there was something new about the statue, he noticed with dismay. Something truly incredible. The delicate line of the breasts was vibrating, as if a hidden bellows were pressing against invisible ribs, lifting the chest. The Virgin really seemed to be breathing feverishly, creating a sense that the eagerness and anxiety of all the onlookers were somehow communicating themselves to her.

'For too long the Holy Land of Palestine has been oppressed by the pagans,' she began to declaim. 'Perhaps you are deaf to the weeping of those people who, like myself, have paid the penalty for being faithful to the one true God?'

Then, suddenly, she began to stare at the bystanders, sweeping her eyes around in a circle and pointing with her hand at the monk who stood mutely beside her. 'And are you deaf to the call of God himself, who through the voice of holy men like our guide ask you to free the land of His birth and His martyrdom?'

The monk lowered his head in agreement.

'Give your hearts, your swords, your riches to this enterprise! March under the banner of Christ! Before it is too late and your souls plunge into hell as punishment for your idleness!' the relic cried, its voice now breaking with the anxiety of this premonition.

Dante conquered his initial impulse to fall to his knees, and stiffened where he stood. He felt as if something had altered in the diaphanous, waxy consistency of the talking torso, as if by the very effort of shouting its cheeks had assumed the colours of life. The movement of the chest was quicker now, too, the breath beginning to falter.

Then the girl opened her mouth. Dante distinctly saw her chest swelling with the act of breathing in, then her high, clear voice rose up once more in the church, ringing out like a song. The harmonious sounds of a Latin psalm spread through the air.

Dante was confused. His initial hypothesis – that he was dealing with a mechanical artifice – seemed to be mistaken. Not even the brilliant al-Jazari could have replicated the image of authentic vitality that the girl exuded.

His eye returned to the little table on which the torso lay, and the slender central foot that supported the table-top. It was impossible that anyone, however slim, could have hidden from sight behind it. And the chest containing the relic and its support was quite plainly empty. Although he hadn't noticed, his mouth was half-open with astonishment, like that of the most illiterate peasant. So this was still the age of miracles, God deigned to send baffled humanity a sign of His splendour. He felt an unexpected warmth rising into his heart. All around the prior the crowd was beginning to kneel, and he too felt himself bending at the knee.

The Virgin's voice had suddenly become sweet and harmonious. She tilted her head slightly upwards as if seeking inspiration among the roof-beams, or as if she didn't want to contaminate her mind with the sight of the excited crowd.

'Just one more day, and you will be able to enrol under the sign of the Virgin!' exclaimed Brandano. 'Prepare your hearts for a long journey to the lands of the infidel. But trust me, God is with us! On the way to Rome, the Pope's blessing will descend upon our heads, just as the Spirit descended upon the apostles before they embarked upon their mission. Trust in the Virgin, O people of Florence, most delightful children of the Church triumphant!'

Beside him the girl seemed to agree with a slow oscillation of her head, as her eyes unceasingly cast her icy gaze over the ecstatic crowd. But something within her seemed to accentuate the torment of her extraordinary injury, like a shadow that had slowly begun to settle on her features in a barely perceptible frown. Her previously calm expression was making way for one of anxiety, as if being dropped back into the convulsion of life after her brief sojourn with the angels were filling her with pain.

The monk too must have noticed those signs of human weariness. He walked over to her and lovingly touched her bare shoulder, as if to ease her fatigue. The relic seemed to take the touch of his hand as a precise signal. It immediately plunged into silence, closing its eyes and mouth, and slowly bringing its hands back to its chest, as though protecting its delicate breast in the sleep that it had been waiting for.

Dante had a sense of a flash emanating from its eyes just before its lids fell closed. A gleam of disgust. But he had no time for reflection. The crowd around him seemed to have received the Virgin's message of reproach, and was growing agitated, prey to a confused desire for redemption. Men and women, excited at the prospect of saving their own souls and with them the Holy Sepulchre, were moving feverishly forward. Shouts and cries mingled with appeals to action, declarations of intent, invitations to join up.

Meanwhile the poet searched for a rational explanation for what he had seen. But he couldn't find one. Only a faint intuition that perhaps it was nothing more than the simple desire to protect the relic and exalt it in a noble setting?

There was certainly no room in the chest for anything else. Perhaps he should give in and lower his pride before what his senses persisted in confirming to him: it was possible that a woman could manage to survive without half of her organs if God had willed it so. But however much he tried to convince himself, he could not rid himself of the suspicion that the chest was not a purely ornamental element, but a device designed to prevent the miracle being observed from the sides.

He tried to move towards the corner of the church, to ascertain whether his suspicions were well founded. But he immediately froze: behind one of the pillars to the side of the church he saw two men in Dominican habits hiding discreetly, staring intently at the scene. He was particularly struck by one of them, with a skull-like face and a mouth like a razor slash: Noffo Dei, the head of the inquisitors of Florence, the shadow of the Pope's representative in the city, Cardinal d'Acquasparta.

His ears fleetingly caught a brief laugh and something muttered by two men in front of him, who, judging by their clothes, must have been wealthy merchants. He thought he heard one of them saying the word 'Toulouse'. He pricked up his ears, but could make out only a few more words before the sounds were drowned out by the excited shouting of the crowds. Had someone seen Brandano in Toulouse?

He turned round in search of a familiar face and noticed Arrigo. The philosopher was standing next to the balustrade, with his usual disenchanted attitude, as if he had only gone there to get a better view. Brandano, meanwhile, rather than moving beyond the little door as he had done the first time, had stopped behind the pulpit and was busy blessing the ecstatic throng. As he did so, he slowly approached the spot where Arrigo was standing and, when he was close to him, the poet had a clear sense that the monk, while tracing his signs of the cross in the air, spoke to the philosopher.

A few words exchanged in haste. Furtively. With the swiftness that is the mark of the devil.

Dante was tempted to walk closer, but now the two men were ignoring each other again. He made for the exit.

At the door he was joined by a *bargellino*. 'Prior, the man you wanted is at the Stinche prison.'

Dante gave a start. What had those idiots done? He had given them an order to find the man for questioning, not to have him dragged to that infernal place. He threw open the door and dashed towards the stairs, dodging the startled guard.

HE REACHED the low, narrow door of the Stinche, which opened in the blind wall next to San Simone. At the top, from the little loopholes of the tower, hung like decorations at the May Palio the strings on which the prisoners hoped some merciful soul might hang a piece of bread. At that moment some of the inmates were in the courtyard, washing skins that had just been tanned in a vat whose foul-smelling water flowed liberally on to the ground.

'A man has been brought here, today. Fabio dal Pozzo, a merchant. Where is he?' Dante asked anxiously, failing to recognise the man among the prisoners. 'I am the prior of the Commune.'

The guard gave a conniving little smile. 'Your friend is already downstairs, with the policemen. Tied and bound.'

'Bring me to him, straight away!' the poet commanded, his voice stifled with rage. Someone would pay for that disgrace, for which he felt involuntarily responsible.

Confused by this unexpected reaction, the man headed towards a wooden staircase leading to a damp corridor, barely lit by some loopholes high above the courtyard. The dense air, foul with the miasma of excrement, took Dante's breath away. Conquering his vertigo, he descended towards the dungeons where the most dangerous prisoners were held, until he reached a larger cell. A repeated heart-rending cry had served as his guide along his short journey.

Before his eyes, half-naked, Fabio dal Pozzo was rocking back and forth, bent double with pain, his wrists bound behind his back by a rope that led to a ring fixed in the vaulted ceiling, before falling back into the hands of one of the two enforcers of justice. One man gave another violent tug, extracting another desperate cry from the prisoner, beneath the complacent eye of the Bargello, who leaned against a pillar, studying the scene with his arms folded.

Trying to vanquish his pain, the poor man had bent even further towards the ground, until he was almost touching the floor with his forehead. Dante rushed towards him, gripping the rope with all his might to try and prevent the guard from torturing him.

Sensing a presence next to him, the man turned in his direction, his face swollen. 'Enough . . . enough . . . I'll talk . . .' he murmured with the last remnant of his strength.

The prior gestured to the guard to slacken the rope. Fabio fell to his knees, his eyes filled with tears. In his spasms he had bitten his lips until they bled.

Dante drew near to the merchant's ear. 'What do you know about your fellow-merchant, Rigo di Cola, and what he has been up to?' he whispered so that the other men could not hear.

The man trembled and a grimace of terror spread across his distraught features. 'Nothing, I swear . . . I barely know him . . .' he stammered.

For a moment Dante was tempted to order another pull on the rope. But something about the man suggested that he was telling the truth. 'And what about the building on the Cavalcantis' lands? It's your work, isn't it?' he ventured.

A twitch running through the man's body told him that his first guess had been correct. 'No . . . the big circle – they were talking about it . . .' the poor man said quickly. He seemed glad to have something to confess at last. 'It was them,' he repeated.

'Why that construction – and why in that place? For what purpose?'

The prisoner was seized by an uncontrollable tremor. 'I

don't know . . . I heard them talking about it, him and the *maestro*. Rigo must have been helping them get a building erected. A circle, that was what they were saying to each other. He was very old and could no longer climb on to the scaffolding or hold the plumb-lines. Then he was killed, and I didn't know what to do. Ask Rigo, he knows everything. I expected someone would come looking for me. And then . . . this . . .'

'Rigo is dead. Murdered, just like the old architect.'

Fabio's face contracted into a grimace of terror. 'But I . . . I don't know anything. In Venice they told me to travel to Florence and stay at the Angel Inn. There someone would make use of my work. I have always travelled under escort.'

Dante studied him carefully. 'You were escorted? By whom?'

'As far as the border with the Piave by servants of *La Serenissima*. Entering the lands of Padua, I had to join a caravan of merchants who were going all the way to Florence. It was there that I met Rigo di Cola. But they weren't merchants, I worked that out straight away.'

'Are you sure of that?'

'Very sure. Even if they were trying to pass themselves off as members of that class. They seemed more like men-at-arms. And their cargoes, too . . . Bales of wool, apparently, but underneath . . .'

'What did you see?'

'At the ford across the Reno, just south of Bologna, one

of the mules slipped and fell, shedding its load. It wasn't just wool. There were iron blades, and pointed staves.'

'And where did these fake merchants end up?'

'I don't know. We parted near the walls of Florence. Only Rigo came with me. My instructions were to stay at the Angel Inn, and then I would have to seek out a monk – Brandano. And help him.'

'Help him do what?' Dante cried, his voice filled with surprise.

'I don't know. They would tell me when I got there,' the other man stammered, stifling a groan. 'I was to work for him . . .'

'Work for him?' the prior asked again, pausing a moment for reflection. 'Do you have any experience of mechanics? Did you put together the trick with the Virgin?'

Fabio looked surprised. 'No . . . why? My skills are of a quite different order. I too am a man of science, as you are,' he added in a respectful tone. 'I am a mathematician. My specialisation is the calculation of fractional relations, on the basis of the studies of the great Fibonacci.'

'Leonardo Fibonacci, the man who taught the Emperor Frederick the secret of Indian calculation?'

'The very same.' Fabio had broken off. His voice was that of someone terrified of not being believed. He moved his head like a crazed animal, in search of something that might satisfy his interrogator. 'Only once did he confide in me. He told me that our circle would conceal a treasure.'

Dante looked away, thoughtfully. Perhaps, if a treasure really was hidden in Florence, complex calculations were required to find it? He looked the mathematician menacingly up and down.

'Yes, that's exactly what he said!' Fabio repeated, encouraged by the poet's attention. 'A treasure. Bound between felt and felt.'

'Between felt and felt?' Puzzled, Dante pinched his lower lip. Meanwhile the other man tried to lift his head to discover some clue to his own fate in the poet's expression. Then Dante stirred. 'What else do you know? Tell me everything!'

'Nothing more, Signore, I swear! I . . . just stole . . .'

'What?'

'From Brunetto's room . . . When I saw he had been killed, I couldn't resist the temptation. He had marvellous instruments, a compass and a massive gold plumb-line – very old things . . .'

'But his papers, the plans for the construction, where are they?'

'I don't know . . . When I walked into his cubicle everything was in confusion – and then that horrible sight . . . But there was nothing apart from his instruments, I swear!'

Dante felt inclined to believe him. The murderer had left behind valuable objects and taken nothing but paper. But perhaps that paper was even more valuable. A treasure, between felt and felt. 'Release this man,' he commanded.

The Bargello had been listening, perplexed. With a nod of the head he ordered the prior's demand to be carried out. As the *bargellini* released the wretched man from the ropes, he walked over to Dante. 'But that rogue has confessed to a theft. And besides . . . Besides, he seems to know about a treasure,' he hissed with a flash of greed in his eyes. 'Perhaps it would be better to give him a few more tugs on the rope and make him spill the beans completely . . .'

Dante glared at him, furious that the head of the guards had managed to hear so much. He was sure the Bargello was groping in total darkness, worse than the darkness with which he himself was struggling. But it was still better for that oaf to know as little as possible about what had happened.

Meanwhile, freed from the ropes, Fabio dal Pozzo had dropped to the ground. Disgust for what he had witnessed merged in the poet's soul with sadness at having seen the degraded application of justice, which should have been the highest aspiration of any human community and the prime concern of anyone in government. What was the sense in having a confession extracted with iron and fire, apart from the interrogator's inability to reach the truth via the logic of reason and the indisputability of the facts? To reduce a human being to this state, guilty or innocent, meant only defeat for those inflicting the violence.

'Set this man free,' the poet commanded. 'And you, go back to the inn and don't move from there for any reason.

You will donate the precious objects that you have stolen to the cathedral works, and you will only leave the territory of the Commune after I have issued the order. But first I want to know one thing from you,' he added, pulling up the man who had fallen at his feet and was trying to kiss them. Fabio managed to stumble to his feet again. Dante took from his bag a folded sheet of paper and a piece of charcoal. He spread the sheet out on a table and handed the man the little stick. 'Summon all your strength, if you can still use your right hand. I want you to reproduce the plan of the thing that Rigo and Brunetti were building.'

The mathematician fixed his swollen eyes on the paper. With an obvious effort he managed to get the image in focus, and then, his hand trembling, he began to trace lines that slowly assumed a shape.

Beneath Dante's eyes, a strange octagonal wheel appeared, surrounded at the vertices by other, smaller octagons.

Curfew

DANTE POINTED the compass again, tracing the ninth circumference. 'And then the Primo Mobile, which instils motion in the heavenly machine,' he murmured to himself. 'As the Greek puts it. And further away . . .'

He lifted up the drawing, bringing it closer to his

face. The diagram of the heavens, Ptolemy's admirable construction, appeared in all its geometrical perfection. 'And further off . . .' he repeated, biting his lower lip. He felt his thoughts growing confused, as if all of the day's exhaustion had fallen upon him all at once. He tensed the muscles in his neck and violently rubbed his eyes, trying to shake off his torpor.

The sound of the door opening attracted his attention. The Bargello stepped warily forward, peering at the writing desk. 'Did you call me? Are you drawing spells?' he exclaimed, pointing at the series of concentric circles that the poet had drawn.

'Equants, Bargello, equants. *Punctum aequans*, the geometrical centre of the orbital circles . . .' the prior replied with disgust. 'But perhaps the celestial mechanism is not something that interests you. I need an escort.'

'To go where?' The Bargello took his time. 'It's late tonight,' he added, looking up at the violet sky, where Venus was already shining brightly. Then, chilled by the poet's eye, he drew his head between his shoulders as if seeking shelter behind the collar of his armour. 'I need to know, to prepare for action.'

'Tonight. We've got to enter a church,' Dante replied crisply.

'A church?' the man exclaimed, alarmed. 'I have no authority to intervene in a sacred place. Neither do you. What are you thinking of?'

Dante swallowed back a scathing reply. The Bargello's reluctance was not without foundation. Bursting into consecrated ground could unleash the most unpredictable consequences. And this wasn't the time to give priests further proof of the instability of the Commune.

'Perhaps you're right. I'll think about it,' he said.

It was better to be alone, at least at the beginning, especially if the Inquisition, as he had seen, was beginning to take an interest in events. They were probably driven solely by the religious aspect of the story, which seemed to be increasing in importance. He wanted to know something else, particularly how a murdered man's final work had reappeared just in time to act as the background to a miracle. And whether there was a connection between those two facts.

Because there had to be, of course: there is a necessary weft that connects all things, which have emerged in an ordered fashion from the hand of God.

Into his bag he put a candle, along with his tinder-box. Then, coming outside, he entered the monastery stables, in search of something useful for what he had in mind.

He rummaged among the tools until he found one of the pegs that were used to remove worn horseshoes from horses' hoofs, and set off at a brisk pace.

THE CURFEW was already in force by the time he reached the abbey. Now darkness had fallen, and the night's humidity was spreading over everything like a sticky veil. No light shone in that corner of the city, far from the main road. But the full moon cast enough brilliance to enable him to find his bearings.

The abbey opened on to a narrow street lined on the other side by the blank walls of market gardens. Behind the building the outlines of the houses of the Cavalcanti loomed darkly. Not one of the few windows was lit, as if the houses had been completely abandoned after the death of the head of the family and Guido's exile.

Dante approached the portal, pushing it to test its resistance. The solid oak surface didn't yield an inch. He tried again, this time leaning all his weight against the door. It vibrated slightly. There must have been an iron bar on the other side.

He rebuked himself for his own impatience. He should have imagined that the miracle would be defended by something better than a mere bolt. The outer wall seemed to be a compact surface, without any handhold all the way up to the narrow windows at the top. The idea of scaling it to reach the rose window above the portal was unthinkable. It would have taken a trick worthy of the great Ulysses to get in there. But even as he paraded through his mind all the books he had ever read, he still couldn't find anything helpful.

A wooden horse, that was what he would have needed, or a way of skirting the defences, such as the ploy that had lost Leonidas the battle of Thermopylae, or that had led to Syracuse falling into Roman hands. There had to be another way through which the monks had been able to pass in former times, without opening the portal.

He walked along the façade and turned into an even narrower alleyway that ran along the side of the building on the right. Here, halfway along the wall, he discovered a small door surrounded by a simple, grey granite frame. This had probably been the original entrance to the building, before the desire for pomp had led to the construction of the new façade.

That defence seemed solid too, but the wood was in worse condition than that of the other doors. Dante inserted the tip of the peg between the two halves of the door, levering them apart by force. With a muffled snap he heard the bar break as the door yielded.

THERE DIDN'T seem to be anyone in the nave. The line of the pillars spread within a forest of shadows, in the moonlight that entered by the large windows. He moved silently towards the apse, where the miraculous aedicule stood enthroned against a background of stone walls.

He lifted the embroidered cloth in which it was wrapped. But beneath it there was still a coil of iron chain. He was already preparing to force it when he stopped, suddenly worried. The incredible spectacle that he had witnessed was still imprinted upon his eyes. He felt as if he were about to confront the divine, and alone, without the comfort of the crowd, by a circuitous route of his own devising.

But he couldn't give up now. There was too much to know.

He attacked the iron links of the chain, which resisted his efforts with unexpected solidity, a sign that the chest was not a simple shelter, but was actually reinforced. Finally one of the rings yielded with a snap. The prior quickly removed the chain and then, conquering his initial hesitation, resolutely threw open the door.

The interior of the chest was completely empty, apart from the little table with the central foot, which was covered by a cloth. Dante felt a contradictory mixture of relief and disappointment. The relic must have been too precious to have been left unguarded, even in a protected environment like this one.

He lifted the cloth. Underneath there was a circular hole through which the walls of the chest could be seen. A doubt arose in his mind, a doubt that had haunted him since his first glimpse of the Virgin. Certainly, this opening in the table might explain the apparent miracle: the rest of the body was hidden under the table, passing through the hole. But how could it remain invisible?

He dropped the cloth into the opening and saw it vanishing, as if swallowed by an invisible mouth.

And yet it had to be there, before him, even if some kind of spell had rendered it invisible. Perhaps it was only his eyes that had been bewitched, he thought. Suddenly a superstitious terror gripped him. Might not the dominion of appearance be the realm of diabolical power? Banished from the luminous reality of the heavens, Lucifer had been relegated to the inferior realms of uncertain visions. Dante thrust his arm under the table and encountered an invisible obstacle. There was something hidden under there, he thought with horror, recoiling from whatever it was that had touched his fingers.

He suddenly withdrew, afraid that the mysterious creature might want to grab him.

In front of him the miracle of Narcissus seemed to be repeating itself: his face was coming towards him out of the darkness like an apparition.

He touched the cold surface. A mirror. And on the other side a second mirror, forming a right angle, its vertex hidden by the foot of the table.

After a moment's reflection he smiled. It was simple, like all good tricks. Put in that position, the mirrors created a niche protected from everyone's eyes, inside which there was room for a woman's body. On the outside, the mirrors showed the faithful not the image of the depths of the case, as they had all believed, but of its identical side-walls.

That was why the Virgin was exposed to veneration inside the case: not to protect its great value, as the ceremony suggested, but to conceal from view the sides of the table, which would have given the trick away.

His smile had now turned into irrepressible laughter. However much he tried to restrain himself, his eyes were filled with tears. He recalled the noble face of Arrigo: he, too, had been hoodwinked like the most gullible hayseed by that vulture Brandano.

SUDDENLY HE thought he heard a noise. He turned to look towards the door of the sacristy, which was now open. A shadow had entered, and was slipping silently through the church.

The new arrival did not even seem to have noticed his presence. Dante crouched even lower behind the aedicule, but the other man had made straight for him. A faint light issued from the door: perhaps there was someone else, the poet thought uneasily.

He decided to try a surprise tactic. Tightly clutching the peg he had used to force the door, he leaped out in front of the man. 'Stop right there, not so much as a breath, or I'll crush your head like a walnut!'

The stranger gave a start and a groan. He grabbed his hood from behind his shoulders and pulled it over his head, attempting to hide his features with his other hand. Dante hurled himself at him, uncovering the man. In the darkness he saw the face of the monk Brandano gleam for a second, before it began to distort in front of his eyes.

Stunned, he realised that he had also pulled away Brandano's noble brow, which was nothing but a piece of painted parchment. Freed from its prison, a lock of hair had suddenly fallen to conceal the man's forehead, as low and receding as that of any common fellow.

Brandano too seemed bewildered, but an incredible spectacle had begun to appear upon his face, like something the poet had read in Ovid's *Metamorphoses*. A sequence of masks flashed across his features, as if his soul were the arena of some demonic battle, as if different creatures were trying to take control of him in turn. A surprised wayfarer, a pious old hermit, a grim abbot, a dull courtier, a tough bodyguard, a wealthy merchant – all passed quickly past Dante's eyes. It looked as if Brandano, having lost the majestic identity that he showed to everyone, was in desperate search of the identity best suited to this unexpected event.

Meanwhile he had begun to retreat towards the door of the sacristy. Dante leaped sideways, blocking his escape route. With a disappointed gesture the monk looked round, in search of an alternative, retreated again until he was almost behind the altar, and then with a sudden movement knocked to the ground one of the tall iron torch-holders in an attempt to hit Dante, who dodged the blow and tried in turn to strike one of the monk's legs with the peg. Simultaneously he watched the door from the corner of his eye, for fear of seeing other adversaries appearing. In the gloom Dante thought he could see a second shadow peering in at him. Suddenly he straightened up and turned in that direction. Meanwhile Brandano had dived backwards.

The outline of a woman had appeared in the door frame, lit by a ray of moonlight. Dante could clearly see her hair, long and loose on her shoulders, as white as a cascade of ice on the crest of a mountain.

Brandano had now run behind the altar, rather than escaping towards the sacristy. There was no way out in that direction, the prior thought, approaching in his turn, careful to cut off the possibility of the man escaping through the side-door.

But the monk was hiding. Dante thought he had crouched down behind the altar, but when he too arrived behind the big stone cube, he discovered with astonishment that Brandano had disappeared. The air still rang with the echo of quick footsteps whose source he could not identify.

Disconcerted, Dante looked round in search of some kind of explanation, but it was clear that the monk had not disappeared by the only visible route, the side-door by the altar. At the end of the apse a narrow scaffold had been erected, which almost reached the top windows. Two of the frames had already been filled with multicoloured stained glass, but the third was still vacant. The rogue must have climbed up there to try and escape across the roof.

Reacting with a moment's delay to this unexpected movement, the poet in turn ran towards the scaffolding. Brandano was trying to escape across the roofs, rather than the streets of Florence, where one of the patrols might have seen him.

The scaffolding, made of poles tied together with hemp, swayed violently beneath the weight of the shadow that was quickly climbing up the wall of the apse. The last boards at the top ended in the frame of one of the windows of the nave, which gave access to the roof. Dante ran towards the opposite side, attempting to cut the monk off, and in turn began climbing breathlessly. Up there, towards the roof-trusses, every sound was amplified by the church's echo, and he felt as if he was surrounded by moving bodies, even though he couldn't see anyone.

He peered through the darkness in search of his adversary. As he did so, the scaffolding swayed again, threatening to crash to the ground. Dante cursed the carelessness with which the work had been carried out, and clutched with all his might at a hempen rope. Then, with one final effort, he reached the top. He ran along the boards to grab the man before he plunged into the void. He couldn't see the monk, but he knew he must be there since the windows – although it appeared differently from below – were a long way from the end of the scaffolding, and only with a super-human leap could Brandano have got to the nearest one.

Dante thought he could see a vague shadow and stopped, clutching the top of one of the poles. All of a sudden he felt exhausted. Until that moment he had been sustained by nervous tension, but now he felt breathless and his legs weak. The pole went on swaying and a sudden dizziness forced him to close his eyes, while a phantasmagoria of sparks exploded in his brain. He felt lost: if he didn't fall, the stranger's blade would finish him off.

He slowly caught his breath. His strength was gradually returning, too. The monk must have hidden at the end of the planks, ready to hurl himself at the prior in an all-out attack if he revealed himself. That was certainly the case. Trusting in his superior strength, Brantano wanted Dante to reveal himself. Only then did the prior realise that, in the excitement of the chase, he had left his iron peg on the ground. He drew his dagger from the pocket hidden in his robes, and waved it in front of him like a recruit on his first day in the Campo di Marte. 'Throw away your sword or you're finished!' he shouted.

The other man remained motionless. Suddenly the poet heard a voice.

'Messere, please, spare this man.'

Dante gave a start. Behind him, as though coming from a long distance away, a melodious voice had rung out, one that he had heard before. The voice of the Virgin of Antioch. He darted round, his heart pounding in his throat. But there was no one there, no one pleading with him.

Quivering with rage, he realised he had fallen into a trap, and that the ventriloquist monk had tricked him. A shadow crossed his field of vision and a heavy blow to the back of his neck knocked him down. A flash exploded in his head, as if he had been struck by lightning, and dizziness took hold of him again.

For a few moments he held his eyelids tight shut, before finally conquering his unease. By the time he opened his eyes again the monk had disappeared.

Then he got back to his feet, summoning all his strength, looking furiously around. But his adversary really had disappeared, as if by magic. He must have fled through the window, but how had he managed to do that? The opening in the wall gleamed in the moonlight several yards away from him. It wasn't possible for a man to make a leap like that. For a moment the idea that Brandano was a shape-shifting demon took hold of his brain once more.

And what if it had all been an illusion? What had he actually seen? At no moment could he have been certain that he had really seen the silhouette of the monk on the scaffolding. He had climbed up there, guided by vague noises and echoes, and above all by his reason, which had summoned the man's image. What if Brandano had never climbed up there, but had instead in some mysterious way – using a trick like the brazen one he employed with the Virgin – deceived him?

He started carefully climbing down. When he had reached

the ground he ran towards the door and entered the sacristy, but it too was deserted. On one side of the room a stone staircase ran up the wall, apparently leading to the monks' old cells. He hurried up the steps, from where a gleam of light seemed to issue. A torch or candle must have been lit on the upper floor.

He walked down the corridor, casting a quick glance into each of the empty cells, then ventured into the last, still clutching his dagger.

The cell was not deserted. Leaning against the end wall, the woman he had glimpsed in the church was standing motionless, staring at him, a flash of fear in her eyes, wiping her hands. She was panting, as if short of breath.

Dante stopped on the threshold, he too breathless from his pursuit. He lowered his weapon, disconcerted by the creature he found before him. She was as tall as he, her intense pallor illuminated by two big, sky-blue eyes.

That face was the same as the one that had appeared in the church, covered by a veil of shiny make-up that was plainly supposed to imitate wax. He raised his hand towards her until his fingers touched her throat. She was not wearing a mask.

Her slender body was covered to below the waist by a cascade of white hair that at first impression suggested a very great age. But this, too, was an illusion. Her hair was flowing and splendid, a snowy torrent worthy of an adolescent angel. There was something unnatural in that beauty, the poet felt, something that could enter the mind and bind it like a subtle poison. He felt the same unease that had taken hold of his mind when he had witnessed the fake miracle for the first time.

The woman had remained impassive. Only in her dilated eyes could he read the terror that still gripped her. A few times she opened and closed her mouth, as if on the point of saying something.

Dante looked around. A thousand questions rose to his lips, now that the very heart of the trick was within his grasp. But he would need time and a more suitable location to interrogate her. Meanwhile he looked round for something to tie her up with, before she disappeared as the monk had done. But the woman didn't seem to want to escape.

'Where have you come from?' he asked her, gasping to get his breath back. She shook her head. 'What is your name?' Again the woman moved her head, this time bringing her hand to her throat. 'You don't want to tell me? Well, you're going to have to.'

She opened her mouth and no articulate sound came out. Just a groan, as she shook her head once more. At last she suddenly gripped the poet's wrist and began drumming with her fingers on his palm.

After a moment of puzzlement Dante thought he understood. He knew of a way with which those without voices communicated among themselves by a system of signs. A

code invented by the Gypsies, who often gave those unfortunates shelter in their tribes so that they could exploit
them as beggars.

'You're . . . you're mute?' he murmured in bewilderment.
'Then how . . .'

And yet he had heard her incredible song during the
display to the people. Unless that, too, was part of a trick.
Like the pleading he thought he had heard on the scaffolding. An act of ventriloquism – that could be the only
explanation.

He gently released her hand from his grip. An idea had
occurred to him. 'Cover your face and come with me,' he
instructed her.

He walked towards the door. After a moment's uncertainty the woman followed him. Now her initial fear had
vanished from her face, making way for the bewilderment
of an animal in a trap. With trembling hands she wrapped
round her head the veil that she wore over her shoulders,
then unexpectedly held out her hand to him, seeking his
guidance.

Dante stepped cautiously outside, making sure there
was no one around who might recognise them. Outside,
the city was in darkness, but the moon, high in the sky,
gave off sufficient light to guide their footsteps, in spite
of the damp haze that rose from the banks of the Arno.

The place they were making for was some distance away.
They had to pass through the city walls beyond the

meadows of Santa Maria Novella. At that hour of night the gates were closed, but the guards wouldn't make much of a fuss, particularly with the encouragement of a few coins.

Dante turned towards the woman to gauge her strength. She was slender and seemed to be in good physical condition, capable of a long walk. But then he remembered a cart, sometimes used by the Bargello, which was kept in the stable of San Piero.

He beckoned to her to follow him and set off towards the priory. He turned right into a side-street, in the direction of the river. Ahead of them, in the distance, he began to glimpse the torches of the Ponte Vecchio. At a crossroads he thought he could see shadows darting along the walls of the building in front of them. But no one seemed to pay the two of them any attention. He was exhausted, his clothes drenched in sickly sweat. They continued on for one final stretch, until they reached the San Piero gate.

Outside the monastery, leaning against the columns of the entrance, two *bargellini* were snoozing. They gave a start at the sound of footsteps and came out in a state of alarm, lances at the ready.

'I am the prior of the Commune,' Dante said brusquely, showing himself in the light of the torch carried by one of the men. 'Step aside!'

The men, after a moment's uncertainty, did as he asked. The poet distinctly saw the irony with which they looked his female companion up and down. But they didn't seem too surprised, as if this only confirmed the frequency with which women were brought into the priory at night.

Having passed through the cloister, Dante walked to a side-arcade. There, as he had remembered, he found the two-wheeled cart, and a horse standing beside it. He roused the beast, which consented to be hitched to the cart without too much protest.

They set off again, once more under the startled and ironic eyes of the *bargellini*. The woman sat on the box next to him, motionless. A new twinge of pain pierced Dante's neck. His old enemy had been revived by the tension and effort of his nocturnal venture. He suddenly felt all the effects of the fight and its aftermath. He headed towards the walls, hoping that he might be allowed through without difficulty.

SOON AFTERWARDS he stopped the cart beside Paradise Gate, in the realm of Monna Lagia. The old Roman villa had once stood in open countryside, but the new buildings now encroached upon it. The reddish mass of the third circle of walls, whose construction was proceeding at a frantic pace, could be seen not far away.

But once they had passed through the villa's arch the atmosphere was as silent as ever, interrupted only by laughter that came at intervals from the cubicles on the first floor.

After making sure that his veiled companion was unrecognisable, Dante entered the courtyard, heading towards the *impluvium*, now transformed into a drinking trough for the horses of the clients. The ancient mosaic in the floor, a ship surrounded by dolphins, was being steadily destroyed by the hoofs of the animals, in an endless shipwreck. By now only the shadow of the ancient forms appeared here and there, amongst depressions and bare patches where weeds grew uncontrolled.

They had almost reached the steps on the other side when a mocking voice thundered in his ears. 'Oh, Prior! Now you're coming to bring me women rather than find them? Or isn't little Pietra enough for you any more?'

Dante turned round with a start, red in the face. A woman with an impudent expression had appeared from beneath the portico, wearing bright colours.

'Lagia, I'm here for other reasons. There's a mute among your women, if I remember correctly. A girl who knows sign language. This woman . . .' he went on, nodding towards the silent, veiled presence, 'is unable to speak. I need someone to help me talk to her. And I want it to be done with absolute discretion, given her aristocratic standing.'

'And why do you bring her to me covered up like that, as if she were a leper?' Monna Lagia replied suspiciously, taking a step back.

'She's not ill. Do as I ask, and quickly.'

The woman waited for a moment. Then, turning towards the women's rooms, she cried, 'Pietra!' Then, with a half-smile, she added, 'You're a good customer, after all.'

A girl's face appeared on the balcony. Recognising Dante, she grimaced.

'Go and find the mute girl, and bring her to my room,' Lagia ordered. The girl merely nodded before disappearing again. 'You follow me, you . . . and the noblewoman,' she said to Dante, glancing ironically at him. 'You always turn up at night, Prior. Your wife Gemma can't be getting much nuptial bliss, even if you have given her children. But in my Paradiso, the beds are sweeter than the houses of Florence, at least that's what everyone tells me.'

'Shut up, woman,' the poet hissed angrily.

Lagia exploded with laughter, slapping her thighs with her hands. 'They tell me you've written love poems to sixteen beauties, but none to her,' she continued shamelessly. Then she pointed her index finger at him. 'People like you would be better off not getting wed at all, if you can't keep your dicky-bird in its cage,' she added, quickly retreating from the prior, who had stepped menacingly towards her.

At that moment Pietra appeared from behind the curtain, and came in followed by a frightened-looking girl, as white as if she had never stepped outside the brothel. As she passed by Dante, she ostentatiously avoided looking in his direction, turning instead towards Lagia. 'This is Martina, the deaf-mute.'

The brothel-keeper raised her chin towards the prior and waited.

'Tell her to ask the woman who she is, and why she has come to Florence,' he began.

Lagia repeated the question to the pale girl, standing in front of her and pronouncing the words clearly. The young woman must have deduced something from the movement of her lips, because she nodded in agreement. Then she gripped the hand of the veiled woman, opening her palm, and began tapping out a mysterious rhythm with her fingertips.

Dante watched, struck by the scene. Meanwhile his mind was wandering in a forest of analogies. He felt a sense of embarrassment welling up in him, as if he were spying on a kind of secret femininity that was gradually being unveiled through this strange colloquium. Perhaps the same embarrassment as Paris felt, he thought, when he was called to settle the dispute between the goddesses.

Pietra too seemed attentive, but although she tried to look away, the poet noticed that her eye, apparently fixed straight ahead of her, was occasionally straying and often settling on him.

The veiled woman had in turn begun to touch the other girl's hand, again with incomprehensible movements. Finally the young prostitute stopped and turned towards Pietra, uttering a series of stifled moans.

'What's she saying?' exclaimed Dante impatiently.

Pietra pulled a contemptuous little face. 'Your friend doesn't seem all that special, Prior. Niece of a monk, if I've understood. She's called Amara. French, from Toulouse.'

'Did your friend ask her why they have come here?'

Pietra hesitated. 'Martina isn't quite sure she understood. She seems to have said it's "for the Emperor's dream". His "last" dream, in fact.'

Lagia intervened, alarmed. 'Emperor? What have emperors got to do with anything? Who have you brought to my house?'

The prior ignored her, absorbed in what he had just heard. Then, turning towards Pietra, he said, 'Ask her about the mirrors.' The girl, after a moment's bafflement, translated the question into that primitive language, which the pale girl hurried to reformulate for the mute. Again Dante witnessed that strange finger-ballet.

'She says that along the way, in Venice, someone taught them magic,' Pietra said, after listening once again to her friend's strange grunts of reply. But her face was uncertain.

Beside him Lagia seemed to be growing increasingly uneasy. 'Magic?' she exclaimed, crossing herself. Dante bade her be silent with an imperious gesture, then Martina moaned again in Pietra's direction.

'What else did she say?' the poet pressed her.

'Nothing,' replied the girl, half-closing her eyes with weariness. But through a narrow gap in her eyelids she continued to stare at him with her bright-green eyes. 'Nothing else. She speaks a strange language, it's impossible to understand it all,' she said abruptly.

He shrugged. Then, after a moment's reflection, he took the mute woman by the hand and set off. Behind him he heard the murmurs of the other women fading away as they walked back across the portico.

Amara looked exhausted. She tried to hoist herself on to the cart by gripping the rim, but stumbled backwards. Dante held her from behind by the hips, keeping her upright, then lifted her on to the box. For a moment the sweet softness of her back pressed against his lips, as a subtle perfume invaded his nostrils. A quiver ran through him.

She had slumped against the back of the seat. Her veil had come away, revealing her alabaster face, which seemed even paler in the moonlight. Her reclining body, unexpectedly full, perspired beneath the light fabric of her dress. Dante was fascinated by the curve of her hips, her long, nervous legs, her half-open mouth, with a drip of saliva gleaming faintly at the corner of her lips.

Dante suddenly withdrew the hand with which he had supported the woman. Was a physical image enough to throw an orderly mind into confusion? And how extraordinarily powerful must Eros be, if the mere vision of his delights was enough to overwhelm all other considerations.

Greatly disturbed, he was about to whip his horse when

he heard the sound of hurried steps beside the cart. Pietra was running silently towards them, looking behind her as if afraid that someone might see her.

He clutched the reins tightly to halt the animal that had just begun to move.

Pietra gripped the edge of the cart as if to hold it back, and was looking at the mute covered by the veil. Then she turned to the poet, after glancing round once more. 'Beware of that woman,' she murmured to him, leaning into his ear.

Dante caught the sharp scent of her breath. But at the same time he thought he noticed a hint of affection in the warning, as if for a moment the girl's hostility had eased a little.

'Pietra . . .' he began. But she interrupted him with a brusque gesture and turned to leave. Her voice was harsh once more. 'Beware,' she repeated. 'She is not as she seems.'

'What do you mean?'

The prostitute cast a hostile glance at the mute, still lying motionless with her head abandoned against the back of the seat. Then unexpectedly she exploded into fits of bitter laughter, full of that vulgar sarcasm that the poet knew so well. 'You'll find out for yourself, my God, you'll find out!' she exclaimed, removing her hand from the edge of the cart and retreating towards the door of the brothel as if sorry she had come.

Dante was unsure as to the best course of action. Beside

him, on the cart, his companion seemed to be slowly recovering, glancing at him from time to time from under the veil, beneath which she had hidden her face once more.

To take her back to the priory would have been impossible. He was almost tempted to turn round and go back to the brothel, to ask Monna Lagia to put her up for a while. But that would have amounted to making her existence public in the blink of an eye, when what he really wanted to understand was what lay concealed behind the trick, and how it was linked to the mysterious deaths.

He decided to return to the abbey. There the woman could remain in hiding, and he would have the chance of getting his hands on the monk as soon as Brandano showed his face again.

DANTE ENTERED the church by the door that he had forced the first time, holding the woman by the hand. Her fingers had slowly warmed up between his. Now when they responded to his grip it was no longer with the fear of a prisoner, but almost with the sweet abandon of a lover.

He led her along the colonnade, towards the door behind the altar. But after a few steps he stopped, pushing her behind a pillar and then squatting down in its shadow. In front of them a man was wandering about the nave as if looking for something. Thinking that Brandano might have returned, the poet moved his hand to his dagger as the shadow came closer.

He was preparing to attack, his muscles quivering for action, but just a moment before he pounced a ray of moonlight from a window lit up the ungainly face of the stranger.

'Cecco!' cried Dante. 'What are you doing here?'

The other man gave a little jump, and stopped. But he immediately recovered his composure, his embarrassment soon erased by a mocking little smile. He raised his head, glancing ostentatiously all round.

'They say miracles happen here. I just wanted to see. You Florentines are really lucky, you know. God comes and writes straight on to your pages. I'm sure that if it rained shit from the heavens one day, in Florence it would smell of violets.'

A red veil fell over the poet's eyes. He gripped the Sienese by the lapel of his jerkin and shook it violently. 'Cecco, did you come here to hoodwink my city along with that rogue Brandano? When there's cheating going on, you're never far away!'

Cecco delicately took Dante's fingers and gracefully loosened their grip. 'I swear I'm here to breathe in the air of the miracle and prepare my soul for the baptistery in St Peter's.'

'What are you doing here?' the poet repeated, trembling.

Cecco's cheerful mask was beginning to crack. His eyes

ran from Dante to the woman, as if uncertain what attitude to assume. 'Nothing . . . I was looking for something . . .' he stammered, embarrassed. He kept his eyes lowered. Then he raised them to the mute woman. 'So you've discovered everything,' he murmured, drawing his head back defiantly. An icy silence fell between them for a few moments. 'Well?' Cecco continued. 'You can't tell me you want to help the populace of this despicable city just to sit on some miserable throne and represent the clique of merchants and cutpurses! Besides, I've used up all my funds and my faction in Siena is doing battle with its enemies. And they will do badly if our only protection is Milady Poverty. I'm not one of those idiots who jump up and down singing the praises of that fool from Assisi,' he concluded, with a hint of his usual mirth.

'Cecco, tonight you will sleep at the Stinche.'

Cecco blanched, just for a moment, then immediately grew cocky again. 'Come on, Dante, you wouldn't do that to an old comrade-at-arms? Don't you remember how I protected your back, at the battle of Campaldino?'

'At the battle of Campaldino all I saw was *your* back, running away ahead of all the others!'

'Which means you can't have been far behind!'

Dante shook his head. 'Who else is involved with you in all this?'

'There's no shortage of them in Italy, people ready to play at being priests,' Cecco smiled. 'And even more if there's the prospect of gain. Join us, my friend. I know your finances aren't exactly flourishing at the moment. We can make a small fortune from the gullibility of these yokels.'

There was a moment's silence. Cecco took advantage of it to nudge the poet.

'Those Florentines can go to hell! What have you got in common with all those pygmies that surround you, apart from the fact that you were born in the midst of them? And wouldn't a few florins in your pocket come in handy? I know your name's in the records of the usurers, as well as on the parchments of the poets.'

The prior's face was darkening by the minute. Beside him Amara had lifted her veil. Once again those enigmatic features pierced him to the core. For a moment he had a sense that she was about to say something, and that even her muteness was a trick. Instead she merely took a deep breath. 'Yes,' he went on, 'they can go to hell. Yet I want to know everything, holding nothing back. Who's responsible for this mess? And who are the people I must join, Cecco?'

The other man gestured vaguely. 'The Fedeli are about to carry out a colossal enterprise that will change the face of the earth.'

'Who's Brandano? And where's he got to? He's the brains behind the illusion, isn't he?'

'He's merely a showman, the kind of wandering player

who charms the peasants at fairs. But he's pretty good, don't you think? He's believable, in those monk's rags. I thought I'd find him here.'

'Who gave Brandano the mirrors for the trick? And who's pulling the strings here in Florence?'

Cecco shook his head. His expression was sincere now. 'I don't know who's running this. I found out about this in Toulouse, when we went there for a change of air.'

'To Toulouse?' Dante said. 'And why Florence after that?'

Cecco exploded with laughter. 'Perhaps they want to pay tribute to the greatness of your city! Or more likely they think there are more priests, more money and more idiots here than anywhere else. Certainly I'd rather have cheated my own Siena, but apparently everything has to be *sub flore . . .*'

The poet gave a start. Where did the old prophecy about the death of Frederick the Second come into it? 'Where did you get the reliquary that you're using for the trick?' he asked.

'Bigarelli gave it to us.'

Dante nodded. His suspicions were confirmed; there really was a connection between the sculptor and that business about the fake crusade. And between that and the crime. The tense expression on Cecco's face suggested that the slashed throat of the victim in the tower was still in his mind.

Dante looked around. 'The reliquary. Where is it hidden?'

Cecco hesitated for a moment, before moving towards a corner of the church not far from the feet of the scaffolding on which the prior had pursued the monk. He bent down and moved something on the edge of what looked like a tombstone. There was the sound of a click, and then Cecco moved the stone aside with remarkable force, revealing the beginning of a staircase that led under the floor. 'It's the old crypt. It's here that . . .'

He broke off. Then, having overcome his final hesitation, he went down first, followed by the poet. The silent woman had also walked behind them, as if she feared being abandoned in the church.

A spacious basement opened up beneath the abbey. Gravestones lay scattered on the tiled marble floor, and Roman sarcophagi were lined up against the walls. It must once have been the cemetery of the little monastic community, but the ravages of time and abandonment were everywhere in evidence.

'This is the secret of the magic,' Cecco murmured, pointing to an object wrapped in a heavy red cloth.

Dante walked over and resolutely uncovered it. The face of the statue, horrible yet fascinating, was lit by the glare of the oil-lamp. The enamel eyes seemed to stare at him with a light of their own, as if they were about to spring into life. He turned around for a minute to look at the woman. There really was a resemblance between the two faces – the same anxious expression – as if some mysterious correspondence existed between the bronze and the flesh.

He carefully worked the locks on the chest, opening the two panels. There was something written inside, invisible to the eye of anyone looking at it from the front. Bigarelli had engraved two words: *Sacellum Federici*.

Frederick's tomb. Or his shrine. Once again Dante raised the lamp towards that bronze face, studying it intensely. The soft features, the long hair, had led him to think it was the statue of a woman. But might he not, in fact, have been gazing upon the lineaments of the Emperor, captured in bronze to carry his image into the afterlife? Might the reliquary have been designed to protect the Swabian Emperor's body on his journey into eternity?

But if that was the case, what was the connection between the sovereign's death and the deeds that stained Florence with blood half a century later?

He went on looking round in that cave of wonders. Next to one of the sarcophagi a crack opened up in the floor, leading to yet another room below. Dante stretched down, lowering the lamp into the passageway. Under the crypt there ran a wide brick corridor that seemed to disappear in the direction of the Arno. The bottom was covered with water.

'It's an old Roman cloaca. It leads towards the old well, in the Forum. Brandano comes along here whenever he doesn't want to be seen,' Cecco explained.

Dante nodded. Brandano really was the king of disappearance. Not just on the roof, then, but here too.

'Now you know everything, my friend. Join us,' Cecco whispered insinuatingly into his ear.

'I can't let you do it. It isn't for this that Florence has trusted in my deeds . . . and in my virtue,' the poet replied with a shake of his head.

Cecco spread his arms in a gesture of comic desperation. By now the woman had joined them. 'Don't lose us. Don't lose her. Isn't she too lovely to end up in the hands of the *bargellini*?'

Dante covered his eyes with his hands. He was about to refuse again, but then a possibility entered his mind. 'What was the Emperor's last dream? What was he building in the lands of the Cavalcanti? What was it that came from beyond the seas, on that broken ship?'

'I don't know. It's something spoken of among the Fedeli d'Amore. Perhaps it's his hidden treasure, as safe as it would be in a felt cradle.'

Dante opened his eyes wide. Between felt and felt: Fabio dal Pozzo had used similar words. He gripped his friend by the shoulders and shook him. 'What is the meaning of the phrase, "between felt and felt"?'

Cecco had turned pale. 'I don't know what you're talking about,' he stammered. 'It was something the Fedeli used to say . . .'

He seemed sincere, Dante thought, disoriented. And

yet the false crusade must somehow be linked to the deaths of all those men. Perhaps, if he had revealed his discoveries to the world straight away, the feeble thread that linked those events might have broken, and he would never know the whole truth.

'For now, the secret remains hidden in the abbey, with that woman,' the prior said at last. 'I shall say nothing. For the time being at least.'

5

DANTE CAME outside at dawn, after a brief sleep filled with restless images. The faces of the living and the dead had merged into a macabre comedy in which Cecco's mocking expression was superimposed over Bigarelli's horrendous injury and the death-ship, weighing anchor again, now sailed with its cargo of corpses towards the lands of the Orient.

He himself must have ploughed through a salty sea, which he thought he could still taste on his lips. The Virgin, too, a prisoner in her gem-encrusted reliquary, had pursued him for a long time, trying to communicate something to him. In the dream, her delicate features had become the horrible face of a monster, as if the wax of her flesh had finally yielded to the glare of the sun.

He had woken up all of a sudden, his forehead gripped in a ring of iron. His old enemy was back, tormenting him by plunging its nails into his brain; although without injuring him too much this time. A light touch, as if to remind the poet of its presence.

So, in Florence he had to find his way to a treasure. He performed a swift mental calculation, but without reaching any definite conclusion. Without having any final idea of the construction, it was difficult to imagine how long it would take to complete it. The 'treasure' – whatever it might have been – might still be in transit, or it might already have arrived in Florence. If that were so, it could not be hidden in the casket designed to receive it. It had to be somewhere else.

Between felt and felt.

An allegory, or an expression to be taken literally?

That might be the explanation. The wool warehouses were all concentrated around the fields of Santa Maria Novella, on the other side of the city.

He hoped the cool morning air might do him good. But the sun was already shining relentlessly, like a ball of fire. He had only been walking for a minute or so, and already he was drenched in sweat, like the humour exuded by the skin in a fever. The burning feeling that had tormented him during the night had flamed up once more.

Further on there was a public fountain, he remembered. He was walking in that direction when he saw a man coming out of a side-alley and heading his way. Dante assessed his chances of turning back, but it was too late.

The man had recognised him, and speeded up to block his path. 'Greetings, Messer Alighieri. It was high time we

met. I was waiting for a visit, but perhaps your engage-
ments have held you up,' he said with a hint of irony.

'I will come to you when the time is right, don't worry,'
Dante replied with a frown.

'But the right time is fast approaching, don't you know
that? It's already the ides of August,' the man replied coldly.
All trace of affability had vanished from his pock-marked
face.

'Domenico, your loan is guaranteed by my brother
Francesco, as you know full well, and by my family's lands,'
said the poet irritably. He wondered why the usurer had
become quite so insolent. Had something happened to
weaken his own position in the eyes of this villain?

Meanwhile Domenico had caught up with him, and
was jabbing at his chest with his index finger. He looked
as if he was about to drum on it, but held himself back.
'It's one thousand and eighty florins. Gold ones.'

Dante shivered. Had he amassed such huge debts? He
knew that figure very well, it had been repeated a thousand
times like a shameful proclamation in all the documents he
had had to sign. But now the usurer's wretched voice seemed
to embody a sum of gold as massive as a boulder. He felt
as if the world were crumbling around him, ready to drag
him down with the ruin that threatened the very walls of
Florence.

He thought once more of Cecco, his haughty refusal
of his invitation. He tried not to listen to this person's

petulant voice, still nattering about maturities and risks. He tried to blank his mind, but Cecco's proposal went on washing around inside his head like filthy water.

In the end, couldn't he too have joined in with this crusade business? Who would it have harmed, except for a pack of wealthy and wasteful merchants, and a corrupt and simoniac Church? Might that really have been a way to get out of the mess in which he had ended up?

'Yes,' he decided. 'Those damned Florentines can go to hell.'

HE REACHED his destination, conquering the fire that burned his guts. The area was occupied with warehouses, but there was no one to load or unload the goods: the bell had just struck nine, and all the porters must have been busy refreshing themselves. So Dante headed towards the wool warehouse. The guard was at the door, sitting on a keg, with an earthenware jar between his feet.

'I don't suppose there's a consignment of felt in the store?'

The man looked him mildly up and down. 'Who wants to know?'

'The authority of Florence.'

'By the Holy Trinity and Saint John!' the man replied, suppressing a yawn.

The poet came closer. The guard read something in his

expression and hurried to his feet, moving back a few steps. 'Only members of the Guild are allowed in the warehouse. And access to the stores is restricted for reasons of commercial security,' he added immediately, looking round in alarm. But there was no one he could call for help.

The prior came closer.

'Perhaps . . . yes, I think so – a few days ago now . . .' the guard stammered, confused, taking another step backwards.

'Show me where it's kept.'

The other man was giving in. 'But I'll have to tell the captain of the Guild,' he whined, disappearing into a little cupboard just behind the door. He quickly consulted a tattered book, then crossed the courtyard to the other side of the colonnade, followed by Dante.

The warehouse was filled to the rafters with goods. Still following the guard, Dante entered that labyrinth and started to walk past the loads piled up towards the middle of the building. The Minotaur's labyrinth could not have been very different from that suffocating inferno, he thought at one point, as he wiped away the sweat from his brow. Finally the man pointed to a pile of greyish bales, tightly bound in hempen ropes.

'Leave me alone,' the prior commanded. 'I have to perform an inspection. Apparently fabric has been brought into the city from Cremona, where there has been an outbreak of plague.'

The guard stepped backwards, crossing himself, and

began to retreat quickly towards the door, vanishing from view without another word.

Having reassured himself that no one could see his movements, Dante began testing the bales, probing the soft mass with his fingers. Reaching the third one, he felt something hard.

With a few quick movements he liberated the bale from its cords. The hidden content was wrapped in soft felt cloths, as Fabio dal Pozzo and Cecco had said it would be. He went on extricating the 'treasure' from its hiding place until he found himself looking at a heavy, compact block, at least two feet by five and more than a span thick. It looked as if someone had hidden a stone slab in the wool.

He delicately cut through a corner of the felt covering with his dagger. A sliver of light from the courtyard exploded with a flash of silver where the felt had come away, dazzling the poet.

A mirror. There was a mirror hidden in the load. A giant slab of mirror, larger than any that Dante had ever seen in his life, not even in the houses of the wealthiest merchants in Florence, or in France, when he had travelled to Paris.

Within a few minutes he frantically inspected the whole load. There were seven more slabs identical to the first, each one carefully protected by felt cloths and hidden amongst the coarse wool. Was this the treasure that everyone was waiting for? They must certainly have been enormously expensive, but he guessed that their value must be more than purely monetary.

One corner of the slab must have been broken in transit. Dante picked up the fragment and put it in his pocket.

He carefully tied up the bales again, concealing all trace of his search. Then he left, brusquely summoning the guard.

The man had followed his movements and would certainly go and nose around as soon as he had left. He came over rather reluctantly, staring at the mass of bales.

Dante turned to him and spoke with concern. 'In the top bale,' he said, pointing at the one in which he had uncovered the first slab, 'suspect rags are hidden. Plague,' and added, 'It must be burned immediately, outside the city walls. I will assign people to carry out the task, as soon as possible. On no account are you to touch it, don't let anyone in, and don't tell anyone what you know, so that the city does not fall into a panic. And now leave, for your own safety.'

Without a doubt, the first thing the ass would do would be to go and tell his friends the news. But at least fear of the consequences would keep him from poking around for a few hours. Judging by the pallor of his face, he looked as if he had believed the story. The mirrors would be safe for a while.

The prior turned back towards the store, trying to

imprint upon his memory the precise point on the shelves where the load was hidden. Then he made for the door, passing once more by the guard, who was anxiously waiting for him. 'There are sure to be other rags in the load. It's not absolutely certain that they come from Cremona, but keep away from them, just to be on the safe side. I'll be back soon, with the chief physician of Santa Maria. And take care that no one gets close: you have to be careful with the plague.'

The man nodded quickly and firmly.

'And now tell me who it was that stored the load of felt,' the poet added imperiously.

The man quickly returned to his tattered book, his brow pearling with sweat. 'Here we are . . . one Fabio dal Pozzo, merchant. The goods come from Venice.'

Dante smiled to himself.

WORK HAD been frantic in Maestro Arnolfo's workshop for some time – an activity that was practically never interrupted, not least because of the need not to let the fire go out.

It was a low basement, filled with the hot dryness that emerged from the kiln in a corner. On the benches, some busy apprentices were pouring on to a brick surface the contents of a crucible that had just been extracted from the flames with a long pair of tongs.

The incandescent glass flowed across the surface. Heedless of the heat, the *maestro* began to trim it with big bronze shears and a shovel of the same material. A few resolute blows and he printed a rectangular shape from the mass, about a foot in length.

'There's another pane for the noblemen's windows, Messer Alighieri. No well-to-do citizen in this city wants the old cloth window coverings any more. It's good luck for us glass-makers.'

Dante studied the cooling pane. 'Is that the biggest sheet of glass that you're capable of making?' he asked.

'You can make them a foot along the side as well, but there's no point. The pane would be too fragile and imperfect. You're better off mounting pieces this size with a strip of lead. You can fill a whole church window with those, as they do in France. And the result is safer.'

'I imagine that in your workshop you make mirrors as well,' the prior went on.

'The mirrors are my greatest boast, the pride of my workshop. Celebrated throughout the whole of Tuscany. Look.'

Arnolfo walked over to a bench, where a workman was mounting a pane of glass a span long in a brass frame. He took the object from the boy's hands and held it up smugly in front of the poet's face.

Dante studied it in silence. His image returned to him as if the surface of the glass were covered by a layer of water, blurring his vision. The mirror of Narcissus must have been like that, so that the youth didn't recognise his own reflection. The background of the image was weakened by the darkness of the lead, in spite of the fact that the light was falling right on his face. He smiled politely as a sign of appreciation. Then he asked, 'Do you have mirrors that are bigger than this one?'

'Bigger than this one? What would you want to do with it?'

'Nothing. I'm just curious to know how big a mirror can be.'

'Not much bigger than what you've seen,' Arnolfo replied. He seemed offended, as if these observations of Dante's diminished his work. 'To increase the size you also have to increase the thickness of the pane,' he began patiently, as if talking to a slightly slow workman. 'Because otherwise the glass breaks as it cools down. But as you increase the thickness, it's impossible to preserve the perfect transparency of the material. Besides, it would be extremely difficult to keep the pane perfectly flat to avoid defects in the reflection, once it's backed with lead.'

Dante nodded as the *maestro* gave the mirror to his workman. 'So, it isn't really possible to make what I suggested? So what would you say about a mirror that was five feet long, and gave a perfect reflection?'

'I'd say you were raving. Either that or you'd found Maestro Tinca's coffers.'

'And yet I have seen one.'

Arnolfo shook his head almost angrily. 'What you're saying is impossible. You must have made a mistake. It isn't possible,' he repeated. But something in his certainty was crumbling in the face of the prior's conviction. 'But you really are sure . . . I'd give everything I own to see what you describe.'

The poet didn't reply, merely staring at the old *maestro*. 'I'm not asking much, just your oath. Promise not to tell anyone about what I'm about to show you.'

Arnolfo's excitement was mounting. He looked like a mystic contemplating a vision. He fell to his knees in front of the poet. 'I call the Virgin and all the Saints as my witness. Nothing of what I see shall ever pass my lips.'

Dante took from his bag the corner of mirror that he had found in the warehouse and held it out to the glassmaker. The man touched the edge of the glass with his fingers to assess its thickness. 'And you say it comes from a five-foot pane?' he murmured with disbelief. Then he brought his tongue to it as if to test its flavour. 'Silver . . .' he said almost to himself. 'Strange.'

'What's so strange?'

'I would have expected something modern, based on lead. And yet it's only silver. If it is as you say, its perfection derives entirely from the extraordinary smoothness and transparency of the vitreous paste.'

'Who could have made it?' the prior asked.

Arnolfo shrugged and went on looking at the piece of

metal. He stroked his bristly chin. 'It isn't from here. Greek, perhaps. Or perhaps made in some workshop in the north, in Ravenna, by someone who's come from far away. I've heard that in far-off Persia they have made glass so thin that it was invisible. Or in Venice, if the legend is true . . .'

'This Maestro Tinca that you mentioned?'

Arnolfo stared into the void. 'Perhaps he was a man who never existed. Or perhaps the greatest glass-maker of all time, who knows? A story that the members of our Guild tell one another, a fairy-tale.'

'What is it?'

'The story of the kiln at the town of Canal. There came to that place a certain Maestro Tinca, from the land of the devil, and he began making extraordinary kinds of glass. Huge, flat panes, even more than two ells in length, the like of which no one had ever managed to make before. Maestro Tinca, glass-maker to the Emperor.'

Dante suddenly shifted his attention from contemplation of his own hand and gripped the man's arm. 'Which emperor?' he asked.

Arnolfo seemed uncertain at first, then straightened his back. 'The great and last one. Frederick.' He had spoken the name clearly as if to challenge him. Perhaps Florence was really full of dormant Ghibellines, as Cecco had implied.

'And what did this Maestro Tinca do for Frederick?'

'They say that two messengers from the Emperor came

to his kiln one night. This was at the time of the Council of Lyon, when Frederick was facing his last battle against . . .' The man seemed to be seeking the exact term.

'The polemicists of the Curia? The Pope?' Dante suggested.

'Yes, perhaps the Pope. Or someone even higher up than that,' Arnolfo suggested enigmatically.

'And who were the messengers? And why at night?'

'Tinca worked by night and vanished by day. He suffered from an eye defect, which meant he couldn't bear sunlight. He saw too much, so he was able to spot every imperfection in the glass. In the darkness he watched over the kiln, taking care that the fires never went out. He had discovered that the quality of the glass is determined by the constancy of the heat. And as for the two men . . .'

Once more Arnolfo stopped, as if uncertain of his own memories. Or uncertain about what to reveal. 'It is said that they were two very senior court officials. And they say that one of the two was the Emperor in person. Perhaps he too wanted to know the master's secret . . .'

'What secret?' Dante exclaimed, fascinated.

'They say that Tinca, just before his disappearance, had discovered the secret of capturing light in mirrors.'

'What?'

'A way of actually capturing the last image reflected inside the mirror. It is said that through alchemy he had discovered a material that reacted to rays of light according to their different sources. The object had to be placed in front of his mirror for a long time – hours, in fact – in bright light, and slowly its image was captured.

'If this were true, the art of painting would be dealt a mortal blow,' Dante observed. Who knew what his friend Giotto would think about it. But might this be the mysterious prize that was being sought so desperately? So much so that people were being killed to get hold of it? And yet this man Tinca had disappeared as well.

'Arnolfo, you swore you would keep all this secret,' Dante reminded him.

The glass-maker touched the metal fragment again, as if stroking a dream. Then he nodded. 'My word is my bond. I respect your will. Perhaps what you have shown me is too precious for a simple craftsman like myself. It could tempt me to emulation, and there is danger in trying to emulate the hand of God.'

At the Angel Inn

THE BIG room on the ground floor was almost deserted. There was only Messer Marcello, seated at a long table. Dante walked silently up behind him. The doctor was eating an apple, but in an unusual way: with his left hand he was crushing the fruit against the table, while with his right he was cutting little pieces away with a knife before bringing them to his mouth. Having noticed the poet, he looked up, still chewing.

'What good fortune brought you to this inn, Messer Marcello?'

'The footsteps of man are written in the book of Time, and the road that has brought you here, and the one I have taken, are also precisely recorded. We could not have done otherwise, neither you nor I.'

'You still haven't answered my question: what has brought you here?'

Marcello moved his head as if to shake off a memory. Or a dream. 'Yes, of course. A vow. Fulfilling a promise that I made many years ago. Paying an ancient debt. But it's also my inexorable fate. It was written that I should be here, now.'

'And the steps that brought Guido Bigarelli to his death were written in his fate as well?'

The old man waited a moment before replying. He seemed fascinated by the last piece of apple, which he swallowed with his eyes closed as if he wished to discover its secret flavour.

'This apple, too, developed from its flower to get here,' he went on. 'Everything is complete in the mind of God. It is only the illusion of our feeble senses that forces us to turn the pages of the book one by one, thus deceiving ourselves that they are not bound in a single indissoluble volume.'

'Certainly the mind of God knows all that happens, and his prescience has wisely imposed repeated and eternal motions upon the universe. But it is his wisdom that has granted our sub-lunar world the infinite variety of becoming, so that we might be free to act and grow. Free to seek goodness. And blind to the things of the future, so that on this ignorance we might base our conscious action.'

'Do you really believe that?'

'Certainly Adam would not have sinned had he known the consequences of his error. But neither would many lofty spirits have sought the means of cleansing that guilt by following the path of virtue. Humanity would have been deprived of its greatest gift, the unsatisfied quest for the truth. Which alone redeems it in the terrible eyes of God.'

The old man exploded in bitter laughter. 'You should be more careful, Messer Alighieri, in expressing your convictions in such terms. I don't think that your love of the truth will be seen in a favourable light in the land of the Inquisition.'

'Florence is not a land of the Inquisition, but a free Commune. For the time being. And I hope for a long time to come, at least while I'm capable of action.'

'You put great trust in your abilities, as if you too can really look beyond the wall of time and see what awaits you there.'

'I don't have the gift of second sight. My foresight is the child of will and learning alone.'

The other man stared at him as if touched, as a paternal light illuminated his face. 'I too have seen spirits like yours – in my youth. Rich in all the gifts that a man might wish for. Strong and ardent in their conviction that they might bend fate to their own will. And yet they were destined to be a source of grief and devastation . . .'

'Who are you talking about?'

'Oh, a long time ago. An abyss of time. In far-off lands.'

'Did you live in the East for a while?'

Marcello stared at a point in the void, behind the poet. His face was illuminated, as if those words had evoked in him the light of distant countries. He nodded his head several times.

'And what did you learn over there?' the poet pressed him. 'What knowledge, what medicines, what magic? Why is that place the origin of the most awful diseases and also the most extraordinary remedies? Is there really a chance, as they say, of extending life beyond the limit of seventy years, as ordained by God in the Scriptures?'

'Yes, in the city of Sidon I myself once knew a man who claimed to have sat at the table of Charlemagne. And another who had accompanied the last steps of Christ at Golgotha.'

'It cannot be . . . !'

'And yet that is what I have seen. And is it not said that

even the last Emperor, Frederick, is not dead, but is still abroad in Germany, collecting men for his final undertaking?'

'You've seen him too? When?'

'Much time has passed since then,' replied the doctor. 'During his crusade. When the Emperor tricked them all,' he added absently.

'Whom did he trick?'

'The pagans. And the bishops in his train. With his allegory. Frederick approached the gate of Damascus, along the stones of the road that leads from Jericho to the city of the hundred towers. Jerusalem the Golden shone in the sun, amongst the jubilant cries of the crowd lined up on the ramparts. Oppressed Christians, insolent pagans, fervent Jews brought together by the same curiosity, seized by the same excitement in the face of the wonder advancing towards them. The Emperor proceeded on foot on his triumphal car yoked to four oxen crowned with laurels. At the four corners of the car walked the same number of chained slaves: a Moor, a Tartar, a white man and the fourth masked as a Triton. Frederick held his golden goblet in his right hand, and in his left he clutched the bridle of a centaur ridden by a man in a two-faced mask that followed the chariot, hammering its hoofs upon the stone paving.'

'A centaur?' Dante murmured.

Ignoring the interruption, Marcello went on: 'The car was preceded by seven girls with lit torches, followed by seven crowned old men in Greek clothing. And then another seven men, with long garments covered in celestial signs, and two horsemen in battle-armour. One carrying in his fist a gleaming sword that reflected the glare of the sun, the other a pile of rope in his arms, tightly twisted into a thousand knots. Bringing up the rear of the procession were five veiled women holding five extinguished lamps, surrounding, as lasciviously as prostitutes, three men, each one holding a book.'

Marcello ran a hand over his forehead as though to erase that vision. His face had hardened.

'Do you understand the meaning of this appalling allegory?'

'Of course.'

'In that case, your perspicacity and learning are truly admirable.'

'The girls waving the torches are the seven liberal arts, and the seven old men following them are the great sages of the ancient era, of whom the Greeks told tales. And the seven starry men are the heavenly bodies that orbit around the earth, that great car on which Frederick places his foot. The four yoked slaves are the three lands subject to the imperial power, and the Triton, the ocean. The centaur, a fusion of man and beast, is a symbol of wisdom, a synthesis of nature and intellect. The two knights are the power to lock away by law, and to liberate by force. And finally the five foolish virgins with their spent lamps symbolise the refusal of faith, along with the three men of the book. The final allegory and the most terrible.'

Marcello nodded gravely. 'So you know who those three men are, that patent mockery of the figure of the magi?'

'I think so. The three masters of the book: Moses, Christ and Mohammed.'

'Surrounded by prostitutes. None other than the Three Impostors, in his heretical philosophy. Frederick entered Jerusalem in perfidy, scoffing with his symbols at the people who lived there,' Marcello murmured. 'But you have left out the two-faced man. Does he escape the blade of your intellect?'

'I don't know, perhaps . . .' Dante began. Then he stopped, seized by the memory of the strange figurehead of the galley. 'And can you reveal its meaning?'

'Not everything that dwelt in the mind of the Emperor is comprehensible.'

There was no point asking further questions.

These were not allegories from fifty years ago, but mysteries from the present day, which he would have to understand to resolve the murder. And Marcello's mind seemed anchored to the past. If he really did have the experience of centuries, now, in his final days, he was heading backwards, lost in nostalgia.

DANTE HAD only just stepped out of the inn when he bumped into young Colonna on his way back.

The student hesitated for a moment, as if he wished to avoid Dante, then continued walking with an arrogant air. 'So, Prior, what brings you to the Angel Inn? Anyone who was going to be killed is already dead,' he said mockingly.

The poet stopped in front of him, blocking his way. 'The murderer has not been found. And there is nothing to say that you can't help me.'

'I know nothing useful. But if I were you, I would search among the priests. Brunetto did not appear to be on good terms with the cowled brethren, and it wouldn't surprise me if your friend Boniface had been pushing him to the other side.'

'Your words suggest that you aren't on the best of terms with the Curia, either.'

The young man assumed a contemptuous air. 'Don't be hypocritical, like everyone in this false city. You know my name. And if you've forgotten it, I'm here to remind you,' he said, lifting to the poet's eye his right index finger, decorated with a big signet ring with a Roman column carved in the seal. 'For years my family has been at war with the Caetani. And the fact that Boniface now wears the papal mitre is certainly not going to improve matters. If he could, he would have exterminated us already. And only the fear of our armies and our fortresses keeps him away from our door. But perhaps . . .'

'Perhaps?'

'Perhaps this time we'll get there first,' Franceschino

went on, intoxicated by his spite. 'When we're all there together!'

'What do you mean?' the poet asked.

But the other man seemed to have realised he had said too much. 'You'll see when the time comes,' he shot back, walking away under the prior's inquisitorial gaze.

At the priory, around midday

DANTE EMERGED from his cell and walked along the loggia. The doors of the other priors' cells were open, too. His colleagues were gathered in an animated huddle. As they saw him, they fell suddenly silent, staring at him with embarrassment. One of them above all, a short man with a thief's grim face, seemed to be hiding something.

Dante walked firmly over. 'What troubles you so, Lapo?'

Lapo arrogantly jutted his chin. 'You do! Apparently you have no time for the Council now, but stroll calmly about the city at all hours of the day and night, in defiance of the rules and regulations. Or have you forgotten that priors are forbidden to leave their rooms for the duration of their term? Do you think that laws apply only to everyone else, the honest sons of the people who elected you as their representative . . . for only another few days?'

'For only another few days, you are quite right,' the poet replied. 'But for those few days the people give me the force and authority to keep the chariot of state on a straight path, and to see off the manoeuvres of the plotters and the wheeler-dealers. The ones who manage to weasel their way into the secret rooms,' he added, looking the other man up and down.

Lapo blushed. He clenched his fists and moved closer, until he could touch him. Dante felt he was about to butt him in the face and jerked backwards.

One of the other priors anxiously interposed himself between the two men, resting a hand on Lapo's shoulder and drawing him back. 'Stop. Let us calm down and establish a date for the next Council meeting, given that we have had the good fortune to run into Messer Alighieri.'

'Tell me, Antonio, what is so urgent that it makes you concerned about my movements?' the poet replied with a hint of irony.

'Cardinal d'Acquasparta . . .'

'The Papal Nuncio? What does Boniface's man want from me?' Dante interrupted, suddenly alarmed. Ever since the Pope's emissary had come to Florence in the spring, and had based himself next to Santa Croce, it was as if Boniface's claw had pierced the city's living flesh.

'The Pope, our benefactor and the high protector of the City of the Flower, is asking for the Commune's help in his enterprise, in return for his vote. And he wishes us to place his apparent and hidden enemies under our surveillance.'

'Speak clearly. Is Pope Caetani after money? Or something bigger?'

Antonio looked around, hoping for the solidarity of his companions. But apart from Lapo, who continued to scowl at Dante, the other three priors were embarrassed and tried to look away. Antonio cleared his throat several times. 'All right, it's a delicate matter. Not to be discussed here in the open, where the ears of strangers might be listening. As a long-standing member, I propose that we call a meeting of the Council for the morning of the fourteenth, the last day of our mandate.'

They all nodded. Dante merely grunted. The decision was easy to interpret: on the last day they would only have to postpone the meeting to grant the Council full responsibility for any resolution, thus sparing those frail shoulders the burden of deciding anything. Idleness was branded on all those faces, like the brand seared into the flesh of thieves. Apart from Lapo, in whom the seed of corruption had come to fruition, turning him into a kind of disgraceful satyr, the perfect allegory for his fellow-citizens.

AN UNUSUAL number of men in armour seemed to be busy around the Palazzo del Capitano del Popolo. Dante recognised the head of one of the three *compagnie del popolo* of San Piero and stopped him on the steps of the building.

'What's happening, Maestro Menico?'

'One of the patrols at the walls has signalled the presence of groups of men marching towards the city, on the road to Prato. They're telling us to be prepared for any eventuality.'

'What kind of men?'

'Who knows, perhaps pilgrims making for Rome, acrobats perhaps, or disbanded soldiers from the Imola militias. Apparently the troops there haven't been paid for months and have deserted, sacking the countryside and heading for the Apennines. But there is a great deal of concern,' the man added, confidentially bringing his lips to the poet's ear, 'that they might be gangs of heretics and intriguers travelling down the Peninsula intent on loot and plunder. We must remain alert.'

'Heretics? And where would so many godless people come from?'

'Apparently plague has broken out once again in the Languedoc,' the other man replied, still in a low voice, 'and it was the enemies of God who put it there, Cathars and Jews with their poisoned tinctures. It is feared that some of them may already have entered the city, as a vanguard for their shady companions. Besides, how could they be kept out with all the gates open, and these vagabonds arriving from the countryside in search of some kind of livelihood?'

Dante could only agree, observing the chaos all around

them. Dozens of strangers were thronging in, searching for a space where they could lay out a cloth for such goods as they had to sell, or loafing about waiting for adventures. Only a few years before, he could have identified by name every single inhabitant in his district, and many of the people in the whole of Florence. But now, after the expansion of the city over the last decade, a gigantic force seemed to have risen from the gorges of the countryside, a deluge that was engulfing houses and roads, flowing beyond the old circle of walls like the Arno when it broke its banks.

'They call it progress,' Menico continued, 'but for me it's just corruption. The world is getting old, and as time passes it brings nothing but new misfortunes. Vulgarity and infamy. Look at them, for example!'

He pointed at three young women dressed in vibrant colours, their dresses cut so low as to reveal almost the whole of their breasts, smiling coarsely at the passers-by, trying to attract their attention.

'Just a few years ago, in the days of Giano della Bella, they'd have been thrown into the Stinche for wearing clothes like that. And now . . .' he observed.

Dante merely nodded. Such complaints were utterly pointless. They bored him.

'And now not even this is enough. Now it's the men who have started pursuing the profession.'

'Sodomites?'

'Bloody shirt-lifters, Messer Durante. Like the ones who fill Ceccherino's tavern every night.'

Dante smiled sardonically. It wasn't the first time he had heard that name. But it wasn't the only meeting place of its kind. The city was full of places where discreet encounters occurred, indecent relations were set up, bodies that Nature had built as a temple were subjected to the most awful perversions. 'They say, in fact, that our city's name is spreading as a byword for such things, and not just for the quality of our fabrics.'

'But they aren't all Florentines, you know,' Menico replied. 'At Ceccherino's most of them are outsiders, and they're still turning up in droves.'

'Who are they? Where do they come from? What are the *sestiere* guards doing about it?' Dante asked.

'What do you expect them to do? They're ashamed even to touch the door,' Menico sighed with resignation. 'Now no man worthy of his good name ventures near the place, not even armed. But it isn't just shame that keeps the guards away. Because you mustn't think we're just talking about effeminate men. No, they're often the kind you could best imagine rowing a galley or yoking two pairs of oxen one-handed. And it takes guts to stand up to people like that.'

The man went on talking, endlessly abusing corrupt and corruptors alike. But Dante was no longer listening. From the very first he had had a sense that the source of recent events lay somewhere far away. His city was like a stage-set, like the canvas cloths used by strolling players as a backdrop to their farces, but in this case it was the setting for a tragedy that had been written elsewhere.

All the actors had come from outside the city. And others might yet be on their way. And if this was all to be done in secret, might not Ceccherino's tavern be the very place?

The words of young Colonna echoed around his mind. 'When we're all there together,' he had said. And those men he was waiting for – where better for them to meet than in a place that not even the local guard dared enter?

HE TOOK the road leading to the Prato Gate, the main thoroughfare of the first Roman settlement. The buildings flanking the paved route, which had grown from the ruins like mould on an animal's decomposing body, were mostly crude one-storey constructions, unornamented, with little narrow windows at street level, barely screened off by a simple cloth cover. Increasingly often, as he went away from the centre, Dante saw between the houses gardens and vegetable plots, most of them reduced to sun-scorched brushwood.

There was no one along the road apart from a few stray dogs sniffing about the place. But from within the buildings he could just about hear all the muffled sounds of humanity confined behind those humble doors, ship-wrecked sailors clutching at floating wreckage.

At last he reached his destination. In the distance he could already glimpse the dark shadow of the boundary walls, dotted at the top by the torches of the sentries. A little way away from the road there stood a series of marble columns, at least five ells high, some still topped by their capitals. In front of them were the shattered remains of a flight of stairs, only two steps of which remained above ground. That ancient space, where once the rites of a forgotten god had been celebrated, had been closed off by a rough wall of volcanic ashlars, producing a large enclosed space extending all the way to the building at the back.

It could have been a priory, the poet said to himself. Or the chapterhouse of a convent. Or the hall of an aristocratic tribunal. Or the court of a barbarian king. Instead it was the place where Ceccherino's tavern had found refuge. The shame of Florence.

At the front, between the two central columns, a low, wide door opened, reinforced with nails and strips of iron. Through the wide chinks at the bottom and the top a flickering light shone, as if many fires were burning inside. Dante pushed the door and walked in.

He sat down on a free seat at the long table. He waved to attract the attention of a waiter, who was wandering among the regulars with a leather bottle of wine over his shoulder, and gestured to him to fill an earthenware goblet in front of him. Dante threw him a coin and picked up the goblet.

Slowly sipping the slightly sour wine, he studied the scene. The room was full of men on their own, an unusual crowd even for a big, well-known tavern like this one.

He had been expecting something of the kind, and yet it was odd that there were no women. None of those women in brightly coloured dresses that you normally found in such places. Not a single female face or voice. And not so much as a skivvy or a waitress, as if by magic everything had returned to the first days of Creation, when the fairer sex still dwelt in the unfathomable mind of God.

He pushed back the bench and leaned against the wall. From there, hidden behind a pillar, he could calmly observe most of the room without drawing attention to himself, pretending to be absorbed in the contemplation of his own goblet. The tavern lived up to Maestro Menico's words.

Great excitement seemed to have taken possession of everyone, a whirl of voices and laughter, a fluctuating motion of wandering bodies like waves on a sea that is only apparently calm, but beneath whose surface unknown depths are seething.

All those men, coupled in twos and sometimes even in obscene threesomes, were groping one another without restraint, groaning and murmuring sweet nothings. An incessant stream of men was going erratically and convulsively up and down the staircase at the end of the room.

Dante was feeling increasingly repelled by what he saw. It was then that he noticed something. Little clusters constantly formed and dissolved as if demonic messengers were shuttling back and forth between the tables, embroidering the weave of evil. But seated at one corner of the long table was a group of four customers who maintained a strangely apathetic attitude. They seemed indifferent to the obscene exaltation of the flesh that exploded all around them. They sat decorously talking in low voices, apparently intent on draining a small leather bottle that had been set in front of them.

Even their clothing didn't seem to match their surroundings. They were wearing ordinary clothes, without the showy colours and without the vents and openings that the others used to expose parts of the body normally concealed from view. Their jerkins, too, were of the normal size, just long enough to cover the lacing of their flies, and not very short like those worn by the others, which ostentatiously displayed their groins, barely hidden by the fabric.

Their faces betrayed no sign of the more or less explicit perversion that marked the features of the other customers. But something in their gestures, more than in the words that did not reach the poet's ear, identified them as outsiders. Perhaps they were the outsiders that Menico had talked about.

All of a sudden the poet heard excited shouting, interspersed with insults. A couple sitting next to him, who until a moment ago had been busy hugging and kissing, had leaped to their feet, arguing furiously. As the tone grew shrill, the two men started pulling each other's hair as they edged towards the far side of the tavern.

Dante picked up his goblet and quickly, slipping along the wall behind the group, approached the seat that had now been vacated beside it, sitting down as if he had just come in.

They didn't seem to notice his arrival, busy as they were following the movements of the two brawlers and exchanging muttered, derisory comments. Dante leaned against the wall once more, taking little sips from his drink.

He managed to catch only a few words here and there, drowned out by the hubbub of the tavern. But however much he pricked up his ears, the meaning of their conversation continued to elude him. Rising within him he felt a growing irritation with the crowd of perverts that whirled around him. How could they go on obstructing the work of justice with their lustful words? When would the hand of God descend to destroy the whole of their kind?

He had instinctively raised his eyes to the sky, as if hoping that the tavern ceiling might split asunder beneath a sudden shower of fire. Otherwise he would see to it himself and would soon order the *bargellini* to clean the place up, and it wouldn't be pretty. He wouldn't leave a single stone of this hovel standing and Ceccherino, burned to a crisp beneath the smoking ruins of his lair, would be a terrible warning to all the remaining pederasts.

'So he still doesn't know anything . . .' one of the four men was saying.

The man sitting in front of him interrupted the sentence with an angry gesture. 'It doesn't seem possible that a whole ship could vanish like a ghost. And after it had been seen inshore.'

'But at least what's left is in our hands. And iron is more use to us than light,' the first man replied with a shrug.

'And gold more than anything!' the third man butted in with a laugh. 'I'll choose the third part of this trinity. As to light, it all belongs to the Emperor. Isn't that what he's looking for?'

'I knew about the others. They will all be at the abbey.'

Dante listened as hard as he could to pick up every detail of this cryptic conversation, fearing that the noise might flare up again, making his efforts useless. He almost failed to notice the hand delicately stroking the back of his neck.

The man who had been sitting beside him must have mistaken the poet's distraction for a sign of encouragement. He repeated the gesture more resolutely. 'So, my fine lad? New here? It's the first time I've seen you.'

Dante turned towards the source of the voice and found himself engulfed in pestilential breath. He saw a long, yellow face with a soft, blond beard and a pair of wild, burning eyes. The man was holding a cup of wine from which he had just drunk. In fact, a thin crown of red drips still soaked the corner of his fleshy lips.

'Leave me alone, my friend. I want to drink on my own,' he murmured, looking away and leaning over his cup. He was still trying to catch the conversation of the four men who had started chatting again.

'On your own? Don't you know that the root of vice and sin lies in solitude?' the newcomer insisted. 'It plants in the soul the seeds of *melancholia obscura*, and puts our humours out of balance, predisposing the body to illnesses and miserable decadence, as Aristotle asserts in *De anima*. Perhaps you want to grow old before your time, shut up behind your armour of pride?'

Dante studied him with surprise.

'You didn't think I was a man of logic!' the fair-haired man exclaimed, clearly satisfied at having attracted his attention. 'I immediately saw from your manners and your clothes that you're a man of letters like myself.'

'Aristotle says nothing of the sort. And certainly not in *De anima*,' the poet declared, trying once more to catch what the four men were saying. He thought he heard a reference to the temple . . .

'Oh, then it must be someone else,' the man snorted, touching Dante's neck with his hand again.

Dante instinctively recoiled, furiously pulling the man's

hand away. He must have hit him hard, because the man shrieked, turning to his companions asking for help, his small eyes filled with sudden hatred. Attracted by the noise, people started looking in the poet's direction. Some of the customers at the back of the hall had risen to their feet and were advancing menacingly.

Dante struck the fair-haired man violently with his free hand and hurled him against the tripod in the middle of the room. The big copper brazier toppled over and crashed noisily to the floor, throwing sparks all around. A chorus of cries of pain rose up from the group of customers closest to it, the ones who had caught the full force of the fire.

The men seemed to perform some infernal dance, as they desperately tried to shake the fragments of burning embers from their hair and clothes. Cursing and swearing, they waved their limbs around, ignoring Dante. But the rest, having got over their bewilderment, still approached, and other customers were joining them.

Dante felt he was lost. A colossus with a cuirass was now only a few feet away, and hurled himself at the poet, trying to grab him by the throat, but lost his balance and crashed to the floor. Dante had the feeling that he had tripped over the foot of one of the men whose conversation he had been listening in on – the foot having been deliberately stretched out between the giant's legs.

The prior took advantage of this to reach the door. He

stopped for a moment in the doorway, looking behind him. He brought his thumbs and index fingers together above his head. 'You cursed sons of whores, unnatural wretches! This is the fire that awaits you, the fire you will know sooner or later.'

The whole tavern had become an infernal madhouse. Only the four strangers had remained motionless in their seats, watching the scene like spectators in a theatre.

As soon as he was outside he began running, afraid that someone might come after him. But the door of the tavern stayed shut, as if it were a kind of inviolable boundary for those who had found refuge inside. As a precautionary measure, however, he flattened himself against the wall of a nearby hut, hiding in the shadow of a doorway.

It was at that moment that he saw two silhouettes emerging from a side-alley and approaching the door of the tavern, after checking with a furtive glance that no one had noticed them. From his hiding place Dante could clearly see their faces outlined in the bright light.

Cecco Angiolieri and young Colonna.

Cecco was the kind of man to frequent such a place. By now his descent along the slope of vice could easily have taken him beyond the bounds of nature. He suppressed a smile at the thought: the hero of Campaldino, with his purple leggings! He really seemed made to pass through that door. But Franceschino didn't seem the kind, it wasn't the image the poet had of him. No, they must be there for some other reason, one that had something to do with the four men perhaps.

He stayed close by the door, unsure what to do. There was no question of going back. Waiting for the strangers to leave and confronting them might mean losing precious time, with no guarantee of honest replies. The two men could have a thousand possible explanations for being in that place, and he had no proof against them.

Perhaps it was better to exploit the little that remained of the day and go back to Maestro Alberto, in the hope that he might have managed to understand something more about the contraption taken from the ship.

THE *MECHANICUS* welcomed him with an expression of disappointment that told him more than a thousand words could have done.

'Still nothing, Maestro Alberto?'

The man shook his head. 'Not really. I think I've worked out some of the connections. And I've rebuilt one of the damaged gear-wheels. Look.'

He held out a gleaming circle of gilded metal, the teeth of which still smelled of the file.

Dante tested the quality of the design, with a quick observation in the light from the window. 'It doesn't look as if your work is in any way inferior to the work of the pagans. But behind the perfection of the form you must now be able to grasp the soul of what you have in front of you. And soon, because the time that this machine is supposed to measure has already been set in motion.'

The *maestro* stared at him, struck by his anxious tone. 'But nothing whatsoever is unknown about its nature . . .' he murmured.

Dante's face lit up with interest. 'And its purpose?'

'A chain of whirling rotations. Gradually accelerated by the reduced diameter of the wheels.'

The two men stared each other in the eye, sure that the same idea was passing through their minds.

The poet was the first to break the silence. 'Just as in the universe the moon's heaven orbits more quickly than that of Saturn, the most remote before one reaches the realm of God. But why?'

'That's what I don't understand. If its purpose were sure-footedly to measure the passing of time, if it were put in motion it would keep a non-human time, closer to a fly's wing-beat than to the beat of a human heart. As if someone had wished to construct a time-keeper to mark the day of people who were not of this earth . . .'

'Perhaps al-Jazari built a clock for the angels?'

'Or for the demons. And besides, there's this detail, here – it's the sign of a genius . . . If I have understood correctly, here the maker's mind really has penetrated the mind of God,' the old man went on, his eyes burning with admiration.

'What's so extraordinary about it?' Dante asked, perplexed. He had seen that hungry, shady expression before. Men who had gone to the pyre because of their hankering to overcome the limits that God has imposed upon reason not illuminated by grace.

'You see this lever and the two lead spheres on the ends of the two little moving arches?'

Dante narrowed his eyes to peer at the tiny detail, then looked quizzically back at the *maestro*.

'It regulates the speed of rotation – so simple, but really the offspring of the illumination that only God can give. The solution to an enormous problem. Don't you understand? Our science too is capable of building a spinning mechanism, driven by the energy accumulated in a curved arc of steel, or supplied by a descending weight. But no one has ever found a way of rendering constant the motion that derives from it, as this machine has done.'

The *mechanicus* went on studying the device admiringly. 'And look here,' he continued, pointing at the hole in a strip of bronze on the side of the contraption. A skilful hand had carved around the aperture the stylised design of a human eye. He glanced quizzically at the poet, as if waiting for an explanation from him.

Dante approached to see better. The circular hole corresponded precisely to the pupil of the carved figure. 'An invitation to look through the hole?' he guessed uncertainly.

On the other side of the aperture there was a bronze frame, pivoted in such a way as to be set at a variable angle. He assessed its dimensions, as a bizarre idea came into his mind. It could hold one of the mirrors in the Virgin trick. He leaned the other way: in front of the other hole there was an identical frame. Confused, he bit his lower lip.

Meanwhile the *mechanicus* had started talking again. 'I thought so too. It could be an unusual model of an astrolabe, and this would be the hole to look at the stars through. But it doesn't make sense. There is in fact a symmetrical hole, on the other side of the machine. But if you look through it, your vision is obstructed by the rotating blades. It makes no sense,' he repeated, shaking his head once more.

'Unless its purpose is to invite people to observe its parts in motion,' the prior remarked.

Alberto bent over the table with his head in his hands. 'Al-Jazari had gone mad. Perhaps the purpose of the machine is merely to celebrate his mastery. A monument to blind pride.'

'An admirable game, but one without purpose. Do you think so many men would have died for that?' The old man looked up at him, disturbed, but before he could comment Dante interrupted him. 'Try to penetrate his secret, Maestro Alberto. You have no idea how important it is.'

'Give me some more time, Prior.'

'Time is the material least available to us,' Dante murmured. The *mechanicus* had leaned over his bench again, with his hands inside the device. Dante looked round.

Hamid stood silently in a corner. He was sunk in prayer, bent over on his little rug. The poet sat down on a chest beside the workbench and watched carefully, his hands twined together under his chin.

He knew it was the custom of Moors to pray towards Mecca, but seeing Hamid prostrate against a wall, immersed in an incomprehensible litany, inspired hilarity in him rather than religious piety.

The slave must have heard his laughter, because he broke off and stared angrily at him.

'Tell me of your paradise, pagan. What is written in the book?' Dante asked him. 'And forgive me for interrupting your conversation with your god.'

He knew he had offended Hamid. But why? he wondered, shaking off that sentiment. The conversation he had interrupted was, after all, merely a dialogue with the void.

'Across the seven skies, the Prophet reached the house of God the powerful and merciful on the wings of Buraq, the magic flying horse. Up there He revealed the secrets of all things.'

'And what might those secrets be?'

'God put a seal upon the Prophet's lips so that nothing would be revealed.'

'Of course! Because he saw nothing. Why should God receive a heretic and converse with him, explaining his intentions to him like the lord of a castle to his bailiff? Flight through the air one might concede, but only as an expiation and a warning to the whole of humanity.'

'Mohammed is the noblest of men, the first and last of the prophets. Who is more worthy than he to visit the higher realms and bear witness to them?'

'God could summon to himself the worst of sinners, just because he had granted him the gift of a higher faculty of the rational mind. A man whose fabric was illuminated by a spark of the supernal light.'

'A man like you, Messer Alighieri?'

Dante shrugged impatiently. 'So your paradise extends beyond the crystal vaults of the heavens. And what is it like?'

'By the stairs that appeared to him, the Prophet – may God's glory be upon him – first ascended through the seven heavens of the seven planets. In the precise order in which the wise astronomers of Baghdad arranged them, with their marvellous vision. Crossing deserts of darkness and light. And the fiery lake of sin.'

Dante shook his head. 'In the order in which the wise men of Greece arranged them, you mean. Aristotle and the great Ptolemy. Those lakes of fire and darkness of which you speak are not the pillars of the world, but something that our eyes might see even if our mind were crushed by the sight of them. God is far from us, and not even your Avicenna could count the paces that separate us from Him.'

The Arab did not reply. Dante's thoughts had slipped once more to the series of crimes. He thought once again of the face of Fabio dal Pozzo, the mathematician. Not even a mathematician could have counted out those paces. So why did it take one to bring that obscure project to its conclusion?

A sudden anxiety had taken hold of him. He hurried out of the door.

He strode down the long street to the inn, as quickly as his strength permitted. As he did so he cursed himself for his short-sightedness. Seized by emotion over what he had seen at the Stinche, he had ordered the man to be freed. It had been a decision that had been dictated not by reason, but only by his sense of guilt at having been the indirect cause of the man's torture. By freeing him Dante had obeyed the desire to erase from his memory that bloody face, those dislocated joints.

But perhaps he still had time to stop him. The mathematician would probably wait until he had recovered a minimum of strength before heading north.

He went on walking until he reached his goal. The ground-floor hall was empty, and he didn't meet anyone on the stairs, either. He climbed to the first floor, where

Fabio dal Pozzo had his cell. Without knocking he lifted the latch and walked in.

It took him only a quick glance to ascertain that the room was completely empty. There were papers on the desk, with geometrical figures and numbers traced on them. He touched his fingertips to the traces of ink, which were still damp. The mathematician must have left the room only a few moments before.

He quickly read the pages that seemed to have been written last: they contained scattered observations, notes on the declination of Venus. In one corner he saw a reddish smudge, as if the paper had been touched with blood-drenched hands. Dante instinctively looked up towards the ceiling. Vespers had just rung, the best time to study the evening star in all its splendour. Perhaps Fabio had gone out on to the roof of the tower to complete his observations. Deep inside he felt an admiration for a man who could not ignore his mind's passions even in a state of terrible pain.

He left the room and climbed the stairs towards the top of the building. At the end of the stairs a closed trapdoor led out on to the roof. He lifted it and poked his head through the opening.

He felt a great sense of disappointment as he saw that the place was deserted. He lowered the trapdoor, but at that moment his attention was attracted by cries from below. Something dramatic seemed to have happened. He dashed back down again.

The cries came from the other side of the ancient Roman walls, beyond which the countryside began. He passed through an arch to the other side of the wall, reaching a group of people bent over something at the base of the tower.

The mathematician's body lay shattered on the stones, amidst a pool of blood.

The onlookers included the innkeeper, who recognised him. 'A terrible business, Prior!'

Dante shooed everyone away from the body and walked over for a closer look. The skull and limbs showed clear signs of the brutal impact against the stone. He looked up towards the distant top of the tower. Fabio must have fallen from the summit, perhaps while intent on his observations.

But when had it happened? The body was still warm, and yet he had not heard the thud of the body, or a cry. Nothing.

'How did you become aware of what had happened?' he asked the little crowd around him. They all shrugged and looked at their neighbours.

Then a boy stepped timidly forward. 'I found him,' he stammered. 'I was coming to take the wine order . . .'

'Did anyone see him fall?'

A new expression of puzzlement floated amongst the dull-witted faces of the bystanders. Dante leaned over the corpse once more, studying the twisted limbs. He turned it delicately over: on its chest, level with the heart, two scarlet-rimmed wounds were clearly visible. One of the two blows must have killed him straight away and, since he had not cried out, this meant it had been the first to be inflicted. The second blow could have been motivated only by the murderer's ferocity. The victim must have known him, since his killer had been able to launch a surprise attack without provoking any kind of reaction.

The innkeeper had come over, trembling.

'Who was in the inn?' the prior asked him, rising to his feet.

Before the innkeeper had a chance to reply Dante had quickly turned towards the door to the tower. The hall was still deserted. He climbed the stairs once more, this time checking each of the cubicles. They were all empty.

The innkeeper had followed his movements. 'I'm not absolutely sure, but I don't think there was anyone with the merchant,' he replied. 'Or at least that's how it seemed to me . . . We could ask the staff . . .'

Dante gestured to him be quiet. It was pointless now. He thought he had worked out what had happened.

The murderer had approached Fabio at the top of the tower and killed him, before throwing his body down below. Then he had climbed the stairs again, taking refuge in one of the cubicles when he had heard the poet coming up. Finally he had made off during the confusion that followed the discovery of the body, taking advantage of the fact that the door to the inn could not be seen from the spot where Fabio's body had fallen. It would have taken nerves of steel not to give himself away. That and a lot of good fortune.

If only he had arrived a moment before, the prior told himself reproachfully, perhaps all this havoc could have been avoided. Good fortune seemed to have vanished from his horizon, he thought bitterly.

The corpses on that mysterious ship, experts in mechanics. And Guido Bigarelli, the accursed sculptor, Frederick II's architect. And Rigo the carpenter. And now Fabio, a mathematician. These men must be connected in some way.

Meanwhile he heard a heavy footstep on the stairs. He stepped out on to the landing, to find the massive bulk of Jacques Monerre coming up.

The poet blocked his path. 'I imagine you know what happened.'

The Frenchman nodded. 'I saw the body,' he replied brusquely. 'An accident?'

Dante said nothing, and only studied Monerre's reactions very carefully. But the man remained impassive, waiting for a reply. 'No,' he said at last. 'A killer's hand put an end to his life.'

Monerre gave a start, glancing rapidly around as if afraid the murderer might be hidden somewhere. Then he stared at Dante again with his one good eye. 'Do you know who it was?'

'No, no more than I know who killed the others.'

'Do you think there's a link between the crimes?'

Dante nodded. There was no point discussing the topic with someone who might be the culprit. 'I need you to tell me something,' he said, changing the subject. 'You said you came from Toulouse.'

The other man silently concurred with a nod of his head.

'And in that city did you ever bump into the monk Brandano, the man of God who is preparing to lead a new and glorious crusade?'

Monerre had been listening without any show of emotion, but the scar on his face seemed yet more vivid against his suddenly pale skin. Nonetheless, when he replied he was perfectly calm. 'No, I don't really think so. Toulouse is a vast city, full of traffic and pilgrims passing through before crossing the Pyrenees on the way to Santiago de Compostela. It isn't possible to know them all, even for someone like myself who leads a relatively outgoing life. But a face like the monk's would be hard to forget.'

Dante nodded, then disappeared into his thoughts.

It was Monerre who broke the silence. 'But why did you ask me that? What does my far-off city have to do with Brandano?'

'Apparently nothing. And yet there's someone who swears he saw him in those places. So I hoped you might be able to confirm this information.'

'Is it of any importance?'

'Toulouse isn't a city like any other. It's a place of great culture and wealth, but also the centre of all major heresies, and the source of constant disturbances on French soil. If the monk really does come from there, and the matter is known to the Inquisition, we may expect that sooner or later they will intervene to stop this dubious adventure.'

The poet stopped, studying the Frenchman's reactions, to work out whether he knew about the hoax. Or whether indeed he was a secret accomplice.

Monerre stared at him. 'What do you think of the miracle we all witnessed, Messer Alighieri?' he asked suddenly, as if he wanted to reveal the trick.

'That's what I'd like to ask you.'

The Frenchman seemed to want to take his time. 'On my travels I have seen things that might have been stranger. I have seen the shades of the jinns, the devils of the pagans, wandering among their red-hot stones. But certainly nothing as weird as that. Only the mythical Phoenix, which is reborn from its own ashes, could match it for unbelievability.'

'If it was real,' Dante murmured.

'If it was, it would be worthy of inclusion in an emperor's treasury.'

'A treasury like Frederick's?'

Monerre gave a start. 'Why do you say that?'

'Because it is rumoured that the Emperor's treasure was

hidden in Toulouse, transported there by his devoted followers after his death, to hide it from the aggression of his enemies and the greed of his heirs. If that is true, the extraordinary relic could come from those very treasure-chests.'

'And yet, Messer Alighieri, where I come from people say that Frederick's treasure was hidden somewhere else,' Monerre replied, glancing at him enigmatically. 'And it is even suggested that it might be here in Florence. And that this is the true meaning of the *"sub flore"* prophecy that has always been part of Frederick's legend.'

'And where might it be hidden?'

'Better than that, *what* is Frederick's treasure? Is there anyone who can answer that question?'

6

Morning of 11th August

As SOON as he left the priory, Dante bumped into a group of local guards. Recognising him, the men came towards him excitedly.

'Prior, we find you at last. A terrible accident has happened, down at the Carraia. A drowned man. We are going to recover the body,' said one of them, making the sign of the cross.

The poet too felt the instinct to cross himself. Death by water was always a harbinger of misfortune in the popular consciousness. And perhaps there was something in that belief, because earth is the place where the body is supposed to find its eternal repose. There is something unnatural about a burial at sea.

But why should the highest authority of the Commune have to take an interest in such an event, however painful it might be? Drownings in the Arno were not rare events, especially in the summer when many people tested its treacherous beds, trusting in the shallowness of the water.

He was about to tell them to approach someone else when a strange presentiment ran through his mind. He immediately changed his decision. 'Take me there,' he called out, following the men.

They moved along the bank of the Arno below the Ponte Vecchio, clambering over the row of water-mills. At that moment the current of the river, almost running dry in the summer shallows, was flowing slowly, often swirling in wide eddies.

On the gravel bed, near the first pillar of the Ponte alla Carraia, a small crowd had formed, all gazing at something and chattering excitedly. Once he had reached the spot, the poet realised the reason for such agitation: stuck in the poles of the last mill he saw a human body, still emerging from the water with each turn of the wheel, like some macabre river god revealing himself in all his dramatic fragility at the top of the circle, drenched with sparkling water, then plunging back into the river once more, immersing itself in its liquid tomb.

There was something extraordinary, the poet thought, in that allegory of incomplete resurrection. As if the dead man were refusing to go to the grave and at the same time the lower powers were denying his return, stopping him each time on the threshold of freedom.

'Why hasn't it occurred to anyone to stop the mill?' Dante cried to one of the *bargellini*, who stood with his arms folded, contemplating the scene.

'The miller is trying to: he's detached the connection with the millstone, but the free wheel is still turning. They are trying to brake it from inside with a pole, before anchoring it with hempen ropes.'

For a few moments the enormous wheel, more than twenty feet in diameter, had actually begun to slow down and the dead man's resurrections had become more sporadic. At last the wheel came to a complete standstill. Two *bargellini* climbed cautiously along the wooden platform supporting it, until they reached the spot where the corpse was jammed. From there, using ropes, they brought their grim cargo down to a little boat that sat waiting on the river.

Dante was standing on the shore. 'Get those layabouts away from here!' he shouted at the *bargellini*, pointing to the gawping bunch of onlookers. As the soldiers set about clearing the field, using the grips of their lances as truncheons, the boat landed. Dante bent over the corpse, which lay face down, its arms spread in a cross and its head hanging over the edge.

He delicately lifted the head, brushing from its forehead the mass of waterlogged hair. As he did so a flood of water spilled from the dead man's mouth, as if his body were full of the liquid that had killed him. Dante immediately let the hair fall back, hiding the man's features once more. He turned round to see whether any of the soldiers showed any signs of recognising the drowned man. But their stupidly curious faces reassured him.

It was the face of Brandano. Or one of his many faces, perhaps, and this time definitely the last. The monk had not had time to assume a studied pose, and now his face betrayed only the anguish of a violent death.

The prior, lifting the body slightly, opened the man's jacket over his chest to give him a quick examination. The corpse was covered with wounds and bruises. It must have struck the river bed with great violence. On one side two red mouths indicated the spot where something had torn the flesh. Dante looked up at the wheel. The poles were fastened to the load-bearing structure by long carpenter's nails. It was probably those that had inflicted the deep, narrow gashes.

He went on studying the body: on one shoulder an unusual tattoo attracted his attention. Drawn in a reddish colour, which looked like a bloodstain on the bluish pallor of the skin, there was the shape of an octagon, surrounded by smaller signs. Dante had never seen anything like it: only some of the smaller markings recalled the symbols with which astrologers represented the various combinations of their art. He remained silent for a moment, meditating on what he could see. Then he bestirred himself.

'Take a cloth, go up to the mill and wrap these poor remains,' he commanded, rising to his feet. In the meantime he had taken his wax tablet from the bag that he carried on his belt, and with the stylus quickly drew a copy of the tattoo.

It wasn't very difficult: since his youth he had been an excellent draftsman, and his knowledge of the mixture of colours had helped him considerably when it came to joining the Apothecaries' Guild. He could have devoted himself successfully to painting, had he wished to do so. His friend Giotto was also convinced of it, and had encouraged him on a number of occasions. Perhaps one day, when he had become something other than he was now . . .

Soon afterwards one of the *bargellini* returned with some hempen sacks. These were used to form a makeshift shroud, in which the poet asked for the man to be wrapped, taking care that his face was covered during the operation. He only felt calmer once the corpse was tightly bound with ropes.

News of Brandano's death would remain secret for at least a few hours. For a while it might prove useful that he alone had recognised the monk.

'Take him to Santa Maria. The Commune will pay for the burial, if no friend or relative appears to reclaim the body.'

The *bargellini* walked away. Meanwhile Dante thought about what needed to be done. So, the monk had not survived his escape along the underground passage. For some reason he must have slipped into the river, and there, weighed down by his habit, had ended up in the vortex of the water-mill, trapped between the spokes of the wheel.

A miserable end for a man who had made skill and juggling the source of his livelihood. Yet that was what appeared to have happened. And judging from the condition of the corpse, the time of drowning must have been more or less the time of Brandano's escape from the abbey.

Nonetheless a voice kept murmuring within him, making him uneasy. The two deep wounds in the man's side might have been caused in the way he had just suggested to himself, but he still couldn't shake off the impression that they were very similar to those inflicted on the bodies of Guido Bigarelli and Rigo di Cola.

And then there was that tattoo, with its unusual astral connotation. But at least Dante thought he might be able to discover its meaning: old Marcello had revealed that he used astrology in his diagnoses. Perhaps he would be able to provide a meaning for the tattoo.

AT THE inn they told him that Marcello must, in line with his custom, be in San Giovanni for his daily prayer at that time of day.

Dante quickly reached the Baptistery, entering the temple by its southern door. He had to pass through the muddle of slums that had accumulated alongside the majestic building over the decades, almost suffocating it with their embrace, and pass the crowd of salesmen who had come to set up their benches even among the graves of the old cemetery that had survived until the present day.

The old doctor was standing up, in the light of one of the windows. He seemed to be plunged in deep meditation, head bowed and eyes closed.

On his time-ravaged face it looked as if the network of wrinkles had been further accentuated over the past few years, digging furrows almost through to the bone. A grimace of pain altered his expression, which usually showed the serenity that comes from a rich life dedicated to the liberal arts. Dante sensed that the man was in unbearable pain, as if a stitch had suddenly gripped his innards.

At that moment Marcello opened his eyes and recognised him. As if by magic his face relaxed, assuming its familiar expression. 'What fair wind brings you here, Prior? Are you too in this extraordinary church for the purpose of worshipping God?'

'No, my reasons for coming here are less noble. I knew I would be able to find you here.'

'You were looking for me? I am honoured to be the object of the attentions of the Prior of Florence.'

Dante thought he detected a hint of irony in the other man's voice, but he continued. 'I appeal to your knowledge of the stars to tell me what this figure represents,' he said, taking the wax tablet from his bag and showing it to the doctor.

Marcello took it, holding it at a distance away from his eyes. 'Over time my pupils have lost their ability to see close up, Messer Durante. As if death wanted to be sure to take me by surprise when the time comes,' he said, forcing himself to focus upon the furrows in the wax. Then all of a sudden he fell silent. 'Where did you see these signs?' he asked after a long pause.

'On a dead man's body. I thought that knowing their significance might help me to establish his identity.'

Marcello stared at him as if attempting to discover a recondite meaning in his words. He went on clutching the tablet. 'They really are unusual signs,' he murmured.

'Symbols of the stars, it seems to me. But what do they mean?'

'As you have correctly understood, the signs surrounding the octagon represent the various heavenly bodies. That is the Sun,' said the doctor, pointing at a little circle. 'And these are Venus and gloomy Saturn.'

'But what does the octagon mean? I have seen other representations of the Zodiacal map, all different from this.'

The old man waited for a moment before replying. He ran his finger along the thin trace left by the stylus on the wax. 'There are many ways of drawing it, but one thing here is truly unusual. Few know this particular aspect of the angular combinations of the stars. The real aspect of one hundred and thirty-five degrees. Only the Arab astrologers are aware of it, to my knowledge.'

'Why "real"? What is unusual about that particular combination?'

'You mean the octagon? It's the shape that God assumed when he wanted to make himself known to man, according to the tradition of the pagans from beyond the sea. It constitutes the doubling of the Tetragrammaton, the name of the ineffable God, the double cube on which the world rests. This is the form that the ancients conferred upon the buildings destined to contain the light of God.'

'His light?'

'Certainly . . . his spirit. Or the traces of his passing. Is it not written in the works of the poets so dear to you that the Grail itself is kept in a stone octagon?'

Dante looked up at the mosaic that decorated the vault, then turned his head. 'The Baptistery too is an octagon,' he remarked.

The other man had followed his eyes. 'It is indeed,' he said.

'In your opinion, why should someone seek to construct a large octagonal building today, on our lands? There is no Grail to guard, after all.'

Marcello turned to look at him in surprise. 'Who is building the thing you describe? And where?' he asked after a brief pause.

'To the north of the city. Something inexplicable.'

'Have you seen it?'

'Yes.'

'And what did you make of it?'

'Little or nothing apart from a general idea of its shape. Apart from . . .'

'What?'

'It was built on the road of death. And death has paid it a visit. Perhaps it was another stage on death's journey, after the Angel Inn. And the marsh.'

'The marsh? What do you mean, Messer Alighieri?'

'The Styx is closer than you think,' the poet said, walking away as Marcello gazed after him.

At the Builders' Guild

DANTE HANDED the piece of paper on which Rigo had sketched his plan for the incinerated construction to Manoello, the prior of the Guild. He was sitting behind his imposing drawing board, which rested on an oak pedestal carved with the symbols of the corporation.

Manoello let a few moments pass with a puzzled expression on his face. He looked suspicious. Then he turned his eyes towards the other two elderly *maestri*, who had risen from their seats to get a better look, as if seeking their agreement. 'What is it?'

'That's what I'd like you to tell me. It's the plan for some kind of building, on which construction was under way. Could you tell me, with your experience, what these drawings refer to? Or what function such an edifice might be designed to fulfil?'

'Why do you want to know?'

Dante took a step towards the desk. He was very familiar with the cloak of secrecy that covered the activities of the Builders' Guild, and the absolute prohibition on revealing anything about those activities to outsiders. But now it was the Commune of Florence that spoke through his lips. 'Because I have reason to believe that this building is linked to a crime. And it is my duty to travel the path of truth, while your duty is to assist me along the way,' he hissed, tapping his finger against the sheet that the *maestro* continued to ignore.

The man looked alarmed. He beckoned the two men over, before finally bending over the drawing. 'An unusual construction. A tower?' he muttered, indicating the outline of the perimeter wall to the first man who had come over.

'Too big,' the other man replied after a brief mental calculation. 'Perhaps . . . it could be a spinning mill. I know they're building huge ones in the north at the moment. Or a drying house for dyed cloths. Or tanned hides.'

'No . . . I know what it is,' a tremulous voice murmured.

The third *maestro*, the oldest, had until that moment remained apart from the others, after darting only a quick glance at the drawings. Dante turned towards him. On his face, as white as a bleached sheet, death had already left its unmistakeable mark. One of his eyes had been blinded by a wound, while the other was barely visible behind its half-closed lid, veiled by a cataract. But now it seemed to blaze with sudden fire. 'A long, long time ago . . .'

'Maestro Matteo, please don't exert yourself,' Manoello interrupted him smugly.

But Dante stopped him with an imperious gesture. 'Where?'

'You see those buttresses fixed on the outside wall, repeating the same figure on a reduced scale? You see the splendid perfection of the crown thus formed?' the old man continued with mounting excitement. 'This building was not conceived for the human race, but as a dwelling for the gods. When Bigarelli . . .'

'Bigarelli?' said Dante. 'He's the one who . . .'

But the other man didn't seem to have heard him. Lost in some inner vision, he kept his claw-like hand on the drawing. 'More than fifty winters now . . . The whole of my life.'

He bent over the papers again, concentrating the last vestiges of his eyesight on the drawings. 'Yes, I saw Guido Bigarelli drawing the plans of the castle, on the Emperor's orders.'

Dante was starting to understand. 'Is it one of Frederick's castles? One of the strongholds with which he marked the frontiers of his kingdom?'

'No, not on the frontiers, but in the centre of the Capitanata, so high up that from it the sea could be seen in the distance. In the bright Mediterranean light. The castle of Santa Maria al Monte.'

Trembling, the old man had risen to his feet, with all eyes upon him. He stopped by the wall at the end of the room, where shelves were lined up, full of rolled-up papers and trunks reinforced with iron bands. After springing open the lock of one of these, he looked inside it for a long time, before standing up again with a triumphant expression, brandishing a bundle of dusty parchments.

'Here it is! My eyes may be weary, but my memory is still intact. I knew they must be here.' He untied the sheets in front of their eyes. 'A copy that I made myself, when I was a colleague of Bigarelli's. In secret,' he added with a shiver, as if fearing that his former teacher might still be able to take his revenge.

Dante bent over the drawings. So, this was the plan for Frederick's masterpiece, the work marvelled at by the pilgrims who returned from beyond the sea, if fortune led them to the Stone Crown, as that mysterious castle was known to the people, a perfect octagon surrounded by the same number of identically shaped towers. A geometrical triumph that was proudly believed to repeat the plan of the ancient Temple of Solomon. And it had been designed by Guido Bigarelli.

'I . . . I saw it,' the old man murmured again.

'You saw Bigarelli drawing on these papers? Are you sure of that?'

'He was the architect who made the designs. But the idea had come to him from someone else. A friar.'

'A friar? Who?' asked Dante.

Rather than replying, the old man bent over the papers once more. He seemed to be looking for something among the faded marks indicating doors and walls. One of the drawings showed the section of a vertical embankment. 'Yes, this is what the great Bigarelli imagined . . . not as it later became.'

The prior gripped the parchment. 'So this plan is different from the real building? In what way?'

'Here, on the ground floor. This continuous wall. That was how the master imagined it, without the windows that were added later. As you see, the ground floor is an unbroken, uninterrupted sequence, without the partition walls that were added later to form a series of halls.'

The prior of the Guild nodded in agreement. 'That's certainly so. The castle would have been better armed and better defended without those apertures. The wall would have been more solid to keep out hostile forces.'

Dante set the paper down on the desk, after looking at it one last time. A sudden intuition had occurred to him. 'Keep them out, you say, Messer Manoello? Frederick was the lord of the earth, of men, of their minds, their souls. His walls were the chests of his guards, the blades of the Arabs of Lucera. He could have slept all by himself in the middle of a field anywhere in his domains, and he would have been safer there than in a room in his palace in Palermo. No, this big blind wall was not designed to keep anyone out.' The poet had risen to his feet, watched with puzzlement by the others. 'Its purpose was to contain something, to hold something that must under no circumstances be allowed to get out.'

Manoello shook his head. 'A prison? No, it was too rich in marble and mosaics for a jail. Besides, Frederick already had prisons in each of his cities.'

'It's too big, one single circular cell,' Matteo added. 'That wasn't what it was for,' he murmured. 'A dark arch, an endless communication trench . . .'

'But what if it was supposed to contain something vast?' Dante pressed, following the thread of his hypotheses. 'A continuous circle, the secret lair not of the Minotaur, but an Ouroboros, the great serpent of time that bites its own tail for all eternity?'

Manoello shook his head disdainfully. 'Frederick certainly wasn't a master of virtue. And all we good sons of the Church share this judgement: that he was the very figure of the Antichrist, sent by Satan to torment us. But you actually see him as a new Minos! What would that stone ring have held captive? Do you believe that the heretic brought back the terrible Minotaur from his expedition to the East?'

'No. But there is something else that needs to be closed away behind massive walls, away from human eyes.

Something beyond the measure of man, just as the limbs of that monster, half-man, half-bull, far exceeded even those of a wild beast.'

'What might that be?'

'Knowledge. And I am sure that you will agree, Matteo,' the poet replied, turning to the old *maestro*, who nodded. 'I need one last favour from you,' Dante continued. 'A quick diagram of the plan of Frederick's castle in its original form, as it has remained in your memory.'

Maestro Matteo exchanged a quick glance with the prior of the Guild, as if asking his permission. The prior gave a swift nod of agreement and the old man went to stand at one of the large tables. He took out a wide sheet of rag paper and began to draw a series of lines, his eyes half-closed as if he were searching the depths of his memory. Then he stopped to contemplate what he had done. After a moment's reflection he added a few details, then scattered absorbent powder over the paper and passed it to Dante. 'This is what I saw, fifty years ago.'

DANTE LEFT the Guild building with few new certainties. Or perhaps none at all. At least now he knew that Frederick's mysterious castle was somehow connected to the events that were troubling him. As was that even stranger construction that had gone up in flames. He looked up at the sky, studying the sun, which was now about to set. Soon the bell would ring out for the curfew. The time had come to put pressure on Cecco.

He headed briskly towards the abbey, once again entering the church through the small side-door, then climbed silently to the upper floor of the sacristy.

Along the way he had not seen a trace of his friend. For a moment he was worried that Cecco might have fled with the Virgin, but then he heard a faint, harmonious sound coming from the end of the corridor. A rhythmic melody, perhaps a dance tune, or a march to accompany a troop of soldiers into battle, but played with a delicate, gentle touch.

Dante stopped on the threshold to admire the woman sitting cross-legged on a cushion, playing a lute. Bent over the instrument, Amara tenderly caressed the strings with her slender fingers. She seemed to be inhaling the vibrations, plunged in the miraculous ecstasy of sounds perhaps inaudible to him. The candle-light played with the whiteness of her hair, turning it into a silvery cascade. Dante's eyes lingered greedily on her perfect face as he felt his heart thumping in his chest.

Suddenly she looked up and saw him. She immediately leaped to her feet, as if afraid. The abandoned instrument rolled to the ground, emitting a muffled lament.

Dante tried to reassure her with a gesture. 'I was looking for Cecco. Do you understand what I am saying?'

Amara nodded. Perhaps she too had felt the heat of the

passion that had been aroused within him, and wanted to escape it? But rather than leaving, as she reached the door she stopped and beckoned Dante to her, indicating a small table in the corner. She looked round anxiously, as if searching for something. Several times she brought a hand to her lips. She seemed to be trying to speak, and kept pointing at the same spot.

The poet came over. On the little table there was a thin sheet of stone, and on it a series of perpendicular lines was carved in the shape of a chessboard. The pieces of the game – tiny ivory and ebony figures – lay in a heap, like the victims of a battle unleashed by the gods.

Amara picked up the black king and set it down in the centre of the chessboard, staring at Dante as though to make sure he was paying attention to her movements. She pointed at the little figure, which bore on its head the sharp points of a crown. At the same time she moved her lips as if trying to pronounce a name.

'A king?' Dante asked. Amara shook her head, then repeatedly touched the chessman's crown. 'The crown. Symbol of power? The empire?' he guessed. The woman seemed still to be waiting for something, as she went on stroking the little crown. 'The Emperor. Frederick?'

The mute woman nodded energetically, her eyes flashing with satisfaction. She picked up the black queen and set it down next to the figure of the king, then put beside them the knights and the castles. Then, with her fingers, she outlined a quick circle round the little group of pieces, as though including them all within a unified whole.

'Frederick's court?' the poet murmured.

Again she nodded. Her little presentation seemed to be over. Dante looked several times from her face to the pieces on the chessboard, in search of a possible meaning. But Amara remained motionless, calmly contemplating her work. Then she stretched her hand out again and picked up another piece from the edge of the table, putting it next to the king, but one square behind him. It was the white queen.

'Another woman?'

A further nod of agreement, and immediately Amara picked up another piece, setting a white pawn next to the queen.

'A son,' Dante muttered. 'By another woman.'

Again the woman stopped, and froze absently once more. And yet those suspended moments clearly had meaning. By standing still, it seemed, she was trying to represent the passing of time.

Then Amara stirred, and looked once more for something among the piled-up pieces. Her hand returned to the chessboard, setting down a white piece, just behind the black king. She repeatedly pointed the piece out to Dante and then, gripping it, violently knocked over the king, which rolled several times and landed on the floor.

Such was the impact that the figure had broken at the

neck. Instinctively, Dante bent down to pick up the two small parts. Someone, striking him from behind, had cast the king to the ground. He held up the fragments in front of Amara's eyes, as if asking for confirmation of what he had seen. 'Someone murdered Frederick? A member of his court?'

Once again the woman nodded.

The prior shook his head. Immediately after the Emperor's death there had been talk that he had been murdered. Too many people had wanted him dead, and it was natural that such a rumour should have circulated. And yet Amara seemed certain of what she had acted out. Perhaps she had heard something different from the usual gossip among the conspirators. He stared once again at the little scene on the chessboard. Amara had used a white piece to interpret the role of the murderer, and the queen. Perhaps white symbolised someone outside the court, someone who had infiltrated it by concealing his true nature.

Then he felt his wrist being gripped. Once again the woman was trying to draw his attention to the chessboard. She pointed to the little pawn, still hidden behind the white queen. She picked it up and delicately set it down in the far corner. Then she looked for two more black pieces, bishops this time, and lined them up next to the pawn, as if to protect it.

'The son escaped? Hidden among . . . clerics?' he asked.

At first the woman shook her head and then, as if she had suddenly changed her mind, she began nodding vigorously. 'And what happened to the little one?' Dante asked.

Amara looked bewildered. She twisted her hands, furious at her inability to find a way of expressing what she wanted to say. Her eyes fell on the little crown that he still held in his hand, and her face brightened. She snatched it from him and set it on the head of the pawn with a triumphant smile.

'The son . . . is going to be crowned?'

The woman nodded. Then, with her hand outstretched, she drew a circle all around them.

'Here? He's going to be crowned here in Florence?'

At that moment muffled footsteps attracted the prior's attention. He turned round to see Cecco in the doorway.

Recognising him, Amara had suddenly straightened and withdrawn to the middle of the room, as if troubled by his arrival.

'Cecco,' Dante said, 'I came here to tell you something.' The other man stopped. 'I saw Brandano today, on the bank of the Arno. Dead.'

Cecco brought a hand to his mouth, his face turning pale. For a moment he glanced towards Amara, then turned back towards the poet. 'Are you sure?'

'As sure as I'm standing here now.'

Cecco leaned against a wall, clearly frightened. 'How did he die?'

The prior waited for a moment before replying. 'Drowned, perhaps. Although other marks on the corpse made me think something worse. As does the expression on your face. So at long last, tell me everything.'

'I've told you everything already.'

'I also want to know what you haven't confessed to me. And you have to talk, at least in the hope of your own salvation, if not for the sake of our old friendship.

'If Brandano has been killed, then the hand of Boniface must be behind all this. His avarice.'

'But why? If the priests really have discovered what you're up to, and if your undertaking was merely a way of getting a few florins out of the yokels, as you said, why would the Pope get involved with a bundle of rogues and set about eliminating them in secret? By now you'd already be in the hands of the Inquisition, you'd be in the pillory in the public square as a warning to the people, and for the greater glory of God. And Boniface.'

'That would be the case if the pontiff really was the righteous vicar of God as he says he is, rather than a money-grubbing sectarian.' Cecco had lowered his head for a moment, before looking up again to stare at the poet. 'There's one thing I haven't told you, my friend. The plan of the Fedeli went far beyond anything that you have seen.'

'Go on.'

'The illusion of the Virgin is merely one stop on a

longer journey, leading to a greater treasure. If Boniface's men have discovered it already, all is lost.'

'What treasure are you talking about?'

'Frederick always took the coffers of the State treasury with him wherever he installed his court. And after the condemnation of his secretary Pietro della Vigna, he became convinced that he was surrounded by treachery and guarded them all the more jealously. But transporting the chests became more and more laborious. After the Emperor's defeat at Parma, when his camp was sacked and it was only by a miracle that the treasure had escaped the assailants, it seems that he decided to hide it.'

'And you know where that place is?' the poet asked in an undertone, instinctively drawing closer to his friend.

'The Fedeli are said to know. Why do you think I got myself mixed up in this lunatic enterprise? Did you think I'd gone soft in the head, as my girlfriend, that whore Bacchina, seems to think? Evidently the secret of its hiding place has somehow reached France, among the Fedeli of Toulouse, but they also say that it is very difficult and laborious to recover. That's why that business with the crusade was organised: to summon the means and men required for the undertaking.'

'And you know the secret of the hiding place?'

Agonised, Cecco shook his head. 'Someone here in Florence was supposed to contact us and guide us, once the undertaking was complete. The Angel Inn was the meeting place. Only Brandano knew the man's identity. Perhaps contact was made, but with the death of the monk the thread is broken. Now what are we supposed to do?' he concluded, twisting his hands.

'Sit firm and stay hidden for the time being. The death of Brandano could also have been an accident – he might have underestimated the speed of the Arno. If he died at the hands of Boniface, the Pope's claws would have reached us already. Perhaps the stranger you were waiting for will show himself.'

Cecco nodded. He seemed to clutch with all his strength at that thin thread of hope. 'But I have heard something about the treasure. Frederick was said to keep it locked in an octagonal building.'

Dante sat down beside the chessboard and thought. If Frederick's much-vaunted treasure was the object of a secret dispute, that would easily have been enough to justify the chain of murders. Locked in an octagonal building. Could the sovereign have kept it hidden in his palace at Castel del Monte? If so, the purpose of the fake crusade became obvious: to assemble a crowd of idiots and drag them along the roads of Puglia, telling them they were going to set off for the Holy Land. And then, having reached the Capitanata, take advantage of the confusion to recover the treasure and hide it among the wagons of the column.

But why rebuild that mysterious castle in Florence? Perhaps to study its secret dimensions, to discover the fake walls behind which the gold was concealed? And if that same Bigarelli had built the original, what need could there be to make a copy?

And why transport all those mirrors, when only two were required for the illusion?

And what about the mysterious machine? And the murdered men?

And then, did Frederick really have an heir, or was it the Emperor himself, still alive, preparing to reappear in all his glory?

HE FELT his head getting heavy, and weariness took hold of him, flickering like the candle-smoke thickening in the air. He slowly slid on to the carpet, propping himself up on his elbows by the chessboard, and closed his eyes in search of rest.

As he slept he must have slipped off the carpet. The cold from the floor had penetrated his bones, and an intense pain was taking hold of his itchy, paralysed limbs. He suddenly felt as if someone had begun to move the mirrors into new positions, in the middle of the room. A horrible geometry of simulated reflections, as terrible as if an unexpected cosmos had taken shape in the space of the room. Behind the glass surfaces he sensed flaming demons, their snake-like tails vibrating like tentacles that slithered along the floor, twining around the candelabras.

He felt himself being pulled upright, even though he still had the languidness of sleep, and he moved a few paces, trying to get away, reaching the corner where he remembered the door of that infernal abbey to have been. But a great roar behind one of the mirrors held him back, petrifying him with fear. At the centre of the octagon a patch of shadow indicated that a great chasm had opened up. A rumbling noise seemed to be emerging from down below, as if massive pillars had begun to crumble, dragging a screaming crowd to their doom. He turned to face the door. From the darkness of that whirlpool a shapeless mass was emerging, and was getting closer all the time. Something terrible was climbing out and his dulled senses could only mark the wait with a continuous and invincible shiver.

Frozen, he stared straight ahead: bigger than a tower, the bearded, two-headed giant from the ship of death had emerged from the crater. And in each of his mouths he chewed with Leviathan fangs the body of a man, violently shaking his head and scattering blood and scraps of flesh all around.

The poet noticed with horror that the two bodies were still alive, writhing in agony, emitting heart-rending cries. Two men crowned with gold, two kings. A father and a son.

7

Dawn of 12th August, at the inn

BERNARDO THE historian set down the papers he was consulting. He rose with a gloomy expression, as if his mind were still absorbed in the thoughts that preoccupied him. He was struck by a fit of coughing that took away the last of his strength. He dropped reflectively back on to his bed. 'Give me water,' he murmured, pointing to a jug on the table. He was drenched in sweat, his cheeks aflame with fever. But before Dante could fill his tin cup, the man grabbed it from his hand, drinking it back in one gulp. He only put it down after he had emptied it. He was shaking violently.

Then at last he seemed to notice the poet. He appeared to have recovered his strength. Bernardo ceremoniously invited Dante to sit down, taking some manuscripts off the only wooden stool.

Once his guest was seated, the *literatus* leaned back on his pillow. 'What can I do for you, Messer Durante?'

'There's something I wanted to ask you, Bernardo. It's

about the life of the Emperor Frederick.'

The other man bowed his head slightly, nodding to him to continue.

'Is it possible that a descendant of his might be alive somewhere?'

The historian shrugged. He seemed suddenly to have noticed an ink-stain on his fingers and began to study it intently, as though it might provide him with the answer. 'It's possible,' he said after a while, finally turning to look at the poet. 'Why do you ask?'

'Because of . . . some things that have happened recently. Just a sense, some vague clues . . . I hoped you might know something more.'

'Frederick was an extraordinary creature, rightly considered the marvel of our times. *Stupor mundi*, as he was called. And there are many uncertainties about him and his life. Many of which I will, I hope, be able to resolve with my writings, but many of which are destined to endure. Even his death was not accepted as a fact for a long time. And not long ago, in Germany, a character appeared claiming to be him, having fled to escape his enemies and returned to save the empire.'

'And did people believe him?'

'Yes, and for several years he wandered about those regions, along with an army of followers, who were ready to die for him. But as to your question, my answer is yes and no.'

Dante waited for him to go on, but Bernardo didn't appear to want to solve the mystery. He went on staring at the poet as if waiting for something. Then he made his mind up. 'The Swabian dynasty, Frederick's bloodline, was extinguished with the wretched Conrad. That's as far as the Emperor's direct heirs are concerned. But Frederick was a man of many passions . . .'

'There is talk of some illegitimate children.'

'Many of them. And even more imaginary ones. There wasn't a woman in his harem who didn't boast of having his child. And the Emperor was not a man to deny certain rumours. He was convinced, in fact, that fertility was one of the attributes of greatness, and that a large number of descendants served to reinforce the dynasty and, at the same time, to placate the appetites and ambitions of the legitimate heirs. He didn't want to lay down his sceptre before the day established by Mother Nature.'

'Could there not have been one who had greater cause than the others to claim the succession?'

Bernardo nodded towards the bundle of papers that lay on the desk. 'Who knows. Maybe one. That's what I'm trying to work out, by studying my teacher's writings,' he replied vaguely.

Dante had a sense that Bernardo knew nothing more on the subject. Or that for some reason he didn't want to tell him anything else. But one thing in the historian's words had struck him particularly. That mention of nature.

'Perhaps Frederick was afraid of being murdered?'

Bernardo gave him a penetrating glance. 'The Emperor was murdered, in fact. By a devious hand, which extinguished this world's greatest hope.'

'The rumour that Frederick was murdered began to circulate straight away, because of both the manner and the suddenness of his death. But there is no proof, apart from the calumnies of the courtiers accusing the noble Manfred of suffocating his invalid father to take his place.'

'And yet Mainardino da Imola had no doubts. He was sure that the Emperor had been poisoned by someone very close to him, someone the sovereign trusted.'

'His doctor, I know, that too has been said.'

'A doctor did effectively make an attempt on his life, after the battle of Parma. But he was discovered. No, it was someone else. Mainardino was certain that he could prove it, if only . . .'

'If only?'

'He had managed to understand how the poison had been administered. Frederick had grown suspicious, and he never consumed anything without first having it tried by his tasters. And yet somehow he was poisoned.'

'Did Mainardino never tell you the murderer's name?'

'No. But he hated him with all his strength. Not only had that man killed a sovereign, but he had also stubbed out any hope of the emergence of a just order of things.'

Dante leaned towards him. 'How can you be so sure?

I too have heard many rumours, but no more, no different from those that always accompany a great man's death.'

'It was Mainardino who told me in person, on his death-bed. And he told me he had never had any doubts about who it was that poured the poison. He disdainfully called him "the incomplete man".'

'The incomplete man? What did that mean?'

'Perhaps it referred to a physical imperfection. Or a moral defect, a *vulnus* in his conscience.'

'And why wasn't the man brought to justice, if his identity was known?'

'That's what I asked my teacher. He told me that his suspicions had run up against an insurmountable barrier: he hadn't been able to work out how the poisoning could have been accomplished. *Certus quis, quomodo incertus*, he wrote. Certain the murder, uncertain the method. Frederick, already ill, had been put on a diet of nothing but fruit. And he drank nothing but watered-down Pugliese wine – all, as I have said, after having everything tried by his tasters, men of his Saracen guard, extremely loyal men. And yet someone managed to pour *acqua tofana* into his cup without their noticing, and without their suffering any harm.'

Bernardo broke off. Dante thought he saw a tear shining in his myopic eye.

'Then, when the Emperor was already in his final convulsions, and his reign was coming to an end, in the agitation of those hours, and as rivalries and hatreds flared up,

Mainardino decided to put off the accusation for a while.'

'And where did that cup end up?'

'I don't know. It disappeared in the confusion that followed the Emperor's death. Mainardino was sure that the murderer had taken it away, to hide the proof, fearing that one day it might be the very thing that revealed the how, the certainty of the who.'

Throughout the morning

YET THERE was another clue enigmatically linked to the crime. The prior quickly made for Santa Croce, and the workshop of Alberto the Lombard.

In his laboratory on the first floor he found the *mechanicus* still at work on the contraption that he had discovered on the galley. He immediately noticed with satisfaction that what lay on the bench was no longer a confusion of brass cogs like the innards of some mysterious animal. They must have regained their position inside the machine; but, far from giving them a recognisable appearance, that made them look even more peculiar.

'You seem to have achieved your goal, Maestro Alberto. Tell me what you have discovered.'

The man turned towards him with a discontented expression. 'I have succeeded in setting the parts back in their places, according to their logical relations. There is a principle of necessity that governs machines, just as there is without a doubt in nature. But if nature is the child of the unfathomable will of God, the possibilities of machines, which are born of the limited human mind, operate according to a more restricted number of combinations. This enables us to go from the parts to the whole, something that would be impossible with a living body once it had been dismembered. But . . .'

'But,' the poet pressed him anxiously.

'But even though the machine has been reassembled and is now able to move, I still can't work out its secret function.'

The instrument consisted of a wooden cube about a foot across, which held the complicated arrangement of wheels. Some lighter parts revealed the damaged areas, which the craftsman had replaced. Over the box, connected by one last toothed wheel to the internal mechanism, lay a long horizontal bronze bar at whose extremities were fixed two balanced semicircles a span in diameter.

'It makes no sense,' Alberto decreed.

Young Hamid had approached too, and watched in silence. 'The will of Allah is also veiled in clouds,' he murmured.

Dante shrugged. 'You said it worked. Show me how.'

The other man nodded, then ran his hand behind the contraption. Underneath, at a point unseen by the poet, a crank-shaped lever protruded from the machine. Alberto gripped it and began to turn it, provoking a metallic whirring sound.

'This crank tenses a steel spiral. Wait.'

He turned the crank a dozen times. Dante had a sense that the resistance of the steel was becoming greater with each turn. At last Alberto seemed satisfied.

On the opposite side from the crank there was a kind of metal butterfly. The *mechanicus* adjusted it by the fraction of a turn, and something inside went off with a ticking noise. Now the upper bar had begun to turn, progressively accelerating the speed of rotation.

Dante watched with agonised interest. The whir of the two semicircles had become intense, like the wings of a gigantic insect about to rise up from the bench. The machine was vibrating slightly, but the weights of the rotating parts must have been measured with extreme care, because the vibration did not alter the balance of the rotation.

'Watch carefully now,' said Alberto, moving the butterfly again. He nudged it another quarter-turn and the rotation of the bar grew even faster.

'The key acts on the internal brake, making it possible to regulate the speed of rotation.'

Carried along by their whirling motion, the two opposing semicircles formed in the poet's eye the image of a complete circle of solid brass.

'But what's it for?' Dante asked. After a moment Alberto

turned the butterfly slowly back, extinguishing the life of the contraption, which came to rest with one final jerk of its hidden gears.

'As I said, I don't know,' he replied. 'It doesn't seem to have any practical use. It just makes those two wing-like objects spin.'

Dante went on studying the object, trying to find a possible answer. 'It couldn't be part of a larger apparatus?'

'I thought of that, too. But it isn't. The whole chain of the internal gears is perfectly arranged to obtain that one effect, and there is no other opening on the box that would enable it to be connected to any other mechanism. And in turn, the moving external part presents nothing that would encourage us to think that anything is missing. No, everything you brought me is here, in front of your eyes.'

Dante had dropped on to a stool. With his elbows on the bench and his chin in his hands, which were clenched to fists, he went on studying the wooden cube. 'And yet the existence of a regulator for the rotation would lead us to suspect some kind of moderation,' he said after a while. 'But are you sure you rule out the possibility that it might be some kind of time-keeper?'

'Prior, no human time could be measured by this machine. Perhaps it really is a spherical astrolabe, but one dreamed up for other heavens, and for other worlds.'

Dante nodded, slowly. He looked up once more, then

stared at Hamid, in the faint hope that the Arab might have something to add. But the boy remained mute, staring suspiciously at the machine. Behind him the curtain that concealed his bed was half-open. Through the chink the poet's eye fell on the manuscript of the *Mi'raj*, open on the humble rug. He sighed. 'And yet I thank you, Maestro Alberto, for what you have done.'

In a corner there was a chest. With the help of the *mechanicus*, the poet rested the machine in it. 'Cover the chest with a sack,' he said. 'I'm grateful to you, and soon I will ensure that your work is compensated.'

He hadn't the slightest idea how he would justify that expense to the Communal clerk, but he would sort it out in some way or other. And he didn't even have a clear idea what to do with that mysterious contraption. But instinctively he felt he had to take it away with him. Too many people knew it was here.

'Don't trouble yourself, Prior. Your city welcomed me when I fled from the persecutions against the Waldensians. See my work as a gift.'

As he was leaving, Dante looked back at the young slave. 'Help me transport the chest,' he ordered brusquely, after asking permission from the *mechanicus* with a nod of his head. Suddenly he had thought of a possible hiding place.

What better refuge than the abbey of the Maddalena? Many things had already been hidden there, both men and objects. If that church was destined to be a receptacle of secrets, he would hide his own there, too.

HE QUICKLY made for the abbey, followed by the Arab with his burden on his shoulders. The machine wasn't especially heavy, but in the terrible heat the boy was soon drenched in sweat. But he went on following the poet without a word of complaint.

On one side of the street the awning of a workshop cast a shadow on the scorching pavement. Dante nodded to the boy to stop, then sat down on the chest that he had set on the ground.

'So in your book, God takes care of the just, seated on his throne. And the unworthy?'

'When he reached the third heaven, the abyss of sins was opened up, and he saw the horrible funnel of the perverted, and the seven steps of their perdition.'

'Seven? According to their sins?'

'And punished according to their crime, with a contrary punishment.'

'A talion. That too you have stolen from Aristotle,' the poet smiled ironically. 'And how did your prophet ascend to the heavens?'

'He was accompanied by the archangel Gabriel,' the boy replied, wiping his brow with the back of his hand.

Dante considered the reply for a moment, pinching

his lower lip with his fingers. 'And why did he need an archangel to support him? Why couldn't he have gone there alone?'

Hamid looked at him quizzically. 'Alone you would burn your wings,' he replied after a while, shaking his head. 'Only a celestial spirit can endure the sight of His Terrible Majesty.'

'Perhaps a celestial spirit will help me, then,' Dante murmured, leaping up again and setting off on his way.

When they were near the old Forum, about a hundred yards from his destination, the prior stopped, sending Hamid away with a coin. The boy set the chest down, looking round in puzzlement, but said nothing. It was not by chance that Dante had chosen that spot by the market. He was confident that no one would have paid them any attention, even in this gossipy city, if they had seen him in the company of a porter with an anonymous burden.

He waited until the slave had disappeared, then hoisted the chest on to his shoulder and set off towards the abbey.

He had encountered some familiar faces on the way, but he had carried on walking, staring straight ahead, and avoided returning anyone's greetings. He arrived at the church just as the abbey bell was ringing out for vespers. Having reached the second door, and having checked that no one was observing his movements, he entered with his load.

Inside it was deserted. He took advantage of the fact and

quickly opened the trapdoor that gave access to the crypt, and climbed down. Remembering where the oil-lamp had been left, he lit it and set off in search of a hiding place.

There were no hiding places in the room. For a moment he thought of stowing the machine in the underground cleft, but was deterred by fear that the water in the well might somehow rise up all that way.

The image of the Virgin came into his mind. In a corner, deposited on an old Roman sarcophagus, was Bigarelli's reliquary, which seemed to stare at him with its terrible *pietra dura* glare. He walked over to it, seized by the desire to observe from close up the fruits of the sculptor's madness.

Then his attention was drawn by the lid of the sarcophagus. The stone seemed to have been moved, and recently, judging by the traces on the floor. With a huge effort, he managed to open it a crack.

Dante was expecting to glimpse ancient, bony remains. Instead the quivering light reflected on a large number of gleaming steel points.

Someone had hidden a bundle of swords in there. He looked round. There were two other sarcophagi in the crypt. He quickly moved their lids, too, discovering other weapons. There was enough in there to equip a small army. New blades, without the slightest trace of rust.

Dante stopped to think for a moment. Then, moving the weapons a little, he made enough room on the bottom to put the machine inside.

He was about to put the cover back in its place when he noticed a movement on the stairs of the crypt. In the faint light of the lamp he saw Cecco. He was clutching a short sword in his hand.

Seeing Dante, he lowered the weapon. 'I heard noises. So you came back, eh? I was about to . . .'

'Why did you lie to me?' the poet interrupted, finishing his work.

A comically pained expression appeared on the man's face. 'What do you mean?' he stammered, scratching his prominent belly.

'The crypt is full of weapons. What are you planning to do with them, if your purpose is only to extort a few florins from the yokels?'

'I knew about those weapons. But I didn't know why they were hidden here, I swear!' He walked over to Dante, throwing his sword aside. 'The Fedeli organised everything, but I don't know the overall plan. None of us has been informed. But if Boniface's men discover it . . .' Cecco looked like a corpse. A violent tremor had taken hold of his limbs. His knees bent and he fell to the floor. 'Then we are finished . . .'

'What does the Pope have to do with it?' Dante replied, immediately alarmed. At that moment the last thing he wanted to face was a clash with Caetani.

The other man bit his lips anxiously and didn't reply. Then he finally seemed to make up his mind. 'The Fedeli have something big in mind.'

'Here in Florence? What?'

Cecco had assumed a circumspect attitude, as if afraid that someone was listening to them. He seemed to have recovered from his initial fear, assuming his usual arrogant expression once more. 'Money, my friend, money. I'm sure of it. That's why they got involved in the illusion, what else? A pile of money, something dating back to the days of Frederick, may God's glory preserve him! So I'll be able to send my father to hell at last . . .'

'What has the Emperor got to do with it, damn your soul?' Dante cried, exasperated. 'You all talk about him as if his shadow had returned to walk the earth. But rather than doing so with the reverence due to the dead, you drag him from his sleep to use him as a screen for your intrigues. What is the purpose of all this?'

Cecco shook his head. 'There are many different parts, like the branches of a great tree. Each of us knows his own task . . . but only the First one knows everything. I, though, have worked out: the imperial treasure . . . the friends are on its trail. And then you can safely bet that much of that metal will end up in my pockets, which have great need of it. And in yours, if you will help me. As you did that time at Campaldino . . .' he concluded, slapping the poet hard on the shoulder.

Dante irritably removed his hand. 'Who is the head of the Fedeli now? Is he the First of whom you speak?'

Cecco shook his head. 'The leader of the Fedeli was for a

long time our friend, Guido Cavalcanti. And perhaps he still would be, if he hadn't been struck by the banishment order to which you put your seal,' he replied bitterly. 'But now the leader is someone far higher up. That is all I know for certain.'

Dante put his head in his hands. All the elements of this enigma were spinning around in his mind like crazed moths round a flame.

'I know they want to avenge the Emperor, I've heard that, too. His death,' Cecco said.

'His death?' the prior echoed.

Bernardo's words had come back to him. 'Cecco, do the Fedeli think the Emperor was murdered as well?'

'That's what we say to each other. Poison, and possibly by his own physician.'

'And how might he have done it?'

'No one knows,' the other man replied with a shrug. Dante felt a twinge of anger. Once again someone had brought him to the threshold of a revelation and then closed the door in his face.

Late morning

DANTE CROSSED the open space that lay behind San Piero, still lined with the ruins of the Ghibelline houses destroyed in the fury that followed their defeat in 1266. There, incorporating large tracts of the old walls, the future Palazzo della Prioria, with its vast tower, was going up. But for now the offices of the Commune were scattered among the little surrounding buildings, which had been let for the purpose.

The clerk of the Commune was based in one of these, at the beginning of the road to the market, on the first floor. On the floor below, and in the basements, lay the city archives, where deeds, depositions and minutes of the meetings of countless assemblies were bound between ornate boards.

'Greetings, Messer Duccio,' said the poet.

The bald man, who had greeted him solicitously, quickly replied with a bow, setting aside the big dossier he was compiling. 'What can I do for you?'

'You know everything about this city. The debits and credits. And above all the activities that go on there, who performs them and where.'

The other man half-closed his eyes with a barely perceptible twinge of pleasure, which he then disguised with a little smile. 'You are too generous in listing my humble qualities. In fact it is the Guilds, with their local registries, that keep precise account of the activities pursued by the affiliates of the various camps. Although it is true that in my office we take general note of everything . . . to give the tax-man a hand,' he added with a wink. 'Those merchants will stop at nothing to avoid paying tolls and taxes.'

Dante looked round. The clerk's room was decorated very simply, with a few items of furniture that had been rescued from God knows where. Even his desk looked like an adapted church pew, and the two mismatched benches were no better. And yet, beneath their shabby exterior, those rooms concealed a detailed collective consciousness of the city.

'Messer Duccio, what do you know about a certain *literatus*, Arrigo da Jesi, who has been staying in Florence for some time?'

The man raised his chin as if his attention had suddenly been drawn by something on the ceiling. He closed his eyes and pursed his lips, repeating the name under his breath. Dante had the impression that he was running through the open pages of a mysterious mental archive, concealed in the folds of his memory.

'Arrigo . . . da Jesi. Of course. The philosopher,' he said after a few moments. 'He arrived from France not long ago. Not much luggage, and in fact he didn't pay any duties, except a small amount for the books and writing paper that he had with him. He asked for lodgings at the hostel in Santa Maria Novella, from the Dominicans. In return he sometimes gives lessons at their school.'

'Are you sure he had nothing else with him? Nothing valuable?'

Duccio half-closed his eyes again. 'No. But he was transporting something unusual, now that you remind me of it. The customs men couldn't work out the sum that needed to be paid, so they turned to my office. A chest with a wheel in it. And some small glass objects.'

'What?' exclaimed Dante.

'Yes, a wooden wheel. Or at least that's how the customs man described it to me, when he delivered his report. More than a wheel, in fact . . . wait!' the man cried, striking his forehead with a hand.

A tall stack of papers had accumulated on his desk. He flicked through them quickly, until he settled on one in particular.

'Here it is, you see?' he said emphatically. 'Nothing gets lost in here! There's the report, with the description of the object,' he added, holding the sheet out to the poet.

Before his eyes, roughly sketched in ink, was the drawing of two concentric octagons.

'You see? A kind of wheel, as I told you.'

'And what did Arrigo tell the customs officer?'

'Nothing. That it was just an instrument he used for his studies.'

Dante had immersed himself in his thoughts, and went on staring at the drawing.

'It's certainly strange,' he suddenly heard Duccio say.

'What?' he murmured, stirring slightly.

'That Arrigo should have been a guest of the Dominicans.'

'What's strange about it?'

'Lots of things, given the way the brothers think. As a young man, Arrigo had been a Franciscan novice, in the days of Brother Elias, Francis's successor. And since there's so little love lost between those two orders – I wonder why he didn't go to Santa Croce . . .'

'Indeed. I wonder why not?'

Midday

THE CLOISTER of the convent adjacent to Santa Maria Novella was full of monks busy with a great variety of tasks. Dante quickly reached the northernmost corner, where a door led to the little classrooms.

He too had been there as a young man, and he clearly remembered the firmness with which the teachers had instilled in them the certain truth of faith.

Of *their* faith. The black and white of the cloaks wandering around was a reflection of the clarity with which the order distinguished truth from falsehood. Even then he had never managed to enter those spaces without a faint shiver of anxiety, when he became aware of one of the monks standing behind him. And that old insecurity seemed to be returning today, he thought with some irritation, as he tried to shake off the disagreeable sensation with a shrug of his shoulders.

Now he was no longer the nervous student getting to grips with God's mysteries; he was the prior of the city, the keeper of the keys – those that closed and those that opened. He raised his eyes, which he had kept lowered until that point, instinctively adapting to the manners of the people he noticed around him, and reached the last cell, from which he heard a familiar voice.

Two benches, on which half a dozen men were seated, most of them tonsured novices, faced a simple desk set upon a three-step dais. Sitting on the chair, Arrigo was busy declaiming from a large illuminated manuscript set on a lectern. In a loud voice, the philosopher uttered the words of the text, slowly, articulating them one by one as though the meaning he sought lay in each one, rather than in the sentence that they formed.

Dante immediately recognised the text to which the lesson was devoted: the Book of Genesis, the narration of the first phases of Creation. He sat down on the end of the closest bench. It was then that he noticed in the audience the thin figure of Bernardo the historian, leaning over his wax tablets and making rapid notes. He glanced up and met the poet's eye. He immediately snapped his tablets shut, nodding Dante a quick greeting.

Meanwhile Arrigo seemed to have reached his conclusion. He quoted the work of some of the Church fathers, lingering particularly over an observation by Lactantius. Then he assigned his pupils the task of preparing a controversy on the subject, to be expounded in the following lesson. As his audience was rising to its feet to pay him tribute, he spoke again, making one final request.

'I would also like you to try and explain how it was

that God created light on the first day, and the stars and the other givers of light only on the fourth,' he said calmly.

Dante walked to the foot of the desk, past the pupils who were proceeding towards the exit.

Arrigo had closed the manuscript. He looked up and recognised the poet immediately. 'Messer Alighieri! And you, Bernardo . . . I am glad you have found the time to listen to my humble dissertation. But come, let us leave this suffocating space. Outside, in the cool shade of the cloister, we will be able to pursue our conversation with greater ease.'

He led them outside. The portico of thin double columns surrounded a luxuriant garden divided into ordered sections, in which the monks cultivated medical herbs for the monastery pharmacy. In one corner a big lemon tree extended its branches towards the shade of the portico, next to a little gurgling fountain.

Arrigo bent down and took a long, greedy sip.

Dante took advantage of this to address the philosopher. 'I didn't expect to find you teaching a lesson on the origins of Creation. I thought you were more interested in the form of our world.'

'The form of the world, as you say, is only the consequence of the manner of its birth: just as each living creature in its adult state is nothing but the necessary development of its infantile form. I am interested in Genesis for the same reason,' Arrigo replied evasively.

'I hear the lesson of the great Aristotle behind your words,' Dante replied, 'and I bow to you. And yet those same Scriptures teach us that not all that has been created endures through time.'

Arrigo wiped his lips with the back of his hand. 'So you too, Messer Durante, accept the thesis of those who assert that Creation was not completed on the first day, but that God attended to it even in the eras that followed, and with different intentions?'

'That much is written in the Scriptures: God added things to the world. But you, Bernardo, what do you think?' Dante insisted.

The historian shrugged. 'I bow to your theology,' he said drily, looking at Arrigo out of the corner of his eye. He seemed embarrassed. Dante had a sense that he was there to speak intimately to the philosopher, and that by coming he had spoiled Bernardo's plans.

Arrigo must have noticed something, too. He smiled reassuringly, laying a hand on the historian's shoulder. 'Come on, Bernardo, the prior knows this kind of thing better than anybody. He was once my pupil, but nowadays his learning is far superior to mine. Don't be shy, if you have any doubts that I might resolve.'

Bernardo bit his lips, glancing from one man to the other. At last he made up his mind. 'You know about the work to which I dedicate my days. There is one point, in the last years of the Emperor's life, about which you might be able to enlighten me better. Frederick's relationship with Elias of Cortona.'

Arrigo closed his eyes for a moment, as if the sound of that name inflamed within him the pain of a wound that had not healed. But suddenly his expression became as serene as ever.

'The Emperor sent him to the East, in the year of our Lord 1241,' Bernardo continued. 'Do you know why?'

'A diplomatic mission. To resolve the dispute between Constantinople and Vatacio of Nicaea,' Arrigo replied after a moment's reflection. He seemed surprised by the question. Dante had a sense that for some reason he had been on the point of not replying.

'That is what they say, and what the chronicles record. But I wonder if there wasn't some other purpose for his mission?'

'I was only a novice at the time. By the time I entered the convent, Elias had already returned from his journey.'

'But didn't you hear anything? A hint, a murmur?' Bernardo pressed him.

'Nothing when I was there. But, as I have said, I was only a novice, devoted to the humblest of tasks. My fellow-monks certainly didn't let me into their secrets . . . if they had any.'

Bernardo bowed his head thoughtfully. He didn't seem very convinced. He looked back up at Arrigo, and the philosopher firmly withstood his gaze. 'So that's how it is,' he stammered. 'Perhaps it really is as you say,' he continued in a louder voice. 'Fine, it's time for me to get back to my work.' He walked away, vaguely nodding goodbye.

Dante and Arrigo watched after him until he disappeared.

'The dispute between Constantinople and Vatacio of Nicaea?' Dante repeated after a moment's pause.

Arrigo smiled weakly. 'Yes. Not so strange, Messer Alighieri. They were uneasy years, dominated by the demons of the manifold. Many kingdoms, many emperors, many gods.'

Dante pursed his lips. 'God is one, Arrigo.'

The other man exploded with laughter. 'Apparently nothing can shake your certainties.'

'Certainly not that one. In fact I'm curious about the question you put to your pupils: whether light is something other than luminous bodies. How do you expect them to respond?'

Arrigo pushed aside with his foot a stone that was in his way. Then he pointed a finger towards the sky. The sun above their heads burned like a furnace. 'Clearly they coincide, and Scripture is mistaken. When the sun sinks below the horizon, light and heat are extinguished. I am sure it is the sun's flame that produces the beam of light, and there can be no light without combustion.'

'Consider the nature of the heavenly bodies,' the prior replied. 'The moon, too, radiates a luminosity, and so do the stars, on clear nights. But no heat comes from them. A sure sign that light exists without combustion. And hence that light is an accident of nature that needs no flame, and could precede it in the order of Creation.'

'That would be the case if the moon and stars gave off a light of their own. But they are merely inert mirrors. Their bright bodies do nothing but reflect the light of the sun, returning it to us from the great abyss of space. *Lucis imago repercussa*, images of light in a mirror.'

'*Non potest.*'

'Why?'

'Because they appear when the sun sets below the horizon, sliding towards the antipodes. From where would they receive the light to reflect, when the mass of the earth is interposed between them and the sun?'

Arrigo couldn't suppress a look of commiseration. 'And yet, Messer Alighieri, there is a very simple solution. Think about it, and you will reach the same conclusions as me.'

Dante had blushed. Just then he could not find the rational explanation that the other man took for granted. He decided to change the subject. 'Did you learn your subtlety at the school of Elias of Cortona?' he tried to joke.

'From him, and from others. But it was from Elias that I learned both the heat of research and the chill of reason.'

'They say that the friar was a close friend of Emperor Frederick,' Dante continued. Arrigo nodded in silence.

'Even helping him with his architectural works,' the poet went on. 'Apparently it was he who designed a very splendid and unusual castle. Castel del Monte, a work whose significance still remains incomprehensible even to experts in the art.'

'Perhaps the art of building is not the one most likely to penetrate its meaning.'

'Which art would be required, then? Or which science?'

'An art that built its forms with learning as well as with stones.'

'Alchemy? Is that what you're thinking of? Is that Frederick's treasure? The one that everyone is looking for?'

'Frederick's treasure . . .' the philosopher murmured. 'Yes, it is one of the Emperor's treasures. But it can be reached only by passing through the door of reason. Think about it, Messer Alighieri. Find the answer to my question. And as for Brother Elias . . .'

'Was he really such a great man as they say? A magician?' the poet said encouragingly.

Arrigo stared at him for a long time without replying. Then he looked away. 'Elias was truly great. Not in the dark sciences, however, but in the bright ones of knowledge. Come up to my cell: there's something I want to show you. Besides, the good friars have served me wine from their vines. A goblet will rinse the dust from your throat, and perhaps the bitterness from your soul.'

Arrigo's cell was decorated as plainly as the poet's own.

But unlike his, it was full of precious manuscripts. About fifty volumes were scattered around the place, lined up on an oak shelf, on the desk and piled up on the floor like little towers of wisdom.

As soon as he had passed through the door, Dante frantically rushed over to examine them. He quickly looked at a number of frontispieces, before suddenly setting down the last volume that he had picked up. Blushing, he turned towards his companion with a word of apology. Wasn't snooping around a man's library like snooping around his soul?

Arrigo had remained in the doorway, surprised at Dante's excitement. 'Don't apologise. Fortune decreed that I should be given the chance to assemble this little collection of the words of the ancients; feel free to use it like a public drinking fountain.'

Dante bowed his head in a sign of silent gratitude, before returning to explore that sea of knowledge. 'Some people would kill to own all this,' he murmured, picking up an illuminated manuscript.

'People always kill so that they may live. And for the wise man, words are the very essence of life.'

'Your arguments seem to allow for a great deal of passion, Messer Arrigo.'

'What if someone were to kill not because he was gripped by the passion of the senses, or by the evil of the soul, or by dulling of the brain, but because in some way he was sure of achieving a greater good, of clearing some obstacle from the path of virtue?'

'No one is permitted to dispose of the life of one of his fellow men, except to defend life and goods against an act of aggression. Virtue is a collective good, and as such it must be defended. Only the people, through their magistrates, have the right to punish those who attack them.'

'Not even if the first cause of that crime was love? You have paid a great deal of attention to that particular sickness in your writings. And great crimes have been committed for love.'

'Crime cannot be included within the natural order of things,' Dante firmly declared.

Arrigo went to a cabinet in the corner, opened the door and took out a bottle filled with amber liquid. Dante had been watching him distractedly, but his attention was suddenly drawn by an object placed on one of the shelves, which flashed brightly in a ray of light from the window.

The philosopher had noticed his reaction. An expression of satisfaction appeared on his face. 'I knew that would interest you,' he said, leaning towards the cabinet again, and beckoning the poet to do the same.

What lay on the shelf was a strange brass lamp, more than two feet tall and octagonal in shape. A little window opened in one side of it, protected by a thick piece of crystal.

The philosopher touched a finger to the metal surface,

as if to run it along its pattern. 'The final work of my teacher, Elias of Cortona,' he said affectionately.

'A lantern?'

Arrigo nodded. 'But one of an extraordinary kind. Brother Elias said its light could cross the sea, even as far as the infidels of Palestine.'

On one side of the strange object there was a little door, held in position by a handle. Dante opened it and peered in. There was nothing inside but a small stove, screened at the back by a parabola, which must have served to concentrate the light towards the little window. He turned towards Arrigo with a disappointed expression.

'It doesn't seem much different from any other lantern,' he remarked. 'Apart perhaps from its size. But I've seen bigger ones on galley-ships.'

'The wonder of it lies not in its appearance, but in the source of its light. This.'

He rummaged in the cabinet again and took out a sealed ampoule. Through the glass a whitish, sandy substance could be seen. Holding it carefully, Arrigo brought it in front of the poet's face so that he could see it better.

'In his last years Elias had immersed himself in the study of alchemy: this powder is his greatest discovery. But he wouldn't tell me its composition, stressing only that it was extremely dangerous.'

'And how does it work?'

'You put the ampoule on the stove and heat it up. It takes only a few moments for it to ignite and give off an astonishing light, white and steady, like the illumination of the sun.'

Dante instinctively held out his hand to take the vial, but Arrigo immediately drew back his hand.

'Be careful. Even the warmth of a hand is enough to bring this compound to life.'

'But if it is as you say, why did Elias not reveal his secret to the Emperor? Such a device could have been used to great effect by his armies, to fight in the dark!'

Arrigo shook his head. 'Elias was a man of peace. Besides, Elias had distilled only this amount of the preparation. Only this.'

'What stopped him?'

Arrigo shook his head. Dante waited for him to go on, but the philosopher seemed lost in thought. He was staring into the distance, as if he had returned to the days of his youth and the dark figure of Elias were in front of his eyes. Dante saw him shaking his head in silence. 'Nothing stopped him,' he murmured. 'There is no need for a second sample. *Omnia in uno*.'

Suddenly he stirred as if his vision had vanished. He delicately put the lantern back into the cabinet, and closed the door.

'Tell me about this wine. Don't you think it's the true nectar of the gods?'

Afternoon, at the priory

DANTE FOUND a messenger waiting for him, wearing the livery of Cardinal d'Acquasparta. The man must have been there for some time, because as he spotted the poet he leaped to his feet with a look of relief.

'His Eminence wishes you to receive this,' he said in an official-sounding voice, handing him a piece of parchment folded in four, tied with a strip of cloth and closed with a seal.

Dante broke the seal and quickly read the message: the cardinal asked him to come as soon as possible to the headquarters of the papal legate, to discuss some confidential matters. 'Why doesn't he ask for an audience at the priory?' he asked crisply, folding up the parchment again.

'His Eminence thinks it's more sensible like this, given the tensions in the city. A visit to the offices of the Commune would give things an official status that would be better avoided. And besides . . .'

'Besides?'

'The question concerns you, personally, Messer Alighieri.'

Dante thoughtfully bit his lower lip. The other man didn't seem inclined to say anything else. For a moment he considered having him thrown in jail, and subjecting him to the same treatment as poor Fabio, to find out more. But he doubted that a fox like the cardinal would have revealed his plans to anyone. Perhaps it was better to take up the challenge and face the lion in his den.

THE CLERIC walked him through the rooms of his residence, opening them up one after the other so that they formed a long corridor. On the threshold of the last door he stopped and stood aside.

Dante walked to the middle of the room, where a huge man was waiting, his insolent features hidden behind a mask of fake bonhomie. He was sitting on a little wooden throne decorated with the insignia of his post. His wide-brimmed hat, with its woven cord, lay on his knees.

'So, Messer Alighieri, we meet again,' the cardinal muttered in his shrill voice, with a hint of laughter that made his double chin quiver. He held out his gloved hand, decorated with a large ring.

Dante took a single step towards him, stopping in front of the throne. Rather than turning towards the outstretched hand he folded his arms. 'I knew you wanted to see me. Why just me, rather than requesting an audience with the whole Council?'

The cardinal withdrew his hand, seemingly undisturbed by the prior's behaviour. Only a rapid contraction of his fleshy lips and a gleam in his eye revealed his true sentiments for a moment. But he immediately resumed his curial pose, his face dominated by a massive nose like the mask of an ancient Roman. 'Because if you want to talk to a man on his own, it makes more sense to address his mind directly than to appeal to his limbs or his guts. And as far as we can tell, you are certainly this Council's mind.'

'It would appear that my humble person is the object of detailed study by the servants of Boniface,' the poet remarked.

'The servants of Boniface are the servants of the Church. The pastors of the people of God. And they benignly lead the herd that trusts in him, firm in the certainty of faith, and standing up to the wolves that wish to massacre that herd to sate their greed. As for you . . .' he went on, raising his ringed hand once more in a menacing gesture. 'As for you, for some time now your actions have given the Holy Church cause for concern.'

Dante rose up to his full height. But those words had sent a shiver down his spine. He had to control himself to keep from looking round. He remembered the threatening black and white figures he had seen at the abbey, their snake-like eyes fixed on the things going on around them. He was sure that Noffo Dei, the head of the inquisitors, was nearby, perhaps hidden in the next room.

'So tell me what you want.'

A smug expression appeared on the cardinal's face. 'To know from your own mouth what your political feelings are.'

'Of what interest could that be to you?'

Rather than replying, the prelate held out a hand towards a cushion set down next to his chair, and picked up a little bundle of papers. He cast a glance at the first, but then looked back up at Dante, as if he was very familiar with what was written on them. 'You are a lover of history, are you not?' he asked; then without waiting for a reply, he continued: 'And you are also curious about those who want to turn history into a narrative, like that fellow Bernardo whom you seem to have started seeing. A man who rummages through the refuse of time with the sole aim of creating a scandal.'

'Recording and rigorously narrating the events relating to a reigning house that has made its mark on the century is a noble project. Why shouldn't it have your approval?' Dante replied.

Acquasparta gestured vaguely, then began waving the papers around again. 'I expect it is as you say. I want, however, to speak not of the story of that sordid tribe, but of your own, Messer Alighieri.'

'Mine?' Dante couldn't conceal his alarm. 'I didn't know I had one that deserved attention.'

'And yet it does. Yours is one of those tales that would have delighted the ancient story-tellers, but which prompts disquiet in the children of goodness.'

'Why?' asked the poet.

'Because it doesn't make sense. And everything that

doesn't make sense is a source of uncertainty. And uncertainty is the seed of disbelief. And disbelief is the enemy of faith, the door through which Satan slips into the homes of men.'

The cardinal broke off, still weighing the papers in his hand and shaking his massive head, then went on: 'It seems as if there are two different people within you, Messer Alighieri. First the young lover of the cheerful life, the poet of sweet manners, lascivious and luminous, all drenched in a dream of impossible love. I too have read your verses about Beatrice, whoever she might be. Because you're not going to try and make me believe that the woman you were involved with is a certain – let's see . . .' He flicked through several pages. 'Here we are, Bice dei Portinari, a poor girl who went on to marry the old man Bardi. Truly very moving verses, a model for all loving spirits. And in fact . . .'

Dante said nothing. The cardinal had stopped again, and now he was flicking through the bundle as if looking for something.

'And in fact,' he continued, 'those verses suddenly became a fashion, and other young enthusiasts, picking up your style, sang of their loves, so similar to your own. And you also gave them a name, didn't you? The Fedeli d'Amore?' The priest stopped again, as if waiting for confirmation of his words.

But Dante remained speechless, frozen in place.

'The Fedeli d'Amore . . . And apparently there's also a leader of this group of yours, your friend Guido Cavalcanti. Or former friend, perhaps? I know you had him exiled, and I wonder why. And then others, all original figures. Like Francesco d'Ascoli, the astrologer. A heretic, a blind leader of his kind. Or that man Cecco Angiolieri, who has now come to your city after spending time as a guest in the jails of his own.'

'You spoke of two people who dwell together within me . . .'

'Oh, yes, you're right. Because all of a sudden, off that noble-minded young man goes to Paris to study. But rather than coming back with his knowledge and learning reinforced, suddenly he disappears. And in his place you appear, Messer Alighieri, the man you are now. The second one.'

'The second one?'

'Another man who, against all of his previous customs, and in contrast with his declared aversion to the vulgarity of the mob, sets off along a difficult path. He begins to enchant the simple people with his ornate words in street-corner meetings, he is elected to insignificant committees, he wastes his genius deciding which streets need mending or which extraordinary taxes should be imposed. And he moves from that fascination with eternity that previously governed him, to mingle with shopkeepers and merchants, climbing step by step a path to nothingness. To where we find you today. Why, Messer Alighieri?'

'Perhaps because within the just man there is the call to goodness, as our great men have taught us,' Dante replied frostily.

'*Verum*. But who are those great minds who have served as your example and your inspiration? Apart, of course, from that man Brunetto Latini, a notorious sodomite who died just in time to escape the death sentence he deserved. And he too drank from the springs of Paris, so much so that he actually wrote his work in the language of that place.'

'Many have loved my fatherland, and are worthy examples. Farinata degli Uberti, Mosca dei Lamberti and Tegghiaio Aldobrandi among them.'

Acquasparta narrowed his eyes to slits. 'Are these the men who inspired you? A Ghibelline leader, pitiless in his fury; a thoughtless lunatic who unleashed civil mayhem with his bad advice; and then yet another sodomite. It would actually seem that this rabble has won your sympathies.'

Dante's eyes flashed and he stepped towards the cardinal, who didn't seem to care greatly about his growing anger.

Once again he waved the report in front of his eyes. 'You know, Messer Alighieri? The men in my secretariat who have been dealing with your case have a theory of their own. Just imagine, they are convinced that everything begins with your father's death. A man whose dealings were not always, we might say, beyond reproach, but who was still able to ensure you, during his lifetime, of that brilliant and lavish lifestyle that you enriched with your songs. Although, once he had been called to the Lord, he meant for you to earn your livelihood elsewhere.'

The cardinal struggled to his feet, snorting as he tried to free his massive body from the arms of his little throne. Then he walked over to the window, inviting his guest to look outside with him. 'You see the fervour of work that pervades your city? How many new buildings, how many streets, how many shops are opening? And for each one a permit, a licence, debits and credits, not gold as in your heavenly Jerusalem, or in the Republic of your philosophers, but at least silver, certainly that . . . I know that you have been in charge of the roads.'

'That's true. But what are you getting at?'

'You were in charge of building a new road to the fields of Santa Croce,' the cardinal continued, pointing to the papers. His eyes were half-closed, as if he had no need to read.

'It was a necessary piece of work, it encouraged traffic to the eastern districts.'

'Oh, very true. But as chance would have it, one of your own farmhouses is there, transformed by a stroke of the pen from uncultivated weeds to building land, for which you Florentines seem to have such an appetite. Chance, certainly. But chance, Messer Alighieri, often favours the audacious, as we have been taught by those pagans upon whom you moulded your own convictions.'

Acquasparta fell silent again, then returned to his chair, as if that brief excursion to the window had exhausted him. He slumped on to his little throne. 'But I, Messer Alighieri, don't agree with my secretariat – for once. I have observed you and I have read you with the infallible eye that tranquillity of the soul gives to those who live the righteous life. And I don't believe that your allegiances derive from the simple desire to enrich yourself by extorting money in favour of your offices. No. It would be as if a venal animal dwelt within you, corrupted either by its insatiable appetites or by a desire for public approval. Were that the case, it would take only a few florins to buy you, enough to pay for your debts and your prostitutes. But within you lies an abyss deeper than that one.'

'What are you talking about?'

'We are convinced that your entry into politics is part of a plan dreamed up over many years by the Fedeli, to infiltrate their men into the highest positions in the Guelph cities. And once they were established, to work in secret for your true purpose, clumsily masked behind rhymes and laments of love: to drag Italy from the righteous dominion of the Church to put her in chains under the supporters of the Emperor. But the Church,' the priest continued, rising to his feet again, this time with unexpected swiftness, 'has over the centuries repelled the coils of the snake that tried to suffocate her, since the days when Charlemagne's successors betrayed the pact conceding the imperial crown to them. And the Church has always defeated them. And the Church will defeat the activities of little men like you. You have pointlessly convened the horsemen of the Apocalypse in Florence to no good purpose!'

The cardinal had raised a threatening finger. He was panting with excitement, his double chin trembling. After groping for words, open-mouthed, he went on: 'You will perish, have no doubt! And you will follow to its ruins the damned rabble of the Ghibellines, ready to betray everyone, starting with the very source of their iniquities: that man Frederick whom you admire so much, and whom they themselves murdered, driven by their greed!'

'What do you mean?'

'The Antichrist was assassinated by his bastard son Manfred, to get hold of his lands and his crown, after Pope Innocent had promised to crown him King of Sicily.'

'You are lying!' the prior exclaimed furiously. 'King Manfred was a noble, courteous man! Only the slanders of your servants paint him as a parricide, but those are words written on water, the fruit of your intrigues!'

'And what do you know about things that happened before you were born, when you were but an insignificant possibility in the unfathomable mind of God? What do you know about what has defined the Holy Church over the centuries? Frederick died in violence and rage, swept away by the same storm of Satan from which he had emerged when that whore d'Altavilla gave birth to him at Jesi.'

Dante glared at him contemptuously. 'If that is what you believe, I should consider myself honoured. A little man like me at the centre of such a grand design.'

'Oh, don't flatter yourself too much, because as you wait for your dream to become reality, we know that your plans are currently heading for disaster. You are in search of Frederick's gold, even more than his return. It would seem that the snake has hidden his golden eggs, and that some people think they know where they might be.'

'And you'd like to be one of those people!'

Acquasparta drew himself up to his full height. 'The Church has the right to that gold, to use it to accomplish the mission that God himself entrusted to her: to pacify Italy beneath the crozier of Saint Boniface. Deliver it to us, and the holy water of forgiveness will fall upon your head. The Church will slaughter the fatted calf, because the prodigal son, who once was lost, has now been found.'

'A calf in exchange for a fortune and a pact that would certainly be pleasing to Boniface.'

'Blasphemer! You believe in nothing.'

'I believe in a single God who moves all things and is not moved. Who reigns in three persons, who is three in one. Knowable not to proof, but to faith and illumination.'

The cardinal laughed sarcastically. 'Even a Patarine, even an Albigensian could subscribe to your words. Perhaps what they say about you is true.'

'What do they say?' the poet asked indifferently.

'That in Paris you supped your knowledge from very strange springs. Including those of the Mohammedans, like Sigieri.'

'Sigieri di Brabante was not a Mohammedan.'

'But an admirer of Averroes, and that's enough.'

Dante came closer, leaning towards the cardinal as if to kiss him on the cheek. His lips brushed Acquasparta's ear. 'Better the light of the pagans than the shadows of your stupidity,' he whispered.

Acquasparta, purple in the face, staggered backwards. 'You will regret your arrogance. We know everything, everything! You, friend of the Antichrist! But not even the four horsemen who accompany him will be able to save you from ruin when the time comes. And we will be the ones who decide when!'

Dante shrugged. 'May the will of God the almighty and merciful be done.'

Only on the stairs did he realise that he had used the formula of the pagans.

THE POET turned off towards the bank of the Arno, skirting the tanners' workshops. He tried to protect himself against the afternoon sun with the veil of his biretta, waving his hand in front of his nose to chase away the miasmas rising from the vats in which the skins were macerating. It was a pointless gesture, but he went on repeating it automatically, plunging further and further into that sticky, tepid wave in which everything was submerged.

His head was filled with the buzzing of the flies that infested the whole district; without noticing, he had left the most direct road to San Piero, seeking the comfort of the shadows in the little vegetable plots behind the Church of the Holy Apostles.

He emerged from the alleyways at the feet of the ramp that climbed towards the Ponte Vecchio. The place seemed unusually deserted, as if a spell had frozen the comings and goings of the crowd that spilled into its arcades at all times of day. Only the quick dart of a fleeing mouse or the shadow of a stray dog disturbed that uneasy stillness.

There was perfect silence, broken only by the cry of a gull from as far away as the sea. Dante could distinctly hear the gurgle of the low water of the Arno, which was now almost running dry. For a moment he thought that the demon of noon had erased all forms of life. Then a breath of wind brought the sound of human voices to his ears.

There was someone at the end of the bridge, beneath the little portico. Two men deep in muttered conversation. Arrigo da Jesi and Jacques Monerre.

Dante began to walk along the row of wooden shops, barred after the end of the working day. The two men didn't seem to have noticed him. They went on exchanging unintelligible phrases, eye to eye, before staring again at the other end of the bridge, as if they were waiting for someone. There seemed to be a secret tension between them.

The prior saw Arrigo clench his fists, as if he had heard something that wounded him. Meanwhile Dante moved, trying not to make a sound. Now the two men were only a few yards away, but still they gave no sign of having noticed his presence. It was he, in fact, who spotted the shadow of a third man arriving from the other end of the bridge. He was walking silently, brushing the stones with the hem of his robe. Tall and with a slightly swaying gait, the doctor Marcello had begun to climb the opposite slope, and was rapidly approaching.

The three men met in the middle of the bridge without any apparent surprise, as if they had arranged a secret rendezvous. After a moment Dante joined the group. He remembered the cardinal's furious words: perhaps the four horsemen of the Apocalypse really had come to Florence.

The men exchanged a silent glance, before Monerre spoke.

'Curious that we should meet in the middle of a bridge, the place where the ancients imagined that the twists of fate occurred.'

'Perhaps because it's on bridges that fate finds it simplest to accomplish its plans, where the path narrows and escape is more difficult,' Marcello suggested.

'And where they say the devil lies in wait for wayfarers to deceive them with his tricks,' Dante murmured, with a sense that there was something strange about this encounter.

'But of course none of us is here to play such a malignant role, Messer Alighieri,' Monerre broke in kindly.

The poet was about to reply, but stayed silent. The other man had resumed staring at the top of the parapet. From where he was now standing Dante could see what it was that had first attracted their attention: a fragment of Roman statue set into the wall. A bearded face with monstrous features like the demons carved into cathedral gutters: two opposing faces profoundly marked by time and neglect.

'You are struck by this Janus head, Monerre?' asked the poet. 'A sign of ancient superstition, from the time of the false and lying gods.'

Monerre turned his one eye towards the poet and stared at him. For a moment he seemed about to reply, then turned his attention back to the statue.

'Our friend seems fascinated by all things double,' Arrigo observed. 'Perhaps because his visual capacity was injured by nature, he is filled with a yearning for completeness that only a pair can provide.'

Marcello was still silent, his eyes fixed beyond the parapet, towards the big mill in whose wheel Brandano's life had ended, just under another bridge. He suddenly stirred, turning towards Dante. 'But perhaps the malignant nature of a bridge lies in its very form, and not in the people who walk across it. Don't you agree, Messer Alighieri?'

'Strange words you speak. They certainly conceal an allegory, but one that my mind cannot grasp.'

'Perhaps I can help you,' said Arrigo. 'If I have understood correctly, I believe Messer Marcello is referring to the purpose of such constructions. And in this sense it is true that they do contain a spark of the ancient arrogance that cast us out of Eden. Because every bridge, by removing a barrier that God has placed in our path, constitutes an insult to his design.'

'Ah, I understand. A subtle observation. But not one that can be shared, I fear. It presupposes that God's design is born complete and definitive, and hence not susceptible to any modification on man's part. But this contradicts the Scriptures, in which it is written that God made man the lord of all creation, to subject everything to his dominion. If he couldn't subject so much as a course of water, then that supposed dominion would be reduced to very little.'

The old doctor shook his head. 'But it is written in those same Scriptures: "You must not eat from the tree of knowledge of good and evil"; so, not everything has been subjected to our rule.'

Arrigo burst out laughing. 'But that tree apart, we would seem to be able to pick the fruit from all the others. And cut them down, if need be, for our fireplaces! In fact, Messer Durante, do you not think there may be more sense in that observation of Heraclitus, to the effect that our days are but the dust of time, lost in the cosmos like the atoms of Lucretius?'

'I believe there exists an order in things. If the world

was put there by chance, what point would there be in reward or punishment after death? And would the Son of God have had to become flesh because of a chance event, and die on the cross only because of a fortuitous aggregation of atoms?'

Marcello gravely nodded his agreement.

But Arrigo calmly returned to the task. 'But do you not see, in that chance, a trace of cosmic beauty?'

'Perhaps, Messer Arrigo,' Marcello replied. 'But this mass of combinations, however immeasurable it might be, cannot be infinite. In far-away Persia, before Mohammed arrived there with his sword, it was believed that all things lived and were consumed for two hundred and sixty of our centuries, before starting all over again in a cycle of combinations only apparently infinite.'

'Twenty-six thousand years? But that vast amount of time is merely a blink of God's eye,' Dante objected. 'How could his infinite power repeat the same thing *ad infinitum*? So however vast it might be, his kingdom periodically returns to zero? And again the six days of Creation, every time, and every time the beginning of light, and his walk in darkness?'

'Why not, Messer Alighieri?' replied Marcello. 'Everything will return to zero and then regain its shape, in a sublime repetition of the same thing all over again. An eternal order will be reconstructed.'

'That is madness, Messer Marcello!' exclaimed Arrigo.

'And these flies that are tormenting us now, will they too re-enter your sublime design? Would they too have to repeat themselves in an infinite cycle? And the mules and donkeys of Florence, and their dung that floods the city?'

'Of course! And you will experience precisely that!' cried the old man.

Dante had been listening attentively. 'So everything will return?' he said. 'Even the murder of Guido Bigarelli? Could nothing prevent it, Marcello? Not a scruple, not a change of heart? Your teaching chains us to evil.'

It was Monerre who broke the silence. 'Perhaps crime too is part of this order. It forms a logical part of a design.'

'And if the crime is part of a higher, infinite design, what's the point of trying to solve it?' Arrigo said slyly.

'To do justice. To bring earth closer to the Paradise we have lost. To draw to earth a spark of God's light,' the poet replied.

'I wouldn't want to find myself in that light,' Monerre said with a note of irony. 'My one good eye is already repelled by excessive brightness, and better suited to dusk than to the brilliance of the stars.'

Dante didn't reply and merely stared at them, convinced that their words contained a deeper significance. No, that had not been a chance meeting, as they had tried to suggest. Perhaps his arrival had interrupted a secret agreement.

Or the elaboration of a plan. Or the verification of an accord?

And perhaps their dialogue had continued even in his presence, under cover of a philosophical dispute, and the three of them were laughing at him. He was tempted for a moment to reveal his thoughts, and ask the reason for their behaviour. But together they were stronger: if his suspicions had any foundation, under pressure they would have backed each other up, defeating all his efforts to reach the truth. Instead he would have to wait, and catch them in his net one by one.

'Nothing will stop the punishment of the murderer,' he exclaimed at last. 'You will see,' he added, raising his index finger. He took a step backwards and then turned resolutely around, abandoning the three men without a word.

Behind him he became aware of a guilty silence. Or maybe it was mockery.

At the priory

PANTING, THE Bargello stopped at the top of the stairs to catch his breath. Then he moved firmly towards the prior. 'There is news, important news. My men have uncovered a secret during a check of the banks in the market.'

While they were extorting money in return for turning a blind eye to all the thieving and trickery that goes on there in broad daylight, Dante thought. 'Tell me.'

'There's someone in the city. A dangerous Ghibelline. Apparently he's come from the North, doubtless to make contact with his colleagues and plot harm to our Commune. I'm waiting for them to reveal his whereabouts, and then I will arrest him and all his accomplices. What you saw at the Stinche is nothing, if he ends up in my clutches.'

'And who might this dangerous demon be?' the poet asked, folding his arms.

'A foreigner, from France, apparently. And I have formed an idea of who he might be. I think you might wish to be present at his capture. As soon as . . .'

Dante firmly raised his hand. 'What I saw at the Stinche is enough to make me recommend that you be prudent. Florence is a land of freedom, where every man – whether he was born there or arrived from elsewhere – has the right not to be imprisoned without certain proof of guilt. So if you want to throw someone in chains, you will need more than market-place chit-chat.'

The head of the guard had turned purple in the face. 'But he's a Ghibelline,' he protested in a strangled voice.

'Don't do anything yet, that's an order. And keep me informed about everything. I will tell you if and when to act.'

Having said this, Dante turned round and headed for the door, with the Bargello's gaze piercing his back.

A short time later, at the Nuncio's palace

THE BARGELLO had practically slipped into the cardinal's room on his knees. Reaching the great mass of Acquasparta, he bowed his head and greedily kissed his ring as if he wanted to eat it. The cardinal smugly withdrew his hand, then sketched a swift blessing on the man's forehead.

'You urgently wanted to speak to me. So, what can I do for you?'

The Bargello bowed again, then cleared his throat. 'I need some advice, your Eminence, on how to perform my office so that my deeds are always welcomed by the Church.'

The senior prelate gave a faint nod of agreement.

'My men have identified a head of the Ghibellines hidden in Florence. But it would appear that the Commune authorities are not so diligent in putting him out of harm's way. I have been ordered to wait, when with a very small investigation I could discover his hiding place. Please give me your advice.'

'Dante Alighieri,' the cardinal hissed, narrowing his eyelids to slits.

The Bargello nodded.

'Pope Boniface's love for the cities that are loyal to him prevents me from interfering in internal matters of yours,' Acquasparta explained, 'so I can hardly advise you to ignore an order from the Florentine authorities. Even if that order might conceal the head of a poisonous snake. Even if that order might fly in the face of all foresight and prudence, and even if no one could reproach you for doing the very opposite.'

'But, your Eminence . . . I would need the endorsement of other priors at least . . .'

'You will have it. And yet you will be able to invoke a state of emergency. It's impossible to ask a man in danger not to defend himself: *nemo ad impossibilia tenetur*. And your actions will have our full support.'

The cardinal clapped his hands vigorously. A moment later the grim silhouette of the head of the inquisitors emerged from behind the curtain. Noffo Dei, rather than coming straight towards him, crept along the wall for a while, as if to avoid the direct sunlight that entered through the window. Then, keeping his hands hidden in the sleeves of his black and white habit, he bowed before Boniface's representative.

'This fine man has come to reassure us of his devotion. He seems to have found the key to the plot that has been causing us such grave concern. Help him by giving him information about the other strands of the problem. Who knows, he might be able to untangle it.'

Noffo bowed, and gestured to the Bargello to follow him.

'Listen well to what he has to tell you,' the cardinal ordered, as the head of the guards walked backwards from the room.

After curfew

'WHY so much interest in the statue of Janus?'

The rooms at the Angel Inn looked deserted. Dante asked Manetto for news of the Frenchman, Monerre. He had spent the whole afternoon mulling over what he had heard on the bridge. Something had sparked a doubt in his mind. And now he was cursing himself for not having gone into the matter, rather than irritably walking away from the challenge like a stupid peasant.

'He isn't here any more,' the innkeeper replied. 'He seems to have moved to another inn,' he added in an offended tone.

Dante pinched his lip with his fingers, as he always did. 'He didn't leave a message of any kind?'

'No. Perhaps my humble lodgings aren't fit for sophisticated foreigners, and I'm not worthy of their trust. He left in the company of two strangers.'

'Foreigners?'

'They didn't speak. But I would swear to it.'

Dante took his leave of the innkeeper. What was he going to do now? He was worried. He instinctively sensed that Monerre was the one most deeply involved in the plot, with his mysterious ways and the affected politeness of a transalpine gentleman. If he really had disappeared, his crimes too would remain swathed in darkness for ever.

Walking slowly, he had turned into an alleyway behind Santa Maria Maggiore, keeping his eyes fixed on the ground. His attention was attracted by a double shadow in front of him. A little way off, two men were walking side by side.

They were foreigners, judging by their clothes, but there was something familiar about them. His curiosity fired, Dante began to follow them. Meanwhile he desperately scoured his memory for an explanation of that sense of familiarity.

Suddenly he remembered. They were two of the men who had sat apart from everyone else in Ceccherino's tavern, apparently uninvolved in the climate of perversion that prevailed there.

He quickened his pace, coming up behind them as they drew near the ancient Roman well.

'Greetings, gentlemen,' he said, blocking their way.

The two men stopped with a look of surprise. 'Do we know each other?' the taller man asked after a moment of embarrassment.

'I don't think I've ever seen you before,' said the other, glancing quickly around as if to check that the poet was alone.

'Don't worry, there's no one else with me. But I have a request to ask of you.'

The foreigners stared at him in silence, maintaining a cautious attitude.

'We have a friend in common, I'm sure of it. And perhaps more than one. I'm referring to Messer Monerre.'

The two men remained silent, impassive, as if that name meant nothing to them.

'I'm sure you know who I'm talking about. Tell him I need to meet him and that I will wait for him behind the Baptistery choir tomorrow night an hour after compline.'

The two men did not reply. Still staring impassively at him, they nodded curtly and went on their way, disappearing at a turn in the road.

The prior watched them until the last moment. He was thinking about how easy it would be to disappear from sight in his city, as if the walls of the houses had been built in tribute to some diabolical design and the streets were really filled with those jinns that Monerre said he had met in the East.

At the priory, night of 12th August.

HE WAS in a terrible state of anxiety. A sense of moral derangement, of torpid sensuality, stirred within him. He was being pursued by Amara's elusive face, almost feature-less, like the surface of a far-off moon.

He paced up and down in his cell, mentally caressing the body of the woman whose splendid figure he had glimpsed on the cart, feeling a tension that refused to assume the form of words, even though he had tried several times to turn it into poetry. He thumped his desk. The violent pain in his fingers brought him back to reality for a moment, driving away those erotic fantasies.

He was ashamed of that instinct. But why? The feeling of love is a proof of noble sentiments, and only a heart rendered superior by learning and virtue is capable of feeling its pangs, of turning a vile sickness of the body into a state of ecstasy . . . and he had to leave her in the hands of that rogue Cecco Angiolieri, with his filthy innu-endos.

Perhaps at that very moment Cecco's hands were running over her body, taking advantage of the darkness and the fact that they were alone. Did he have to consent to a girl in his city being exposed even to rape, perhaps, with no one to apply the rules of common courtesy on her behalf?

All of a sudden he closed the wax tablets and jumped to his feet.

THE CITY streets were deserted. Dante was very familiar with the route of the night patrol, which was mapped out with the sole purpose of protecting the houses of important families. He had no difficulty in avoiding their measured pace when he spotted them in the distance.

Having drawn close to the abbey, he peered into the street ahead of him for the last time to make sure no one was there. Approaching the corner of the building, he thought he heard a metallic sound, followed by the quick, rustling footsteps of someone leaving in a hurry. He waited a few moments, but complete silence had fallen once more.

Only then did he open the little door. Inside, the nave was in total darkness, apart from a faint beam of moonlight that caught the tops of the windows. He reached the door of the sacristy and walked in.

The first room was empty. He quickly climbed the stairs to the corridor with the old cells along it. Here, too, contrary to what he expected, he didn't encounter a living soul. Cecco and the woman seemed to have disappeared. They might even have fled.

A confused emotion took hold of him. He was reassured by the idea that they might be far away. It meant that the plan to defraud Florence had now been abandoned. The burden that weighed upon his conscience over his failure to reveal the plot grew lighter. But his hopes of exposing the murderer were fading, too. Now that Brandano was dead and his accomplice had vanished, another thread in that mesh of clues and shadows had been severed.

But beneath the surface of his rational reflections he

felt a twinge of disappointment: never again would he see that woman, who had escaped him for ever.

Then he spotted a glimmer of light coming from a little passageway leading to the stairs of the abbey tower. His heart leaped in his throat as he started running again, charging up the narrow stairway towards the top. When he reached the final flight, he stopped, panting, beneath the rough arch leading to the bell-tower, which was lit by a candle in a niche in the wall. The wheels of the old bells still hung from the roof-beams, and beneath them someone had arranged some cushions. In the total silence of the night he could hear the breathing of the figure that lay on that improvised bed under a thin organza veil. The shape of it . . . At that moment the woman, taking a deeper breath, stirred in her sleep, turning on to one side and revealing her back.

The gentle curve of her hips appeared in all its splendour. She seemed to be dreaming. Her hands, joined in her lap, brushed her private parts with a tender and barely perceptible gesture. As if she were trying to protect herself.

'Psyche waiting for the hand of Eros,' Dante thought excitedly, as Amara began stirring in her sleep once more, stretching her legs voluptuously. For the first time he could see, right before his eyes, all the splendour of a body that he had only guessed at before, when it had been hidden by her clothes.

He approached slowly until he could touch the bed.

The flickering light of the little flame seemed to bring the thin fabric to life. Trembling, he stretched out a hand, slowly revealing the body. Amara appeared before him as clearly as an ivory statue.

He felt a flame blazing up inside him, and his breath quickened. The woman, moving again, had turned round, revealing her lap, still veiled. Her quivering eyelids revealed that her sleep was coming to an end. Her eyes, which looked as if they were made of clear glass, flashed a few times; then, after a shy gesture of fear at the sight of the man leaning over her, a mysterious, distant smile appeared on her mouth, the like of which Dante had only ever seen on the statues of ancient goddesses.

She stared at him for a few moments, then slowly spread her arms. The prior fell to his knees before her. He felt her hands brushing the back of his neck and drawing him gently towards her half-opened lips.

Her mouth tasted of sleep and honey. Dante abandoned himself voluptuously to the kiss, trying to wipe away the smile that still hovered before his eyes. Breathing in the woman's breath, he began to peel back the thin cloth that covered her breasts. Freed from their constraints, her erect, excited nipples stretched towards him.

When he began to loosen the sheets around her belly, Amara gripped his hand with unexpected strength and stopped it from going any further. Then she rose slowly to her feet, still keeping him at a distance with her fingertips.

He took a step further, trying to grab hold of the creature who went on eluding him, but once again she escaped his grip, taking refuge in a corner of the cell, beside the candle-flame.

At last, with a slow movement, as if she was dancing, she herself shook away the last of the cloths that still covered her belly, displaying herself to his gaze. Dante brought his hand to his mouth, his lips half-open with surprise.

Before him was a being of god-like form, the monster described by Ovid, male and female at the same time, a living hermaphrodite sprung in all its albino glory from a page of the *Metamorphoses*.

A strange sensation had taken hold of the poet, a mixture of horror and desire. He took a step back towards the door, but stopped on the threshold. The creature had spread its arms, revealing all the pallor of its body. A big feath-erless bird. That must be what the angels look like, he thought, the ones that form a crown of praise at the summit of the sky.

The creature moved again, beckoning him, approached him in all its dazzling nakedness, and began once again to stroke his face with its hand, as cold and white as snow. Attraction and repulsion alternated within him. The gentle-ness of the gesture and the sweetness of the facial expression were those of a woman in love. But as Amara began to approach him again, he saw with horror that the creature's male member was also in a state of excitement.

Unable to react, Dante discovered that he was torn between two desires, like the monster that was stretching its hands towards him. Then, with an effort of will, he gripped the organza veil that lay abandoned on the bed and wrapped it delicately around the ivory body, conquering the desire to press it to him and possess it. Now that it was no longer naked, its duality too had vanished and Amara had become female once again, by the same magic that had made a male of her a moment before.

Still bewildered, Dante dashed from the cell and ran away without a backward glance. On the stairs he encountered Cecco, standing on the bottom steps with his arms folded. The poet raced past him without saying a word, avoiding the sarcastic glance that the other man darted at him.

He was sure that Cecco knew everything, and that he would make a fool of the prior. But he would have time to settle his accounts, he said to himself, choking back the insults that had risen to his lips.

Different considerations now flooded his mind. His confusion and his impotent rage diluted his arousal, and the voice of reason returned to speak in his ear. Amara was a man . . . was also a man. And what if in her masculine condition she was really the one who was due to come – Frederick's heir, the one to restore his throne? Bernardo hadn't known, or hadn't wanted to be more precise about the sex of the heir. Perhaps because he didn't know whether Bianca Lancia had given the Emperor a boy or a girl? Or because it was in a single descendant that the two sexes were united, and the new Emperor would put his dual natures on the throne?

He shook his head to rid it of such an insane idea. Amara didn't look more than twenty, and she would have had to be at least fifty to have been born of the Emperor's seed. But Dante didn't seem certain even of that. Had his own teachers, the great writers of antiquity, not told of fabulous creatures with the gift of immortality?

He ran away, into the street, like a wounded animal in search of its lair.

At the priory

DANTE NERVOUSLY crumpled the sheet on which he had written only a few lines. He looked at the thin ream of pages that lay on the desk: soon it would be finished, and he didn't know whether he would be able to get hold of another one. He would have to go back to working in his mind alone, exploiting the book of memory.

A violent spasm struck him behind the eyes, with its fiery finger. He closed his eyes tightly, waiting for the cloud of flaming sparks to fade away.

As he held his fists tight against his eyelids, he thought

he was aware of a movement behind the door and of a hand touching the latch. But he didn't have the strength to turn round. When he finally did manage to do so, he saw the visitor who had come in and was waiting motionlessly, leaning against the door-post.

'Pietra . . . is it you?' he murmured, recognising the woman's slender outline. In the light from the little candle on the desk she barely stood out against the darkness. 'How did you get in?'

'Lagia's women always find open doors. I also have friends among your guards,' she replied with her vulgar chuckle.

Dante struggled to his feet and walked over to the girl. He stretched out a hand to touch her cheek, but she recoiled, turning her head away.

'Don't touch me. You haven't paid.'

The poet lowered his hand. The girl stared at him with her deep-green eyes. The mass of dark curls, loose on her shoulders, framed her face. He thought there was a slight luminescence to her eyes, which were caught by the flickering light from the candle. For a moment the sweet phantasm of Amara was superimposed over those hard features, hiding them from view.

Pietra carefully studied his feverish face. Then she exploded into coarse laughter. 'So you tried it on with that woman? Her too?' She laughed again, scornfully. 'And did you enjoy yourself?'

'That's enough,' Dante said, feeling sick to his stomach. 'Wouldn't you like a real woman, so you can forget that other one?' Her feline appearance was accentuated by her short, straight nose and her full lips. She wore a light tunic over her thin body, with the narrow hips and the broad shoulders of an adolescent boy. She leaned against the wall, her body arched, her erect little breasts stretching the cloth of her garment. 'Don't touch me,' she repeated, stretching her hand towards him, as if to establish a boundary between them. Then she looked all round the room, her eyes finally settling on the scattered papers. 'More words. That's all you know how to do. Say words.'

'They are the consolation of the man on his own. His words.'

'You want to be on your own because you're afraid of being abandoned,' Pietra replied mockingly. Dante was about to answer, but she didn't give him time. 'Words, on your own.' She picked up one of the pages and furiously threw it into the air. 'So many pointless words.'

The burning vice still gripped the poet's brow. Tottering, he dropped on to the bed.

Pietra had been following his movements. 'That illness of yours again?' she asked coldly.

He didn't reply. The girl stepped forward until her breasts brushed his forehead. Then she passed a hand behind the back of his neck, pressing his face delicately against her own body and gently stroking the tendons on his neck.

Dante caught the perfume of her skin, a mixture of cheap essences from the other side of the Arno and a hidden, subtle stench that rose up from her belly. He closed his eyes, surrendering like a child in his mother's arms. He felt his eyes filling with tears, and sobs shook his chest. Then he felt a feeling of warmth stirring within him.

He looked up. Pietra, ceasing her caresses, brought her lips down towards his. Then she caught his mouth in an endless kiss as his hands rose up her legs, raising her tunic to her belly. He kissed her taut, freckled skin, then drew her on to his bed, tore off her clothes and plunged into her body as if entering a dark sea.

He REMAINED motionless for an incalculable length of time. The girl, lying next to him propped up on her elbow, studied him with an enigmatic expression.

'Pietra, I . . .'

'Don't say anything,' the prostitute broke in, putting a finger to his lips. 'Don't keep ruining everything with your words. Don't say anything more,' she murmured, kissing him again. But now her mouth was cold. He thought she was only obeying the rules of her profession, when the time came to say goodbye.

'Why did you come?' he asked in a low voice.

She didn't reply, merely shrugging. 'Who knows. Perhaps I felt like seeing you.' She was hurriedly getting dressed, her thoughts already elsewhere. In the doorway she turned towards him again. 'You are in danger. You and the other people involved in this business of yours.'

'What are you talking about?'

'You know. Lagia told the Inquisition everything. They talked about you.'

'What did you find out?'

'I only heard a few words. But you've got to get away from here,' the girl said again with an unexpected flash of tenderness in her eyes. 'They were saying that your plan had been discovered. They talked about an "accursed son".'

Dante ran over to her and grabbed her by an arm. 'Are you sure? Is that what they said?'

She pulled away from him and escaped along the portico.

Left on his own, the prior began thinking furiously. So Acquasparta knew about the plot to restore the imperial dynasty. But did he also know the name of the "accursed son"? Perhaps not, given that he expected a confession from Dante: he seemed sure that the poet was in on the secret. Could it be that in the recesses of his mind he held all parts of the secret, and just hadn't noticed yet? Was he really a victim of a joke played by fate?

8

After midday, 13th August

H E MUST have fallen asleep without noticing. And yet he felt as if he had closed his eyes only for a few moments, yielding to the confused hubbub of sounds and images that seemed to rise up from the wooden floor. He felt as if the ancient, uncovered tombs of the dead buried in the church lay beneath his feet, as if their shades had risen up to him, to watch him and spur him on to action. When he opened his eyes again, the cell was flooded with light. He looked around, his mind still fogged, trying to calculate from the height of the sun how much time had passed. That star had already passed its zenith and was beginning to fall towards the west. He leaped to his feet, trying to impose some order on his thoughts.

Meanwhile the sounds and voices around him were becoming more clearly defined. There was a frenetic coming and going under the portico. Dante walked to the door and threw it open.

One of the Bargello's men appeared breathlessly in the doorway. 'Please come! There's been another murder!'

'Where?' Dante asked, alarmed, dashing outside.

'In Santa Croce. At the house of the Lombard, Maestro Alberto.'

'What happened?'

'Maestro Alberto . . . He's been murdered in his work-shop – come!'

The prior set off, fury poisoning his blood. The *bargellini* tried to escort him, opening up a path through the crowd, but their long lances were too cumbersome for the job, so he reached the door of the workshop on his own. The man lay on the floor, drenched in blood, beside the tools of his trade still neatly arranged on his workbench. As far as Dante could tell, nothing had been touched. The cases and cabinets had not been forced, as if the murderer hadn't been interested in their contents. It seemed that whoever had killed the man had taken nothing away.

'Where is Hamid, his servant?' he asked the Bargello, who was standing in the doorway.

'He made off after murdering his boss. The whole of the local guard is on his tail. He won't get away for long,' the head of the guards replied triumphantly. 'We've checked, but nothing's missing. Upstairs in the bedroom there's a little coffer full of florins. It was not a thief, but the vengeful hand of his servant that killed him.'

Dante grimaced with disappointment. If the *bargellini*

got their hands on that innocent boy, nothing could save him, he thought bitterly. Not even his own authority as a prior, which would shortly expire. In a corner he saw that poor wretch's prayer-rug, and on it the book.

He picked up the volume and went on looking inside it. Whoever it was that had killed the *mechanicus* with two knife-blows to the neck must have been looking for something else. He congratulated himself on his far-sightedness in putting the device in a safe place.

At the same time he went on thinking furiously. Maestro Alberto hadn't been part of the conspiracy, and yet his death was plainly linked to the strange plot that was unfolding in Florence, something to do with the great Emperor. And clearly to do with the mechanism that the victim had reconstructed.

But the murderer hadn't looked for anything in the workshop, a sign that he knew the machine was no longer there. So why had he killed? There was only one logical answer: he wanted to ensure that the only man capable of constructing a similar mechanism lost his life. It was the secret that he had wanted to snuff out, rather than Alberto's life.

The murderer? Dante suddenly thought back to the mechanic's wounds, so similar to the ones that had killed the others. Why one murderer? The same pattern seemed to be repeated in all the corpses: two blows a short distance apart, only one of them fatal. And what if two people were in fact responsible for the crime? Two men accustomed to fighting and striking in pairs, capable of attacking from both directions, leaving the victim unable to defend himself. Accustomed to sharing death as they were prepared to share everything: bread, their horse, a woman . . . A sudden idea flashed into the poet's mind. The crazed fragments of the plan seemed to assume a definite shape: in his memory he ran through the dialogue on the bridge. Of course, that must be it. The statue of Janus reappeared before his eyes.

But if that was so, perhaps there was still a chance of interrupting that chain of horrors. He leaped to his feet, passing before the disconcerted eyes of the Bargello.

He reached the Angel Inn. On the ground floor he met the landlord, who was busy decanting wine from a big jar.

'Is Messer Bernardo upstairs?' Dante asked as he passed, making for the stairs.

'No, Prior, he went out a short while ago. I think someone was waiting for him outside.'

'You didn't see who it was?'

'No. Messer Bernardo seemed to be ill. He asked me if anyone had come looking for him. I told him they hadn't and he sat down and asked for something to drink. But he was obviously waiting for someone. Every now and again he got up and went to the door to look outside. Then, the last time, he waved his hand and left. But I didn't see who was with him.'

Dante nodded, then headed for the little room on the first floor. The door was unlocked, as if Bernardo was not afraid for his possessions. Perhaps he thought no thief could be interested in written pages, or that in a city of thieves no one would bother to appropriate knowledge, Dante thought bitterly.

There was really nothing in the room that anyone could have stolen. Just a modest chest at the foot of the bed, with a few rough items of clothing. Bernardo must have been in a hurry when he abandoned the work he was busy with: the *Res gestae Svevorum*. Open on the desk was a thin, bound volume and beside it some sheets of cloth-paper and an ink-well.

He started reading out loud: 'The name of this book is the *Cronica federiciana*, and concerns the affairs of my sovereign, the wonder of the world . . .' Dante looked up for a moment, then back down to the parchment. '. . . whom I, Bishop Mainardino, saw, and whose memory I leave to the just: compilation commenced in the year of Our Lord Christ MCCLV.'

Startled, he raised his eyes. 'The *Chronicles* of Mainardino,' he murmured. 'Frederick's great biographer. So it really does exist. Bernardo wasn't lying.'

He quickly scanned the pages, frantically running through years of exploits and glory. The almost miraculous birth at Jesi, the struggle for the crown. The triumphal entry into Jerusalem of the hundred towers, the triumphs and the defeats, the insatiable desire for knowledge and the splendour of Frederick's court. His poems . . .

He skipped to the last page. The bishop's solemn prose sang out the end of the Emperor in the tones of a classical drama. The agony of illness, the false hopes of apparent recovery. The troubled tangle of passions and rivalries around his death-bed. Then he was startled to see a note that Mainardino recorded as if in passing: '. . . news was brought to Frederick of the death of a little son of his, a novice with the Franciscans. And Frederick wept over him.'

Shortly after this the bishop returned to the affairs of court. Dante stopped to reflect, biting his lip. Could this be the son of Bianca Lancia? But if he was dead, upon whom did the Ghibellines rest their hopes? The whole venture of Rome was based on the charisma of the imperial blood. And wasn't it the return of the clan of the Antichrist that Cardinal d'Acquasparta was so afraid of?

Fascinated, he began reading again. Page after page of deeds, of pain, of glory, which his mind drank in as a thirsty man drinks water. At last, having finished the manuscript, Mainardino described the poisoning of the Emperor, 'killed by the hand of the incomplete man, who was' . . .

Dante turned the page, hoping that the text might continue on the other side. But the sheet was blank: and the last scrap of parchment had been carefully torn away, as if to remove the final lines that mentioned the murderer's name.

If someone had been seeking to protect the man responsible for the crimes, why not get rid of the whole previous page, or indeed the whole book? Why hide only the name of the murderer, when it would have been possible to erase all traces of the crime itself?

Or had it been Bernardo himself, perhaps to remain the sole guardian of so terrible a secret? But if he was about to make his work public, why destroy the very text that could have backed up his claims?

He had to find the historian at all costs. He looked around, trying to find some answer to the doubts that haunted him. For a moment he had imagined himself close to the solution of the mystery. Or at least to the discovery of the guilty man and his shadowy accomplice.

But Bernardo's disappearance dealt his theory a fatal blow. If the man was one of two murderers, he would surely be far away by now. The poet suddenly felt uneasy. Apart from the book, there were no objects of value in the room, nothing that a thief could not easily have abandoned without regret. If, on the other hand, his theory was incorrect, then at that moment Bernardo was close to the deadly blade, and with his death the last chance of solving the mystery would be lost for ever.

He turned towards the stairs, in the hope of seeing the shadowy figure of the historian, safe and sound.

Down below, someone was sitting at the communal table.

Dante climbed down the stairs and silently walked up behind him.

But somehow the man must have noticed his presence. 'Welcome, Prior. Sit down,' he heard the man whisper.

The prior threw caution to the winds. He walked past the table and stopped in front of Marcello. The doctor was sitting there with his eyes closed, motionless, with a big book in front of him. On the corner of the table there was an hour-glass: all of the sand had collected in the bottom half, as if the man had spent some time immersed in his work.

'You seem to be able to see in the dark, as cats do,' Dante exclaimed with surprise.

'Your step is light, and yet it has an unmistakeable tone.'

The prior moved slowly along the edge of the table, trying to make out, by the faint candle-light, what Marcello had written.

The old man, still without opening his eyes, twitched with impatience. 'Stop hovering around me and sit down at my table. Have you found the key to that tangle of clues that you talked of?'

'No, not yet.'

'And what about the intentions of Frederick the Great – have you reconstructed his plan? What dwelt in that mind of his before Death came for him?'

Dante cast his eyes down and bit his lip. 'I don't know,' he admitted.

'For God's sake, Messer Durante, how difficult was it to say those three words?' the old man exclaimed triumphantly, suddenly opening his eyes. 'And yet they're enough to moderate your pride, to bring you back within the realms of the human. "I don't know"! Sculpt them in bronze above your front door!'

Dante clenched his fists, conquering the impulse to get up and leave. 'It sounds as if you know much more than I do,' he said.

The old man picked up the hour-glass and tipped it over. His face had softened, as if he wanted to apologise for his sarcasm a moment before. 'The certainty of my knowledge comes from the passing of time and things that I have seen and measured,' he added mildly.

Dante shrugged. 'The certainty of knowledge!' he repeated angrily. He was leaning on the table, head in his hands. He stared at the sand that had just begun to flow. 'It is only an illusion, just as time is an illusion of our senses,' he added bleakly. 'Look at these little grains. Like these, the grains of our time run out in hours and days. And what do we know, lost in this dust?'

'Are you losing your faith, Prior?'

'No . . . but never more than in these last hours have I felt I was wandering amongst mirages. Even my star seems darkened, with its useless light,' Dante replied through gritted teeth.

'And it will happen as it is written in your stars. Triumph, if that is what awaits you. Or defeat, if that is what the heavens decree.'

'I don't believe in predestination. If I fail it is because of the weakness of my reason and my virtue, not because of some cold spark that gleams far away.'

Marcello contemplated his last words for a moment. Then he shook his head and with an angry gesture struck the papers in front of him, hurling them to the ground. 'Not a cold light, Prior!' he cried. 'But a noble echo of the divine splendour. The light that calls all things into being and gives them names. Before Adam's voice. Before Creation itself. *Fiat lux*, His first act!'

As it descended, the bundle of papers had fallen apart, revealing sheets covered with calculations and astronomical symbols. Dante's attention immediately revived. 'You should take greater care of your writings,' he exclaimed, bending down to pick up the fallen pages. 'Great works of ancient genius have been lost through careless gestures.'

'Nothing will happen that must not happen. Nothing will happen that has not been written from the first day in the book of destiny,' Marcello insisted, his voice breaking hoarsely. He held out his hands to regain possession of the notebook.

Dante, after rapidly realigning the pages, tried to read a little of what was written on them, but the other man snatched them from his hands, as if fearing contamination. He was surprised by the old man's impetuosity. 'Do you really believe that we are governed by an unknown force, even in our most ordinary acts, in contempt of the freedom conferred upon us by the Creator?'

'The freedom granted to us is the same as that granted to the acorn to become an oak. It is only the limitation of our senses, deceiving us into seeing alteration where there is none, that forces us to see the whole of destiny only in fragments.'

'But that would mean that the very movement of our bodies is an illusion,' Dante objected. 'And yet we are surrounded by the most obvious proof of the contrary, precisely in these heavenly bodies upon which your science is based. Does not the sun rise every day; does not the moon wane with perfect precision every month? And even if those bodies were fixed, does not their light at least move, carrying their image to us?'

'No! Light is not the propagation of light, as the pagan al-Kindi proclaims! It is without motion, fixed like the stars on the First Day!'

'Then in those stars man could have read of the pomp of Babylon, the pyre of Ilium and the furrow that first marked Rome, and the throne of Peter and the second Empire, and Frederick the Great and finally this very night, and our meeting . . .'

'Who tells you that this is not the case? If . . .'

'You are blaspheming, Marcello! Adam was created free to choose between good and evil. And if that were not so,

God would have tempted our progenitor solely to witness a spectacle of degradation that already played out in His mind.'

'Then look at this!' cried the old man, beginning to draw a square on the parchment. 'You will have the summary of your life, and all that awaits you in what remains of it. And you will have the pain you deserve!' He went on scratching nervous lines, turning the original square into a complex grid. He delineated the series of Houses, then arranged within it the symbols of the planets. He worked from memory, without reference to calculations of any kind.

He must have had a prodigious mind to remember the angular positions of every heavenly body on the ecliptic, Dante reflected admiringly. Or else he must already have drawn that diagram in the past, and now was simply re-transcribing what he had discovered in his secret studies.

But before the poet could express his doubt, Marcello had finished. 'Here are the signs of your hour on earth, Messer Alighieri. The blazing sun in Gemini, in the final surge of inconstant spring, which governs your ambiguous, dual instincts, or couples with wavering Mercury, the lord of your thieving science of ancient knowledge, and vain as he. Your insatiable concupiscence, governed by the star of Venus in exaltation in Cancer; your ferocity, turned blood-red by leonine Mars. And then . . .'

'I see you have spied well on my life so far,' the poet broke in mockingly. 'There are many in Florence who could give you a much more concise account!'

'But no one else could show you what remains of it.'

Dante stretched out a hand to pick up the parchment, but the old man's energetic hand clamped it to the table.

'Nine is your ruling number. The same number that governed the destiny of Frederick, who died in the face of the ninth two-headed shade.' The prior wasn't sure that he had understood, but before he could say anything the other man continued. 'At the age of nine you experienced your first illumination, at eighteen the ravenous bite of lust. At thirty-six you will know the despair of banishment. You will die far away in exile, a death without the comfort of hope. That is my prediction.'

Dante had listened to the last words with his lips tightly pursed, as rage and perplexity filled his mind. 'And you, Marcello? Where is your death written?' he replied with derision. 'Or do you have certain knowledge only of the future of others?'

'My end is written, as they all are. In the hour and the place set out by the stars, and which I know already. It will be a liquid death that carries me off, governed by the liquid sign of Pisces. From water I have come, like all human beings. To water I will return.'

Dante silently gripped the chart. Then he clenched his fingers as if to seize his fate in his fist.

Night

THE REAR corner of the Baptistery almost touched the old buildings that crowded around it, separated from them only by a narrow alleyway. At that point the mass of stone completely concealed the cathedral of Santa Reparata, and not so much as a faint glimmer from the torches in the square reached as far as that.

Dante had been waiting for an hour now. A cry rang out at regular intervals, perhaps an invalid wailing out his anguish. Or perhaps someone being tormented by demons. He slipped slowly down the wall of the building until he was sitting on his heels. A torpor born of heat and exhaustion held him in its grip. He felt his mind wavering, at the portal of dreams. And yet sleep, which lay in wait somewhere behind him, seemed to want to stay at a distance, as if his mind was as yet unwilling to free itself from his exhausted body, which was now on the point of complete collapse.

After drifting into unconsciousness for a moment he opened his eyes, watchful once more. He thought he had heard light footsteps approaching. Then a dark outline interposed itself between him and the exit to the alleyway. This new danger revived his strength. He rose to his feet, clinging against the wall, motionless and alert. He clutched his dagger and prepared to repel the intruder, if he was someone other than the person he was waiting for.

The figure that appeared in front of him was completely enveloped in a cloak of light linen that covered the lower part of his face. On the man's head was a hat of woven straw like those worn by country people, pressed down over his forehead and leaving only the eyes visible.

And yet the prior had immediately recognised the unusual visitor, who stared at him heedless of the steel point brandished only a few inches away, even though a single torch barely pierced the darkness of the loggia.

Monerre came forward and stopped a few feet away.

'I know you've been looking for me,' he said.

Dante waited for him to continue. Then he leaned towards Monerre until his lips almost brushed the man's cheek. 'I know all about your machinations. Not a hoax for money, as your movements might have led us to believe. That was just your cover, in case anyone grew suspicious about you, or worse still, discovered the trick with the Virgin.'

He stopped, waiting for the Frenchman to reply. But Monerre remained silent and merely stared at him. The poet felt himself becoming increasingly irritated. 'In fact, there's something even more perfidious about your plan, I'm sure of it. Whoever came up with it wanted the trick to be discovered, to reinforce the conviction amongst your enemies that they were only up against a bunch of second-rate crooks. And I too fell into that trap, but only briefly.'

Monerre's eyes glinted. 'And what do you believe now?' he said softly, finally breaking his silence.

'Your plan was quite different: to repeat the pattern of the Fourth Crusade, when men, lances and horses were recruited for the Holy Land, but were instead unleashed against the Eastern Empire, with a view to loot and plunder. Your scheme was the same: to unite the faithful, stir them up for the task, fill their minds with dreams of salvation and booty. Conquer their simple minds with the glimmer of a miracle. And meanwhile fill key posts with trusted Ghibellines. And then, on the way to the Holy Land, this was your true objective: Rome! To take it by storm, as once Constantinople had been taken. After assembling your army in the squares of the great city, pretending to wait for the papal viaticum, it would have been an easy matter to cause utter chaos merely by revealing, through a half-closed door, the light of a gold chalice, a tabernacle encrusted with jewels . . .'

The Frenchman was staring at him in silence, his one eye flashing in the darkness like a cat's.

'There, the Colonnas and other big Roman families would be ready to provide their armies to back you up, just to escape Boniface's claw-like clutches, helped by the money of the men of *La Serenissima*!' the poet went on. 'That was the plan of the Fedeli, wasn't it? That's the treasure you're all inventing tales about: the coffers of St Peter's.'

'Come with us, Prior.' Monerre's voice had become calm and distant. But there was a hidden fervour in his words.

'And not only theirs!' Dante cut in.

'Come with us,' Monerre repeated. 'We will avenge the last Emperor, the murdered eagle.'

'With you? With the Order of the Templars?' hissed the prior.

Monerre stiffened. Then he nodded slowly. 'How did you find out?' There was no disappointment in his voice, only surprise. The embarrassment of a little boy caught playing a forbidden game.

'I was sure of it, listening to your words. The story of your travels and that practice you told me about, of sharing a single mount between two horsemen. That is the trick of the Templars: not to quicken the journey, but to have a horse that is always fresh when the moment comes to attack. That was how you disconcerted the pagans, the reason why you always won your battles with half the number of forces. The practice that you turned into a symbol on your seal.'

A pale smile lit up the Frenchman's face. 'Our seal – you are right. And so many poor fools believe that it symbolises the poverty of our order . . . Come with us,' he repeated for the third time. In the faint light of the lantern his scar stood out like a mark of the devil on the shadowy face.

'To bow down and worship the hideous Baphomet, the vile two-headed god? I clearly remember your praise of Janus, your other secret symbol. The double demon who dwells in your hearts, who is even made the figurehead of your ships, like the one lost in the marshes of the Arno.

You heap nobility on what is merely a path of heresy and perdition.'

'So the ship arrived!' the Frenchman exclaimed, interrupting him. 'And where . . .'

'It arrived with its cargo of death. Is that what you were waiting for?'

'You don't understand, Messer Alighieri.' Monerre shook his head. Then he looked up, as if to draw inspiration from the stars that filled the firmament. 'How far your judgement is from the truth, and unworthy of a mind like yours. One of our most sacred symbols is the head with the double face. But it is no pagan idol . . .'

'Then what is it? A symbol whose features pervert the precise harmony of Creation? What could be sacred about that?'

'Peace, Messer Durante. The highest aspiration of righteous minds, which you yourself have celebrated in your writings. Those two faces, which together contemplate the whole of the horizon, symbolise a supreme accord made in the lands that witnessed the birth of Christ.'

'The *Pactio secreta* . . . but that's a legend,' Dante said, caught by surprise.

'No legend. In Jerusalem, in Frederick's presence, amidst the fury of battle vainly being waged against the enemy armies, an accord really was reached between us and the Islamic sages. It isn't written on the parchments, but the image that we have borne with us since then marks its

316

intangible seal. The figure's two faces represent the West and the East, different but united in a single idea of peace. Facing opposite directions so that nothing escapes their gaze.'

Dante listened attentively, as unease rose within him. 'You have betrayed your mission, which was to redeem the Holy Land,' he said frostily.

'No, Messer Durante. We have only betrayed the vain ambitions of little men for something much higher. A truly universal empire.'

The poet's certainties were beginning to waver. Perhaps the Templars and the Republic of Venice, which seemed to be behind the plot, really had a plan even greater than the sacking of the holy city.

'That great project has come to nothing,' Monerre continued. 'Broken like the spine of the imperial family. But it is now possible that it will be repeated and taken to its conclusion, and that the legitimate Roman emperor, Frederick's heir, will return to the throne of Rome. Come with us,' he added sorrowfully.

'Frederick's heir . . . You're imagining things.' Involuntarily Dante heard the firmness of his own voice faltering. A doubt was beginning to form in his mind. A hope . . .

'No, he exists. He is alive and ready to reveal himself to the world by guiding this enterprise and celebrating the glory of his ancestor by bringing Frederick's greatest project to its conclusion: fixing the boundaries of the world.'

'What do you mean?'

'His great unfinished work.'

'But who is the man you are talking about?'

Monerre opened his mouth for a moment, but then said nothing. He took a step backwards, as if preparing to say goodbye. A moment later, though, he began talking again. 'A man whose identity we have all sworn on our own lives to protect. The last son of Bianca Lancia, the only woman the Emperor loved. Brought up far from the court and then locked away in a monastery, with monks loyal to the Emperor, to save him from the hands of the Pope and then those of Manfred, his ambitious half-brother.'

Dante thought for a moment about what he had just heard. 'The heir referred to in Mainardino's *Chronicles*, the proof of whose existence Bernardo came looking for in Florence?' The other man stared at him impassively, his lips pressed tightly together. 'Is he the one you want to put on the throne? And is he what you're killing for?'

The Frenchman remained silent as he stepped back. 'Come with us,' he said once more. 'You still have time!'

After Monerre had disappeared around the corner of the Baptistery, Dante sat down on one of the sarcophagi that lay next to the southern portal of the church. The stone still held the warmth of the blazing sun.

He tried to give meaning to what he had just heard. Monerre had struck him as sincere when he outlined his plan and sought his complicity. And yet there was something about it that did not completely convince him. A faint tremor in the voice, every now and again, as if his words were marked by a hint of desperation.

Something must have put a stop to that perfect plan. The murderer's hand had begun to strike the pillars of the future edifice, unpicking the weft of the scheme. But if the murderer's intention was to shatter the dream of the supporters of empire, it was not impossible that Boniface lay behind his bloody hand.

A shiver ran down Dante's spine. Then he thought he heard footsteps behind him and turned his head.

Something dark enfolded him, blinding him. For a moment he was aware of a sharp stench of mildew, as a hand pressed the cloth against his mouth. He tried to jump to his feet and free himself. He distinctly felt the mass of a body behind him and instinctively swerved to the right, trying to escape its clutches.

From behind, a blade sliced at the makeshift hood and slipped around his shoulder. He felt the cold steel brushing his neck and a sharp pain rising from the base of his throat. Then his assailant drew the weapon back to strike again.

Meanwhile the poet had managed to tug himself free; he blindly flailed his arms in front of him, trying somehow to strike his attacker. But his hands met only air. The man must still be behind him, he thought with terror, and went on clutching at the cloth that blinded him.

He threw himself forward, trying to break free. But fear

made his movements slow and clumsy, so he merely pulled like a yoked beast, sure that in a moment he would once again feel the bite of metal. And this time the wound would be fatal. But all of a sudden he felt a weakening in the grip that held him, as if his enemy's fingers had suddenly been forced open. Carried on by the impetus, he staggered blindly forward for a few paces before stumbling and falling. When he was on the ground he turned convulsively on to his back.

By now he had finally managed to shake away the cloth. For a moment the external darkness prolonged his sense of impotent blindness, then his eyes slowly regained their sight. Standing in front of him he recognised the imposing figure of Arrigo.

The philosopher was bending over him. He looked as if he was about to start attacking him again. Kicking out desperately, Dante dragged himself along the ground, retreating a few feet. Then he managed to spring up and unsheathe his dagger.

But Arrigo didn't seem to want to threaten him. He stretched his hand out towards the poet, showing him that he was unarmed, and addressed him calmly. 'Do not fear, Messer Alighieri. Your assailant has fled. He made off in that direction,' he said, pointing towards the dense network of alleyways behind the Baptistery. 'How do you feel?' he went on, staring at the wound.

Dante touched the source of the pain at the base of his

throat and, drawing back his fingers, saw they were covered with blood. Holding his hand over the cut, he took a step backwards until he stood at a distance from the other man, who seemed to want to help him.

Arrigo understood and stopped. A smile passed across his lips. He spread his arms again. 'I'm not the one who was trying to kill you.'

'Someone was. And you're the only person I can see.'

The philosopher's mouth tightened for a moment, and then his features relaxed. A shrewd light flashed in his eyes. 'That's true, but go back to what you know: the world is full of things that we can see and which have no bodily form. The rainbow that colours the sky, the wind that fills the sail, the song that touches the soul with its sweetness. And also things that exist and which we cannot see, like the network of infinitesimal particles that makes up our bodies, the earth and the whole of the universe.'

The poet, after a moment's uncertainty, lowered his weapon. 'The atoms of which you speak are unfeeling grains of sand, fragments of a mindless void. But the blade that tried to kill me is sensitive enough.'

Arrigo had pulled a piece of linen from his bag. He took a step forward and held it out to the poet.

'So tell me what you were doing here, since I am prepared to believe that you did not come here to attack me,' Dante went on, bandaging his wound as best he could. 'At this time of night, in defiance of the curfew . . . and of prudence.'

'You will have noticed how the same forms change as they are filled with the breath of light, or as shadows cast their veil over them.'

'It is a common experience.'

'And yet I wanted to see what shape your Baptistery would assume when the shadows fell upon it.'

Dante stared at him in surprise, then glanced back at the dark, imposing mass behind them. The big stone octagon towered over the shacks that spread out from its northern side. 'And what did you learn?'

'That this one, like so many of your religion's monuments, is far more useful in the darkness.'

The prior was not sure that he had understood. But he was overcome with emotion, and reached out a hand towards the old teacher's shoulder. 'Our religion, Arrigo? I thought your speculation had stopped on the threshold of apostasy. I thought you were not lost.'

Arrigo smiled again, but his expression had turned cold. 'There is nothing inside that stone drum, nothing but the darkness it contains. But it might be precious for that very reason.'

'How can I help you in this madness, whatever you mean?' Dante said.

But Arrigo seemed not to have understood. He gripped the poet tightly by the arm. 'You have the key to that door!'

he shouted. He looked desperate. 'Give it to me, and I will let you have some of my glory!'

For a moment Dante thought the philosopher had gone mad. His eyes were wide. He jerked away from his grip and took a step back. The other man did not try to follow him, but kept his hand stretched out as if he could still clasp him in his arms.

Suddenly he stirred himself. Dante saw him moving his head around, confused, as if he had just emerged from a dream and was trying to regain his bearings. Then he turned round to face the Baptistery. The prior saw him walking with his shuffling gait to the bottom of the wall, where he stopped and spread his arms out wide. Arrigo remained motionless for a few moments, a theatrical parody of the crucifix that he had been mocking a moment before. Finally he slipped off to the side, disappearing round the corner, in the same direction as Monerre.

Dante leaped after him, trying to catch up with him. But when he turned the corner, there wasn't a trace of the philosopher.

9

Afternoon of 14th August, at the priory

THE LAST meeting of the Council of Priors had been called for the third hour. Sitting at the long table in the hall, Dante wasn't listening to the low murmur of words that the others were exchanging under their breath, as if afraid that he could hear them. Several times he had caught a meaningful look between them, but his thoughts were too wrapped up in the events of the previous night. He was beginning to pursue the trace of an idea that had flashed through his mind, but the line suddenly dissolved in a thicket of inconclusive hypotheses.

The meeting had been dragging on for hours now, scattered over an apparently endless multiplicity of meaningless by-laws. For a few moments, though, something had begun to irritate him, piercing his reflections with a shrill noise.

'And now we come to signing the minutes . . .' The words rang in his ears. One of the priors had come over to him, holding out an ink-well and a quill.

'I have no time for your papers!' Dante exclaimed.

'But it's the administration's bimonthly report,' Antonio, of the Cloth Merchants' Guild, stammered from the other side of the table. 'It is your explicit duty to sign it, as a member of our assembly. We can't pass on the file unverified to the next group of priors . . .'

Lapo Salterello defiantly held the ink-well out to him. Dante leaped to his feet, striking his hand against the little receptacle and spilling its contents in a dark pool on the table. Then, to everyone's bewilderment, he suddenly turned and headed towards the door without a word.

Baffled, the five men stared at one another. Then Lapo picked up the quill and dipped it in the spilt ink. After taking one last look at the others, he made a few jottings at the foot of the page, at the point where the poet's name appeared. 'Not a word,' he laughed, turning towards the door. 'You all saw him sign.'

The shadow of embarrassment on the faces of the other four melted into smiles.

DANTE HAD left the hall in exasperation. On the stairs he was almost knocked over by a breathless messenger running towards the door. Dante gripped him by the arm and stopped him.

'What's going on?'

The other man must have recognised the prior, because

he bowed. Then he glanced anxiously towards the door, from which the excited voices of the other priors could still be heard. 'I've been sent by the Bargello; I have a message of the greatest importance to pass on to the Council,' he said with great agitation, and made as if to set off running once more.

Dante gripped his arm again, holding him back. 'First tell me what your message is.'

'The Bargello has sent me to say that his men have surrounded a group of rebels, Ghibelline heretics, at their hide-out at the Maddalena. He's about to smash his way into their den and take them all prisoner. He asks to have reinforcements ready in case of an emergency, sounding the martinella bell to summon the forces from the Oltrarno.'

The poet bit his lips, trying to conceal his anxiety, and let go of the man's arm. 'Return to your tasks immediately. I will pass your message on to the Council. Don't worry about anything else.'

Unconvinced, the messenger glanced nervously at the door. For a moment he looked as if he was going to insist, but in the end he decided to turn on his heels and go back whence he had come. Dante paused, worried that someone might have heard his words. But the priors were all immersed in their meeting, which continued amidst jests and laughter. Trying to pass unobserved, he made for the stairs, looking straight ahead and avoiding the eyes of the guards who had witnessed the scene from the court-yard.

In the cloister he bumped into the secretary of the Commune, who seemed to be looking for something.

'Messer Alighieri, the very man. I thought you would want to know.'

'What?'

'You asked me to find out about the pilgrims in the Angel Inn. One of them, Messer Marcello, has been seen preparing to leave. He requested a mule from the stables at the Porta Romana, and some strong men to carry his luggage.'

'Has he already left?' Dante asked, disappointed. 'I'd given orders that no one should be allowed to go.

The secretary shrugged. 'He hadn't been accused of anything.'

For a moment the prior assessed the chances of ordering someone to be sent in hot pursuit of the old doctor. He couldn't have got far. But what would have been the point? For him finally to expiate his guilt in Rome, and bring all his fancy notions with him. Events at the abbey were far more important.

Outside San Piero he didn't notice anything different about the normal comings and goings of merchants and craftsmen on their way to the Ponte Vecchio. Luckily the news did not yet seem to have spread. Perhaps he still had time to take control of the situation, in the last hours of his authority. Yes, he would try to stop the Bargello by appealing to the higher interests of the Commune.

So he would gain time to allow Cecco and Amara to get to safety.

He ran along the road leading to the church, guided by a buzz of conversation that was growing more and more intense.

At a bottleneck in the street he had to stop, his way blocked by an old woman with a bundle of wood on her bent back, hobbling slowly in the same direction. He tried to slip between her burden and the wall to get past her, but without success. After his second failed attempt he panted, exasperated, 'Let me pass, old woman! To hell with your wood!'

Instead of stepping aside, the woman turned round to look him in the face. 'Why do you insult me, Prior? I'm helping the good people of Florence. There's going to be a pyre of heretics, down by the Cavalcanti Tower. It's my seasoned wood, good for making white smoke!'

'Who do you want to burn, you witch? Think of your soul instead!'

'Why don't you think of yours!' she retorted, showing no wish to move. 'Or are you running to their aid?' she added, a flash of malice lighting up her cataract-clouded eyes.

Dante furiously pushed the bundle aside. The woman fell on her backside with a flurry of curses. 'Damn you to

GIULIO LEONI

hell!' she cried as he began running once more.

He had run almost two hundred yards when he was forced to fall on his knees and gasp for breath. In front of him, at the end of the alleyway, he saw a whirl of torches outside the door of the church. Vespers had been rung shortly before, and it was still light enough to see. Those flames had a more sinister purpose, he thought as he began running again.

The road outside the portal of the abbey had been filled by a crowd of armed men. It looked as if a sample of the whole of Christendom had assembled in the churchyard, ready to set off on the crusade. Looking quickly around, Dante recognised the livery of the French pikemen of Acquasparta's guard, and of the Genoese crossbowmen, as well as the *bargellini* and the district guard. The heavy armour of some Teutonic mercenaries also peeped out here and there, along with the rough garments of peasants armed with pitchforks.

Blood-soaked bodies lay on the cobbles. As he ran, he passed one of them, gaunt and in the grip of death. He was lying open-mouthed, his face in the road.

Suppressing a groan, Dante leaned over him. Bernardo the historian had been struck in the back, and there were two bloody gashes just below the base of his throat. Dante quickly made the sign of the cross, before closing Bernardo's eyes. So he too was part of the conspiracy, even if his time was running out.

Or had Bernardo become involved in the clash by accident? Heedless of the risks, Dante headed on towards the open portal. Spotting him, some of the men had dashed towards him, swords drawn. Over their chain-mail they wore tunics in various colours, different from those of the other soldiers. Dante dodged the first of them, who wore a leopard's head on his chest. Then, bending down, he managed to escape the grip of a giant with a lion's head embroidered on his jacket. He was about to pass through the portal when he bumped into the chest of a third armed man who had emerged from the shadows. Dante slipped to the floor, just in time to see with terror that the man had bared his sword and was preparing to strike him. He just noticed the wolf's head that he wore on his helmet, before instinctively shutting his eyes.

He was saved by a familiar voice. 'Messer Durante, have you come to see justice at work?' croaked the Bargello in an ironic voice, restraining the guard's arm. 'It does you an honour: true to your duty until the final hour. But you could have saved your strength. The Council has already elected your successor.'

Dante had regained control of himself, even if his heart was still pounding with emotion. He got rapidly to his feet and brushed the dust from his clothes. 'My mandate ends at midnight. Like my authority. Tell me what's happening, straight away. Why are these forces being deployed without an order from me?' he asked, pointing at the crossbowmen who were furiously operating the cranks of their weapons, which rested on forks held by their fellow-soldiers.

'A plot to endanger the security of Florence has been discovered . . . Prior. Under the appearance of proclaiming a crusade, the Ghibelline leaders have assembled men-at-arms, certainly to overturn the Commune and the laws of the people. The leader seems to have been that man Brandano, a false monk and a heretic. And as for the Virgin . . .'

'Who gave the order to intervene?' Dante interrupted angrily. 'The secular arm is subject to the authority of the priory. No one can usurp its rights!'

'No one has usurped them,' the Bargello replied, rising to his full, small height. 'It was your colleagues who gave me the order to act, after granting an audience to the Holy Inquisition, at the palace. That's why the Pope's men are here as well . . .'

Dante lowered his head in anger. Now that his mandate was about to expire, the crows were ruffling their feathers. He should have been more cautious. And from midnight onwards it would be vital to arouse no suspicions.

At that moment the crossbowmen, having completed their laborious loading operations, had begun to launch their projectiles at the gaps between the crenellations and the little loopholes that opened in the tower. It was impossible to tell who or what they were firing at, apart from a few shadows that could be glimpsed up above. Nor did there seem to be anyone coordinating the firing; everyone seemed to be shooting on a whim. Laughter and salacious comments made the atmosphere even more unreal, as if what was going on were a macabre game rather than a deadly attack.

The first salvo, fired off pretty much at random, had missed its target. Many arrows had flown over the tower and disappeared, while others had struck the wall, scattering fragments of brick and dust. Shouting with excitement, the men began to reload their crossbows.

Those Genovese don't seem to live up to their fame, Dante thought. And the Commune had bled itself dry to acquire their services, the lazy bastards. At that moment a sudden uproar broke the silence. Something shattered at the very top of the tower. A cloud of dust swelled up and then slowly began to fall. Then, accompanied by a series of loud crashes, a small section of the crenellations leaned dangerously outwards, before collapsing on the heads of the besieging forces with a rumbling roar.

Dante was still busy assessing the effects of the firing from the crossbowmen. He instinctively gripped the Bargello by one shoulder, pulling him beneath the canopy that covered a shop doorway. They fell over one after the other, as the great collapse crashed in front of them and a hail of detritus thundered down on the wooden floor.

In the narrow square not all of the besieging forces had

managed to find shelter. Shouts and laments emerged from the cloud of dust and rubble, confirming that more than one had been hit.

The poet struggled painfully to his feet. 'Damned heretics, we'll kill you all,' the purple-faced Bargello brayed beside him. He sat there legs akimbo, panting with rage and fear. An adversary hitherto obscure and impalpable had suddenly emerged from the shadows, revealing himself to be a dangerous flesh-and-blood enemy.

'You thought they were going to infiltrate your guards, like the Turks in the carnival procession?' mocked the prior.

The other man coughed violently, trying to rid his throat of dust. They found themselves at the centre of a bedlam of fleeing men, blinded by the dust and seized by terror that the collapse might be repeated. Meanwhile those men who remained unscathed tried to reorganise themselves, dragging the wounded to shelter. A company of archers had retreated to the mouth of the three lanes that led into the piazza, and from there had resumed firing at the tower. Fiery arrows rained down on the stones and exploded in a shower of sparks.

Some projectiles had entered the narrow loopholes, others had become stuck in the roof-trusses. The strips of resinous cloth wrapped round the tips smoked in the air. A cry of pain, followed by the shadow of a body falling far below, indicated that at least one of the arrows had reached its target, amidst the jubilant cries of the bowmen.

Here and there on the roof the poet saw red dots flaring where the arrows had struck and pierced the wooden covering.

Meanwhile he reflected anxiously upon what he had to do. Through the wide-open door of the church he glimpsed the blurred silhouettes of other men moving around. He impulsively threw himself forward, emerging into the abbey cloister through the unhinged door.

Spurred on by his own impetuosity, he gripped the door-post and looked all around. Having recovered from the confusion that followed the collapse of the building, the others were running, too. The place was swarming with armed soldiers scattered around the open space of the portico, wielding their swords to finish off the wounded men and women who fell to the ground amidst wails and cries of terror.

All was lost, for Cecco and the others. How could he stop the coming massacre? His own authority would expire in just a few hours. Seized by impotent grief Dante wrung his wrists beneath the sleeves of his robe.

But he could not yield to despair, he decided. He moved cautiously on, taking shelter behind a small pillar. All around him the ground was covered with shattered corpses. Someone, still in his death-throes, was groaning softly, trying to creep towards an unreachable shelter. None of the bodies on the floor wore any of the liveries that he had seen outside. The attackers must have overcome their victims without too much difficulty: the dead weren't wearing armour, and there was no sign of any weapons on the ground, suggesting that God's army had not had time to grab the swords hidden in the crypt.

Trails of blood marked the route of the assailants, who now raged on the stairs of the tower. From inside, at the height of the first landing, more groans could be heard, and pleas for mercy. Dante withdrew still further into the shadows, uncertain what to do. Whatever idea he might have had as he entered that slaughterhouse, it was too late now. Everything was lost, and for ever. He was about to make his way back out again when he heard a quiet voice from the darkness behind him.

It sounded like someone mumbling prayers, a confused and incomprehensible murmur in which the prior could make out only the word 'damned' obsessively repeated in the midst of other imprecations. He cautiously approached the source of the voice. It was a man crouching behind one of the pillars, who seemed to be pleading with the wall of the portico. When Dante came up behind him, he saw the man suddenly rising to his feet and turning towards him, as a purple flash split the dense darkness.

Dante felt a hand covering his mouth. He instinctively raised his arm, diverting the dagger-blow. He became aware of the sweetish taste of blood behind his lips. Then with a desperate jerk he escaped from the man's grip, hurling himself forward in a bid to strike a blow of his own. The movement had impelled him into the open, dragging his adversary with him. The light coming from the flaming roof suddenly lit up their faces. Before him, his face distorted with anguish and his face covered with blood, stood Cecco Angiolieri.

Still trembling with excitement, Dante leaned against one of the pillars. He lowered the weapon, staring at the man in disbelief. His friend was wearing a plumed helmet worthy of a Roman emperor, and thick leather armour. But underneath it he saw the puff of the jerkin and the usual purple stockings. Half god of war, half satyr. A joker as usual.

Cecco seemed pleased to see him. Still quivering, he hugged Dante, covering his cheeks with kisses like a delighted dog. 'My friend, I knew we'd make it! The Fedeli always help each other.' Then all of a sudden he turned suspicious, casting the poet an inquisitorial glance. 'Were you the one who gave the order to attack us?' he added.

Dante felt it was more of an aggrieved reproach than a question. 'I should have done it when I saw the head of the snake that is currently unwinding all its coils. But now you must flee, you must all flee! Where is Amara?'

'I . . . I don't know,' Cecco stammered, adjusting his breeches. 'We split up after the troops broke in. I saw her escaping towards the tower . . .'

The cries and mayhem continued above their heads. Cecco looked up for a moment, before staring at Dante again with a despondent expression. 'The slaughter and great havoc,' he muttered pompously, moving his blade in a circle like a bad actor on a stage.

The whole upper part of the tower was in flames, like a gigantic torch in the night. The heat had even begun to char the soft tufa from which the building was constructed, and which was now being carried away in an infernal cloud of sparks. If anyone had taken refuge up there, by now they were scattered ashes.

Something stirred on the first floor, where a loophole opened up on to a small stonework landing. Two men had appeared there, attracting the attention of the other men further below.

One gripped a human figure by the hair. 'Look who I've found!' he cried mockingly. With a violent jerk he pushed the body beyond the overhang and left it dangling in the void. 'The Virgin of Antioch . . . all of her, ready for a second miracle!'

The woman uttered a moan of terror, her bare feet kicking in the void as her hands waved desperately around in the air in search of purchase. The other man stepped over and stripped her clothes off her with a broad grin, revealing her true nature.

'But she's a monster!' he cried with horror. With both hands he brandished the sword he carried at his hip, raising it above his head and bringing it down with all his might.

The blade struck Amara in the loins, penetrating her

delicate flesh and shattering her backbone. A rain of blood and innards plunged down below. From her open lips there came only a sigh, followed by a soft bleat like that of a slaughtered lamb, as her chest was drenched in blood. Her arms jerked around in one final spasm, as if in a desperate bid to fly away from her pain. She was still alive, the fallen angel in the hands of the dwellers in Sodom. The man who was holding her shook her violently, sniggering, and then let go. The mass of hair slipped through his fingers like a bundle of dead snakes, then fanned out as the body plunged far below.

Trembling uncontrollably, Dante covered his face with his arm. A stormy sea roared in his temples. He had to lean against the roof-beam to stay upright. Beside him Cecco gave a muffled sigh.

It was that wound that brought the prior back to reality. He turned towards his friend, staring in bewilderment at the bloody remains that lay piled up a few feet away from them. 'Move yourself or you'll be finished, just like that woman!' he hissed, shaking him by his arm.

Cecco remained motionless, as if he was deaf. 'She wasn't a woman . . .' he stammered. He had taken a few steps forward, emerging from his hiding place. He stared at the body, his eyes bright with a strange form of lust.

'Follow me!' Dante commanded, pushing him towards the door. 'But first help me to recover something precious.'

'Money?' panted Cecco, suddenly animated again. 'The

treasure? So you know it exists!' he exclaimed.

'Maybe more than that. The key to a kingdom.'

Cecco stared at him, disconcerted. There really was something precious in the abbey. And something very dangerous. Something that the poet could not abandon at any cost. Al-Jazari's machine, hidden in the crypt.

When the disorderly troops had overcome the last of the resistance and turned their attention to plunder, it was just a matter of time before they reached the sarcophagi. And the Bargello had seen the machine, albeit in pieces, and would be able to recognise it and denounce Dante as a co-conspirator. It would be like handing the enemy his head on a silver platter. The machine had to disappear.

He stopped on the threshold, holding Cecco still just behind him. There didn't seem to be anyone inside, the shouts and footsteps were further off now. He slipped silently towards the basement entrance, pulling his friend after him by the hand. In the crypt he lifted the slab and, with Cecco's help, pulled out the chest. During the operation Cecco had continued to stare greedily at the object, but Dante had ignored all his silent questions.

'We have to get out along there,' he said, pointing to the cavity at the end. 'Help me – two of us will be able to do it.'

Conquering the horror that the fetid opening aroused in him, he slipped into the passageway. There was no time to get hold of a torch, and the air was so thick with fumes that a flame would have made it impossible to breathe. At the end he spotted a little tunnel leading from the wall. He began to move forward on his hands and knees, feeling his way along the stone. The vault of the tunnel was so low that it forced him to lower his head until he was almost creeping along.

They proceeded in the most total darkness, trusting their instincts. Cecco followed him as a blind man follows his guide, while the hurrying feet of the soldiers echoed above their heads like a distant tremble. The air was getting hotter and hotter, filled with a powerful stench of burning, indicating that the smoke from the fire must have penetrated all the way down there.

Dante made his way onwards, filled with nausea and a growing sense of vertigo. His guts were getting tighter and tighter. Beneath his fingers he recognised the regular roughness of a brick wall: that meant they were underneath the tower. Followed by Cecco, who was still cursing everyone and everything, he started to climb along the passageway, which was so narrow in places that the chest could hardly pass through.

The air was getting more and more impossible to breathe, and the prior felt anxiety mounting within him. He had set off on this journey with no guarantee of success, and a growing feeling of suffocation was taking hold of him. Behind him he heard his companion's panting breath.

He was gripped by fear: if the passageway led nowhere, or if it was blocked, would he be able to turn back? If Cecco was exhausted and collapsed, his body would prevent any possibility of reaching safety. Or if the chest got stuck . . .

The spectre of a horrible death flashed before Dante's eyes. Ideas became muddled in his air-starved brain. Beginning to panic, he was tempted to turn back. He thought he couldn't hear Cecco any more. Perhaps he had stayed behind, not daring to carry on. Perhaps the chest whose weight he could still feel was merely a hallucination. And if . . . if Cecco had followed him into this trap specially to get rid of him? Mightn't his scoundrelly coarseness, his affable buffoonery, be merely a mask that he wore to conceal the muzzle of a murderous beast?

He was about to lose control of his movements when he started to feel a faint draught on his face, barely perceptible at first, then gradually more apparent. He climbed the short flight of steps and emerged in the Forum well.

Panting, his companion emerged behind him. Cecco's face was a mask of sweat. He looked disorientatedly around as he got his breath back. 'Where are we?' he asked in a stunned voice.

Dante had recognised the pool of calm water at his feet. 'In the old Roman well,' he said, pointing to the narrow flight of steps that led into the open. 'We should be safe here.'

'Damn it . . .'

'Who are you angry with, Cecco?'

'That old hangman – my father. It's his fault that I've ended up like this . . . Damn it!' Fear had made Cecco's voice even shriller than usual. 'If I ever make it back to Siena, I'll throw him down the stairs, I swear I will. He'll give me every last *scudo*, if I have to drag it out of him with my fingernails. I'll carve him to pieces, I'll eat him up and then I'll shit him into the Arno . . .'

As he said this Cecco waved his arms around, flailing to left and right with his dagger, which he had drawn from his belt. He seemed to be plunged in a battle with the shadows, as his grotesque mask became more and more tragic. His face, too, beneath the waving pennant of his helmet, had grown sombre. He went on trembling, in the grip of an uncontrollable fury. He prodded the poet's chest several times with his index finger. 'I'm fed up with the company of Poverty. When will our time come, my friend? And by the way, what's in there?' he said, pointing to the chest, suddenly suspicious. 'You haven't told me yet. Are you going to keep it all to yourself, are you going to steal from an old companion-at-arms?'

As he spoke, with a rapid movement he gripped the lid of the chest and opened it. An expression of disappointment appeared on his face as he shifted the machine to make sure there was nothing hidden underneath it. 'A clock – all this for a damned clock . . .' he mumbled, passing the back of his hand over the cut in his forehead. 'And . . . the treasure?'

'There is no treasure, you idiot!' Dante cried, exasperated. 'It doesn't exist, it has never existed! Only death, the shadows and this inferno. Look!' he added, gripping him by his tunic and forcing his head all the way round.

Cecco coughed, trying to escape his grip, then sagged as if all his spirits had abandoned him. 'The treasure . . . doesn't exist,' he said disconsolately. 'They've tricked me. Me, the master.'

Stupefied, he had slumped down on his backside. Dante couldn't suppress a smile. 'Head for Pistoia, you fool. For the Eagle Gate,' he said in a low voice. 'All the units are assembled around here, and no one will pay you any attention. Wait for night to pass, and at dawn mingle with the peasants leaving for the countryside. You'll be able to do that if fate's on your side.'

Suddenly Cecco leaped to his feet, like a cloth puppet pulled by a string. He threw himself on the poet, hugging and kissing him. His eyes were moist with joy, faced with that hope of salvation.

Dante looked away and broke free from his grip. He was suddenly able to express the doubt that had been tormenting him. 'Why were they killed?'

Cecco stiffened, a grimace of surprise on his face.

'What did old Bigarelli have to do with your plans?

And what about those unfortunates on the galley?' the prior pressed him.

'Nothing! I don't know what you're talking about,' Cecco stammered. He had become circumspect once more. He glanced nervously behind him, as if fearing an ambush.

'There's no one here,' Dante reassured him coldly.

'I told you, and I swear on the life of that sainted woman Becchina, my lover, and the horns she puts on my head.'

'Cecco, I know everything. Monerre told me all about the plan. But who did you want to put on the throne? One of those already dead? Or . . .'

'So the Frenchman didn't tell you? And now you want me, your old friend, to show you his cards?'

'It's what you're best at, it seems to me.'

'Oh, there's no one better than you at cheating!'

'Who is it, Cecco?' the poet yelled, gripping him by the collar and shaking him violently.

'Arrigo,' Cecco moaned, trying to break away.

Dante tightened his grip still further. Beneath his hands, his strange friend's face had begun to redden. On his own face he felt splashes of spittle from a mouth desperately gasping for breath. Then suddenly he let go. 'Arrigo!' he spluttered. In the end it was just as he had expected. It had to be that way. According to reason, which is never wrong. The one who had always been in the back of his mind. Arrigo, with his defective leg, the mark left on him by the evil one. Arrigo, the 'incomplete man'.

Cecco seemed about to add something. He stood there rubbing his neck, trying to get his breath back. But all of a sudden he turned round and made off in the direction indicated by Dante, who saw him vanish in swirls of acrid smoke.

After a moment the poet stirred. With one final effort he hoisted the chest on to his shoulders and headed for his destination. There, in Arrigo's cell, he would find all his answers.

He looked around: the whole area was swarming with armed men, but no one noticed him. Pressing his face against the chest, he headed onwards, hoping that no one would recognise him. In all likelihood he would be mistaken for one of the looting assailants.

At that moment, in the distance, the roof of the flaming tower bent beneath its own weight and fell in on itself, taking with it the floors in between. Dante instinctively looked round, just in time to see a mass of incandescent beams collapsing, sending intermittent flashes of light through the loopholes in the wall, as if a crowd armed with torches was dashing down the stairs. All that remained at the top was the circle of charred crenellations, an enormous fireplace belching smoke and red flashes, like the jaws of a dragon trying to bite the sky.

Sensing the impending collapse, the besieging forces had already retreated, leaving their victims' bodies scattered in the courtyard to await the devastation of the fire and raining masonry. There were no enemies left to kill now, and the fire put a stop to any opportunities for looting. Without waiting for an order, the regular units were assembling, while the volunteers had already dispersed.

Some groups of soldiers passed by, ignoring him. They were making excited comments about what had happened, like a hunting party returning from the chase. Dante had gloomily sat down on an old Roman stone to get his breath back, and meanwhile he listened to the horrible boasts and jokes of the mob, still delighted with their slaughter. All that remained all around was the agitated motion of the local *vigiles*, who had come with pumps and buckets to keep the flames from spreading to the neighbouring houses.

After getting his breath back, Dante set off quickly on his way. When he reached Santa Maria Novella the main portal to the church was barred. Only a little torch beside the arch had been lit against the coming night. But one of the side-doors was still open, and the prior slipped inside, walking quickly down the deserted nave.

From the church he passed into the cloister, and from there to the corridor with the cells along it. Arrigo's cell was barred from inside. He knocked without receiving a reply. He put the chest on the ground and tried to shake the door, hoping it would open. From the other side he heard the metallic sound of the latch, refusing to budge.

He was gripped by fear that Arrigo might have escaped. Perhaps he sensed that he had been discovered. Or, having learned of the destruction of the Maddalena, perhaps he had decided to make his getaway to save any aspects of his plan that could still be rescued. Or perhaps he was in search of some other victims, to finish his plot once and for all, Dante thought with a shiver.

But where could Arrigo be? He leaned against the door again, pushing harder at it. As he crashed into it for the second time he felt the latch yielding and entered.

The cell was plunged in darkness, barely attenuated by the faint gloom that filtered through the closed shutter over the loophole. He paused for a moment on the threshold, waiting for his eyes to accustom themselves.

'Arrigo, I come with the authority of Florence to make you account for your crimes,' he announced, his hand raised like the statue of a classical figure of justice.

After a while he was able to see more clearly. He made out the profile of the philosopher sitting on the little stool by his desk and could just make out the whiteness of the paper. The man seemed to be busy writing something, in spite of the lack of light.

'Arrigo, justify yourself,' he added, walking towards him. His resolute tone was crumbling. The absolute certainty of Arrigo's guilt that had held him in its sway and brought him here was wavering in the face of the enormity of what he was about to do.

Perhaps he had been wrong to have blind faith in Mainardino's writings.

If Arrigo really was the natural son of Frederick, then his veins flowed with the most noble blood that the world had known since Charlemagne. Was it right to apply, to a being privileged by God's design, rules created to hold together a clutch of merchants and peasants? Was it right to consign to the noose a man within whom dwelt the hopes of the restoration of the empire, the supreme construction of the human spirit, an earthly mirror of the divine order?

And what if the *Chronicle* had been right and Arrigo really was an impostor? Might he not have derived a dream of peace and grandeur from that very imposture? Might he not have been a great emperor in any case? The long-awaited greyhound coming down to administer justice to the wolves?

His hand fell limply back against his side. The vulgar faces of the Council of Priors, the haughtiness of Cardinal d'Acquasparta, the ferocity of the Inquisition, the decline of the morals of his fellow-citizens – all of this could have been righted by this man, whose work he was now preparing to bring to an end. Perhaps his bid had failed. Manfred and Conrad had already lost their part of the game, but hope was young. It was still possible to try.

To stop him at the peak of his venture – would that not have been the real crime?

Should he not instead throw himself at Arrigo's feet, put all his ingenuity, his will, his knowledge at the service of this great work? Be the counsel, the voice of the new Frederick, the one who holds and discloses his heart with the keys of wisdom and virtue. Correct his errors, rectify his imprudence, pick up where the plan of the Fedeli had failed . . .

And then to sing all this in his work and give it the form of a journey of the spirit, from the darkness of despair to the light of order regained, order's bridegroom. And to be crowned poet in San Giovanni!

He stepped forward again until he could just touch the man's shoulder. Arrigo sat with his head on one side as if sleeping, his hand abandoned on the paper in front of him. Dante ran to the window and pulled open the shutter to let in what little brightness remained outside. The last of the evening light poured into the small room, slightly softening the shadows.

Arrigo was dead. In front of him, set down on the paper on which his hand had written a few lines, lay a cup still moist with wine. Dante noticed a sharp smell, the scent of the grape mixed with something metallic. A thin trickle of reddish spittle fell from the corner of the philosopher's mouth, an unmistakeable sign of the poison that he had swallowed.

Dante delicately slipped from beneath the lifeless hand the sheet of paper on which, in an unsteady hand, Arrigo had written a few words: '*Omnia tempus corrumpit, non bis in idem datur hominibus.*'

Time corrupts all, men are not granted a second chance.

The poet's eyes filled with tears. 'Why didn't he wait for me?' he cried, waving his fists at the dead man. In Arrigo's half-closed eyes the light of dusk reawakened an unexpected appearance of life. He seemed to be staring with detachment at the goblet from which he had drunk his death. Only now did Dante notice how magnificent it was, something that had escaped him in the agitation of the moment.

The darkness was deepening. He drew his tinderbox from his bag and lit a candle on the table, then brought the goblet to the flame to take a better look. It was gold, the size of a Eucharistic cup.

'It really is . . .' he said to himself with disbelief. A lump in his throat stifled the cry that had risen to his lips. He ran his fingers along the delicate pattern of the goblet, a garland of roses and laurel leaves along the rim, above four imperial eagles with their wings outspread. A precious piece of work, truly worthy of the lips of an emperor. The eight faces of the goblet recalled the perfect shape of the temple in Jerusalem. But also Frederick's old unfinished fortress and the building burned in the land of the Cavalcanti.

There were Greek characters carved around the eagles. So it had been engraved in the East, perhaps in Constantinople. But someone had disfigured it, roughly carving three Latin characters with a sharp piece of iron: '*F R I*'.

The gift from the Emperor of Byzantium, renewing his

allegiance and protection. The cup from which he had drunk on his last day on earth. *Federicus Rex Imperator* . . .

A shiver ran down Dante's spine. He quickly set the object down on the desk with great reverence. The gold seemed to have become incandescent, and burned his fingers. A cup not of life, but of death. The one used to kill Frederick. By a coward, an 'incomplete man'.

Once again emotion took hold of him, and his eyes filled with tears. A great roar like that of a waterfall filled his mind, as his consciousness seeped away.

HE CAME to his senses disorientated, with no idea how much time had passed. He was lying on the floor, all his limbs aching from his fall. A few hours hence his mandate would come to an end: he had to get back to San Piero and arrange the transfer of duties to the new priors. But before he did that he wanted to restore order to the blood-drenched ruins. Starting with Arrigo's body, lest it be abandoned to the fate reserved for the remains of suicides.

He would spread the rumour that the philosopher had succumbed to an incurable illness, on his way to an impossible salvation in Rome. Anyway, that idiot the pontifical doctor wouldn't be able to tell a drowning from a death by fire.

The tension of the most recent events was easing, leaving him with a sense of emptiness. That vista of ruins was the end result of all his efforts, he thought with despair. The force of his reason had been able to do nothing to resolve the enigma. Like an idiot standing open-mouthed watching the performance of an acrobat, he had observed the fatal events unfolding without knowing how to intervene in any way.

Perhaps Marcello had been right about the total, blind predestination of human life. By some inscrutable irony of fate, two men had drunk death from the same precious object. The second by his own will, the first the victim of the perverse desires of others. Both now dust in the eternal cycle that hangs over us all.

Dante leaped to his feet, bumping his head against the desk. He wanted to cover Arrigo's face before calling anyone. His feet struck something on the ground that he had not seen. Mechanically he stretched out his hands and picked up a big notebook. He brought the manuscript to the candle flame.

It was a folio manuscript, more than a hundred parchment pages sewn together: *Decem continens tractatus astronomiae.*

The great work of Guido Bonatti. The most important astrological book of modern times. And Bonatti had been Frederick's astrologer. Another ghost from the past returning, as if from the realm of the dead the Emperor had ordered his court to assemble for one last time in Florence, the city that had always escaped his complete dominion.

The touch of his hands had instinctively become more delicate. The poet flicked admiringly through the first few pages. Arrigo, then, had been so deeply attached to the science of the stars as to possess this most precious of works. And what was more, he was capable of making notes on it, as borne out by the many observations written in the margins in a narrow, nervous hand, quite unlike the regular Caroline script of the anonymous copyist who had transcribed the text.

Unusually similar to his own, he noticed as he read the observations jotted here and there. There was something about the author of those notes that made him seem close to Dante in a completely unexpected way, as two pilgrims in a foreign land reveal themselves to be fellow-countrymen even before they have exchanged a greeting or revealed their names. That harmony of the soul that binds all the citizens of Plato's Republic.

He went on flicking through the manuscript until he reached the final pages. Two whole bundles of paper had been added to the binding, partly covered with jottings and observations in the same hand that had written the notes. A new chapter, *Liber undecimus de amplitudine rei universalis.*

The width of the universe. The author of the notes had not merely noted the text then, but had sought to complement it with an organic treatise. Dante's admiration grew as he read on. Had Arrigo himself been responsible for these jottings?

He stared again at the dead man's profile: the nobility

of his features could easily trace him back to the ancient Swabian race. Perhaps he too had been deceived by his own image, when he had found himself looking at it reflected in the mirror, and had desperately wanted to believe in an unfathomable fate, when he measured the tracks of the stars – a fate that seemed to summon him to be next on the throne of an imagined father.

The throne of Frederick.

Dead. Murdered.

A new possibility took hold of the poet's mind; what if Arrigo had killed himself not because of the failure of his plans, but out of remorse for some long-distant crime, a shadow that had dogged his steps for fifty years? Could he have been the Emperor's assassin, the 'incomplete man'?

Reading Mainardino's pages he had thought the metaphor referred to a physical imperfection, or perhaps to a moral defect. But what if the bishop had, with the words 'an incomplete man', meant someone who had been only a boy at the time? And what if that boy had acted as a blind instrument of other people's wickedness, out of hatred for a father who had inexplicably denied and insulted him in the person of his beloved mother?

That ancient pain might have paved the way for a tragedy that had exterminated a clan and devastated the empire. Until the final act, which had happened before his eyes, when men had come to Florence from the four corners of the earth only to meet the frozen mask of death.

And that city, Dante's city, which he felt pulsating beyond the walls of the convent, was the stage for all this. Through the walls that hung above him, gripping the dead Arrigo and the living Dante in a strange stone embrace, he seemed to see the streets and the walls, the houses, the locked doors, the great sack of wickedness and evil always on the point of overflowing. And he heard no footsteps. For this was the city of Dis, its gates guarded by demons.

With that same goblet, Arrigo had killed the man he believed was his father. But how had he done it? After the barons' conspiracy Frederick had become extremely suspicious, and had his food tasted by loyal Saracens. And even if the poison had been diluted, to act only after a certain delay, others would have died with him. Had that been so, the rumour would have circulated straight away, while there was nothing to suggest that anyone had accompanied the Emperor to the realm of the shadows.

Perhaps Frederick had fallen into the trap as a result of some distraction, a little flaw in his otherwise perfect circumspection, perhaps trusting the bastard son he had grown used to seeing around him since his childhood, the boy he now ignored . . .

The poison aconite acts through contact, he recalled. During his studies he had seen the spasms of a rabbit after aconite was poured into its ear. Could there have been some sort of spike hidden in the stem of the cup, which pierced the sovereign's finger?

The gold's brilliance filled the little cell. Dante very carefully picked up the object again, raising it to eye level as though in a mute act of offertory. Again he ran his fingers along the engraving, seeking the point that the Emperor's lips would have touched as he took his final sip. But he discovered nothing that confirmed his hypothesis.

He closed his eyes, his thoughts still focused upon the Emperor. Now his body lay embalmed in Palermo. But where was his heart, once torn from his body? Did not an echo of his mind still resound there in the cell, even more powerfully than it hovered around his decomposed tissues, the rags of his royal garments locked up in his sarcophagus?

Perhaps that was the deeper meaning of Michael Scotus' prophecy: 'Sub flore morieris.' You will end your days in Florence.

Like his great architect. The man who wanted to build his tomb. In all likelihood the building that had gone up in flames on the Cavalcanti lands had been designed as a cenotaph for the Emperor, a great monument apparently built to celebrate – but in reality to hide – the crime.

Had that been Arrigo's plan? To have himself crowned in that replica of the Castel del Monte, decorated with the magic mirrors that would endlessly have replicated his glory, granting it eternal life in an extreme repetition of the same image, over and over again.

With a shiver Dante glimpsed the madness within the

plan: Nero had had a throne built for him, which followed the movement of the sun. Arrigo wanted to be that sun himself, at the still centre of a dazzling planetarium.

He had opened his eyes again, and the splendour of the goblet, still gripped in his hand, filled his mind once again.

He thought of his own work, still unfinished. Clear proof of his limitations as a poet, he reflected bitterly. Might that have been the solution he had sought so hard for his vision of Paradise? A vast golden goblet, the same one used in the sacrifice of Frederick, but wide as a thousand skies, where the souls of the blessed swam in a bath of eternal purification?

Horrified by his own blasphemy, he slammed the goblet down on the table. It was then that the silence was broken by a metallic click. He looked carefully at the goblet. The candle-light clearly emphasised its outline. The symmetrical flow of the handles and the curves of the grip formed a pair of human faces. The shade of the two-headed man that Marcello had spoken of. The ninth shade . . .

What did it mean? Dante picked up the goblet and set it back down on the table, listening attentively. Once again he thought he heard the same faint metallic sound. He repeated the gesture: the little carved column actually seemed to give a little. So this jewel had not been cast as a single piece, but was made in at least two parts. He performed the same action again, pressing the bottom with increasing strength, then slumped on his stool in disappointment.

Nothing had changed in the appearance of that deadly chalice. There was no secret spike to wound the drinker's finger.

His whole theory was collapsing in the face of the evidence. And yet he was sure that in some way that was what had happened. He struck his forehead with his fists, desperately looking around the cell for something that might suggest a solution. Then an idea came to him.

Nine. The number which, in the view of old Marcello, united their destinies. He began to press the goblet down on the table. At the fifth attempt a barely perceptible crack opened up inside the bowl. That was how the wine, had the cup been full, would have made contact with the poison hidden in the grip. Each time the cup was set down on the table the hidden mechanism brought death a step closer. After the cup had been supped nine times death was a certainty.

That would have deceived even anyone who had noticed the small movement of the stem, apparently a flaw in the casting. And besides, who else would have dared bring the goblet to his lips? It was used only by the Emperor, and he alone could have fallen into the trap. That was how death had struck both the father and the man who thought he was his son. Or desperately wanted to be.

That was how Arrigo had been poisoned by the assassin, who had resorted to a mocking repetition of the ancient crime.

Dante looked anxiously around. Now he knew why the assassin had ripped only the last lines from the *Chronicles*: in the murder of the heir he wanted the poet to read the proof of Arrigo's guilt. And if he hadn't discovered the secret of the goblet, Dante would have fallen into the trap, believing – like the others – in the suicide of a murderous, defeated and desperate pretender.

A crime concealed for half a century was emerging before his eyes. Perhaps the star that marked his birth and governed his path truly was remarkable. Perhaps Marcello was right: there was a route carved through everyone's life, and life was nothing but blindly walking along that route.

He took from his bag the wrinkled sheet on which the astrologer had traced the boundaries of his fate, the limits of his glory and of his grief. Before his eyes that network of lines and points danced through the flashes of a blinding headache. He began running his index finger along the signs that bound his destiny. All the way to the malign square of Jupiter, in which Marcello had read the augury of his exile. He ran a hand over his forehead, then shook his head.

The plan of the horoscope blazed in front of him, with Marcello's notes. Those characters, that thin handwriting . . .

A sudden idea had flooded his mind. He threw himself on the manuscript of the *Decem continens*, comparing the two scripts. Even by the flickering candle-light the lines of the pen that had drawn the symbols of his destiny were identical to those left by the hand that had jotted down the text, the only one that could really have attempted to complete the *Decem continens.* That of its author, the greatest astrologer of his day, Guido Bonatti.

Dante shivered at the thought of the person who had prophesied his misfortune. But then he suddenly sat up, banishing the thought from his mind. No, those marks on paper could accomplish nothing. He was sole arbitrator of his own fate.

He gripped the sheet of paper furiously, planning to rip it up. He started tearing the edge, then stopped. In doing so he had turned the piece of paper over and now he noticed something for the first time.

The doctor had sketched his horoscope chart on a sheet taken at random from his bag. In the excited discussion in which they were immersed he hadn't noticed that he had used the back of one of Bigarelli's drawings, taken from the sculptor's studio after his death.

The weight of truth crashed down upon him. He was the murderer. But why? He yelled his question at the deaf stone walls, at Arrigo's motionless body. Then his attention returned to the drawing that he still clutched in his hand, trembling with excitement.

The poet sat down at the desk and unfolded the paper beneath the light. A large octagon, with other, smaller octagons nestling in its corners. Castel del Monte, with its crown of towers. But there was something else, too, something to do with the maps he had seen at the Builders' Guild.

Various signs had been added to the diagram of the rooms and corridors: eight lines traced in blood in each of the eight rooms, each one marked with a phrase, '*lucis imago repercussa*', and an angle measurement. A thin ink-line linked the reddish marks together, as if to indicate a trajectory uniting them in a chain.

'Reflection of an image in light . . .' Dante murmured, biting his lower lip. The discovery seemed to have conquered his pain, as if the excitement of the soul could defeat each of the body's weaknesses. 'Eight reflections . . . in eight mirrors.'

He went on studying Bigarelli's drawing, fascinated by the perfect geometry of the lines that crossed the plan, indicating strange positions of objects and the relationships between them. If truth is revealed in the beauty and harmony of the figure, then that drawing, in its symmetry, must contain a truth similar to beauty.

There was a note in characters so small as to be almost invisible. Even Dante's eagle eye was strained to the utmost as he tried to decipher it. The figures seemed to relate to the construction. He tried to follow the line traced by the pen. It was as if Bigarelli had been trying to indicate the wild path of a force, an image repeated from mirror to mirror in the great blind drum of the castle, until with one final deviation it reached the centre of the construction, in what must have been the inner courtyard. Here, suggested with a few lines, was the diagram of an object, some wheels. And then a particular detail, out of scale and circled by a red line: an axle with two half-moons facing one another and a human eye observing one of the two ends.

Lucis imago repercussa . . . An idea was forming in Dante's mind. Something he had read in the *Chronicles* when scanning their pages in Bernardo's cell. Something that was now rising to the surface of the prodigious lake of his memory: 'It reached the Emperor on the threshold of the great proofs. And wise Michael it was who found the way, contrary to the opinion of his astrologer . . .'

Then his face brightened, as he suddenly raised his head. *Lucis imago repercussa.* What Frederick the Great hadn't lived long enough to find out. Now the door of that awareness was right in front of him, and it was about to close.

So his eye moved to the still-locked cabinet, covered by piles of precious books. He forced the lock with the tip of his dagger. Elias of Cortona's lamp. Now he understood the meaning of it all. That was why the copy of Castel del Monte had been made, why the mathematician Fabio dal Pozzo had been called in to perform the calculations . . .

That was what Arrigo had been trying to tell him, by the walls of the Baptistery, precious to him only because of the darkness that lay beneath its vault. A great black lake of darkness that the philosopher needed in order to realise the father's ancient dream.

Not the rebirth of the empire, wrecked in the storm of time. That was the plan of the men from the north, from Venice, the Templars. Arrigo had only been helping. Generously, he had invested his heart in the bid. But his mind was elsewhere, lost behind another dream. A dream that even Dante was only now beginning to understand.

He was filled with sudden anxiety. Penetrating that secret – was it not the same as penetrating the secret of God? He felt his eyes welling up, and a knot tightened his throat like an iron hand. He burst into tears, defeated by his grief.

'And is this what you wanted?' he asked with a sob, turning towards Arrigo.

'What's going on, Maestro? Are you unwell?' he heard a voice say on the other side of the door. With a massive effort of will, Dante restrained his weeping. 'Nothing!' he answered abruptly. 'Just a bad dream,' he added, hoping the nuisance would go away. But then he saw the door half-opening.

A monk clutching a lantern had appeared in the doorway. He peered innocently in, glancing back and forth between Dante and the corpse. 'But . . . Prior, what are you doing here? And Messer Arrigo . . .'

'Is dead, Brother. *Sed non a Deo advocatus.* He chose, with unhappy hand, to rejoin the spirit of his ancestors before his time. He took his own life,' the prior concluded, seeing that the other man was still staring at him in disbelief.

At these words the monk brought his hand to his mouth in a gesture of horror. 'A suicide, here, in a sacred place . . . I will have to alert the abbot,' he stammered, staring at the dead man.

'Do that. But later. First send for someone from the Misericordia, with the dead-cart.'

The monk stared at him in alarm.

'The funeral must be held straight away,' the poet explained to him. 'It would not be good for your monastery to be dragged into a scandal. I want the body to be taken outside the walls, with tapers quenched.'

The monk nodded and disappeared.

Perhaps an hour had passed by the time the announcement was made that the people Dante had called for were at the door. The abbot himself had come, with a worried expression on his face, to bring him the news. He glanced rapidly at the dead man, then suddenly looked away as if he feared being contaminated by the sight of it. Behind him a little group of friars crowded into the doorway, craning their necks to see.

'Wrap the body in a canvas and take it below,' ordered Dante.

With a nod of his head the abbot did as he asked. The

brothers seemed eager to free themselves of the inconvenient presence of the corpse, and quickly disappeared with the body.

The poet hoisted the chest with the mechanism on to his shoulder and followed them in turn, after picking up Elias' lamp wrapped in a cloth.

Outside the monastery he saw the dark outlines of two members of the brotherhood hidden by their cowls. One of them held the poles of a cart with large wheels, covered by a black canvas under which the monks had already placed Arrigo's body.

'We're here, Brother,' said the other man, who was holding a small oil-lamp. 'What are those?' he asked in a puzzled voice, staring at the chest and the bundle.

Without replying, Dante put his load on the back of the cart, beside the feet of the corpse. 'Follow me. To the abbey of the Maddalena.'

'That's where we've just come from. The war has lately been putting a great strain on our resources,' the other man replied, perplexed.

The prior took the oil-lamp from his hand. 'Come, I'll take you there. First we have to load up a few things,' he said as they set off. Behind him he heard a puzzled murmur.

At last the taller of the two men steeled himself. 'Messere, what's going on, is this a joke? Have you swapped a hearse for a rubbish-cart?'

'Do as I say, and have no fear. I am the Prior of Florence

and there is a logic to my actions. Nothing of what you see contravenes the rules of your order.'

He quickly made for the wool warehouse, along with his grim-faced followers. In the lodge beside the barred door, the guard had been asleep for a while. He dozily emerged, with an irritable expression that quickly turned to alarm when he saw who it was that had interrupted his slumbers.

'What . . . what do you want?' he stammered in terror. He looked as if he was about to faint from the horror inspired in him by this procession of ghosts. His trembling subsided only once he had recognised the poet.

'The cloths of the merchant Fabio dal Pozzo. I have to confiscate them. Stand aside, I know the way.'

Then, without waiting for any reaction from the still-confused man, Dante stepped into the labyrinth of heavy oak tables, guiding the dead-cart down the narrow passage-ways until he reached the spot where he had deposited the Venetian's felt fabrics. In the storehouse, filled to the rafters, the air was so hot it was almost impossible to breathe.

'Help me bring these bales down. Be very careful, they contain something fragile and precious. Take care not to drop them.'

Now that he had the slabs in front of him again he realised quite how big they were. They wouldn't fit on the cart. Quickly, and beneath the eyes of the two monks who looked on in alarm, he gripped Arrigo's body under the arms and lifted it into a sitting position. Then he pointed to the slabs wrapped in the felt, ordering them to be placed edgeways next to the corpse.

The brothers of the Misericordia were growing more and more startled. Beneath the weight, the axle of the cart groaned dangerously. 'They're as heavy as marble!' exclaimed one of the two, sweat-drenched beneath his cowl, while the other, assisted by Dante, began to push the cart. 'What on earth is in there?'

'A dream,' the prior said quietly, wiping his brow. 'A dream dreamed by a great man.'

'We'll have to inform the captain of the Misericordia about all this.'

'Tomorrow. Tomorrow we'll have time for everything.'

The little funeral cortège re-emerged from the portal of the warehouse, passing once more in front of the trembling guard.

Outside, the darkness was softened by the moonlight. Dante pointed towards the Baptistery. With a jerk, the cart set off behind him.

At a turning in the street ahead of them a district patrol appeared. At the sight of the hooded figures they quickly stepped aside, making the sign of the cross. The prior passed by them without so much as a glance. For a moment he thought the two monks were about to turn to the armed men and tell them everything, but instead they said nothing and went on pushing the cart.

In the distance the road opened up towards Santa Reparata. In the background the great marble drum of the Baptistery stood out against the black sky like an imperial crown wrapped in a starry cloak. Dante anxiously quickened his pace.

They stepped out into the deserted square, amidst piles of building material. Further on, a corner of the walls of the future Duomo was already beginning to rise from the earth.

He walked resolutely towards the side of the Baptistery. There was someone in front of him.

'Greetings, Messer Alighieri,' he heard a voice say from the shadows. 'I knew your obstinacy would bring you here sooner or later. The exact hour of your madness was indicated in the stars.'

The man was sitting on one of the Roman sarcophagi that leaned against the Baptistery wall. His face was hidden by the hood of his travelling clothes, but Dante had recognised him straight away. He took a few steps towards the doctor.

'Greetings, Messer Marcello. I too knew that we would meet one day. Or perhaps I should call you by your true, ancient and famous name.'

His words had provoked no reaction in the man.

'Guido,' Dante continued. 'Guido Bonatti. Astrologer to kings and emperors. A man who knows the path of the stars – and a murderer.'

Still the old man did not reply. He merely looked up as though seeking in the darkness the stars that the poet had mentioned. 'Its form is perfect,' he murmured, nodding towards the drum of the dome that loomed above him. 'A pointless perfection, as always when the acts of men seek to ape nature,' he added.

Dante had caught up with him now. With a nod of his head he ordered the two monks to stop. The cart came to a halt by the sarcophagus.

The astrologer lifted a corner of the cloth and looked carefully inside. His eye stopped first on the severe face of Arrigo, then on the chest at his feet. He turned to the poet. 'So it was in your hands. I should have known,' he said, pointing at the bag containing the machine. 'I was sure I had destroyed it.'

'Alberto the *mechanicus* put it back together . . . before you dispatched him to the afterlife.'

Guido Bonatti nodded. 'He was good at his job. I saw what he did, in his workshop. As good as the devils who made this,' he said, pointing once more to the machine.

'Like that man from the East, the one you murdered after being welcomed on to the galley. Was it in Malta that you boarded it? Or had you mingled amongst the passengers since the vessel's departure, far beyond the sea?'

'I was in Sidon when word reached me that the vile plan was once more under way. I persuaded those men that I could be useful.'

'You carried out a massacre just to kill one man.'

'His mind had to be obliterated. And his memory. Nothing else mattered.'

'Not even the lives of all those innocent men that you wiped out with your terrible poison, the same one that you used to kill the father and the son?'

'No one is innocent,' Bonatti said with a disdainful shrug. 'Arrigo wasn't Frederick's son. Only in his insane pride had he been able to imagine such a thing.'

'Arrigo wasn't the Emperor's son by blood, but he was a worthy son of his intellect, and for that reason alone he would have deserved to live and rule. For his devotion to Frederick's mind. A devotion that you exploited by flattering him, making him believe that his imperial destiny was confirmed in the stars. That was why you showed him your treatise on divination. And then you made him toast his enterprise with the marvellous goblet that had belonged to his father. The one that killed him, in the same way as it had killed Frederick.'

'My treatise . . . a life's work,' Bonatti said, his voice thick with sadness. 'Lost.' But then he shrugged, and returned to his mocking tone. 'And why did I do it? I loved my Emperor. Can you tell me, Alighieri?'

'Yes. I know now. I know everything now,' the poet exclaimed triumphantly. 'Because Frederick was launching an enterprise that would have destroyed all your certainty.'

'And is that why you're here?' Bonatti asked. 'With him,'

he added, pointing at Arrigo's body without looking at it.

'Yes. He too has the right to see what I will see.'

The old man shrank at these words, as if struck by a sudden gust of wind. 'And what do you think you will see?' he asked angrily after a moment.

'Frederick's dream. The Kingdom of Light. He summoned the best minds of his court to prepare the enterprise. Elias of Cortona to use his alchemy to create a light that would match the light on the day of Creation. Michael Scotus to study how it might be done, and Leonardo Fibonacci to measure the result with his calculations. And Tinca the *maestro*, with his admirable glass. And from the East al-Jazari with his machines, and Guido Bigarelli, to erect the testing ground. To discover how far light travelled during the six days of Creation. He wanted to know the width of the universe, to measure the realm of God.'

Bonatti nodded slowly. 'Frederick was a mad blasphemer. A champion of the impossible. If light had a motion, it would continue for ever, heading towards a horrendous, infinite void. All certainty, all stability of the creation would collapse. All this had to be stopped. It was written in the stars that I was the one to do it.'

'You are the madman. The measurement of the created universe would have been the supreme work of human genius, a song of praise to God.'

The astrologer had leaped to his feet with unexpected

agility, moving towards him. Dante took a step back. But Bonatti did not seem to want to attack him. He was staring at something behind him. The poet instinctively turned round: the double wound on the bodies of the murdered men returned to his mind and he feared that the second murderous hand was hidden behind him.

But there was no one there. Bonatti was lost in contemplation of a group of stars low on the horizon. 'Scorpio is rising . . . So it was written, so it will happen,' he murmured, closing his eyes, his voice suddenly distant. 'All the wickedness of the Moors and their necromancy can do nothing against the admirable architecture of Creation, motionless light and its stable confines.'

'It was not the Moors who sought the truth, but the best minds of our century, of our race, of our faith, of our tongue! And many of them have been extinguished by you!' Dante replied angrily. 'It was not your certainty, but your power that led you to kill.'

The old man clenched his fists in front of him, as his mouth struggled to reply.

'How old are you, Messer Bonatti?' the prior pressed him. 'Haven't you lived through most of this century? And after so many years, in which you have seen and known everything, you wanted to deprive yourself of the greatest experiment of all? I challenge you to this test: in the Baptistery, with its perfect geometry. That which was not possible in Puglia will happen here,' he continued resolutely, pointing his hand towards the marble mass behind them.

'Like Saint Thomas you want to seek the truth in blood,' the astrologer replied. 'That blood will extinguish the infernal fire of your pride, it will temper your arrogance. I do not fear your challenge. So enter the temple, if you dare to profane it with your confused science.'

'By the northern door. In the Baptistery they are finishing off the big mosaic in the dome, and it is left open to allow the workmen in and out.'

Behind them the two monks had been watching in silence, their puzzled expressions hidden by the hoods over their faces. The group slipped along the side of the Baptistery, passing into the narrow alley that separated it from the nearest buildings, which leaned against its perfect form like ragged beggars.

'Push the cart in and then leave us. I will deal with the transport of the corpse,' the poet commanded. 'Return to the battleground and bury the remains of the Virgin of Antioch, beyond San Lorenzo.' His voice was tinged with grief. 'And respect them, because her end was more atrocious than her guilt. As for what you have seen, forget it all.'

Bonatti had remained apart. As soon as they were alone, his hand trembling with excitement, he lifted aside the heavy length of felt that protected one of the slabs, then brushed the icy surface with his fingers, like a blind man using the sense of touch to seek confirmation of his imaginings.

By the faint moonlight that entered through the windows, Dante found a candelabra and with a few strokes of his tinder-box lit the candle stumps. Then he turned towards Guido Bonatti, who had sat down on the edge of the baptismal font. He looked exhausted, covered with sweat, as if his great age had suddenly revealed itself. He struggled to breathe the thick, heavy air, staring at Arrigo's lifeless eyes.

The poet pulled Bigarelli's diagram from his bag. But the astrologer, having sprung back into life with unexpected force, had already begun striding across the Baptistery floor, as if that same diagram had been imprinted on his mind in symbols of fire.

'A thousand times I have read that diabolical plan, a thousand days I have woken with its image before my eyes, a thousand nights I have descended into the darkness bringing it with me. You don't need that filthy scrap of paper. Put the first mirror there!'

In a corner Arrigo's body, wrapped in its shroud, seemed to be watching their movements. The edge of the cloth had slipped down, revealing his face. It was only right that he should be there, Dante thought. Less than two hours had passed since his death, and his soul was still wandering on the borders of the realm of shadows. He could still see.

One by one the eight slabs were placed against each of

the walls. Bonatti followed the perimeter of the construction, outlining the angles from memory as if marking on the stone the trace of one last, extraordinary horoscope. Dante followed him, checking with a candle that each mirror caught the image of its companion on the right and reflected it precisely to the one on the left in a circle of repeated images.

'Do you really think there's any point to all this?' the astrologer said, arms pressed to his chest as he waited for the last slab to be put in place.

'Yes. I'm sure of it,' the poet replied, checking in the candle-light the point where Elias' lamp was to be placed, facing towards the first mirror.

He cast one last glance at Arrigo. His hands trembled with excitement as he opened the little door of the lamp. Then, with a more resolute gesture, he brought the vivid flame to the little bottle.

The white powder caught fire with an incandescent flash. Concentrated by the brass shield, the ray seemed to bounce against the glass surface. All around them a phantasmagoria of light lit up along the walls of the Baptistery like a crown of flames. The splendour of Elias' light set the dust aflame, transformed by the rays into a galaxy of stars. Vague in the shadows above them still hung the face of Christ the Lord surrounded by the angelic hosts, mute witnesses to the events below.

'There they are!' cried Dante to his adversary, showing

the strips of light reflected from one glass surface to another. 'There are the rays of which al-Kindi speaks. The light has run from one mirror to the next!'

'You are wrong! The circle of flashes all around us appeared in unison, and not by degrees. It proves not motion, but the sempiternal motionlessness of light. Omnipresent and constant as its creator.'

The prior shook his head violently and freed the spring of the machine. The toothed axle began to rotate, slowly at first, then faster and faster. He brought his eye to the slit in the side opposite the one holding the lamp. The halo of light shone all around, but the thickest darkness lay within the opening.

Bonatti too had drawn close to the observation point, and stepped back with a mocking expression. 'Behold the darkness that punishes your ignorance, Messer Alighieri!' he spat disdainfully. 'I have been familiar with the nature of this devilry since Michael Scotus demonstrated its working. If the light passed through the teeth of the two opposing wheels, that would be proof of its motion. But it was merely the illusion of his hazy mind. None of this will happen.'

Dante bit his lips uncertainly. The growing roar of the gear-wheels filled the air as the thrust of the spring increased the speed of the rotation. The fins of the regulator were rising and the braking action had begun. Soon the axle would reach its anticipated speed and stabilise.

Meanwhile he went on looking through the slit, but couldn't see anything. He ran his hand over his sweat-pearled brow, as the bitter sensation of defeat began to weigh upon him, heavy as a boulder. Then all of a sudden a flash, followed by a flood of dazzling light, spread from the slit and exploded in his face. He instinctively raised an arm, shielding himself from the glare that seared his retina.

As he tried to react to his momentary blindness he heard a muffled groan from beside him. He had a vague glimpse of Bonatti staring in alarm at his face, illuminated by the flash.

'The light of God!' Dante cried, still shielding himself from the glare. 'It moves . . . as everything moves!'

The shape of the heavens, that sought-after realm of the just that had always eluded his words, was there in front of him right now, full of the splendour of creation. In his still-dazzled eyes the octagon drawn by the flashing lights seemed to dance in supernatural motion.

'Frederick was right!' he cried.

The astrologer shook his head firmly, several times. He had closed his eyes tight as though trying to keep from seeing anything. 'You think you are victorious?' he said after a long silence, broken only by the frantic roar of the spinning mechanism.

'Yes! And here, in San Giovanni, here is my crown!' Dante replied, still staring drunkenly at the flashing light.

The image of the glory of the heavens, that image that he had sought for so long, was there now, in front of him, the Comedy was finally about to find its epilogue. 'This was written by God in the nature of the boundless splendour, this my words will represent upon parchment, this men will read for their ultimate edification!'

Guido Bonatti looked petrified. 'It isn't . . . it isn't possible!' he stammered, moving towards the poet. He groped with his hands in the void, as if trying to grasp the rays of light to stop them. The poet stepped aside to let him look through the slot.

The astrologer shook his head for a moment as he began to bend towards the eyepiece. Then with a jerk he stepped back, crying out and covering his face with his hands, as if a living flame had escaped from the machine. An expression of despair replaced the sneer that he had worn a few moments before.

'What have you to say about this sign, Messer Bonatti!' the prior scoffed. 'In what fallacious horoscope will its form now feature?'

The old man's long hair, caught in one of the circular rays, looked as if it was on fire. Slowly he slipped on one of his gloves.

'This is a work of magic. It isn't true . . . it isn't . . .' he stammered. His left hand, now revealed, gleamed in the light. A silver hand.

The 'incomplete man'. The cursed man of Mainardino.

Dante saw him activating something on his wrist with his good hand. His index and little fingers suddenly extended, turning into a pair of sparkling tongues.

At the sight of them Dante stepped backwards. Bonatti raised the weapon until it crossed the ray of light. The steel flashed in the brilliant light. He looked like an angel with his sword of fire.

'Do you know this weapon, Messer Alighieri?' the old man murmured, his voice suddenly calm. 'Forged in Damascus and tempered in the blood of the prisoners by the caliph's executioner. A man who had once been a thief, in his first life, mutilated by the butcher's axe. It was for him that the craftsmen forged this hand, so that he could perform his duties.'

He had brought the two fingertips to his face and studied them carefully, as if he were only now discovering their singularity. 'Another creation by those demons whose ingenuity you seem to love so much, to blind condemned men with a single blow. Do you see how the distance between these two fingers repeats the precise distance between a man's eyes?'

He moved the weapon towards Dante's face as though allowing him to check his words for himself. The poet stepped back once more, until he felt the cold stone of the wall behind him. The blades were approaching him dangerously, those blades that had killed so many men with their parallel jaws.

He lifted his arms in a bid to defend himself somehow. But Bonatti seemed not to want to strike. He stared with fascination at the blades plunged in the flood of light; then he bent over them with a sudden movement, piercing both his eyes. Horrified, Dante watched a scarlet flood pouring from the double wound, as the old man withdrew the blades without so much as a moan, his face reduced to a mask of blood.

'If thine eye offend thee, pluck it out. So commands the Scripture. And so it is done. Not even the Emperor can defeat the plan of God. There is nothing your magic can do against my science,' he gurgled, his teeth clenched in spasm.

Then he turned round, letting his arm drop along his side, and staggered forward. Dante ran up to help him, but Bonatti seemed unaware of anything, locked away in his own world of darkness and perfect repetitions. He stoutly brushed away the poet, as if he had sensed his presence through the scarlet veil that had deprived him of his sight.

He advanced towards the centre of the Baptistery. Dante watched after him, paralysed with emotion. He saw Bonatti approaching the baptismal fonts full of water, and stagger on to the edge of one of them. He swayed for a moment, seeking a hold in the void, then fell head-first into the round basin, plunging in to the knees. The water seethed with the old man's efforts to re-emerge, and his legs waved desperately around. Beneath the shining waters his hands couldn't find a grip and slipped on the smooth surface of the ancient Roman marble.

For a moment Dante didn't react. He stood motionless, staring at that liquid death that punished the murderer precisely in line with his own premonition. Perhaps it had been right for such a thing to happen, bringing to an end the destiny begun half a century before.

Then a shock of rage dragged him from the torpor that had seized control of him. Bonatti would triumph, even in his despair, if his plan were accomplished. And the water would fill his lungs, passing through the grin of his lips. He would have the death of which his false science assured him. And he would triumph over Dante for ever.

He ran towards the basin, grabbing Bonatti by his ankles and trying to pull him from the water, now reduced to a bloody froth. The man's body resisted, weighed down by the liquid that had drenched his long garments. Dante set his foot against the font and pulled with all his might. One of the little columns broke beneath the thrust, but the poet managed to maintain his hold until he dragged out the astrologer's body.

Bonatti was still alive. He saw him propping himself up on his elbows, the mass of wet hair sticking to his head and hiding the mutilation of his face. Beside him, Dante tried to stay upright, his hands resting on his knees, panting with exertion.

They stayed like that for a few moments, before the astrologer suddenly rose to his feet as if some demonic power had taken control of him. The poet remembered what he had heard: sometimes dead bodies are possessed by the spirit of hell and brought back to life with its breath.

He saw Bonatti walking slowly towards the still-open door, leaving a bloody trail behind him, and disappearing in the maze of alleyways towards the north.

'Liquid death refused you, Guido! Your science was inexact, as blind as your spirit!' he called after him, but Bonatti did not seem to hear him.

All around him the strength of the crown of fire was waning as the phosphorous mixture lost its strength. Now all that remained was a pale shadow of the triumph of light that had illuminated the Baptistery with its splendour.

Dante bent and picked up the weapon, still covered with blood and scraps of bone. Al-Jazari's machine was coming to rest with a final whirr.

Then he was overcome with emotion. As he slid down the wall, he felt his own senses sinking into the void.

As HE came to, the poet found himself submerged in darkness that was barely attenuated by the moonlight flowing in from the windows. Some time must have passed, but how much? He felt a rough hand shaking him, and a harsh voice calling his name.

'Wake up, Messer Durante! What happened?'

Dark shapes stirred around him, wandering through the

empty space of the Baptistery. He recognised the squat outline of the Bargello, armoured from head to toe.

'What happened, Prior?' he heard him repeat suspiciously. 'All this blood . . .'

Dante tried to get back on his feet, summoning the last of his strength.

'The guard at the Porta ad Aquilonem called for help, thinking a fire had broken out in San Giovanni. When we got here the Baptistery was shining in the night as if a thousand torches were burning inside it. What happened?' the head of the guards asked for the third time, pointing to the machinery in the corner and the mirrors still resting against the niches in the walls. 'And who broke the balustrade of the fonts? Was it you? Have you gone mad? You will pay for this,' he announced, with a hint of satisfaction in his voice.

Dante didn't hear him. He went on staring at the darkness beyond the wide-open door through which Guido Bonatti had disappeared. Twice he thought he saw his shadow swaying in the distance, among the graves of San Lorenzo.

'And what is all this?' the Bargello asked, pointing to the machine and the mirrors.

The prior picked up Elias' smoking lamp and looked at it carefully. A deep sigh emerged from his chest. 'Light. The light that dreams are made of,' he replied.

Then he walked slowly towards the night outside, beneath the stars.

AUTHOR'S NOTE

THE MACHINE dreamed up by Michael Scotus and realised by Arab mechanics, although plainly imaginary, is not entirely implausible. It broadly follows the lines of the one made by the Frenchman Armand Fizeau around the middle of the nineteenth century to determine the movement and speed of light.

The device is based on the use of two toothed wheels welded, slightly out of plane with one another, to an axle so that each interval between two teeth of the first wheel corresponds to a tooth of the second. After having set the axle to rotate at high speed, a ray of light is projected against the first wheel: this passes through the slit, is reflected against a mirror placed some distance away, and returns towards the second gear-wheel, which has by now rotated far enough to offer the light a new interval. By calculating the relation between the space travelled by the teeth of the gear-wheel and that passed by the ray of light, it is then possible to establish its speed to a good approximation.

Bearing in mind the relative simplicity of the apparatus,

the Frenchman's intuition could have been anticipated by the wise men who made the crown for Frederick the Great. That this did not in fact occur may be a source of regret for the historian, but does not greatly disturb the story-teller.

On the other hand, there is no need for the ray of light to travel along an octagonal trajectory, as imagined in the story: but so fascinated was I by the idea that the mysterious Castel del Monte might have been a kind of thirteenth-century *tokamak* that I risked presenting it as such to the reader.

GLOSSARY

al-Jazari (1133–1206) – the greatest machine-maker and inventor of a famous Persian family who made automata; he is best known for writing the *Book of Knowledge of Ingenious Mechanical Devices*, in which he described how to construct fifty mechanical objects

al-Kindi (c.801–73) – Islamic philosopher, scientist, astronomer and physician, known for trying to introduce Greek and Hellenistic philosophy to the Arab world and considered one of the greatest philosophers of Arab descent

Cecco Angiolieri (1260–c.1312) – a dissolute poet from Siena, born into a wealthy Guelph banking family and an acquaintance of Dante – they fought together at the battle of Campaldino (see below), where Angiolieri did not distinguish himself; he addressed various bantering sonnets to Dante, but their relationship subsequently deteriorated as his life became ever more turbulent astrolabe – an instrument used by classical astronomers and navigators to predict the position of the sun, moon, stars and planets and to measure local latitude and longitude; it consisted of a disc marked in degrees along the edge, a pivoted pointer (alidade), a pierced rotating disc (rete) with a projection of the ecliptic plane, and various 'flames' showing the position of the stars

bargellini – armed guards (of which the Bargello was the head) responsible for maintaining order in the Republic of Florence

Beatrice/Bice dei Portinari – the woman who takes over from the poet Virgil as guide in Dante's *Divine Comedy* and also appears in his *La Vita Nuova*; Dante met and fell in love with the real Beatrice in Florence, and although she died in 1290 (three years after marrying the banker Simone dei Bardi), continued to dedicate work to her throughout his life

Guido Bigarelli – thirteenth-century sculptor. He is known chiefly for the font in the baptistery of Pisa

Guido Bonatti – thirteenth-century Italian astronomer from Forlì, astrologer to the court of Frederick II and the most famous astronomer of his time throughout Europe; he was mentioned in Dante's *Inferno* and wrote

The Book of Astronomy, offering rare glimpses into the working life of a medieval astrologer

Boniface VIII (c. 1235–1303) – Pope of the Roman Catholic Church from 1294 until 1303; born Benedetto Caetani, he was elected Pope after Celestine V renounced the papacy, and pushed papal supremacy to the limit, leading to bitter quarrels with Philip IV of France and, indeed, with Dante, who portrayed him in the *Inferno* as being destined for hell

Campaldino – a battle on the banks of the River Arno between the Guelphs (led by Florence) and the Ghibellines (led by the commune of Arezzo) on 11th June, 1289, in which the twenty-four-year old Dante fought for the victorious Guelphs (see below)

Castel del Monte – a thirteenth-century castle in Puglia, built by Frederick II between 1240 and 1250 in the shape of an octagonal prism (possibly as an intermediate symbol between the square – representing the earth – and a circle – representing the sky); it is now a World Heritage Site

Cavalcanti – a prominent Florentine Guelph family, of which the poet Guido Cavalcanti (c.1255–1300) was a friend of Dante, but had to be exiled by him for factionalism; Guido is celebrated for his poetry exploring the philosophy of love, written in the *dolce stil nuovo* ('sweet new style')

Cerchi and Donati – the Cerchi were a leading Florentine banking family, head of a Guelph consortium, who were increasingly at odds with the Donati family, leading to virtual civil war between the rival 'Whites' and 'Blacks'; this ended in victory for the Blacks and exile for many Whites, including the Prior of the Republic of Florence, Dante Alighieri

Council of Lyon (1245) – the Thirteenth Ecumenical Council, at which Pope Innocent IV announced the deposition of the Emperor Frederick II, although he did not have the means to enforce it

Elias of Cortona (c.1180–1253) – Minister General of the Franciscans and a disciple of Saint Francis of Assisi, to whom various alchemical manuscripts have been attributed

Fedeli d'Amore (The Faithful of Love) – a secret sect of poets, led by Guido Cavalcanti (see above), struggling against the despotism of the popes and devoted to *Sapienta* (wisdom); Dante tried to contact them in 1283 by writing a poem to them and was eventually invited to join the group

Leonardo Fibonacci (c.1170–1250) – Italian mathematician also known as Leonardo of Pisa, renowned for spreading the Hindu-Arabic numeral system in Europe (as described in his *Book of Calculation*) and for the number sequence named after him, in which after 0 and 1 each subsequent number is equal to the sum of the previous two numbers

Frederick the Second (1194–1250) – Holy Roman Emperor 1220–50; Italian pretender to the title of King of the Romans from 1212 and unopposed monarch of Italy from 1215; he was known as *Stupor mundi* ('the wonder of the world') for his wide learning and was one of the foremost Christian monarchs in Europe during the Middle Ages, but his dynasty lost its influence after the death of his son Conrad in 1254, although there were continuing rumours of the attempted advent to the throne of another son

Giano della Bella – a wealthy, aristocratic Guelph politician who became the leader of a popular Florentine revolt against the magnates during the 1290s; having aroused the hostility of the guilds and the grandees, he was forced into exile

Guelphs and Ghibellines – rival factions in thirteenth-century Italy, supporting the Pope and the Holy Roman Emperor respectively; the Guelphs (to whom Dante belonged) comprised middle-class merchants, shopkeepers and traders, while the Ghibellines consisted of an alliance of leading merchants and the feudal nobility. In 1300, after their victory at Campaldino (see above), the Florentine Guelphs themselves split into two factions: the Whites and the Blacks (see Cerchi and Donati above)

guild – a professional and trade association in medieval Europe; there were seven 'great guilds', fourteen 'lesser guilds' (craft guilds) and seven liberal arts guilds in Florence, setting the standards for the occupation in question and granting privileges and protection to their members; in the novel the Builders' Guild is specifically mentioned

Inquisition – a series of Roman Catholic bodies charged with suppressing heresy throughout Europe from about 1184; they were a response to the threat presented by large popular movements such as those of the Cathars and Waldensians in France and northern Italy, which were viewed as heretical by the Catholic Church

Jubilee – on 22nd February, 1300 Boniface VIII convoked a holy year of 'great remissions and indulgences for sins' for those who visited the basilicas of Saint Peter and Saint Paul in Rome and confessed their sins; this started a tradition in the Catholic Church that continued every twenty-five or fifty years; Dante is reputed by some to have visited Rome in 1300 for this purpose

Kitab al-Mi'raj – The Book of Ascension, a Muslim book written in Arabic about the ascension of Mohammed into the heavens, after his one-night journey from Mecca to Jerusalem; it was translated into Latin in the mid-thirteenth century as the *Liber scalae Machometi* and is believed by some scholars to have influenced Dante's *Divine Comedy*

Monna Lagia – the brothel-keeper in the novel is possibly named after the Monna Lagia who had a relationship with the poet Lapo Gianna and who is mentioned in poems by Dante and Cavalcanti

Bianca Lancia – an Italian noblewoman whose full name was Bianca Lancia d'Algiano, she became mistress and (reputedly on her deathbed) wife of Emperor Frederick II; her last son was thought by some to be the 'lost' heir to Frederick

Liber scalae Machometi – see *Kitab al-Mi'raj* above

Mainardino da Imola – Bishop loyal to the Emperor Frederick, and author of the *Chronicles*

Oltrarno – a central district of Florence located south of the River Arno (from the Italian meaning 'beyond the Arno') and containing many of its historic buildings

Pietra – in 1296 Dante composed a series of verses to one Donna Pietra, who was possibly named for her stony indifference to him (*pietra* being Italian for 'stone'); it may have been a reference to Pietra degli Scrovigni, daughter of a Paduan money-lender assigned to the circle of usurers in Dante's *Inferno*

prior – the Florence in which Dante lived was a republic, governed by an elected Council of Priors, comprising six members, based on the previous Priors of the Guilds; in the novel Dante's term as prior is due to end shortly

Michael Scotus (c.1175–1234) – one of the foremost philosophers, mathematicians and scholars of the thirteenth century, who rose to prominence as an astrologer at the court of Frederick II and translated some of the Arabic works of Averroes and Avicenna; he featured among the magicians in Dante's *Inferno* and in the work of Boccaccio and Sir Walter Scott

La Serenissima – the Republic of Venice, from its title in Venetian: 'the Most Serene Republic'

tokamak – a device for creating controlled thermonuclear fusion energy, invented by Soviet physicists during the 1950s

The Virgin of Antioch – also known as Saint Margaret and Margaret of Antioch; she was scorned by her father for her Christian faith, tortured when she refused to renounce it and, after various miraculous incidents, put to death in AD 304

TRANSLATOR'S NOTE

THE KINGDOM of Light, like its predecessor, *The Third Heaven Conspiracy*, is scattered with embedded quotations and references from Dante's *Divine Comedy*. While many of these would be instantly familiar to Italians – as quotes from Shakespeare might be to us – even the most alert English-speaking readers couldn't possibly be expected to spot them all. To take a couple of examples: towards the end of Chapter 1, Dante says to Lapo: 'But anyway, in church with the saints and in the inn with the gluttons.' The phrase comes from *Inferno*, Canto XXII, ll. 15–16:

> *. . . ma ne la chiesa*
> *coi santi e in taverna coi ghiottoni.*

In the passage in question, Dante and Virgil are being escorted through Hell by a group of ten demons. Here the church, in Dante's throwaway proverb, represents heaven, and the tavern hell – a theme that will be picked up in Leoni's novel.

Perhaps more obviously, in Chapter 9 Dante finds his way obstructed by three armed men wearing the insignia of a leopard, a lion and a wolf. These are the allegorical beasts which, in Canto I of the *Inferno*, block the poet's path to salvation, representing (in the poem, not necessarily in the novel) lust, pride and avarice. And towards the end of the same chapter, Dante orders that a funeral be conducted 'with tapers quenched'; the Italian phrase, '*a lume spento*', is from *Purgatorio*, Canto III.

These are just a few of the allusions buried in the book – and if readers are tempted to track down others by returning to Dante's great work, that may well be part of the author's intention.

www.vintage-books.co.uk